ASK AGAIN, YES

Named a best book of the year by *People, Vogue, Parade,* NPR, and *Elle*

———

"An epic of intertwined families redeemed by their enduring compassion for one another." —*O, The Oprah Magazine*

"A rare example of propulsive storytelling infused with profound insights about blame, forgiveness, and abiding love." —*People*

"A beautiful novel, bursting at the seams with empathy." —*Elle*

"Keane's gracefully restrained prose gives her characters dignity. . . . Shows how difficult forgiveness can be—and how it amounts to a kind of hard-won grace." —*Vogue*

"Keane writes with acute sensitivity and her characters are consistently, authentically lived-in. . . . Smartly told." —*Entertainment Weekly*

"Tender and patient, the novel avoids excessive sweetness while planting itself deep in the soil of commitment and attachment. Graceful and mature." —*Kirkus Reviews* (starred review)

"A gem of a book." —Taylor Jenkins Reid

"I absolutely adored *Ask Again, Yes*. . . . I'll read everything she writes." —Liane Moriarty

"Mary Beth Keane is a writer of extraordinary depth, feeling, and wit." —Meg Wolitzer

"I devoured this astonishing tale of two families linked by chance, love, and tragedy. . . . A must-read." —J. Courtney Sullivan

"Stunning! An absolutely brilliant, gorgeously written novel by a fearless writer." —Lisa Taddeo

Also by Mary Beth Keane

Ask Again, Yes
Fever
The Walking People

THE

HALF

MOON

a novel

Mary Beth Keane

SCRIBNER

NEW YORK   LONDON   TORONTO   SYDNEY   NEW DELHI

Scribner
An Imprint of Simon & Schuster, Inc.
1230 Avenue of the Americas
New York, NY 10020

First Scribner hardcover edition May 2023

SCRIBNER and design are registered trademarks of The Gale Group, Inc., used under license by Simon & Schuster, Inc., the publisher of this work.

For information about special discounts for bulk purchases, please contact Simon & Schuster Special Sales at 1-866-506-1949 or business@simonandschuster.com.

The Simon & Schuster Speakers Bureau can bring authors to your live event. For more information or to book an event, contact the Simon & Schuster Speakers Bureau at 1-866-248-3049 or visit our website at www.simonspeakers.com.

Interior design by Hope Herr-Cardillo

Manufactured in the United States of America

10 9 8 7 6 5 4 3 2 1

Library of Congress Cataloging-in-Publication Data

Names: Keane, Mary Beth, author.
Title: The half moon : a novel / Mary Beth Keane.
Description: First Scribner hardcover edition. | New York : Scribner, [2023]
Identifiers: LCCN 2022037896 (print) | LCCN 2022037897 (ebook) |
ISBN 9781982172602 (hardcover) | ISBN 9781982172626 (ebook)
Subjects: LCGFT: Domestic fiction. | Novels.
Classification: LCC PS3611.E165 H35 2023 (print) | LCC PS3611.E165 (ebook) |
DDC 813/.6—dc23/eng/20220808
LC record available at https://lccn.loc.gov/2022037896
LC ebook record available at https://lccn.loc.gov/2022037897

ISBN 978-1-9821-7260-2
ISBN 978-1-9821-7262-6 (ebook)

To my first loves, Annette and Catherine

Right and wrong were shades of meaning, not sides of a coin.

Louise Erdrich, *Love Medicine*

one

Malcolm Gephardt could tell the bar was busy even from a block away, even from behind the filthy windshield of his Honda. The night was damp, the sidewalks along the center of town laced with dirty snow that had been refusing to melt for near a week. Most businesses had heeded the weather forecast and closed in advance of the coming storm, but when Malcolm approached the traffic light and saw his own squat, brown-shingled building at the bottom of the hill, something lifted in his chest and he leaned over the steering wheel.

"Oh," he said aloud to his empty car. Something was different about the place tonight. He felt a pull of energy, that singular happy chaos that can only be found inside a crowded bar when the music is good, people are running into friends, and the whole place is cozy despite the bone-cold world outside. He tried to imagine himself a stranger, tried to see his place as a stranger would. His place. *His.* Did it look welcoming? Was it just his imagination or did the light spilling onto the street give the whole façade a faint glow? Yes, he decided as he slid neatly into his parking spot and felt a thrill of hope, of faith, shoot through him for the first time in weeks: in himself, in his town, in these people, in life, in destiny, in following one's intuition. It was a good town, a good bar, and he was okay, he said to himself silently, like a prayer. *Half Moon* the old wooden sign above the door read, punctuated by a carving of a crescent moon (people loved pointing out the mistake) that had gone black and moldy over the years, and which Malcolm had scrubbed and then retouched with bright white paint the day after the deal went through.

Tonight, there were two people outside, smoking, and another woman just standing there, shivering. A positive sign. But it meant he couldn't go around to the side entrance because they'd spotted him, were already lifting their chins to him, and now as he approached he had to say all the things: how's it goin how you feelin looking good yeah more snow coming what a winter I guess nobody's goin nowhere for the weekend hope to god we don't lose power what'll we do without the TV ha ha ha. He had to shake hands, kiss the women hello, pretend he didn't know what they were talking about when they asked how he was doing, and made serious faces. And when he told them he was good, he was fine, as if he didn't know what they could be referring to, he had to do a better job pretending when they asked him again not ten seconds later.

All of this was far more difficult without a two-foot-wide bar sitting between him and the person asking. It was more difficult than it used to be, that was for sure. But why? Because he believed he knew himself, he supposed. Because he believed he knew Jess. He held fast to the good feeling from a moment earlier and told himself to keep going, to get through the night, and then maybe there'd be another one just like it. Lately, he'd been having thoughts. While at the stoplight on Wappinger a week ago, the sunset a purple bruise above Tallman Mountain and the wide Hudson hidden beyond, he thought, I could keep driving. I could turn right and head for Mexico. Turn left and make for Canada. All he had to do was keep filling the gas tank. He was handsome and charming and people liked him instantly. This was a fact he'd known about himself his entire life, and it would give him an advantage if he were to turn up in some Québécois village looking for work. His mind glanced at how much money was in the safe, how much room was left on the credit cards. He itemized everything in his house that he considered dear, but what was there that he truly loved? The coffeepot? His leather chair? Then the light turned, the thought evaporated without taking root, and he arrived at the bar feeling off-kilter, like he'd been on the verge of saying something important, but he couldn't remember what.

As he chatted with the people standing outside, he allowed himself to hope for twenty people inside. Twenty would be a decent night, and if there were twenty people in there, he told himself to not immediately wish there were forty. He refused to look through the window as if it might bring bad luck. Thirty maybe. There might be thirty. It was the coming snowstorm. Gallagher's and The Parlor hadn't even bothered to open. Primavera, next door, seated their last table at seven sharp. He wasn't sure about Tia Anna's or the new Thai place. If he had to close, he'd close, but until then he'd pull pints.

"He's here," Roddy said as soon as Malcolm stepped inside, and he felt his optimism wobble for a moment. As always, there was a note of urgency in Roddy's voice, something in the timbre finding a frequency above all the conversations and reaching Malcolm like a tug on his sleeve. Forty people. More. His friend Patrick was there. Siobhán, too, and God love her she was bouncing a hip to the beat of whatever was coming out of the jukebox. His friends had been calling and dropping by his house a lot more often since Jess left, and even if their cheeriness was a performance, he appreciated it so much that one recent Saturday, when he woke up to Patrick and their friend Toby banging around his kitchen looking for coffee filters, he sat up in bed and felt pressure in his throat like he might cry. He and Patrick had been gently making fun of Toby for almost forty years, but there he was, sniffing the creamer he found in Malcolm's fridge and searching for an expiration date. Were they calling Jess, too? Siobhán was, probably. Maybe some of the others. But no one raised the subject, no one wanted to talk about anything explicitly. If there were sides to be taken, they let him know in small ways which one they were on.

"Malcolm!" Roddy called over. "Hey!"

Malcolm nodded at Patrick and Siobhán and held up a finger to let them know he'd be just a minute. Roddy had been getting on Malcolm's nerves from almost the first minute he started working at the Half Moon, but he seemed honest, his uncle had vouched for him, and Malcolm reminded himself that honesty was what he needed most after the disaster of the previous year, when he found out that John had been stealing money since probably the very first day Malcolm took over, just folding stacks of bills and shoving them into his pocket, running only the credit card tabs through the register. This, after all the times Malcolm had covered for him when they both answered to Hugh Lydon. All the coke John shoveled into his nose. His wife on the landline wondering where he was, though she already knew, and then turning her rage on Malcolm because he was stupid enough to have answered the phone. He hadn't thought twice about keeping John on when it went from Hugh's place to his place, and stealing was how John had thanked him.

Emma, his best bartender, was the one who told Malcolm. It was eleven in the morning, and they had a hundred balloons to inflate for a private party. She took him by the arm and pulled him into the women's bathroom. For a second, when she put her warm hand on his tricep and locked the door, all his synapses fired. He didn't want to think about what his expression told her when she stood close to him, because whatever she saw there prompted her to raise her hands as if to tell him to relax, as if to tell him in his dreams, maybe, to get over himself, that she would shelve *that* conversation for another time, that first she needed to tell him something. She held a finger to her lips and listened, to make sure no one was passing in the hall, but the servers were busy with the helium tank, André was cutting long strands of ribbon, and the chairs were still upturned on the tables like a forest of mahogany legs.

She told Malcolm that she didn't want to be a narc, but she started watching John because he wasn't putting his tips in the jar, and look at André working two jobs, and Scotty with a whole slew of kids, she could never remember how many. She certainly wasn't giving up every weekend of her youth just so this joker could take money out of her pocket. She told Malcolm that when she called John out, he offered her three hundred dollars on the spot.

"Was he pulling this when Hugh was here?" Malcolm asked.

"I doubt it!" Emma said. No one would have messed with Hugh Lydon. With Malcolm, however, the bad seeds saw an opening.

John left without a fight, a sign of guilt, and Malcolm needed to fill his shifts. Roddy's uncle was a regular, a union boss, Cement and Concrete Workers. Huge guy, with a face the color of a raw porterhouse. Jess used to cross paths with him once in a while when she was newly out of law school and working for Laborers' International. Every time he saw her, he pointed finger guns and shouted, "Malcolm's girl!" Jess forgave him for never bothering to learn her name because she so enjoyed when the other attorneys looked at her as if to say, We can't believe you actually know this guy. Roddy was a good boy, the uncle told Malcolm, very smart when he applied himself, but he'd dropped out of college after two semesters. He wasn't a drinker, the uncle said. He wasn't into drugs as far as the uncle knew. Get him away from the computer and he was fine! His dad had split years ago and he needed more male role models in his life. Would Malcolm do him a favor?

"Malcolm!" Roddy called again. What Roddy's uncle failed to mention when he was talking the kid up was that Roddy was annoying. His whole vibe was nervous, and that feeling was contagious, coming from a bartender. It could infect the entire place. Malcolm thought he'd lose that nervous energy once he learned his way around, but he hadn't, and lately it was worse than ever. That night, he was behind the stick wearing a ratty T-shirt that said "Byte Me" and had a picture of an old 1980s floppy disk underneath. There was a dress code, Malcolm told him when he hired him. Wear dark colors. Shave. Comb your hair. Jesus.

Malcolm wasn't ready to deal with Roddy yet, though he wondered for a moment if whatever Roddy wanted had to do with Jess. Maybe she'd called the landline. Maybe she was still on the phone, holding until he showed up. But who called the landline anymore except Malcolm's mother, who had the number memorized since he started working there twenty-six years ago, or around the Super Bowl, the old-timers who were laid up after hip surgery but wanted to buy a box. Would Malcolm cover them? Of course he would. Of course. But try getting money out of them after they lost.

Maybe she was there somewhere. He glanced around.

No Jess at the bar. No Jess at the high-top she liked best. No Jess bullying people by the jukebox. She'd memorized the codes for the songs she hated, and in the old days, before the updated system, she would sit there and make sure no one pressed the combination of numbers that would serve up "Piano Man."

But one look at Roddy's face and Malcolm could see it was a problem with a customer. He took a quick glance around at the various clusters of people. Most were laughing. There was a group playing darts. "Gephardt!" someone called over, and he turned to find two of his buddies from the gym. He saw an old neighbor from his mother's block. A guy from the barbershop. He saw his friend from the deli with a new girlfriend. Cute. Everything seemed fine. Seemed better than fine, actually. He clapped a few backs on his way through the room, and felt his own back clapped in return. There was joy in the air. People making themselves at home. Did the group by the window seem too rowdy? He watched for a moment. They'd hold for a few minutes while he collected himself.

And then he saw Hugh's guy, Billy, sitting alone at a two-top, sipping a whiskey. They made eye contact, and Billy raised his glass as if to say cheers. Cheers to the crowd. To the money the night would no doubt bring in. Malcolm's stomach heaved. Ignore him, he told himself. Just keep going.

He nodded hello to Emma as he tossed his keys in the usual drawer. Her hair was up in a high ponytail, and he really tried not to keep track of these things, but she had a beautiful neck, and in the one second he allowed himself to look, he followed a tendril of hair that had slipped loose.

"How long has—?" Malcolm lifted his chin toward Billy's table.

"A while," Emma said. "Waiting for you to show up, I think."

He pulled on his tight shoulder to stretch it and then remembered Jess saying that was what he always did when he was worried. He hated getting to the bar so late, but his mother had come by with a meat loaf. She'd looked in his fridge like he was twenty-two again, living in his first apartment. After they ate, as she wrapped the leftovers for him, Malcolm had a vision of Jess rolling her eyes. "I gotta go, Ma," he said eventually. "You okay to get home?"

"What the heck are you talking about am I okay to get home?" she asked.

In the old days, on Fridays, the construction workers would have started arriving by four. By six they'd have moved on and the commuters getting off the train would take their places. Around seven he used to start looking for Jess, in case she wanted to have a beer and a sandwich at the bar before she kissed him good night and said she'd see him later. Jess had warned him about making changes, but how could he have guessed the depth of love people had for broken-down, sticky barstools? Who would have believed they'd want to keep listening to the same songs on the jukebox over and over and over, as if music stopped being made in 1996? And he didn't do even a fraction of what he dreamed of doing. He stuck to things that were relatively cheap and quick. But it turned out people didn't want things to be nice, they wanted them to be familiar.

The only demographic that got stronger once Malcolm took ownership was the underage crowd. The moment he took over, they started trying to get in after ten o'clock with their New York State dupes and their good friends from Ohio and Florida. But a bar full of kids didn't help the bottom line because they ordered straight sodas for a dollar and then brought their drinks to the bathroom, where they pulled nips out of their pockets and mixed their own. They worked on animal instinct, these kids. It was like a call went out the very hour the bar changed hands, and next thing they started showing up with little bottles clanking in their purses.

"I'm sure every generation thinks they invented that move," Jess said, when he brought that detail home.

Where is she right this second? Every time he thought about it and realized he didn't have the answer, he felt as if he'd taken a flying leap off a ledge without having a clue where he'd land. Up until that week she'd been staying with her friend Cobie, who lived on West Twenty-Third Street with her wife and their two sons. Cobie made sense as a person to go to: a college friend, one of the few close friends who was entirely Jess's, without any connection to their hometown. But a few days earlier, he called Cobie because Jess wasn't answering his calls or responding to his texts, and Cobie told him that Jess was, in fact, back in Gillam.

Look at that, Malcolm thought, she was inching her way home.

To Malcolm's ear, Cobie pronounced Gillam like she was holding her nose. The one time aside from their wedding that she'd come to Gillam was to meet Malcolm, fifteen years earlier, and she kept pointing out things that she found interesting. That there were seven Catholic churches within five miles was interesting to Cobie, and that so many business names were Irish. She found it interesting that so many cars had a union local displayed on the bumper, and as they walked through town she called out each one they passed—carpenters, sandhogs, scaffolders, ironworkers, steamfitters—as if she never knew these jobs existed. How much do jobs like that pay? she wanted to know. What were the benefits? How long could a person do a job like that?

"Why?" Malcolm asked. "You gonna start digging tunnels?" Jess gave him a look that said, Watch it. He was sick of Cobie's observations. He thought she was a snob.

But it was *interesting* that Jess was back in Gillam. She probably wanted to meet up, but she was so stubborn. Well, he had a few things to say now that he'd had space to think. He wouldn't let her back in without a conversation, that was for sure. He had a memory of her in her twenties, just as they were getting together, how she used to stand with her friends but keep her eyes on him while he worked. How he felt electrified by that, astonished, really, given how brightly she shined and how proud everyone was of her going to that good school, her hair gleaming down her back, the breathtaking perfection of her profile when she turned to talk to the person next to her. Everything he did—mixing, reaching, leaning over the bar—he felt more acutely knowing she might glance over at him for a moment.

Since Cobie told him Jess was in Gillam, he'd been picturing her against the backdrop of her mother's floral wallpaper, the two of them settling in to watch *Dateline*. He imagined her mulling over how to approach him, how to apologize. He remembered the first time he drove her home. She was not quite twenty-four and he was twenty-eight. They hadn't done anything yet, though he decided at some point that night that he had to kiss her, and didn't understand why he hadn't already. They were four grades apart, just enough to have missed each other in high school. He'd overlapped with her older brother, Mickey, but Mickey was two years younger than Malcolm and played soccer and took all honors classes. Only the name rang a bell. Jess was beautiful and funny and a little different from the other girls. When she stood near the bar, something inside of him wobbled; he became clumsy and self-conscious when normally he felt graceful and fluid, like his movements had been choreographed to precisely fit the narrow space of his workplace, his stage. He couldn't remember ever feeling self-conscious before meeting her.

9

She told him she had an apartment in Manhattan but came to Gillam every few weeks, to see her parents and go out with her high school friends. On the night when he drove her home for the first time, she sat at the bar and they talked. When her group went to leave, he suggested she stay, keep him company.

The thing he remembered most about dropping her off at her parents' at four in the morning was not the kiss, whatever that had been like, but that she hopped out of the car and ran to the front door like a little kid. She took the concrete steps two at a time, pumping her arms like a high hurdler. When she got to the door, she turned and waved at him before disappearing inside. Not a flirtatious wave. Not a demure Miss America wave. It was a dorky wave: palm wide, vigorous back and forth. Alone in his car, the stink of the bar on his skin as always, he laughed. What a weirdo.

She'd probably been driving by their house every day since she came back, looking for his car, trying to think of a way to approach him. Well, let her sweat, he thought. I'm not going knocking. No way.

The music was catchy. More people were starting to sway. He made his way over to Patrick and Siobhán.

"Look at his place," Patrick said as Siobhán gave Malcolm a long, tender hug, the kind he imagined she gave her children when they woke from bad dreams. "Packed to the gills."

Malcolm ignored that, hoping to imply that the bar was full all the time, but then remembered that Patrick knew, of course. His oldest friend, he could read Malcolm easily and knew almost from the start that things were not going as Malcolm expected them to. He and Siobhán had their six-year-old's birthday party there a few months earlier, hired a magician, told Malcolm it was because Eamon loved the mozzarella sticks at the Half Moon and so would his little buddies. They invited parents, too, no doubt so the bar bill would be substantial. Malcolm wouldn't take Patrick's money, but then he found it in an envelope in his car, in the compartment where he kept his nicotine lozenges.

He looked around at the table where Billy had been sitting, and noted it was empty. He just wanted to be seen, Malcolm knew. He just wanted Malcolm to know that he was keeping close tabs.

"Date night?" Malcolm asked, flagging down Bridget, the waitress, to bring his friends another round.

Siobhán glanced at Patrick, and Malcolm caught a whiff of panic.

"Yeah, sort of," Siobhán said, but when Malcolm looked at Patrick, Patrick wouldn't meet his eyes. Malcolm gestured toward the empties in front of them. "Sorry about that," he said as he plucked them up, said he'd send someone to wipe down the table.

"Oh, don't worry," Siobhán said.

"Yeah, don't worry about it, Mal."

"I'm usually here earlier. My mother came by with food."

"Do whatever you have to do," Patrick said. "We can hang out later. When you get a minute."

"Yeah? Okay good."

It had been over four months since Jess left. Seventeen weeks to be exact. Thanksgiving with his mother, his sister, his brother-in-law who was on the wagon, his three near-feral nephews. He got completely hammered, and his mother, who'd normally give him a little reminder about genetics and his line of work, only guided him upstairs to his high school bed and tucked him in. She had a pot of coffee and a plate of eggs ready for him in the morning and didn't say a word.

Christmas he spent with Patrick and Siobhán because his mother went to his sister's in Boston. New Year's at the bar. In his own house, he kept the TV on nonstop for company. When his friends came by, they let themselves in through the back slider, something they would never do if Jess were around. It was a shock at first. With adulthood and marriage came a turning in toward one's own unit, but now, it seemed, he was everyone's worry, and part of him suspected these friends, grown men, all in their mid-forties, loved the excuse to leave their families on a Saturday afternoon and claim they were checking on Malcolm.

"Malcolm," Roddy said now as Malcolm approached the bar. "Hey."

The whole place was full from end to end, and from one group came a sudden swell of people singing. Others joined in from all the way across the room, and it became a call-and-response, a song everyone knew. You might not know how you felt about the song if you were alone in your car, but sung in a local pub? With a drink in your hand? Alongside strangers? Pure magic. The problem was that if Malcolm wanted the same thing to happen the next night, and the next, just having the thought in his mind and looking for the right moment would make it impossible. The warmth, the feeling of camaraderie, even the night sky swollen with snow—it was like chemistry between people—surprising, impossible to predict—but once the charge was in the air, there was no force more powerful.

He wanted to take a video and text it to Jess. See? he'd write. Didn't I tell you?

Roddy's expression seemed worried, but Malcolm refused to let him ruin the moment. Back in January, someone unscrewed one of the urinals from its mount and tossed it out the kitchen exit, where it broke into a dozen pieces. In Malcolm's history tending bar, it was the third time someone had ripped a urinal out of a wall. This time, at least, the person had turned off the water. Malcolm still couldn't figure out who'd done it. Someone who knew his way around a stop valve and who carried a wrench in his pocket. That night, when Roddy had come up behind him and told him the urinal was gone, just *gone*, he looked so upset that Malcolm knew if he said the wrong thing, Roddy would cry. He was certain of it.

"Why would they do that?" Roddy asked, following Malcolm to the men's room. "I don't get it."

"What do you mean? There's nothing to get," Malcolm said. He turned to study the kid. "Drunk people do stupid shit. You need to calm down."

But the urinal incident seemed to make Roddy even more anxious, more on edge during his shifts. Now, as Roddy tried again to flag him down, to get him to stop and listen, Malcolm turned and gave him a look of total faith, of confidence.

"That guy is here. Was here."

"I saw him."

"And also—"

"Roddy, I need a minute," Malcolm said, and then he looked around as if to say, I don't see anything happening here that you can't handle for one minute. He opened the door to the basement storage room and felt his way down the stairs in the dark. It was musty down there, low ceilinged, a row of kegs on one side, towers of boxes screaming brand logos against the opposite wall. He pulled the string that turned on the light, and raised his hands to the crossbeam above his head. He listened and felt relief bloom and grow inside his body. It would all be fine, he told himself. Heels clicked on hardwood, chairs scraped the floor. He ran his hands over a stack of tablecloths enclosed in plastic, looked at the jars of cherries, olives, vac-sealed drums of mixed nuts that wouldn't expire for another two years. A full bar. He wanted one minute to soak it in, to remember.

He'd been working at the Half Moon for twenty-four years when he bought the place, knew it better than even his childhood home. He knew the smell of it, the way the light looked at different times of year, in different weather. It was at the Half Moon that he learned how to fix a running toilet, how to solder a pipe. He got strong at the bar, bringing case after case of Bud Light and Ultra up from the basement because Hugh wouldn't add a light beer to the draft options. He learned about cash there, how to accept it, how to turn it away. He learned how to handle the sales reps, which ones would fork over free branded glasses and napkins and throw a few packs of cocktail straws on top, just because they liked shooting the shit for ten minutes. He learned that though he could drink for free at any bar in town, he'd drop more in tips in those places than he'd ever have paid had he come in as a regular customer. He learned how to talk to anyone, how to find common ground. He learned how to be a vessel for people's worries, their complaints, and he learned that he'd better not have any worries or complaints of his own. He learned how to be friendly to women without crossing a line, he knew how to make them feel beautiful without being a sleaze, and he learned how to walk those same women back when they crossed the line, without insulting them, without embarrassing them. He learned to hide his shock at some of the things they said to him, these perfectly normal-seeming women, these women in their nearly identical faux leather jackets and their wedges, their hair in banana curls like they were all heading to some pageant for middle-aged women, the things that came out of their mouths when they had too much to drink or if they'd been wronged by their boyfriends or husbands. He learned it was possible to appear to the world as an average, ho-hum person but to actually harbor thoughts that human strangers didn't normally share with one another, until they sat at a bar for too long on a Friday night and encountered a bartender they considered attractive.

"I mean, these are *mothers*, most of them," he reported to Jess after. "They have little kids at home." He saved all his judgments for later, for her.

But Jess never wanted him thinking badly of these women. She insisted that they shouldn't be judged for reaching back to their youth for a moment, chasing a temporary high. When she took this position, he felt baffled. Did she want to say these things to a near stranger? That wasn't the point, she said; the point was to try to understand wanting some of that intoxicating energy in their lives again for thirty seconds, what harm, because the truth was that most of them would wake up to a pile of dirty laundry and kids demanding a snack. Jess had seen it crush their female friends in a way that Malcolm had mostly been shielded from. She had a friend who, when Jess asked how she did it all—the kids, the house, a job, the cloth napkins at holidays, and so on—lifted a finger to her lips and pulled open a drawer in her bedroom dresser to show Jess where she'd been stockpiling Percocet, collecting it from friends who'd had C-sections but were afraid to finish their prescriptions.

"But you still want a baby," Malcolm asked. "Even knowing that."

"Yes," she said, without hesitation. "Very much so."

What had he said in response? He couldn't remember.

The snow was really coming. The air outside was heavy and still.

He thought, she might text if she's worried. She didn't like weather.

He heard the creak of the storeroom door opening, a hesitant step down.

"Malcolm?" Emma's voice. He looked up at her from the bottom of the stairs. She was in her usual work uniform: black jeans, a black shirt, black boots that reached to mid-shin.

"Yeah?" he said.

"Just come," she said.

Emma filled Malcolm in as they crossed the short distance between the storeroom door and the knot of energy by the window. "It's Tripp," Emma said. "I've never seen him like this." Tripp was around sixty, Malcolm guessed. He was on the short side but broad. He'd been coming in for years, always paid cash, never ran a tab. He always sat by the window, put a few twenties on the bar, and left as soon as the twenties were gone. But tonight was different. Once he drank through his pile of cash, he added more. As they approached, he was waving his arms as he ranted about something, and Malcolm could see in the heaviness of his movements that he was very drunk.

Emma told Malcolm that she overheard him asking Roddy how often the draft lines were cleaned. He asked what detergent they used on the glasses. He said to no one in particular that he might call the board of health, that he knew a guy, that it didn't take much to pull a liquor license. When Emma heard him ask Roddy for a Jameson, she put a pint glass of ice water in front of him instead.

Then she sighed, and Malcolm knew they were about to arrive at the more immediate problem. "I don't know what they were talking about, but next thing he called the tall guy over there a 'smug little shit.'"

Part of Malcolm wanted to laugh—every twenty-five-year-old male was a smug little shit—until the crowd parted and Malcolm saw how angry the guy was.

"Guys," Malcolm said. "Hey." He made his way to the center of the knot. But it was too late. A surge of raw energy raced through the air. He could smell it as clear as the coming storm: someone was about to get punched.

Malcolm put his hand on Tripp's arm to stay him. He was way too old for this nonsense. Tripp used to take a car service straight from work to the bar on Friday afternoons and as soon as he ordered, he'd take off his tie and drape it over his knee. But it had been a while since he'd come in, now that Malcolm thought about it. He was not usually one to pick fights. The worst he ever did when he had a few drinks was go on about how one day he was going to buy fifty acres in Peru and move there, land was cheap and beautiful. He was going to step out of his life and into another. He'd be off the grid and closer to nature. He'd get healthier, more balanced—a state that was impossible to achieve in the New York metro area. He said most of the parcels near the Sacred Valley had mature fruit trees—fig, guava, apple. The melt running off the Andes brought potable water. He'd put up solar panels and get his exercise doing real work, on the earth.

A lot of people had a go-to subject when drinking, a touchstone—an ex-wife, a failed music career—and moving off the grid was Tripp's.

"If it were that easy, everyone would do it," Malcolm remembered saying one time, when Tripp had launched into his favorite topic.

"You would do it?"

Malcolm laughed. "No, not me. What am I going to do with fifty acres of guava trees? I'm just saying a lot of people feel exactly like you do."

He couldn't remember what Tripp had said in reply. He glanced over at Patrick and Siobhán, to see if they were watching. Just like that, the magical bubble had burst.

The young guy widened his stance, screwed his face into a grimace, and drew his elbow back. "Hang on," Malcolm said, but then the kid released, and next came the unmistakable sound of meat on meat. The wave of energy surged forward, tickled the back of Malcolm's neck. Tripp slumped.

Nick, the bouncer, caught the young man's second punch mid-flight, as Malcolm tried to get Tripp out of there. But Tripp wouldn't move.

"Roddy," Malcolm said. "Help." Nick was dealing with the young people, telling them to gather their things and go.

Together Malcolm and Roddy marched Tripp through the swinging door to the kitchen, where they sat him on a folding chair. André was lowering a fry basket into oil. Scotty was breaking down boxes in the corner. "No way," André said, taking one look. "Have Nick toss him."

Malcolm checked his watch. "It's only nine thirty. I'll get him a cab but I want him to sober up a bit. God, I hope no one calls the cops."

"I'm not babysitting," Scotty said. "I need to get out of here before we're snowed in."

"Me too," André said.

Emma, watching from the door, said nothing.

"Hey, Tripp," Malcolm said loudly, right near the man's face. "Where do you live?" He ran his own company, implied he had a lot of money. Malcolm was almost certain he lived in the big Victorian at the end of

Acorn Drive, but he wanted Tripp to confirm before he packed him into a cab and sent him there.

But Tripp only pressed his cheek against the cool stainless steel of the walk-in. He closed his eyes.

"Roddy," Malcolm said, feeling a headache coming on. "You see a guy getting this banged up, you can't just pour whatever he asks for."

"I was trying to tell you."

"Tell me what? That there's a drunk guy at the bar? Dealing with the drunk people who come in here is the whole job." Malcolm sighed. "What about his tab?"

"Cash as he went, like always."

"And the others? That younger group?" He could tell by Roddy's face that they'd not paid. He looked at Emma and didn't even need to say anything. She immediately pushed through the swinging door that led back to the bar to catch them before they left.

Roddy was silent for a moment. "I didn't know you were going to kick them out."

"Just go," Malcolm said. "Start busing."

Out front, the night's momentum had come to a halt. Some new faces had arrived, but it was as if they could sense they were out of the loop, and they didn't settle in like the earlier crowd had. People were closing tabs, shrugging on their coats. There'd be no more singing. No more dancing. The night was skewed early. Everything that would have normally happened between 8:00 p.m. and 4:00 a.m. was being compressed into a much shorter period, because of the storm. After another forty-five minutes, the only patrons left were Patrick and Siobhán. Malcolm turned the music way down.

"Hey," he said as he made his way over to his friends. He saw that they'd already settled their bill.

"That guy almost got his ass kicked," Patrick said. "He owes you."

Malcolm sighed. "I'm sure that'll be his first thought when he wakes up." He sat down with them. "Haven't broken up a fight in a while."

The bell chimed on the door, but Emma called out that they were closed.

"So, Malcolm," Patrick said, with an expression like he was working up to something.

"What's with you two tonight?"

Patrick and Siobhán had some sort of silent communication, and then Siobhán turned her whole body toward him. He'd known her since they were fifteen years old, when she started hanging around his group, crushing on Patrick.

"Mal," she said. "When's the last time you talked to Jess?"

"Why?"

"We wanted to make sure you knew. Before you hear it around."

Malcolm waited. He felt the blood coursing through his body slow down. He heard his heartbeat in his ears. Behind him, Emma was tipping everyone out. The new waitress left, shouted goodbye from the door. She'd been there since Christmas, but Malcolm still found her crying in the walk-in every few days. He had to deal with Tripp. He had to clean up. And the snow was coming down harder now. He thought about what would be auto-deducted from his account over the next day or so, what sort of dancing he'd have to do to get through another month. But as he sat there, watching his friends' faces as they worked out the best way to tell him something difficult, everything happening in the bar at that moment seemed to be taking place at a greater distance, and something blurry in his peripheral vision stepped into clear view. He felt his chest get hot. He felt every inch of his six-foot-three frame, the width of his shoulders. And then, not one second later, he was so exhausted that the idea of stretching out on the sticky floor and going to sleep appealed to him.

"You and Jess," Siobhán said, "you haven't been talking, have you?"

He didn't bother answering, since she clearly knew more than he did. He felt dead limbed, like he'd just sprinted up several flights of stairs.

"You know she's here? In Gillam?"

"Yeah I heard that," he said, realizing he'd only assumed she was at her mother's house. Cobie had never actually said that.

"Meg Whelan saw her driving down Madison yesterday evening. As a passenger, I mean. Not her car."

"Okay."

No one spoke for a beat.

"Just say it," Malcolm said.

Patrick cleared his throat. "You know my friend from college? The one who moved here right around the time you bought this place?"

"Neil," Malcolm said.

"Yes," Patrick said.

"Bad divorce," Malcolm added. The floor beneath him felt less solid than it had a moment before.

A standard guy in a golf shirt. Nothing special, as far as Malcolm could recall. He showed up at the Half Moon with Patrick one time, both of them already pretty loose. Toby was meeting up with them, too. They'd been making the rounds to give Neil a sense of the town's offerings, and Patrick had saved the Half Moon for last, so they could really settle in. But Malcolm had been distracted that day, had argued with a vendor, and the feeling of being behind was becoming more and more familiar. After, he remembered thinking he should have been more welcoming.

"I knew it," he said, though he had not known it, not even close. What they'd come to tell him—it was obvious now that the visit had a purpose—would have been anyone else's first suspicion, but not Malcolm's. He tried out the idea sometimes, but only to remind himself that he wasn't dumb, that he'd considered all possibilities. But it just didn't compute. They were having trouble, but they were a pair. Jess's face, her body, her moods—they were all as familiar to him as he was to himself.

Malcolm tried to conjure up Neil's face so he could study it, this near stranger, but it was just too far-fetched, that a person he didn't know at all could have anything to do with the person he knew best.

"Who told you?"

"Him. Neil." Patrick looked away.

"He told you? Not her?" Malcolm studied Siobhán. "Did she tell you?"

"She's not answering my texts."

"So it might not be true."

Neither Patrick nor Siobhán could think of something to say to that.

"It's true," Patrick said finally.

"We didn't want you to feel stupid," Siobhán said. "We thought best you hear it from us. But I think we should keep in mind what Jess has been through, and—"

"How does she even know him?"

Siobhán looked down at her hands. "They met at our house—"

"Like barbeques and things? I met him there, too. There must have been something else."

"You know how it is. We get together on a Saturday and you're here at the bar. Jess always comes. And so would Neil this past year or so." All three of them looked around the bar as if seeing it for the first time.

"But did they talk? I don't understand."

"He's a lawyer, too," Patrick said. "Big firm. Graduated law school around the same time Jess did. I guess they have mutual friends."

"I knew that," Malcolm said. "I remember that. Somebody from her old study group is at the same firm he's at now." He had little facts tucked away about everyone. Not gossip, he didn't like gossip, but conversation pieces should a person turn up at the Half Moon feeling low. "And what? You're telling me it's serious?"

"Well," Siobhán began, but Patrick shook his head almost imperceptibly, so she swallowed back whatever she was about to say. Malcolm was relieved. Which would be worse, that it was serious or that it wasn't? What an odd question. He didn't want details. He wouldn't be able to take them in. All these weeks he'd been running through the things he'd done, the ways he could have been better, but really Jess had been deep into a story that spun away from him entirely. He could feel his pulse as it pushed his blood through his body.

"She's going through something," Siobhán said in a near whisper. "That's what I keep telling myself. She's going through something that the rest of us can't understand."

"I can't understand it? You're including me in that?"

Roddy was wiping down the bar. What a night it had been. If Malcolm could capture lightning in a bottle every time, he'd be okay. But if he couldn't, what then? He couldn't operate a place that was only half-full three nights a week. He was forty-five years old and he'd never had any other job. And he was good at this one. But middle age was looming and he could already see the headline that would arrive with it: that a person could be extraordinarily good at something and still fail at it.

"It's my fault," Siobhán said. "I didn't like to think his girls wouldn't know anyone in school. So I always told Patrick to include him."

Malcolm stood. "You know what? I can't do this right now."

Last time he spoke to Jess was a full month earlier. He was carrying a bag of groceries into the house when he saw her name light up the screen of his phone, so he dropped the bag on the counter and two apples rolled out, bounced to the floor. He stabbed the button that would bring her voice to him. She asked how he was, how the bar was, his mother. His answers must have been brief and she must have heard frustration in his voice because she pulled up short of whatever she called to say, said she had to go. "Jess!" he shouted into his phone, but she was already gone. When had she ever stopped herself from saying something? And then he understood she'd been crying. In their whole relationship, he could count on one hand the number of times he'd seen her cry, and each of those times had to do with their plot of garden remaining bare while everyone else's bloomed so large and wild that they had to work to keep it in check. Follicles too few. Numbers too low. Canceled cycles. Illogical insurance requirements. Waiting to zero out. Waiting longer. Failure to implant. Failure to thrive. Hoping her period would come soon. Hoping it would not come. From the very beginning he was afraid to be specific when they talked, in case he'd get some detail wrong. Little pastel-colored boxes of medication and supplements on the counter, filling an entire shelf of the fridge. Jess on the phone with the insurance company, her color-coded folders spread across the kitchen table, insisting the clinic had already sent a letter, reciting the names of medications like she had a doctorate in pharmacology, like she was fluent in a language he didn't understand. Overhearing her every Saturday morning—her paperwork time, as she called it—saying, sure, she'd be happy to hold, saying she'd already been holding for an hour, and then lowering her head to rest in her arms.

Jess telling Malcolm that she didn't fucking know what she wanted for dinner, because she'd been on the phone all fucking day, and then saying sorry, she was sorry, she was just frustrated. Malcolm standing beside her chair with a feeling like he was apart from something. Like if he reached his hand out to touch her, there'd be something in his way.

When was the first time he had that feeling? The night at her friend Rachel's wedding, in the restroom of a yacht club in Hyannis. He thought about that night a lot since she left. She'd asked him to come with her, to hold her dress. She unzipped and lifted the gown over her head, handed it to him, and then opened the little cooler bag she'd stashed at the coat check. He folded her dress over his arm and could feel the warmth of her skin coming off the material. Once undressed she panicked. The sink edge was too narrow. The drain plug was missing. What if everything disappeared down the pipe? Before he could think of a solution she dropped to her knees, and unfolded a triple layer of paper towels on the tiled floor. When she was satisfied she placed her little bottles of saline and powder on top of the towels, her needle and plunger, too. "Can I help?" he asked as she mixed the contents of one tiny bottle with another.

"I got it," she said and smiled up at him, no doubt having the same memory he was having right then, of Malcolm sweating through his T-shirt the one and only time he'd done an injection for her, a trigger shot that had to go into her back, which she couldn't reach. Once it was done, he remained seated on the closed seat of their upstairs toilet until his heart stopped racing while Jess pressed her open palm to her back and counted to thirty. "Doesn't it seem like a doctor should be doing this?" he asked that night.

The wedding in Hyannis was the first time she had to give herself an injection outside of their home. They hadn't been through everything yet. It was still very much the beginning, though they didn't know it at the time. She'd canceled dinners, wriggled out of business trips, but their friends' wedding date couldn't be changed and couldn't be skipped. When the save-the-date came, she thought she'd be pregnant by the time the day arrived.

Looking at her crouched on the floor, her expression so determined, he felt a swell of love for her, for what they were trying so hard for. He watched closely as she took hold of her belly, as she pushed the needle in. There was a nine-piece band in the other room. The walls thumped with sound. The swell of flesh above the elastic of her underwear looked vulnerable and pale. She was worried all the medications were making her chubby, but he thought she looked so pretty that night.

"I set a timer for the next one," she said without looking up. She'd need three shots in all, spaced about an hour apart. "But I can handle it now that I have a system." She gathered up the paper towels and told him to go have fun.

"I can hold your dress again."

"No, it's fine," she said, and rose onto her tiptoes to kiss him before stepping back into her heels.

An hour later he was just leaning across the bar to order a drink when he looked over and saw her walking toward the bathroom with her little bag tucked discreetly at her side. That wedding was the first time he put a name to the worry he'd been feeling, the vague sense of panic he had that he was forgetting something, that there was something he needed to do.

But they'd stopped all that. The bruises on her belly faded. The binder that sat on the windowsill for almost seven years was moved to a desk drawer. Malcolm would never again have to jerk off into a plastic cup in a fluorescent-lit room. He'd never again have to walk down the hall to let the nurse (always young, always female) know his cup was labeled and waiting.

He thought, at first, they'd go right back to the way they were before. He thought she'd start stopping by the bar again, to surprise him. He thought she'd start grinning at him again, looking at him like she knew a juicy secret. It'll take a while, he told himself, have patience. But then she was gone.

"I'm sorry, Mal," Patrick said at the Half Moon as Malcolm's wheels spun. "I thought maybe you knew. And I'm sorry we did this here. I thought telling you here at the bar would be better, but now I'm thinking this was a bad idea."

"I told you," Siobhán said.

"Yeah, she did tell me. I thought you'd feel sort of protected here— your house is crazy lonely right now, buddy—but Siobhán disagreed. Anyway. I'm really sorry."

"It's fine."

"No, it isn't. You want help turning chairs or anything? The snow is picking up."

"I'll do it," Malcolm said, but he didn't move. He had questions form- ing, but he didn't want to ask them. Despite how mixed up he felt, he also detected some calm at his center for the first time in many weeks, a pinhole of light that would help make everything easier to read once he had the energy to think about what his friends had said. He'd learned over the seventeen weeks since Jess left that waiting for something to happen was exhausting, as if a door slammed four months earlier were still slamming, and he was still standing there, flinching, body tensed, waiting to find out what would come after. Now he knew, he supposed. In a tiny way, it was a relief.

Siobhán and Patrick were the last customers to go, and when they opened the door, the snow swept through the vestibule and into the bar.

"How's our friend?" Malcolm asked Roddy.

"He left," Roddy said. "Must have gone out the kitchen exit."

"Really? It's all ice back there."

Malcolm walked through the kitchen, opened the door that led to the alley, and squinted into the dark to make sure Tripp wasn't splayed out with a broken leg. He turned on the flashlight on his phone and took a few careful steps out. He shined the light in every direction. Jess, he thought. Jess and Neil? Who started it? Did she place herself in just the right spot, give him a sign that she wouldn't object? Or had he caught her in a certain mood and then she hadn't known how to rewind? The motion sensor went on, and Malcolm watched the snow fall through the cone of light. For a moment he forgot why he was out there, what he was supposed to be doing. The alley was empty except for the dumpster, a few dozen boxes flattened and tied up with twine, a pile of broken packing crates that had been sitting there for at least a year.

"You're still here," he said to Emma when he returned to the main room. It was an early night for all of them, but with the snow suddenly falling faster, he was starting to feel as if they should have closed hours ago. Emma had to drive to Yonkers. The bridge would be backed up. Roddy was counting his cash, and everyone else was gone. Malcolm sucked in a little, worried he was getting a belly. Jess said he'd be able to carry it when the time came, he had that kind of frame. She said it like it was inevitable because his father had had a belly, his uncle, both dead now, struck down by heart attacks in their forties. He dropped his hands to the edge of the bar and held tight. Emma was looking at her phone, her fingers flying over the screen like she was playing an instrument. He could offer her a place to stay if she was worried about driving in a snowstorm. She knew his house was empty. No big deal. They'd get home pretty early. They could watch a movie if she wanted.

"You okay to drive in this? You're welcome to crash at my house." He tried to say it casually, as if the thought had just entered his mind.

For a moment, when she looked up and locked eyes with him, a hundred and one calculations passed over her face, but in the end she said she'd drive slowly, her tires were brand new.

"Great," he said, not sure if he was disappointed or relieved. "Good. Be careful."

The plow passed as Emma left. Malcolm took one last look around. "All set?" he said to Roddy as he put on his coat. He held the door for Roddy to step through first, and as he turned to lock it, it occurred to him that he should offer Roddy a lift home.

"Good night," he said instead.

"Yeah good night," Roddy said, and then: "hey, I been meaning to say, you know, better late than never, sorry about Jess. That was her friend, right? The lady you were talking to?"

"Roddy," Malcolm said. "You and I aren't talking about Jess."

"Oh," Roddy said, his cheeks instantly flushing bright red. "Sorry."

And then, watching the kid lope up the street in only his windbreaker, hunched against the storm, threadbare sneakers, he felt like a monster. Here was this boy, less than half Malcolm's age, who could not even choose a playlist when Malcolm asked him to last week. He had his life savings rolled up in his jeans pocket. His uncle claimed he was smart, that he was a whiz with computers, so what the heck was he doing with his life? Malcolm had promised to look out for him.

A moment later, Malcolm pulled up beside him. "Want a lift?" he asked.

"I'm good," Roddy called over, without breaking stride. "I prefer to walk."

It was so unexpected that Malcolm laughed.

I prefer to walk, Malcolm repeated to himself as he drove away.

two

In May of 2004, they were twenty-five and thirty, which meant they were not too young, not even close. The show *Friends* was about to air its final episode, and the characters' faces were on buses all over the city. The baby would be born when Jess was twenty-six, well into adulthood, a solid education under her belt. Cobie was having friends over and was distracted by assembling snacks and straightening up while Jess watched for Malcolm's car from her bedroom window. "I'll be back in a bit," she called out to Cobie when she spotted his black Nissan, and ran down the stairs and around the corner, where he always got lucky with parking. When he found a spot, they walked to Duane Reade and, shocked by the prices, picked the cheapest test. But then as they waited on line and Malcolm read the small print on the box, Jess knew that no matter what the result, she wouldn't trust it because it was half the price of the others, so she told him to hold their place while she went back and picked the most expensive. When she returned, he pulled her close and kissed the part in her hair. "Don't worry," he said.

"You don't worry either," she said, circling both arms around his waist.

Waiting ahead of them were ten other New Yorkers getting bits and pieces of daily life: mascara and Benadryl and condoms and greeting cards and toothpaste. It was a beautiful spring night.

She didn't want to take the test at her apartment because Cobie was home and would have questions. Malcolm was surprised that she'd said nothing of her suspicion to anyone else, not to Cobie, not to anyone, and felt moved by it, a secret that was entirely theirs alone. So they walked the city for over an hour, the box shoved into Jess's bag, until she couldn't take it anymore and suggested running into the bathroom of a Pizza Hut they'd passed as they were walking through Times Square. "I'm coming, too," Malcolm said, following her. "You think I'd wait outside for this?"

On the phone with him earlier that day she said on a scale of one to ten in terms of being sure she was at an eight, but now that she was about to actually pee on the thing, an eight felt overly dramatic. "So where are you now?" he asked. "A five?"

"More like a three," she said. She made him turn around and plug his ears because she didn't want him to see her pee but she also didn't want him to hear.

He laughed, "I've seen you in more compromising positions."

"I don't care!" she said.

She was two weeks late. She was unusually tired. Things smelled weird but this was Manhattan and there had been a stretch of hot days.

"What now?" he asked as they huddled close together to look at the stick.

"The directions say it can take up to two minutes." Out in the jam-packed restaurant, a song he loved was playing over the din. He hooked his fingers in her two front belt loops and pulled her close. He'd once come out from behind the bar at the Half Moon to dance to this song. A woman made an offhand remark that there was nothing better than a big man who was light on his feet, and Malcolm asked if anyone would like to see what that looked like. He touched his tie, had a moment of stillness, and next thing he hunched his broad shoulders and took off.

The crowd clapped to the beat and made a circle around him. He danced faster, better. I love this guy, Jess thought that night. After one chorus he went back behind the bar as if nothing had happened. Remembering that, Jess understood that before the song was over, they'd know. Someone banged on the door, and Malcolm shouted that it would be a minute.

She peeked early, showed him, but they held their reactions until they got outside, away from the long lines of tourists ordering stuffed crusts to-go. It had gotten dark in the short time they'd been inside.

"I'm supposed to be upset, right?" she said. "You're supposed to be upset. We're supposed to ask each other how this happened. Then I'm supposed to say you don't have to feel obligated. Are you upset?"

She studied him under the bright lights of Times Square, a false daytime at night. He didn't seem upset. He was unflappable. She'd seen it at the bar and she was witnessing it now.

"Nope," he said. "Are you?"

"No."

He was built to take a blow, rock back on his heels for a moment, maybe, but never fall. We can do this, she thought, and knew he was thinking the same. She didn't know how, it would no doubt get complicated, but she knew in her heart that they could. The sidewalk was thick with people. Usher was on the ten-story screen above them, saying how much he loved New York while "Yeah!" played in the background. There was no mystery; they both knew exactly how it happened. She forgot to renew her birth control prescription. To get a fresh pack of pills before heading to Gillam for the weekend she'd have to wait at Health Services for probably over an hour since she didn't have an appointment. If she waited, she'd miss the best train, and she wanted to get to Gillam as soon as possible, get to him. Hours later, when she told him, he said it was fine, he'd pick up condoms, or they could skip it this time, it was up to her. But she didn't want to skip it. What could happen? One little time. But then it turned into several times, because she stayed the whole weekend and he never got around to buying condoms and she didn't make it to Health Services until Monday.

"I want to marry you, Jessie," he said. "Not because of this. I wanted to anyway but I was thinking about how I'd ask." He paused. "You are—"

"What?"

She knew why she loved him, but she wasn't sure why he loved her. He appeared to be struggling with something, finding the right word, nailing down an exact thought, and even seeing him struggle opened something in her and she knew that his was the name written onto her soul, no matter what came next. "You're kind and funny but there are a million women like that. You're smart, obviously, but it's not that either. You're different. You see things differently. It's like I knew you right away. I'm never more myself than I am when I'm with you. I don't know how else to describe it."

"Malcolm," she said. "I'd marry you tomorrow."

"So let's," he said, sweeping her up roughly.

"Careful! The baby!" She laughed, and he clutched his head as he stared at her midriff.

"Holy shit."

"I never wanted a wedding. Like in a hall with centerpieces and stuff. That's not me. I've never once had a fantasy about a wedding dress."

"I know."

"The courthouse sounds perfect to me. Quick and easy. Walk to lunch after."

"Well, maybe a party at the bar, right? Something low-key?"

She laughed, "Of course." And then her expression changed. "Oh God. You have to come with me to tell my parents."

"Will they want us to do it in a church? My mother will definitely say something about that but she won't really care."

"Well, yeah, but—" She laid a hand on her stomach. "I think that ship has sailed."

"What about school? We have to find a place to live."

"I'm done after finals. I'm about to accept that position with Laborers'

International. I take the bar in July. We have nine months to get ready. Well, eight I guess. I think my mother will help as long as we're close by. It can work."

"And Hugh has already said something about wanting to retire. He asked if I'd be interested in buying the place."

"And you would be interested, right? You love that bar."

"Yes," he said. "This is going to be so good."

Twelve years later, when Hugh finally announced that he was buying a house in South Carolina, that he couldn't take winters in New York anymore, not with his aching hip or his neuropathy, Malcolm figured that was it, he'd forget about all the hints he'd dropped over the years and give the Half Moon to one of his dipshit sons. Malcolm would have to find a job for the first time in twenty-four years. But one morning before opening, when Malcolm was going through receipts, Hugh came in, bypassed his usual chair, and sat on a stool like a regular.

"Malcolm," he said, laying his meaty hand on the bar, his wedding band so deeply embedded into the fat of his finger that Malcolm didn't know how it wasn't cutting off his circulation. "Here's what I'd like to see happen." His face was swollen and red, a drinker, though Malcolm had never once seen him drunk.

He took a pen from his pocket and wrote two numbers on a napkin. The first was the price for the business alone, and the second was the price for the business with the building included. The building didn't look like much, and needed a lot of work, but a stone's throw from the city meant it had real value. Then he coughed into his fist for half a minute, hacked and growled and wheezed. When he stopped, he rested his hand on his enormous belly, and told Malcolm he'd give him time to think about it.

"You okay, Hugh? You good?" Malcolm put a glass of water in front of him.

"Fine, I'm fine."

Hugh wouldn't admit it even if he knew that very hour would be his last, but they had their lines to say. Hugh had known Malcolm since he was a kid, had known his father, though he never wanted to talk about Darren Gephardt when Malcolm brought him up. Hugh said if Malcolm didn't have the money, or if the bank wouldn't back him, they'd work something out.

Later, as he watched Hugh wedge himself into his Cadillac, the steering wheel toylike in his giant hands, Malcolm wondered what would have happened if his father had not died at forty-three. Would Malcolm have eventually managed Gephardt's, his father's bar? Would he have inherited it by now? It was a block from Penn Station, and Malcolm could still feel the energy of the place, the people and personalities that swept through. Cops and criminals drinking side by side, women who sat so primly at the bar but whom his father said to stay away from once he turned sixteen and they started eyeing him.

When it wasn't too busy, his father used to take meetings at a two-top in the back and once, during a big renovation when the bar was closed for a few weeks, a man Malcolm had never seen before pulled aside the thick plastic dust flaps at the front and approached his father cautiously, as if he needed permission. It was the day after Malcolm's ninth birthday, and he'd just gotten in trouble for firing a nail gun he found lying on a windowsill. When the adults were distracted, he pressed the trigger three times—three loud cracks—and like magic there were the nailheads, shining like jewels on a wall that had just been taped and mudded. His punishment was to sit in the corner and do nothing for one hour, but a guy called Truck who worked for his dad slipped him a jumbo bag of Lay's. From his angle on the floor he entertained himself by looking at everyone who walked by outside.

"Look at this kid," his father said to Truck, and shook his head. "He's enjoying himself."

The man who came in approached his father and Truck just like their old Jack Russell, Lucky, did when he wanted his belly rubbed but was afraid to come too close in case he got a kick instead. Malcolm couldn't hear what they were saying but his father's voice seemed different, cold. He felt worried enough to put down the bag of chips, rub his greasy fingers on his sweatpants, and glance down the street to see if he might spot his mother returning from her errands. Nothing bad would happen if his mother were there. The man hated his father, it was obvious. And he seemed more nervous than adults usually were. His dress shirt was untucked, his tie askew. His father made no effort to make him feel at home like he usually did when people came into his bar. Malcolm got a scared feeling in his belly. He should shout, he thought. He should do something. But next thing his father nodded toward Malcolm, all three men looked over at the small sawdust-covered boy in the corner, and without discussing it they stepped into his father's office and closed the door. They still hadn't come out when Malcolm's mother returned.

"Darren?" Gail called, when Malcolm told her where they were. She tapped lightly on the office door with her fingernails, tilted her head to listen.

"I'll see you at home," Darren said, without opening the door.

"What were they doing?" Malcolm asked his mother on the drive home. "What were they saying?" He tried to explain what he'd seen, what a scary face his Dad made at the guy, scary mostly because Malcolm had never seen it before so it seemed like his own dad was a stranger for a second, but his mom said it was nothing, it was business, his dad was his dad and he loved him.

Hugh had three sons, and not one of them had ever worked at the Half Moon. Not one of them had ever held a family party there or shown up half in the bag. They didn't ask their daughters to get up on the bar to dance a reel as Malcolm's sister, Mary, had been asked to do by their father many times when Gephardt's was booming, a success story right there in the shadow of the busiest train station in the world, so busy that Malcolm's mother learned how to drive on highways and parallel park so they could go to the city to see him. Otherwise they never would.

"Where did all that money go?" Malcolm asked over the years, tentatively at first but then more bluntly. He'd seen the photos. He'd heard the stories. Muhammad Ali had eaten a meal at Gephardt's within a week of returning from Ireland, where he barely beat Al Lewis in eleven rounds. A famous actor had come by and, sick of waiting, drank a warm beer a stranger left behind. Malcolm's mother had been living so carefully since Malcolm was eighteen that it was obvious there was no surplus, no retirement account, no special accommodation made for a career so vicarious that one was always having to borrow from Peter to pay Paul.

"But Muhammad Ali," Malcolm said to his mother once. "The place must have been pretty popular for him to go there."

His mother scoffed. "Your father knew his driver! They grew up together. Can't pay bills with stories."

"But I thought—"

"And the rent was going sky high. We couldn't have held on to it if that's what you're asking, there was no way. Not without your dad . . ." Her sentence petered out, as if she couldn't quite figure out how to phrase something.

"What?"

"Well, he was a bookmaker, of course."

"Really?"

She looked at him. "You knew that."

"You always said that bar was a mint."

"Well, it was. But that part of it?" She passed her hand in front of her face as if waving away cigarette smoke. "I couldn't keep that up."

Once in a while, Little Hughie came by the Half Moon at his father's bidding, but he walked through the place like a foreigner in an unfamiliar land. Malcolm would greet him warmly, ask how he was, but Hughie always seemed uncomfortable, so Malcolm didn't bother with him much beyond that. Would be nice if he stayed for a drink, remembered some funny things about high school, but Hughie always had to be somewhere. Rumor was when his boys turned eighteen, Big Hugh warned them to never let him catch them drinking there, embarrassing themselves. He wanted them to be businessmen, wear suits every day. But wasn't Hugh a businessman? Malcolm thought. Wasn't he in fact better off than those guys in suits because he didn't answer to anyone? In addition to the drinking, the nightly peeling of someone off a stool while that person either wept or cursed at you, Hugh said he didn't want his boys feeling the weight of a stack of cash at the end of a night. It was too tempting for a young person, and giving in to that temptation was shortsighted. Something about that nagged Malcolm, who was the same age as Little Hughie and sat next to him in American history their senior year. Malcolm remembered Hughie giving a two-minute speech on the wedding of the rails, and watching as the sweat beaded at his hairline, ran down by his ear. Malcolm went up there next and winged it, having completely forgotten he was supposed to present that day, and the podium was dotted with Hughie's sweat. Malcolm got a B and Hughie got a C.

But Hughie did a summer enhancement program at Columbia when they graduated, the same summer Big Hugh taught Malcolm how to change a keg, how to free pour, how to make his own syrups if the bar ran out. "Surprised your father never showed you," Hugh said once, and more than two decades later, Malcolm still thought about him saying that—his exact expression and tone—every time he changed a keg.

"He was proud, your father," Hugh said another time, out of nowhere, or so it seemed, until Malcolm noticed a news story about a shooting outside Penn Station on the TV over the bar. "Some people thought he was arrogant."

"What do you mean?"

"Probably because he bought that bar in the city instead of up here.

He didn't think much of this place, I don't think. I'm sure he thought it was very small town compared to Gephardt's."

Malcolm turned to look at him, but Hugh was still staring at the TV. "He had a steak on the menu for like thirty bucks at Gephardt's. Keep in mind this was in the seventies. You didn't hear of that kind of thing in an Irish pub."

"You were there? You never said you went there."

"Oh yeah, I was there a lot of times."

"So you knew my dad pretty well?"

Hugh seemed to consider his words. "I knew him." He turned to Malcolm. "Did he ever say anything to you about me? Or about the Half Moon?"

"I don't think so," Malcolm said.

"Really? Nothing?"

Malcolm shrugged. "No."

Hugh nodded, and Malcolm hoped his feelings weren't hurt. Maybe he should have told Hugh that his dad loved the Half Moon, but the truth was he never remembered his dad acknowledging its existence at all. He only had eyes for the city and often said if it weren't for Gail, who insisted on a yard as soon as Mary was born, they'd be living somewhere downtown.

"So you remember it? Your dad's place?"

"Yeah, of course I remember it. I was eighteen when he died." After Gephardt's it became a more generic sports bar called Over Time. They took down the photos of the Irish countryside and replaced them with signed posters of athletes.

"I was just wondering if you visited him there. If he let you and your sister there when you were growing up."

"Yeah he did. Why?"

"Jeez, Mal, no reason. I'm just asking."

Once in a while, especially when Malcolm was younger, Hugh would comment that his own boys weren't as wise as Malcolm, and he'd tap the side of his nose. It was a compliment, Malcolm always told himself after, and couldn't for the life of him figure out why it unsettled him. Everyone knew being wise was a good thing.

Alone in the bar after Hugh made his offer, eleven thirty in the morning, a tower of receipts on the spike, Malcolm poured one small scotch and drank it slowly as he looked at the yellow sunlight pouring in through the windows, falling on the beat-up tables and chairs. The temperature was brisk but the forecast looked lovely for that whole week, and he thought about how nice it would be to sit outside. Then, with Hugh's words still echoing, he saw it right before him: everything the place could be. Stonework, string lights, umbrellas, patio heaters through November, blankets they could lend if people got chilly, like they did in Germany, according to Jess, who'd been there. He'd have half-moons stitched into the corners. Maybe on the umbrellas, too. He could have T-shirts available for sale like they did at bars down the shore.

It was a risk that they could just barely take on. As manager he made a salary they could rely on. As owner he'd have to look at the net profits each month, invest what he could back into the business, and take whatever was left as income. To do even that much, they'd have to cash out another portion of Jess's retirement savings.

"It's really just a question of money," Malcolm said. He'd taken the night off and had dinner ready when she walked in from work. She was exhausted. She'd been fantasizing about a cold glass of wine since three o'clock. After running to catch the 5:46, the train ended up sitting in a tunnel just outside Hackensack because of system-wide signal problems. When the train lost power and went dark, the woman in the seat next to her started taking small sips of air like she couldn't breathe. Jess asked if she was claustrophobic, and offered the bottle of water she'd been drinking from, assured the woman she wasn't sick or anything. The man across the aisle informed them that she was probably cleithrophobic, not claustrophobic—a common mistake. When he turned away, Jess mimed gagging herself, and the woman almost smiled.

By the time she got to Gillam, it was after seven. At first she thought Malcolm being home was just a nice surprise—they rarely ate together on Friday nights—but then she realized it was because the day he'd been waiting for had finally arrived and he wanted to talk it out.

"Just money," Jess repeated.

"You know what I mean."

She didn't know what he meant—money was *the* question.

He'd made pasta in a cream sauce. Hunks of chicken. The pots and pans he'd used were washed and drying on the rack. As soon as she understood that he didn't simply have André pass two meals out the alley door of the Half Moon, she softened. Malcolm taking over the business felt inevitable, especially when Hugh said his sons had no interest, but he had to see that the building was way out of reach. She didn't have to sit down with the numbers to know that much. She understood the potential it had, yes, but a big renovation would require even more money.

"I don't know. Hugh said he'd work something out with me if I wanted to buy both," Malcolm said. "A side deal."

"No way," Jess said, incredulous. "I really don't want to be tied to Hugh Lydon. Do you?"

"We go way back! It wouldn't be like that with me. It would be fine."

Jess thought of the guys who worked for Hugh in varying capacities that no one ever discussed. Men twenty years older than Malcolm, or maybe the same age, it was impossible to tell. They were the type of men who barely spoke but cried at ballads on St. Patrick's Day. When they came into the bar, Malcolm served them, never charged them, never asked any questions. They ran errands for Hugh, collected rent on apartment buildings he owned in the Bronx that he never referenced but André knew about somehow, said the places were complete holes. The guys came in for extra security on big nights, and Jess had a memory of the one called the Grog hitting on her even though she was newly married to Malcolm, who was twenty feet away. Pleasantly buzzed, she was waiting for the bathroom, leaning against the wall. She closed her eyes for a moment, and when she opened them, he was standing in front of her. He put one hand on her hip as if to ask her a question, and she put her hand over his and gave it back to him like she was apologizing, like it was awfully tempting but she was a good girl.

It was as if Malcolm didn't even hear her. "That second floor would pay for itself pretty quickly. I was thinking I could get an architect to see about getting the roof reinforced to bear weight. I could put up some sort of wood panel, something to block out that ugly section of the parking lot. There's a nice view up there if you don't look north. It would have a different vibe than downstairs."

She put her fork down. "You want to hire an architect? With what? It's a stretch to buy the business alone and keep it exactly the way it is. And if you so much as change one tiny thing, that crew of old-timers you're counting on to buy twenty drinks a week will take it personally. Remember when the Brew Pub got new menus? People lost their minds. It was the exact same food, just printed in a different font. And even if everything stays exactly as is, Hugh's profit won't be your profit because you'll be mortgaged to the hilt."

"No shit, Jess." Malcolm pushed back from the table. Why isn't there any money, the expression on his face asked. In the world of bad investments, wouldn't nearly seven years of fertility treatments be right at the top? At first they could keep up with whatever insurance didn't cover by going to his safe deposit box, handing over a brick of cash. But it didn't take that long for the box to empty. All that money—just gone. He stopped himself from saying it aloud, but they knew each other so well that the air between them became legible, and she could read it anyway. He sat there with his arms crossed, his wide shoulders tensed, pretending he'd forgotten what it was he was going to say, but her gimlet eye took it in, every last word.

They didn't talk about it all weekend. Instead they talked around it, a half-moon-shaped sinkhole they were both careful to avoid. On the Sunday after Hugh raised all of this with Malcolm, and after Malcolm raised it at home, she went for a long run and left on the kitchen counter printouts of other bars being offered for sale, scattered around the county. They were all asking less than what Hugh was asking for the Half Moon, but when he looked closely at the thumbnail photos, he could tell they were either smaller or in bad locations or total dives that would need to be gutted. There was no energy in these places, he said. No magic. Plus it meant something that it was the Half Moon, the place he knew best. It meant something that Hugh had handpicked him. There'd be a story to tell.

"Well?" she asked on Sunday night. Something had to be decided.

"I want to do this," he said. He turned toward the window but it was dark out, so it was like standing at a mirror. "I just feel like you had your shot and I'm sorry it didn't work but now it's my turn."

"What in the world does that mean?"

"I mean—"

But she knew what he meant, and she knew he wouldn't say it.

"Malcolm," she said, approaching him from behind and laying her cheek against the center of his back. "You deserve everything. Of course you do. But we just do not have the money right now. I know you think that's my fault—"

He sighed. "Of course I don't think it's your fault."

"Well, in any case, it's not there. We've already drained everything we can drain. But we can swing the business. You deserve it and you've earned it."

"For now, yeah, okay," he said, turning to face her. "Maybe we can strike a deal to buy the building down the road. Maybe he'll even write that in. The right of first refusal."

She raised an eyebrow to say she was impressed, relieved that this particular argument was over for the moment.

"I've been researching," he said.

He hadn't planned on doing anything behind her back, but on the other hand he was certain she'd eventually understand that in business there were moments when opportunities had to be seized. She complained of meetings all day, meetings about meetings, but his line of work was different. Information was packaged inside euphemisms, everything made pleasant and polite until it suddenly wasn't. Deals were made on handshakes. Oaths sworn over drinks. Shortly after he and Jess came to a grudging agreement, and Malcolm called Hugh to tell him that after giving it much thought he wanted to buy only the business, Hugh stopped by to clear out his personal items from the storeroom. It was ten days before the closing. They ended up talking about the building once again, all the potential it held. Hugh told Malcolm that he'd hold on to it for a while, but then he'd have to sell. And then what? Where would that leave Malcolm? Malcolm thought about his mother saying the rent on Gephardt's shot sky high after the lease was up. It was a point he'd made to Jess but Jess wouldn't budge.

"Why didn't you ever do anything with upstairs?" Malcolm asked, and Hugh reminded Malcolm that the place was a broken-down diner when he bought it in 1973. He already brought it a long way. He thought about turning upstairs into an apartment, but his interest faded when they ran up against permit issues and, really, he didn't want to deal with anyone calling him in the middle of the night to say the music was too loud. The bar was packed four nights a week plus pretty much all day on Sundays. What more could he ask for? But a young man like Malcolm?

There were a dozen ways a person with vision could make something fresh of the place. And then, running his massive thumb along one of his unruly eyebrows, he offered a private loan so that Malcolm could buy the building, too, without putting any additional money down. The underwriters at the bank would need to know the provenance of a sudden, large deposit, so they'd call it a gift, but between Malcolm and Hugh, just the two of them, they'd work it out. Large gifts were taxed pretty steeply, but Hugh said they'd bundle all that in the repayment, not a big deal. Malcolm immediately understood that making the offer had been the whole point of dropping by. It was simple, really.

"I mean, can you think of it as yours if you don't own the building, Malcolm? That's what I'd ask myself if I were you."

"Jess isn't so keen on the idea. She—"

"Jess? I thought you two might have . . . I don't know. Haven't seen her in a while. I didn't want to ask."

"We're good," Malcolm laughed, but felt a little shaken at the bottom of it. Him and Jess? "She's working a lot. Like everyone."

"I really think you should consider it."

"I will."

Malcolm didn't get a lawyer for the closing, out of respect for Hugh. He couldn't ask Jess to come with him because she'd find out about his side deal, and then what would he do? Stand there looking at his shoes while she asked Hugh a hundred questions? And also, there might not be any going back now, even if he changed his mind, even if Jess made him. As soon as he told Hugh that he wanted to buy the building after all, he set something in motion, and later that very afternoon Bronx Stevie dropped off a check. "From the boss," he said simply, and then asked for a Guinness. When Malcolm opened the envelope, he found a check written for an amount far larger than the one he'd written when he and

Jess bought their house, wiping out all of their savings. Included also was a letter to the loan officer at the bank, explaining Hugh and Malcolm's long relationship, confirming the money was a gift, free and clear.

"The letter is for show, of course," Bronx Stevie said, and Malcolm was surprised he'd read it. The envelope had been sealed.

He waited two days to deposit the money. Jess always looked at their month's-end balance, so he waited until the new month. Rumor was that Hugh bought each of his sons their first homes, and though Malcolm was not naïve enough to think Hugh thought of him as a son, twenty-four years of working for him must mean something.

After, they celebrated with a bottle of bourbon Hugh had been keeping for a special occasion. Hugh's lawyer whistled when he saw it, hung around for one, and when he left, Hugh went to his car for a box of cigars, which he offered around the bar. He and Malcolm sat on side-by-side stools, smoking, drinking, talking about the old days, the craziest nights. The time they found a gun on the floor, just lying there under a chair alongside a crumbled napkin. The time someone left an urn of ashes. The time a woman unzipped her dress and stepped out of it, her breasts absolute perfection where they sat in her bra, a silvered C-section scar above her panties, the inscrutable expression on Malcolm's face when he simply picked up the dress and handed it to her like it was nothing, no big deal, and told her the floor was filthy so she should probably just put it back on. And then, when she did put it back on, right there in front of them, how he'd suggested gently, "Is it time to call it a night?"

There were stories Malcolm had forgotten, but they rose up again unbidden like they'd taken place the day before. He felt so full of joy that he wanted to call Jess, tell her to get down to the bar because there was finally something to celebrate. The bar was his! Officially. Not just in spirit but in name and deed. A place he loved. His. He wanted to ask her if she remembered the night she won the ladies' darts championship. He wanted to ask her if she remembered when that band called her up during their session, put her on the spot, and she surprised everyone with the most clear-throated rendition of "The Parting Glass."

"I didn't even know you knew that song," Malcolm said at the time.

"Everyone knows that song," she said. "Everyone here, I mean."

Her voice was strong and unwavering, and the whole place had hushed to listen. You are full of surprises, he thought that night, looking at her. She had something other women didn't. She was entirely herself, she never looked left or right to figure out how to be. She could be wild sometimes—dancing and laughing like the rest of them, walking barefoot through town with her high heels hooked on her fingers. But she could be intensely quiet, too. If someone was telling her something important, or if she sensed something was troubling them. If she had something on her mind. He looked over to the corner where she stood to sing that night, but instead of a band set up there was a four-top, three seats taken.

People still talked about their wedding party at the bar. How fun it was despite the short notice, Jess a sober bride. It started at two in the afternoon and by the time everyone left it was dawn the next day, Jess sleeping in a chair with Malcolm's suit jacket draped around her. Malcolm's roommate had moved out several months before, so Jess moved in with her overnight bag, said she'd get the rest from Cobie's when they could borrow a truck. Hugh apologized that he couldn't be there, but he gave them the party as his gift—a table spread with appetizers and a steep discount on the open bar. He had John hang a sign on the door that said the Half Moon was closed for a private event. Cobie had filled the place with flowers, mason jars full of daisies. Jess's high school friends had gone in on little bottles of champagne as favors, and Gail Gephardt made the cake. Jess's parents stayed for about two hours, sipping drinks, still shell-shocked, Malcolm supposed. He tried to put himself in their shoes and decided it was nothing to feel insulted about. Jess's mother was more disappointed than her father, for her girl to have all that promise and then get herself bogged down with a baby before she'd had a chance to find her footing. To be tied to a local bartender for life. "Ouch," Malcolm said when Jess reported that, and she instantly went pale. "Oh my God, why did I tell you that?" She hugged him. "Because it's insane and she doesn't mean it. When she's worried she lashes out."

Gail Gephardt kept glancing over at the Ryans during the brief cere-mony at the courthouse, making sure their faces didn't imply Jess could have done one bit better than her boy. After, the parents all agreed that it would be nice to get a priest to bless the union. Gail said a baby was always good news no matter what the circumstances, but Maureen Ryan didn't say a word about that.

Everyone knew about the baby coming, though Jess's mother had cau-tioned her not to tell anyone until she was at least twelve weeks along.

"Why not?" Jess had asked. They were young and beautiful. Everything was ahead of them.

Malcolm said he wished his father were still alive to celebrate, and Hugh put his drink down on the bar, as if hearing the thought said aloud took the wind out of him. "You're a lot like him," Hugh said after a moment. "Except—"

"Except what?" Sometimes Malcolm got the feeling they'd known each other better than Hugh ever let on.

"I don't know." Did you like him? Malcolm wanted to ask, but it felt far too pathetic, hoping his long-dead father was a person people liked. When Hugh finally left, wishing him the best once more, Malcolm picked up his phone to call Jess but got a shock when he saw the time. The closing had wrapped up around two, Hugh's lawyer had left around four, and it was already eleven thirty. He texted instead.

What are you doing?

Half asleep. Signed and sealed?

All good

Heading home?

In a bit

Let's celebrate this wknd

Yes definitely

He picked up the near-empty bottle Hugh had left behind and looked at the label.

"Surprised he opened this one," Malcolm said to Emma, who was behind the bar. "The price of it."

"Isn't it yours now?" she said. "Technically?"

"Oh," Malcolm said, stunned. And everyone around them, everyone tuned in to the special thing that had happened that night, the meeting of a fate, the shaking of its hand, all laughed.

What if they hadn't gotten married so quickly? What if that baby had been born? It was like those Choose Your Own Adventure books he used to love as a kid, where you could follow a dozen different paths to a different conclusion, each road forking again and again.

The doctor said it was perfectly normal. It happened more than people knew. As many as fifty percent of pregnancies, often before the woman even knew she was pregnant. Between fifteen and twenty-five percent of recognized pregnancies. And it could be for no reason at all, or at least no reason a doctor could isolate. The important thing to know was that there was nothing to worry about. Jess was only twenty-five and the picture of health. When the time came and they wanted to try again, it would more than likely all be fine.

Although they were knocked down, surprised by how sad they were, they agreed that good had come out of it. They were bound now. They loved each other and had no regrets. Jess recovered fairly quickly. She started the job with the union. She took the bar exam and passed with flying colors. She said she didn't know how much she was allowed to grieve, given that it wasn't something she'd been trying for or even wanted, and that she'd only been nine weeks along. Malcolm told her it wasn't a question of being allowed, she felt what she felt, there was no rule book. Mostly, he was surprised. They both felt sort of guilty, like maybe they'd done something wrong—stayed out too late or tried to do too much in such a short period—but Jess said she felt better day by day, so Malcolm did, too. They agreed they had to get a bigger apartment and then, eventually, a house. Though they could have handled it, they were sure, now at least they could plan a little. Be ready. Now at least they knew what to expect.

three

Malcolm woke around noon on the Saturday after the storm to the sound of a loud crack, followed by a crash. His mind bleary, he thought for a moment that the noise came from inside the house, but then he heard another crack and looked over in time to glimpse a large, dark shape passing his bedroom window. The image of a body came to mind, someone jumping from the roof. It would be high enough to break a few bones, maybe, but not to die. Plus, no person could have gotten into the house without him hearing. Not Jess, in any case. If Jess so much as drove down their street, he'd feel a chord struck deep in his chest and he'd just know.

And then he remembered what Patrick and Siobhán had told him the night before. He tried to sit square to it, tried to take a good look, but it was as if what they said—about Jess, about Patrick's friend Neil—existed behind thick glass. In daylight, from the bed he considered more hers than his, since she used to always be in it when he came home at night, her long body turned toward his side, it felt absurd that she was sleeping, perhaps, at that very moment, in a place that was unfamiliar to him. That she was showering, or moving through rooms she felt at home in, while he, if he visited her, wouldn't know which door led where. For one second, he thought he might have dreamed it entirely, but then he noticed his clothes from the night before in a heap by the bathroom door, the topography of their bedroom so different without Jess's lotions and compacts and makeup brushes and multivitamins spread over the top of her dresser. Without six-and-a-half-years' worth of prescription bottles and hormone creams. Without her bangles and hoop earrings.

He looked at his phone. No new texts. No missed calls. He googled her name as he did most days, and there she was, Jessica Gephardt, senior counsel, wearing a blazer, her hair neater than it was in real life.

He looked back at the last text she sent, nearly a month earlier.

Malcolm, I canceled Dr. Hanley going forward. He's charging us full price for the last two sessions because he held the hour but we didn't show.

No abbreviations. Perfect punctuation. What about the therapy sessions before that? He wondered if she went alone, and whether that was ethical, talking about him in couples therapy when he wasn't there. She found Dr. Hanley because she thought he'd help her remind Malcolm of what they were working so hard for. But instead Dr. Hanley wanted to start way back. "There isn't enough time for that," Jess blurted out during their third session.

That she'd used his full name bothered him—not Mal, but Malcolm. Before last night Patrick had been suggesting Malcolm go to her, as if that didn't occur to him every single day. But when he pictured it—pulling up to Cobie's building, waiting on the stoop like a delivery boy while Jess decided whether to come out or not: screw that. And what would he say? She left him. If anyone should be doing the seeking, it should be her.

As he lay in bed, still looking at her LinkedIn photo, it dawned on him that the fact that no one had asked for her lately meant they probably all knew. No one asking for her was the best evidence that what Patrick and Siobhán had told him was true.

As soon as he got out of bed, he noticed the house was brutally cold, and when he went to the window, he saw two huge tree limbs on the ground below, just lying there in the snow, joint to joint, like a pair of lovers who'd spent themselves and then fallen asleep. There were two matching blemishes left behind on the tree. He pulled the comforter off their bed, wrapped it around his bare shoulders, and walked down the hall to one of the front windows. The Bennetts' mailbox was gone. Gerry Kowalski's little two-door hatchback was just a lump. The Colemans' collie was outside, and all Malcolm could see of him was his head hopping above the surface of the snow now and again while Jon Coleman stood in his open garage door blowing into his cupped fists. There was not even a tire mark in the road, no sign that the town plow had passed. Everyone's winter-bald gardens were buried under a blanket so clean and new that even Mike Dunleavy's trash-heap yard looked as tidy as a postcard. The sky was blue, cloudless. The tops of the row of evergreens across the street leaned in the wind. The temperature was expected to drop into the teens by nightfall and stay there for several days.

He wanted to call her right then and tell her it was time to come home. She was embarrassing herself, he would say, everyone knew what she'd done, but there was still a chance to work it out. There'd been a blizzard and enough was enough.

He tried once again to picture Neil Bratton. Jess was sleeping with him? Malcolm made himself picture it. He felt absurdly naïve, but was it possible they were just good friends, had a bunch in common, and people had drawn their own conclusions? He listed their shared interests on his fingers. They were both lawyers. That was one. He moved to his second finger but he couldn't think of anything else. He tried to decide whether it mattered. Malcolm had slept with what was probably considered a lot of people. God knew they didn't all mean something to him. And if he slept with someone new today, or ever, that person would never mean what Jess meant to him. It wouldn't mean that person really knew him, or would have any sort of say in his life. Jess was usually the one who told him how to think about things, how to see them, and he was trying to understand what she'd done the way she would if she weren't Jess, and he wasn't Malcolm, and Neil Bratton was a stand-in for anyone, and the people they were thinking about weren't them.

Maybe for Jess it was just mechanical, a joining of bodies without really knowing each other. If so, he could possibly get over that. But she would have confessed more easily, if this thing with Neil Bratton meant nothing. She was not a liar, so the seriousness of whatever was between her and this guy, this stranger, was the only thing that explained her silence. In a lineup of kneecaps or elbows, he could pick out Jess's from a group of a thousand. From fifty yards away he could tell her exact thought by the set of her shoulders.

Or not, it occurred to him. Or not.

A memory skittered through him, how he'd been brushing his teeth with the bathroom door open one morning and in the mirror he'd seen Jess lift his work shirt out of the hamper and press it to her face. He was about to ask what she was doing, when it hit him. He tried to never mention Emma at home, but maybe it was the omission of her name that pointed Jess to his interest. But interest wasn't a crime. Nor was the way his belly tightened when he passed close to her in the narrow space behind the bar. When Emma asked him a question, she didn't immediately doubt his answer, and that felt good. When she reported a problem, she looked at him with an expression of total faith that he would figure it out. One time, once, he stood so close to her as they were looking at an invoice that he could feel the light down on her arm brushing against him. She held perfectly still and so did he. Then Roddy came in and Malcolm shifted away.

In the days since Cobie told him Jess was in Gillam, he'd been tempted to drive by her mother's house, but he held strong. Every time he passed her block and didn't turn, he felt like he should be applauded for his self-restraint. How stupid he felt now. What a joke. He'd have been out on the street imagining every lighted room had her in it, when she wasn't even there. The night his friends came by specifically to tell him that she was not, in fact, at her mother's house, was the night he chose to drive over there and see for himself. The roads were getting worse by the minute, but he put the windshield wipers on the highest setting, leaned over the wheel to glimpse between the strokes, and turned onto her old street. Normally, he loved the drive home from the bar late at night, the feeling of being up and out when everyone else was asleep. It was like time outside of time, whenever he cruised around after closing, looking at the quiet of everything. But on that night, the utter stillness felt like a warning. He reached the crest in the road where he could glimpse her childhood home, where the first time he slept over—just a few hours after going down on her in her twin bed, an INXS poster taped to the wall—he tried to leave through the kitchen with only a brief hello, but Mr. Ryan stopped him, told him to sit. He had meant to go home before Jess's parents woke up, but he must have fallen asleep because next thing the room was full of light and Jess's bedside clock read eight thirty. Eight thirty meant he'd slept over. He was a guest of the whole house.

As they talked, Mr. Ryan folded a crust of bread and pushed it into a soft-boiled egg. A yellow drip landed on his beard, and Malcolm tried not to gag. He sipped the orange juice Mrs. Ryan made out of a frozen cylinder of concentrate, and wondered if the conversation was just a ruse, whether Mr. and Mrs. Ryan were just acting nonchalant until Jess emerged, and then they'd both get scolded. He was far too old for that, but he knew from his own house that girls were never too old to get scolded, and it would be wrong to leave now and have Jess take it alone.

And then Jess walked into the kitchen, freshly showered, in sweats and a T-shirt, her skin rosy, her green eyes bright despite only four hours of sleep. He could see that she was surprised he was still there, nervous about what her father might be saying.

"He didn't sleep in Mickey's bed," Mrs. Ryan said to her daughter, as if Malcolm couldn't hear them.

Jess's father was pretty sick by then, though no one knew it. Malcolm remembered him running his fingertips across his chest that morning, back and forth, sort of absentmindedly, as if feeling for something.

When Malcolm recollected that for Jess several years later, she said he made it up.

"How old are you?" Mr. Ryan asked Malcolm point-blank. Far too old to be sitting here, Malcolm thought. A four-and-a-half-year difference seemed greater in those years. At twenty-four, Jess still had one foot in childhood, despite two years of law school under her belt. Despite an apartment in the city. Jess's high school bedroom was downstairs and her parents' was on the second floor, but the house was not big. She'd refused to go to his apartment because she thought his roommate was weird, and they'd have to take a taxi from the bar because Malcolm's car was in the shop. Her house was walkable, she said, though it turned out to be a longer walk than he expected. "You said it was right up the road!" he complained, but she just laughed. "You're sure your parents won't wake up?" he asked when she opened the back door and paused to listen for a moment. The house was dark and silent.

"They didn't wake up last night," she said.

"Wait," he said, drawing up. "What?"

"I'm kidding," she said, rolling her eyes.

"He slept on the couch," Jess told her mother, by the sink. He'd glimpsed an old sofa in the little nook off the hallway and figured that was the couch she meant. He got nervous for a moment, as if he might be asked to prove it—what blanket did he use? what pillow?—but Jess's mother nodded and accepted that explanation so readily that he understood she didn't care whether it was true or not.

That was fifteen years ago, he realized as he rolled to a stop in front of the house. Her car wasn't there. He stared at the blank space in her mother's driveway as if waiting for something to appear, some bit of evidence that would prove Patrick and Siobhán wrong, some sign that she was in there with her mother, thinking about how to come home to him.

When he parked in his own driveway just three minutes later, the whole block, the whole town, felt lonelier than it ever did in daylight. He got out but when he turned toward the door, he found he couldn't go in, not yet. It was one thing to get home in the wee hours of the morning, collapse into bed, wake up, and rush out the door for another day. But it wasn't even midnight, and he wouldn't be able to fall asleep. He sat on his front step, the small awning over the door protecting him from the snow, and drew out the cigarette he'd bummed from Scotty an hour earlier, with this exact scene in mind. The temperature wasn't that cold. There was no wind, though the news said that was coming. The snow made a whisper-soft crystalline sound as it fell. He hadn't smoked in years, but right then, his empty house waiting behind him, he wondered if it were possible to change, to end up in a life completely different from the one he thought he was in.

He should have followed her that day. He should have stopped her from getting in her car and talked everything out with her, like Dr. Hanley said was important. But he'd just let her go. Because he was shocked. Why else? Because his feelings were hurt. Why else? Because he didn't know what to say.

He didn't know how much he depended on her habits to set the pattern for his days until they were gone. He never knew what he was supposed to do with himself when he was alone, and wondered what people did who lived by themselves their whole adult lives. He'd not eaten a single meal inside his house since Jess left. Days off he texted his friends to see what they were up to, see if he could get himself invited over to their houses or else peel them away from their families for a few hours. If that didn't work, he knew at least one bartender in most of the local places, and could go from one to the next, never a shortage of available spots. He could eat a sandwich at the bar; he didn't even need to talk to anyone. The sound of people talking all around him was enough company, far better than ESPN droning on in his empty living room.

On Halloween, the day that Jess left, he went to work as always. People filed into the Half Moon dressed as rock stars, as ghosts, as characters from TV shows everyone recognized, and there were moments when what had happened earlier that day was too surreal to be true. She'd taken the day off to organize the closets, she said. And she really had organized. He went to the gym around noon, and when he came home, he threw his keys on the hall table and noticed her duffel bag by the door. But he was distracted. It had been a tough week at the bar. His food supplier had to float him for the second time in a month. He'd already switched to a bar-food-only menu, no fresh vegetables, only stuff that could live in their walk-in until the apocalypse. The next step was scrapping food entirely and simply giving out bags of chips. More worrisome: he'd missed a payment with the Guinness guy—missed three payments, actually—but the last time was the delivery guy's fault. He didn't grab the check even though Malcolm left it out for him. They reported him to the state liquor authority, the alert went out, and since then he had to pay cash on delivery with all the booze suppliers. He owed the guy who came around in his beat-up van to clean the draft lines. He owed the soda guy. He owed the trash removal guys. He was owed his cut from the ATM and the jukebox, but the guys who ran them were so young he felt cheap going after them for it.

And then they ran out of vodka, a stupid miscalculation on his part, so he sent Roddy up to the liquor store to buy whatever vodka they had, full price. Instead of grabbing a variety, Roddy returned with six bottles of Absolut, and of course the next person who ordered asked for Ketel One and soda and the one after that asked for Stoli and anyone under forty-five wants Tito's and everyone acts as if everyone else's favorite vodka is garbage even though no human can actually tell one vodka from another.

Did a feeling of dread come over him when he noticed her duffel in the hall? He could hear her moving around up in their bedroom. He flipped through the mail and then threw it on the table next to his keys. As soon as he climbed the stairs and walked into their room, he saw that she was packing her old roller suitcase, too. "Malcolm," she said, as if she was surprised to see him.

"Are you going somewhere?" he asked. But then it hit him, what was happening, and he did the thing she hated whenever he was reeling on the inside. He made his body a suit of stone. He crossed his arms and pulled on his tight shoulder as if he'd not asked a question, as if he weren't waiting for an answer.

She took a deep breath, and he felt the hairs at the back of his neck rise.

"Just for a while," she said. "To think. Mal, there's so much that we need to—"

"To think," he repeated, and she nodded, looking up at him like she was making herself brave, like she was ready to answer anything he might ask her. He could see her pulse flickering in her slender throat, her long dark hair swept up as it always was when she was around the house. But he was too surprised to ask another question.

"I can't deal with this," he said. "Not this week. Do you even know what's going on at the bar? I can't."

He gestured at her little piles of clothes and shook his head as if to say this—leaving—was what they promised each other they'd never do. They'd never even joke about it. They were family, thick or thin. And yet.

She turned back to the suitcase. The headache she'd been nursing for days coalesced into a fine point behind her brow.

If he'd been paying attention, he would have figured it out the day before. She'd cleaned out the drawers of the bathroom vanity. She got a giant black trash bag and threw out every half-empty hair product and lotion. She was about to throw out all the unopened pregnancy tests but something stopped her. Instead, she opened one, peed on it, examined her face in the bathroom mirror while she waited for the line to appear. It had been two years since her last pregnancy test. She tried to remember what she used to think about as she waited, whether sometimes she thought of errands she had to run and what she might eat for dinner, or whether she always, every time, imagined what it would feel like to push out a baby and hear her shocked wails, have her placed on her chest for the familiar smell of her body, the only home she'd ever known. This is air, she'd whisper to her baby. That's light. Those are people, like you. She opened another test and did it again, though there was barely enough left in her bladder to saturate the stick. She imagined what she'd do if two lines appeared. She'd read the stories, women conceiving when it made the least sense. A hundred thousand dollars spent on fertility but lo and behold one weekend in Puerto Rico when she was not even ovulating did the trick. If that stick displayed a second line, whose baby would it be? Cold shock rolled through her and she clutched the edge of the counter.

She needed to tell him about Neil. She needed to tell him before he heard it from someone else.

"Malcolm," she said and stood up. "I know it's not a good time, but I need to clear my head. I just don't think the way we are right now can go on any longer. Before I go, I need to tell you something that I should have—"

"Those are mine," he interrupted, looking at the set of earbuds in her hand.

The rest of her sentence was cut off as if he'd clapped a hand over her mouth.

"These?" she asked, holding up the earbuds.

"They're mine," he repeated. He wasn't going to ask where she was going or why, but she could see in his stance that, by God, those earbuds would be the hill he chose to die on.

"I think they're mine," she said. "See?" She showed him the dot of nail polish she'd used to mark them, to differentiate them from his.

Packing he could take. The fact that she was leaving he could take. But that little dot of nail polish sent him over. He pounded down the stairs, and when he slammed the door the whole house shook.

Ten minutes later he was back, rooting around for something or maybe working himself up to a question.

"You don't want to know where I'm going?" she asked when he didn't say anything.

"Nope," he said.

"Well, I'm going to Cobie's," she said, her voice catching.

"Go to the fucking moon if you want," he said, and left the room again. He went downstairs and she imagined him pacing, cracking his knuckles, trying to decide what to do or say. She thought she'd hear the sound of his car starting, him driving away, but he stayed. He's hurt, she told herself. He's angry and feels stupid. Just as she would feel if the tables were turned. Just as anyone would. They'd talk, surely, after a cooling-off period. They'd talk after they got used to having a little space from each other. Then she'd tell him everything.

As she finished packing, little kids started ringing the doorbell, crying out, "Trick or treat." She listened to Malcolm make a big deal about costumes, imagined him waving to the parents standing at the curb. Amazing, the way he found a different thing to say to each kid. She alone knew how hard he must be working to sound friendly and normal. But why? Was it a positive attribute, or was it pathological, that desperation to shield the world from his personal business? Listening to him, no one would guess what was going on in his life, his house, at that very moment.

Jess carried her suitcase down the long flight of stairs, and seeing the effort it took felt like a jolt through Malcolm's bones, that feeling like missing the last step. He watched her heave it into the trunk of her car, somehow, he didn't think she'd be able to do it, and then he just stood there while she went back for the duffel, also packed tight.

The craziest thing, the thing he couldn't stop thinking about after she was gone, was that as he was driving home from the gym, he thought she might come over to the bar with him, help him judge the costumes and award prizes, throw a few darts if she was having fun. It had been such a long time since she went there just to hang out, and she loved

Halloween. They'd been moving around each other without seeing one another lately, but that week she'd touched his arm as she passed behind him at the sink. She'd reached for him in her sleep and fitted her body around his. He thought things were getting better, but actually, all that time, she was saying goodbye.

What did he do in his house for two hours, alone, before he left for the bar? Aside from answer the door over and over and over again. It was lost time. The last thing she said to him was a warning not to leave the candy bowl outside because one bratty kid would just dump the whole thing in his bag. And then they looked at each other across a distance of maybe ten feet—she on the front lawn, he at the door, and he thought, Jesus Christ, she's micromanaging the candy bowl even now.

He almost never drank at work but once he got to the bar that Halloween night, he did two shots, quickly, before the party started, and then three more, spaced about thirty minutes apart so he was never drunk, exactly, just better able to contain thoughts of Jess in a corner of his mind. He gave out the prizes for best costumes, singles and groups. He thought he was being normal, being fun even, but then Emma's mouth was by his ear, asking if he wanted to take a break.

"I had a rough afternoon," he said, standing close to her as he took in the delicate frame her collarbones made for her shoulders, the way her shirt skimmed her body. He was about to tell her what happened, that he and Jess had separated, he guessed, if that was the right word, but they got interrupted by a group of women a little older than Malcolm who'd come dressed as a nineties girl band and wanted a photo with him. So he smiled, and they leaned against him and cocked their hips, and then they huddled over phones and after a moment asked for another photo, just one more, a slightly different angle. He wondered how old their children were, if they had children. He wondered if they were divorced. He could tell which ones among them had once been hot, and which had blossomed later, after marriage, after motherhood, perhaps, a rare trajectory.

He considered telling them that they had a few good years in them still, despite their age, and that's when he suspected he might be more drunk than he thought he was. Emma guided him to a stool, told him he could be the master of ceremonies from a seated position. And then she brought him a pint of water and a plate of fries.

He half expected to arrive home hours later and find Jess there, waiting for him. "Sorry about before," she might say, her voice hoarse with sleep. "Can we talk about it tomorrow?" But inside, the house was as empty as it had been when he left, a dirty coffee mug in the sink.

He thought, at first, that he might never have to tell her about his side deal with Hugh. One day, when business was booming and they were organizing their assets, he'd present her with a nice surprise.

But she wouldn't leave it alone. Hugh sent a fruit basket to the house along with a card that referenced the smart decision Malcolm had made, the good bones the place had. Jess kept leaning across the counter to take another look at the message, asking Malcolm what it meant.

"He just means best of luck, I guess," Malcolm said, shrugging. But there was something in the construction of the message. She kept re-reading it like she was dowsing for water, going around with her rod, poking surfaces.

At first, he could see, she honestly didn't know. But then, two days after closing, while Malcolm was sleeping and she was getting ready for work, it dawned on her.

"Did you buy the building? Did we? The contract I saw only included the business."

She never woke him before she left for work, but that morning she shook him until he opened his eyes. She asked him to please sit up.

So he told her, and she went pale, stared at him for a long time. She asked if he'd hired a lawyer, and when he said he had not, she went even more pale. He thought for a moment that she'd hold back, that she'd see that it wasn't all that different from what they agreed to except they'd have to shoot some money over to Hugh, too. And for that they owned a building! A building with enormous potential! But after a moment of silence where it turned out she was only gathering her strength, she asked everything at once: the terms, the payout structure, what happens if he defaults. She asked to see what he signed.

"I didn't sign anything. We did it on a handshake."

She pressed her palm to her forehead and stood there for a moment, staring at him. He'd never known her to be at a loss for words before.

"You left me out of things, too," he said, before she could start.

"What did I leave you out of? I never hid anything from you!"

"Give me a break," he said. "You knew I didn't want to take everything so far. You knew I didn't, but you kept making appointments. Last time you had your baselines taken before I even knew we were doing it again. That was sneaky."

"Sneaky! The window was so small, and getting smaller every single day. You want to think about everything for a month, but there was ab-solutely no time for that. I'm not a mind reader, Malcolm. I thought we wanted the same thing. If you were *that* against it, you could have made yourself heard."

"I wasn't against it. I just—it was like a vacuum that sucked up every-thing."

"You're obsessed with how much it cost. To have a child. Ask anyone what they think their child is worth, and they'll tell you she's invalu-able."

"I'm sure they would! But we don't have a child, Jess. So this isn't the same. And anyway, *what I meant* was that it was sucking all the joy from our lives. It was all we ever thought about. But sure, money, too. You act like that's superficial or something but people like us—people like you and me—we can't afford multiple big dreams. We can only afford one.

And I just wonder why it had to be that one. When it was very clear to everyone except you that it wouldn't work out."

"Then why did you go along for so long? If you were so sure it wouldn't work?"

"Because," he said, and looked at her like the answer was so obvious he'd never bothered putting it into words.

"Because?"

"Because it's what you wanted."

The possibility that Jess loved this guy shifted something, and for the first time in seventeen weeks, for the first time since putting his head down and deciding he'd just keep going until she came around, he looked up and noticed that he'd long since wandered off the path he was on, that he didn't have any idea where he was. To distract himself he did his ritual calculations, his morning routine, like daily affirmations but with the opposite effect: What was left in the freezer? What was left in the storeroom? He was still standing at the window with the comforter around his shoulders, but in his mind he could see everything. The drop bag had some heft to it for the first time in ages, and of course it was the one day he probably wouldn't be able to get to the bank. First, he had to retrieve it from the safe at the bar. It had been a few years since he'd skied, but his gear was still in the attic, unless Jess had tossed it in a purge. Would the bank even be open?

Gas, electric, and cable for the bar were all scheduled to go through on Monday. Those same bills were due on the house the following week. The minimum payments were due on two credit cards. Jess's student loan would auto-deduct from their joint checking. He was behind with Hugh once again. The first time he fell behind, Hugh's guys had come by the bar, asked for Malcolm. Roddy fetched him from the back, but when

Malcolm emerged, they nodded a greeting, nothing more, as if they just wanted to lay eyes on him and make sure he knew they were there. They sat at the bar, had a drink each without speaking to anyone, and then left without paying.

It was fine, he figured, all good, at that point it had been not quite a year since he bought the place, and Hugh was like an uncle to him, and like an uncle he was probably just reminding him of what they'd agreed upon.

Malcolm decided to move money around and get square with Hugh, carry a balance elsewhere. He did inventory of their shed one morning and itemized everything worth anything. He had expensive saws, a nice road bike he hadn't used in years, a retro ceramic barbeque, a collection of power tools. He had a stack of expensive bluestone pieces under a tarp, leftovers from when he put in the walkway around front. Two hundred square feet of mahogany flooring, a kayak. He had two fifty-pound coils of bright copper wire that they found in the basement after they bought the house. He sold it all and arranged pickups while Jess was at work. But even as he was clearing things out, accepting cash, he knew he'd have the same problem the following month, and the one after that.

He couldn't ask his mother for help. He imagined her trying to comprehend the amount of money he owed. She didn't know anything about his deal with Hugh. All she knew was that he bought the place and she was thrilled for him. And then to that amount he added Jess's student loan debt, which never seemed to get any lower, and what they owed the third fertility clinic they'd used. Their sessions with Dr. Hanley added up to a small fortune every month, and Jess's insurance covered only a quarter of what he charged. "But that's a necessity," Jess said, when they were trying to figure out what to cut, and Malcolm knew better than to ask if she was sure Dr. Hanley hadn't made things worse.

The world was different now, he'd tell his mother. But she wouldn't buy it. His sister had given her a set of expensive face creams years ago, and those creams had been in a position of pride in her salmon-tiled bathroom ever since, never used. One day, when she died and he was in charge of clearing the place out, he'd probably throw them in a dumpster along with everything else she cherished. She worked in the kitchen at the local elementary school, and every Friday she brought home some of the food that was going to be discarded. She always had an assortment of little cling-wrapped bagels on her counter, boxed strawberry milks, and yogurt squeezes in her fridge. He imagined telling her the situation he was in while she arranged for him a mismatched sandwich: peanut butter and jelly on white bread to the left and bologna on a roll on the right.

Do your best, she'd say. But he was already doing his best. He was at the bar in person sixty hours a week. He booked live music. A DJ. Live music followed by a DJ. Eighties nights. Dance instruction. Ladies' nights. Paint and sip. Speed dating events. Trivia night. Guest bartenders. On and on and on. He took out ads in the local paper. He bought a sign that was hung on the fence of the Little League field, along with several other local businesses. He was cheerful. Welcoming. He never let on that things were tough because who wanted to hear that? No one. Not when they were out to forget troubles of their own.

"How's it going at the Half Moon?" his mother asked him from time to time. "Getting a good crowd?"

"It's spotty," he admitted about a year in. "The new place that opened on Oak didn't help. They pull the same crowd." Which was really surprising, he didn't add. The place on Oak was a brewery, gleaming stainless steel drums of their own lagers and witbiers. He predicted the guys in their thirties would go for that, but he didn't expect the other age groups to like it over there, too. It didn't make sense that the old-timers who were annoyed at him for updating a few things at the Half Moon were over there studying hops and unmalted wheat. It didn't make sense that the near-broke twenty-two-years-olds were forking over ten dollars for a pint.

"Yeah? But you're okay?"

"Oh fine. Yeah. I'm doing fine. Don't worry."

Malcolm was eighteen when his father died, nearly an adult. Everyone seemed to have liked Darren, but Malcolm's clearest memory was of him getting pissed once when there was no milk in the house. He slammed the fridge so hard that the half-empty bottles of condiments stored on the door rattled. Malcolm also remembered his dad making fun of him for getting March and April mixed up on a test he took in—what? Second grade? Charm was a performance for other people, Malcolm had learned. He came alive as soon as he stepped inside his bar every night.

Malcolm fell behind with Hugh again, just a few months after the first time. He still didn't quite understand how; the money was there and then it just wasn't. The laws of simple addition and subtraction didn't seem to apply to the Half Moon's checking account. He'd look at the balance, jot down the amount, run a few quick calculations. But then he'd look again and there'd be only a third of what had been there the day before.

Hugh's guys came to his house. One of them knocked, though the doorbell was right there. His clothes and the stench of tobacco seemed totally out of place against Jess's hydrangea, the bold turquoise of their welcome mat. Jess came downstairs when she heard a voice she didn't recognize, took one look, and knew everything. She was quieter than normal, listening. The tall one—Billy was his name—smiled like it was a regular social visit, while the other one hung back.

"Listen," Billy said. "Malcolm." He tried to steer Malcolm outside to talk privately, but Malcolm shook him off. His house. Jess looking on. Their laundry tumbling in the dryer. He was livid.

"What's the plan?" Billy asked.

"Don't worry about it," Malcolm said.

Billy laughed. "I'm not worried about it," he said. "Are you?"

"I'm working it out with Hugh."

"You're working it out with Hugh? I talked to him this morning."

"Great."

"He didn't mention it."

What would they do? Malcolm wondered. What would they really do?

"Why did you ever agree to his terms?" Jess asked at least one hundred times.

She believed Hugh had tricked him. That Hugh had marked him and circled him and went in for the kill. That he'd never liked Malcolm nearly as much as Malcolm believed he did. She had no evidence to point to, it was just her gut that told her. But why would he have tricked Malcolm when he could have easily gotten someone else to buy the place? And Jess always asked whether he was sure about that. It was true that no one knew the Half Moon like Malcolm did, but someone else would have done research about the rest of the market, what was changing, new places opening up. Someone else would have hired a lawyer, made sure there wasn't something big they were missing. Someone else might have gotten in touch with the various vendors to make sure that the contracts in place would carry over, and they would have found out that even if Hugh had stayed on, his contracts would have expired because one company buys another, which buys another, and next thing your supplier is not a buddy from the Bronx whom you've known for forty years but a global conglomerate with satellite offices in your area. Surely, Malcolm insisted, Hugh had no idea about the new place opening on Oak, how successful it would be, how the local paper would say it was exactly what Gillam needed.

Once Billy left, Malcolm called Hugh directly. He figured it would be best to face the music head-on, cut out all those middle guys. Maybe they could work out a plan, a different schedule. How many hours had they spent together at the bar, Hugh giving advice, Malcolm taking it. But the phone rang and rang. He tried Hugh's cell. He tried his house in Gillam, in case he was in New York for some reason. He sucked up his pride and called Little Hughie, left a voicemail to say he was looking for Big Hugh.

Now, in the place where Billy had pulled his car up to the curb that day several months earlier, the snow looked to be waist high. He'd pulled a rabbit out of a hat after that visit, but he was behind again, and it had taken far less time to get there. He should be doing something. He should be solving this puzzle, but instead he was stuck in his house. Where was the plow?

Already the silence was suffocating. He looked at his phone: no texts.

And come to think of it, the house was quieter than quiet: no hum from the heating vents, no ambient vibrations. He walked downstairs. The face of the cable box was blank. The clock on the microwave dead. He flicked the hall switch up and down and up and down as if he might get better news if he just tried one more time. The couch looked different in the silence. The chairs, too. He wondered if power was out all over town. His phone was at nineteen percent. He tried to remember how much gas he had in his car. He thought of the pipes snaking through the walls of the Half Moon, of the portable generator he'd bought last winter but which was completely useless to him if he couldn't get there to set it up.

He dressed in layers. An absurd amount of clothing. He didn't bother with a hat but as soon as he stepped outside, the rims of his ears stung like they'd been pinched. He tromped across the yard to the shed and when he opened the door, he remembered that he left his snow shovel at the bar. He looked around for the garden spade. He found a rake. Tarps. Canisters of gasoline. His face was freezing. The Kowalski kid might shovel for twenty bucks. Mrs. Kowalski kind of liked him, Malcolm knew. She was cordial on their street when they met as neighbors, but when she came to the Half Moon, she always put her hand on his arm when she said hello.

He swept enough snow off his car to be able to open the door, and then he turned on the engine and blasted the heat. The gas tank was half-full. He put his phone on the charger. He could walk to the bar, maybe. Would be good to get his heart pumping. Or he could walk to Siobhán and Patrick's house. It was just two blocks over. But what would they be doing, trapped inside with their three kids, everyone in pajamas, giving him concerned looks? Siobhán reminding him that Jess was still Jess, no matter what. He imagined cereal floating in milky bowls, trying to talk to them but a kid always interrupting. The car was so nice and warm. He stayed there with his eyes closed until his phone reached fifty percent.

Back inside half an hour later, he sat on a kitchen stool and made columns. What he owed, what he had, what he needed. He heard a groaning sound from above and paused for a moment to listen. Ice in the gutters, maybe. Ice in the pipes. What could he do? He opened the cabinet doors under the sink. He went down to the basement and turned off the water main. When he got back upstairs, he turned on the water in the sink to drain the pipes. He filled every pot with water and set them on the stove. He went upstairs and filled the bathtub. Then he returned to his spot at the counter and made a list of dream projects, calculated what those projects would bring in.

He did twenty push-ups.

He backed up to a kitchen chair and did two sets of dips.

He checked the junk drawer for matches to ignite the pilot on the stove, but there were no matches, only a half-empty box of trick birthday candles way in the back with the crumbs.

He walked over to the bookcase and skimmed the titles for something he'd never read, something Jess had left behind, but the silence was too distracting. He opened a box of granola bars and ate four in a row. He pounded a glass of water.

He lay on his back in the living room for a while, deciding whether to text Emma. He could phrase it in a way that implied he was checking on the whole staff, not just her. He decided against it. He noticed dust under the TV cabinet and stood to get the vacuum before he remembered it wouldn't work. Sighing, annoyed with himself, he stepped into his boots once again and carved a path to the Colemans', to borrow a shovel. He spent an hour shoveling, sweat soaking the layers under his coat.

When he was finished he made a bet with himself about whether the power was back on. He looked up at the heavy black lines strung overhead and decided, yes, he could sense current running there. To buy extra time he walked the shovel back to the Colemans' even though Jon said there was no rush. He hung around Jon's garage for a minute— clearing his throat, stomping the snow off his boots—in case Jon got the idea to invite him in for a drink. When he gave up and returned to his own door, he opened it slowly and felt genuinely surprised to be wrong, the lights still dead, the silence more silent than it ever was when there was electricity flowing through the wires.

Okay, he said to himself. Something had to be done. He couldn't very well pace inside his house until the power returned. He went upstairs and pried open the door to the attic crawl space. He used the light from his phone to look for his skis, and as soon as the space lit up, he wanted to drag Jess back from wherever she was hiding to look at how cluttered it was up there, how she'd just been shoving stuff in willy-nilly and now he couldn't find what he needed in an emergency. He wanted to call her to let her know that he didn't care whom she slept with, but what had she been thinking tossing their old camp chairs on top of chafing dishes on top of Christmas decorations. How dare she ever scold him for where he threw his keys. He started picking things up at random, throwing them to the side. The sound of things crashing felt good, so he threw harder. Boxes of papers, bags of shoes, appliances he couldn't even identify.

There was baby stuff from her girlfriends that she'd kept, oh my God, she'd kept. Slowly, he drew from the gaping mouth of a shopping bag a knit blanket and then another, and then another, how many blankets could one baby possibly need. Another bag held tiny one-piece rompers with snaps that ran from toe to neck. A half dozen. More. The bag had no bottom. He went down on his knees among these soft things and looked through all of them for a second time. He pushed his face against a green towel that had a frog's head as a hood, and for a moment he saw a child wearing it, damp from the bath, hair dark like Jess's, like his, pale eyes and long lashes. All the adrenaline he'd felt a moment before leaked out of him, and he dropped to both knees. He counted to ten.

He saw there were two small swings, plus a thing with a sitting basket and spinny toys attached to the rim. She'd pictured a child playing in these contraptions, he knew. He put that on one side of a scale and on the other side he put Neil Bratton, but he didn't want to think about it long enough to see which side weighed more. No skis. He closed the crawl space door and returned to his spot at the upstairs window. No one was out, not even little kids making snowmen.

He texted a few friends. He typed in names like tossing a ring over a table of bottles, hoping one would land around a neck. But one by one they got back to say they couldn't get out, their street hadn't been plowed, it was so cold, nowhere was open anyway.

He watched TV on his phone and tried not to think about the fortune it would cost in data. When the show ended he went over to the liquor cabinet because he had a flashback of his brother-in-law giving him a bottle of Macallan two Christmases ago. Then he remembered taking it to the bar. He did inventory of what was left, little half measures. No gin. Some rum. There was a bottle of sweet vermouth at the back of the fridge. He returned to the couch and stared into space. He got up again, went to the freezer, and found a near-empty bottle of vodka, what was left gone syrupy, so he passed the bottle between his hands for a minute. When the viscosity looked normal, he went back to the liquor cabinet and found an unopened jar of olives. He was too lazy to dig out a martini glass, or a shaker, so he mixed everything in a highball glass. He took it to the couch, and as soon as he sipped it, he wished he'd done it right. He made himself drink exactly half and then he dumped it.

He fell asleep on the couch with his coat on at 7:30 p.m. When he woke up around midnight, his shirt was still damp with the sweat he'd worked up while shoveling. He climbed the stairs to his bedroom.

And then, lying on his side of the bed in the complete dark—no stars that night, no porch lights coming through the trees from neighboring houses, the streetlamps all dark—he heard a voice calling his name over and over, so regularly, in fact, that it had become part of the background noise of his mind. He heard it only because of the darkness, the silence, because his mind was circling and circling, looking for a place to land. Once he tuned in, he saw Siobhán, her face downcast at the bar, saying something about feeling bad. He saw the new guy, Neil, in her backyard, in the same golf shirt Malcolm always pictured, though that couldn't be right. Malcolm saw him leaning down to lift something. A child.

Neil Bratton had three kids. And the youngest was only two.

"Wait a second," he said aloud, and sat up.

He checked his phone. No missed calls. No texts.

four

Just before Jess met Neil, before she found out the name of his street and typed it into the map on her phone, there was San Francisco.

The route to Neil's house, when she eventually traced it with her finger, reminded her of a child's drawing of a staircase. Sitting in her silent bedroom, Malcolm at the bar, the novel she was trying to read winged over the arm of the chair, she thought how easy it would be to break off a little portion of herself and climb those crooked steps, see what might happen. It would only be a small detour from regular life. The thing between them, whatever it was, might be the kind of thing that vanished as soon as it was spoken aloud.

But before Neil came San Francisco, which arrived at the worst possible time. The bar was newly theirs, two months since Malcolm signed a sheaf of papers without bothering to let her know the details, without really understanding them himself—he was so goddamn cocky, everything he ever wanted in life he'd always just smiled and gotten. If he were the one who wanted a baby as much as she did, then they would have one. She was sure of it. But what he wanted most in his life was to own a bar, to be able to say, *I have a place of my own over in Gillam.* And not just any bar.

Other places had become available over the years, but there was always something wrong with them. The light, he said. The location. A feeling he got in his bones. Hugh had been dangling the promise of his eventual departure for years; all Malcolm had to do was wait.

At some point after Hugh told him that the time had come and Malcolm was still pretending to be merely thinking about it, he started calling it a restaurant. "What restaurant?" Jess asked as she was filling the kettle. "I thought we were talking about the Half Moon." Earlier that evening, when she was searching for dried oregano, she came across a half-empty bottle of FertilAid. It felt like running into an old friend with whom she had an unresolved disagreement. She went to throw it out but found she could not. Instead she fished out one pill, swallowed it, chugged a glass of water. And then she tucked the bottle way back in the cabinet where she found it.

"We are," Malcolm said, and set his face in a way that told her he would not break, no matter what. Whether he was rebranding it for himself or for her, she couldn't tell. Beller's Steakhouse was a restaurant. The Half Moon was a bar that offered a glorified children's menu just so it could keep its liquor license. Calling it a restaurant should have been her first clue. Her second should have been that he wore a jacket and tie to the closing. She'd just started a new position in the legal department of Bloom, a left-leaning media company that owned a suite of magazines and cable channels, totally opposite the conservative firm she'd just left. There were meetings she couldn't miss, being so new, and as the mortgage loan officer from the bank pointed out, Malcolm could simply sign for her as proxy. She was just gathering her things for a lunch meeting when he sent a photo of himself standing in front of their bedroom mirror.

Aren't you just meeting at the bar? she replied.

Yeah, he wrote. Wanted to look nice. Big day!

You look great, she wrote back and felt a sudden punch of guilt, considered coming down with a stomachache so she could hurry to Penn Station and make it to Gillam on time. He looked so happy. It was a big day for her, too, she supposed. Though everyone would describe the place as Malcolm's, it was equally hers.

Jess preferred the work she'd been doing at Laborers' International but switching to a private firm made more sense. The salary was better; she could keep up with her loan payments and save a little on top. In a few years she'd likely make partner, as long as she paid her dues, and like most firms they needed more women. At thirty-two, on their seven-year wedding anniversary, she threw her dial of pills in the trash and told Malcolm she was ready. He'd been saying all along that he was ready whenever she was, all she had to do was say the word.

Six months later she went to see a fertility doctor her gynecologist recommended, because of her age. By then she was thirty-three.

"My age?" Jess had said at the time, sitting on an exam table and thinking her legs needed to be moisturized.

"I know," her doctor said. "Fertility has not quite caught up with modern life."

At the first clinic, on the second page of the packet of paperwork they sent, was the usual trio of questions she dreaded: How many children did she have? Zero. How many times had she been pregnant? One. Age at the time of first pregnancy: twenty-five. That she'd miscarried was not worrisome, every doctor always said. The important thing was knowing she could get pregnant.

Jess's insurance required four IUI cycles before each IVF. She was game the first time—who knew? She was willing to give it a whirl. She was far from panicked. A lot of women she knew had taken a while to get pregnant.

But after the four IUIs failed, just as the fertility doctor said they would, and after the first failed IVF, the lead doctor at the clinic wrote letters to Jess's insurance carrier to explain why intrauterine insemination would never work for Jess's particular problem, that they had to go straight to in vitro fertilization next time. She had diminished ovarian reserve, only a fraction of the number of eggs left in her ovaries that she should have at her age. And on top of that, the quality of her eggs was not good. Poor egg quality, her doctor told her, was closely associated with chromosomal abnormalities in embryos, which usually resulted in miscarriage. He recommended genetic testing before any future transfer of an embryo to her uterus.

Dr. Mann's mustache was so long that sometimes he chomped on it when he spoke. It was hard to decide whether a person like that was totally trustworthy. Could he say why she'd miscarried her first pregnancy? No, definitely not, to even guess would be pointless. On the wall behind his desk were photos of him holding various babies, all success stories. "But I got pregnant without even trying," she said.

"You were twenty-five," he said.

Jess took the news as if from a distance, like maybe they'd gotten her labs mixed up with someone else's. She'd been getting annual pelvic exams for a decade. She was a normal weight. She ran four or five miles a day. She bought organic tomatoes and ketchup because she read an article once. She was never sick. And then, slowly, it sank in. Her body might not be what she thought it was.

The best the insurance company would do was reduce the required number of IUIs to three. The only other option was to pay out of pocket, but the expense was absurd, so she went through the three cycles of IUI again, this time more impatient to get to IVF. Once they got there everything looked precarious but more or less normal until the transfer, which was canceled because of the four decent eggs they'd retrieved and fertilized, none turned into blastocysts. That was year one.

Every morning for the six and a half years they spent trying, Jess woke up and her first thought was of her ovaries—what they were up to in there. Time seemed bent in all the wrong directions. A week felt like a month, a month felt like a year. The meditation instructor at the acupuncturist's office—an elderly woman who wore sexy deep-cut blouses and tight jeans—said to always begin the day with positive affirmations, but Jess couldn't stop herself from scrolling through regrets. She should have started earlier. That was always number one. Right after they lost that first pregnancy they should have tried again. She should never have smoked, not even at weddings, not even on big nights out. She shouldn't have had so many Diet Cokes. She once wrote out a rough estimate of how many she'd had in her life, starting around eighth grade, right up until the present day, and the number made her weak. She should never have so much as tasted that no-frills powdered iced tea her mother used to buy in drums so big that their cat could climb inside when it was empty. She should have been the kind of woman who nursed a club soda and didn't in fact spend so many nights of her late twenties doing flaming shots at the Half Moon while she waited her turn at darts. Or maybe it was just the opposite. Maybe she could have used more fun and less studying, less worrying over that incomprehensible law school loan, which became real to her only after the first entire year of payments didn't change the balance whatsoever. Why had she stayed up so late working on papers, keeping herself awake with gallons of coffee when she could have been sleeping, making her body a safe haven? She never should have gotten into a hot tub, especially in rental houses down the shore.

After two years, they switched to a clinic that struck better deals for people paying out of pocket. She had to wait six weeks to even get an appointment, and then figuring it all out—the financials first, and then getting new baselines with new tests—took another two months. And did it work? It did not, despite all their talk of new protocols, success rates. They switched to a third clinic in year five.

Seeing the picture of Malcolm in his jacket and tie, getting ready for the day he'd been looking forward to since he started working at the Half

Moon, it hit her that despite recent tension between them, she should have planned a party. He was forty-three and she was nearly thirty-nine. After so many years of disappointment, they could have used a celebration. She'd pressed snooze twice that morning, had struggled to get up and into the shower. Had she even wished him luck? She regretted not pausing for a moment to tell him that she was proud of him.

But after it went through and she discovered the details, the swell of love she felt while sitting at her desk that morning of the closing drained away and was replaced with a rage so all-encompassing that sometimes it was only as she was falling asleep and felt her body relax that she noticed how tightly clenched her muscles were from jaw to shoulders, down the long plane of her back.

Jess found herself at Bloom because she needed to get away from her own failure to thrive. Every day at the law firm after not making partner left her feeling more deeply embarrassed than the day before, like everyone in the entire building was talking about her. She lost weight because instead of gobbling a sandwich at her desk each day she started walking over to the park to sit on a bench and study the people who passed by. Of all things she kept remembering a moment in law school, a mock debate in front of the class, how easily and deftly she'd won, how her professor had given her a nod to acknowledge she'd done well, how she and her classmates had gotten drinks after and how smart and strong and beautiful she felt that afternoon. But there was something crucial about her life that she didn't know then, and the present-day Jess wanted to reach back and shake her. If it were possible to send that girl a message, what exactly would she say?

She started doing strange things. One day she bought an ice cream cone from a truck parked on Eighth Avenue, but it was too sweet and after a few licks she didn't want it. Instead of walking it to the garbage bin on the corner, she simply dropped her arm and let it go. No pedestrian stopped or glared. No passerby expressed condolences—what was worse than dropping a fresh ice cream cone? The taxis and buses and trucks and cars and bicycles and mopeds all continued along the avenue at the exact same frenzied rate. Only the machine-sharp edges of the swirls sagged until they disappeared. Another afternoon she walked all the way to the High Line and noticed a group of young people lying on a sliver of grass, their pant legs and sleeves hiked up to soak in the sun. It was spring, the first sunny day after a week of gloom, and she decided that she would also like some sun, so she took off her blouse, unbuttoned it top to bottom as if she were sitting on the edge of her bed, and stretched out in a pencil skirt and a navy bra that she told herself looked like a bikini top. She set a thirty-two-minute timer on her phone, and when the timer went off, she was surprised that she'd fallen asleep, her purse tucked under her head as a pillow, her stomach itchy for the rest of the day because the skin there hadn't gotten sunlight in probably ten years.

One afternoon a woman pushing a stroller sat on the other end of the bench where Jess was sitting, scooped up the baby inside, and placed the child on her chest. The baby stretched out an arm, a tiny fist, and then settled. From four feet away, Jess could feel the baby's warm weight, the sweet smell of her scalp, and felt the breath go from her body as if she'd jumped into a lake of icy water. The mother turned to her for a moment—not so young, Jess could see—and smiled.

When they told her she was not making partner, she knew she was supposed to be a good sport. It's better, actually, they all implied. Less face time with difficult clients, plus partners had to buy in, and this way she could keep her salary and not bother with that. They wanted her to stay, they made that clear. Not all firms were so generous. But to be passed over at almost the exact same time she and Malcolm reached the end of their fertility effort—for Malcolm to have reached *his* end, more accurately—seemed too coincidental to be unrelated. The powers that be would never say it, of course, but Jess knew the main reason she hadn't made partner was because she'd taken herself off cases that required travel. She didn't want to deal with explaining her bag of medications to a TSA agent, and she didn't want to worry that they'd keep her cooler bag open for so long that the meds would be ruined. She didn't want to go hunting for a monitoring facility in Savannah or Austin or Denver to have her follicles checked. Who knew if those clinics were even good? How many hours had she spent lying on an examining table with her knees pulled to her chin while back at the office her admin kept her calls at bay? After, she'd close her eyes at her desk, will her mind empty, and then picture some wheel deep inside her body turning at exactly the correct rate. Maybe someone had looked in and seen her, assumed she was asleep. She knew what they were thinking: she doesn't even have kids.

When she brought the news of not having made partner to Malcolm, he pointed out that it was just a title, and it meant something that they wanted her to stay. He said working at the firm was still better than the years she'd spent working for the union when she was fresh out of law school, but what he meant, Jess knew, was that the money was better, and though he never said it, she also knew that Malcolm believed all lawyers did more or less the same thing.

"Are you friendly at work?" Malcolm asked when she was trying to figure it out. "People like you?"

Jess felt her face get very hot.

"I'm just asking," he added. "That's the main thing, right? No matter what kind of job you're in."

"And here I thought the main thing was competence."

"You did?" Malcolm said, her tone completely lost on him. He was distracted, searching for a missing scratch-off in the basket where they threw the mail. "I really don't think so."

In nearly seven years of trying, she had two chemical pregnancies, eight months apart, that disappeared around week four. Where did they go? Vanished. Like the ribbon of a balloon that slipped out of her hand. She had one ectopic pregnancy in their third year. She went for a long run while it was still inside her, and she couldn't stop herself from hoping that if she ran hard enough she might shake it loose, send it to a place where it could live.

She had one miscarriage of a baby that was in the right place, a robust seven weeks along, floating in there exactly as it should have been, but then its heart simply slowed to a stop, like it had shown up at the wrong house, the wrong party, and then turned around and left.

After that one, they had to wait four months before even getting baselines for a new cycle because she was still showing positive for HCG. The next cycle was canceled at retrieval. The one after at the transfer.

Eighteen months after losing that pregnancy, she was pregnant again. She didn't celebrate until she reached week ten, even in her own mind. Mostly she felt dread, like she'd better move through her days with great tenderness. She stopped exercising. She stopped carrying the laundry basket up the stairs and asked Malcolm to do it. She left flats of water in the trunk of her car until he got home. She bought milk by the quart instead of by the gallon so it was lighter to carry. At eleven weeks she felt more confident and told her mother and Siobhán. The baby forums she was on, the private Facebook groups, the Reddit threads—all reiterated what her mother told her when she was twenty-five, that twelve weeks was the moment she could feel sure that the "baby dust" they were always wishing upon one another, strangers in dark rooms, typing their dearest hopes into a box, had actually worked.

And then, eleven weeks and five days, a dull ache across her abdomen. Livid spots on the toilet paper when she wiped. "No," she decided, closing her eyes and pulling up her underwear like she'd seen nothing, knew nothing. Malcolm was sound asleep—his wallet, keys, phone, and a small pile of coins on the bed table next to him, as always. But then she stood at the kitchen counter a few minutes later and felt a wet heat bloom between her legs.

"Malcolm!" she shouted, dropping to a crouch. He came clambering down the stairs, fear on his face.

He took one look and knew. "You're okay," he said, getting down on his knees to hold her, fumbling with her phone to get past the password and find the clinic's number. "You're okay, you're okay, you're okay."

That time, Malcolm had gone so far as to say that he liked the name Nora for a girl. Dennis for a boy. Without telling her he was going to do it, he moved his childhood dresser from his mother's house to their house one morning while she was at work. The dresser was still covered with old Mets decals, baseball cards he'd pasted so carefully when he was ten or eleven.

Eleven weeks and five days, almost the moment it went from being an embryo to a fetus. The doctor shared a few theories and then repeated what they'd heard before: it was a sign that a healthy pregnancy was possible. "How do you figure that?" Malcolm asked, incredulous. This clinic was an hour-and-a-half drive from their house. The doctor said that with every setback they learned more, made an adjustment.

"Oh sure," Malcolm said after, when they were on their way home. "Of course he wants us to keep going."

"You think he's lying to us?"

"Not lying, exactly. But—" They crossed the Tappan Zee Bridge, and Malcolm took the first exit. He pulled into a park that overlooked the Hudson. "Want some air?" he asked, and then he got out of the car and walked toward the water.

"You know when we were growing up, there were those couples who didn't have kids?" he asked when she caught up to him. "My mom's friend Annie used to give us two-dollar bills when she visited. Mary and I used to always argue about whether a two-dollar bill was real money or not."

"My aunt Linda, too," Jess said.

"Exactly. So for them—" Malcolm seemed to be turning over what it was he wanted to say. "I assume they wanted kids. Maybe that's wrong but I assume they did. So they did whatever you could do forty years ago, but then your options ran out pretty fast and you accepted it. It just wasn't possible.

"But nowadays there's always going to be someone who'll say maybe you can, as long as you do x, y, and z and take this cocktail of drugs and do this and that. If you want a baby, even if you have less than a half-percent chance, there's a doctor who will come up with a protocol."

"And thank God, right?" Jess asked, even though she knew that was not the answer he'd come to.

"I guess," Malcolm said. "In some ways, okay, thank God. But when does it end? There's you, and there's me. That's enough for me. I just want you to know that. I think we're going through a hard thing, but once we're past it, we can have a great life. We've been doing this for a long time. I think you and I alone make a family. Don't you think so?"

Part of her was glad he was as shaken as he was. Sometimes she wondered if she was grieving alone.

"Of course you're enough for me, Malcolm," she said. "Of course we're a family. I've loved you since the first second I saw you. This is just something I always expected for us. It's hard."

"I know it's hard," he said.

They looked at the water for a moment longer, and then he turned to her and grinned. "From the first second, huh? That's called lust, Jessica," he teased, and pulled her close.

He believed they'd resolved something, she knew. He believed they'd come to some sort of agreement.

Two weeks later, she pulled into their driveway after work to find his old dresser sitting there on the curb, in the dark, like a lonely child whose parents had forgotten about it. She parked and considered for a moment the fact that he was the person she knew better than anyone, but she had absolutely no inkling that this was the task he'd set for himself that day. That this was the day he'd settled on as the day all hope was lost. Nora with the scraped elbow. Dennis who liked to sing in the shower. Did he lay his hand on top of the dresser and bow his head for a moment, or did he bull forward as was his way? When she walked upstairs to look at the spot where it had been sitting, she saw that he'd opened the window a few inches to let in the fresh air.

Of course it made sense that Malcolm buy the bar. Long before Hugh told him that it was time, he often stayed up another hour after getting home from work, dawn nearly cracking the sky, just to jot down ideas, changes he'd make to bring it up to date. Sometimes when Jess picked up the iPad they shared, there were tabs open to bars in Los Angeles, Reykjavík, Tel Aviv. Photos he took screenshots of and emailed to himself. Sleek wood, chrome, leather. Against these beautifully lit images Jess always placed a thought of Malcolm's car: balls of wax paper from deli sandwiches, wads of nicotine gum, empty soda bottles, and little threads of tobacco, like sand that gets everywhere after a day at the beach.

When she made her pitch about donor eggs, he was taken aback. "I told you, Jess. I'm done. I can't take it anymore."

"What do you mean you're done? That's not really something people say on this subject."

"Well I'm saying it."

"A donor egg would still be your DNA. Is that the issue?" Not that his DNA was all that award winning, she wanted to add. His father dead of a heart attack at forty-three, his mother's recycling bin always stuffed with empty jugs of Carlo Rossi.

"No."

"Why?"

He held up his hands as if to say he was sorry. Sorry he felt that way. Sorry he couldn't explain why.

"Adoption then," she suggested, without adding that she'd already done some research and learned it could take years. *More years*, Malcolm would say. She read an essay by a woman who fostered a child for eighteen months. He came to her as a five-month-old baby boy who lit up her life.

After a few weeks with him, she submitted all the adoption paperwork and in the meantime fed him his first solid foods, watched him figure out how to crawl and then walk. It's happening, she was told. It just takes time. He called her Mama, and also said the words "hi," "bye," "dog," "ball." And then suddenly he was taken away. The birth mother wanted him back. The writer's heartache was raw, as was Jess's as she read it. She knew she'd never survive that.

"No, Jess," Malcolm said. "We tried our best."

"But we didn't try our best. Hello? I'm literally listing all the other things we can do."

She made an appointment with Dr. Ianucci and though she practiced how she'd put it, what coded language she'd use, when the time came, she was blunt. She wanted to know if there was any way to do it by herself. A donor egg, fertilized with Malcolm's sperm. "Well, yes," the doctor said, slightly confused. "A donor egg would be a very smart next step."

"No. I mean, is there a way to do it so that Malcolm thinks it's ours. Both of ours. I mean can we go through the motions. You'd just slip a different egg in there."

She waited a moment.

"Or a donor embryo if that's easier. It must happen, right?" There were shady dealings in every corner of business, why would fertility be any different?

"Jessica," the doctor said kindly.

"Jess."

"Jess. If you were interested in having a child on your own, that's one thing. But no, we're not going to mislead Malcolm. Every couple goes through this, and you've been through more than most."

By San Francisco, she'd already had a talk with herself about what exactly could be done about the deal Malcolm had made with Hugh, what could be done about *them*. She was so sick of every conversation finding each of them braced for the other's reaction. When she heard his car turn in to their driveway, she made sure she was folding clothes, peeling an orange, occupying her hands so she wouldn't have to greet him. Once, she held her phone to her ear, signaled to him to stay quiet, and then stepped into the front room and had a loud, one-sided phone conversation about liability and insurance with no one on the other end. She cut herself off mid-sentence, pretending to have been interrupted. She didn't come out until she heard him turn on the TV. When she organized her thoughts, the top bullet was the fact that they couldn't go on the way they were for much longer.

Her new job required so little travel there was no way to wriggle out of the conference in San Francisco. Malcolm wanted to do a few tune-ups to the bar right away, and at the top of his fix list were tiny things that had driven him nuts for an entire decade. Light fixtures that didn't work. Certain floorboards that moved like seesaws when people walked across the ends. But one thing led to another, which led to another, as Jess knew it would, as it always did, a warning she spoke aloud and which Malcolm took as a sign of her enduring pessimism. The handyman couldn't fix the lights, so Malcolm called an electrician, whom Jess let in on her way to the train one morning. Later, the electrician called to say he needed to show them something, he'd meet them there the next morning. Malcolm got up early, Jess called her office to tell her team she'd be late. It was so hot out, one of those days when walking one city block meant her hair would stay damp all day.

When they arrived at the bar, the electrician showed them a bundle of wires that Jess knew she was supposed to understand were dangerous, but he might as well have shown her a bunch of bananas for all she could intuit about them.

"Is it just this one spot?" Malcolm asked.

"No," the electrician said.

"Can we get away with it for a while longer?" Jess asked, and he looked horrified, like she'd asked him to murder someone.

"What about the panel?" Malcolm asked. "It's pretty new. I remember when Hugh had that put in."

"Malcolm," the guy said, and Jess realized they knew each other, he was probably a regular. "It's not that it's old but it's way overloaded. AC alone and the thing is maxed. You need to update all of it if you don't want the whole place to go up one night."

And Malcolm said, "Okay, yeah, of course, go for it. What else can we do?"

"It's been this long," Jess said and turned to Malcolm. "If you didn't look into fixing those lights, we wouldn't even know about it."

"But I did, and so we do know about it," Malcolm said, and then turned to his electrician friend. "Can you work mornings? I can't close. Show me what you'll need to open up."

"Wait," Jess said. "Hang on."

But Malcolm looked at her as he rarely did, only two or three times in their whole relationship, a look that said he was one second away from losing his temper. And if she knew him at all, being that close to revealing some deep part of himself in front of an acquaintance, a customer, meant he was at the very, very end of his rope. A muscle in his cheek was fluttering.

"Let's talk later," he said to her. "Don't you have a train to catch?"

"Love that guy!" people said when they found out Malcolm Gephardt was her husband, as if she were married to a celebrity, as if they knew him nearly as well as she did. Then they inevitably told some story about Malcolm that she'd never heard, two o'clock in the morning, a packed bar, someone jilted, someone wronged, Malcolm to the rescue. People couldn't imagine him at home, couldn't imagine him without a clean shave, a perfectly pressed shirt, sleeves rolled up. They couldn't imagine the damp towels he always left on the floor, the coins he left in little piles all over the house. They ended up in the dryer, in the vacuum. He used paper towels to blow his nose. When he went to the bathroom upstairs, he always called down to her to "give it a minute," as if she had any notion of going in after him.

On the morning Jess had to leave for San Francisco, they were down to three digits in their joint checking account, and off the top of her head she could think of two fairly significant bills that still needed to be paid. Seeing that number sent a shock down her arms to the center of her palms. "There's a debit from the supply company," she said, scrolling through their transactions on her phone. She was standing by the front door with her suitcase, looking out for the corporate car service that was picking her up.

"Which one?" Malcolm asked, but with such perfect airiness that Jess knew he knew.

"The one in Jersey," she said, making her voice even so he couldn't accuse her of picking a fight. She was merely stating a fact. She waited for him to say that he'd been there, it was his charge, that he knew money was tight but there were things he needed. The bar came fully stocked, but he'd always wanted those oversized wineglasses that looked like fishbowls on stems. Hugh would never agree to them, and Malcolm always said that when he had his own place the first thing he'd do would be to upgrade the wine list and try to attract a clientele that appreciated it. All at once, she knew he bought those dumb glasses. They were the only ones at the supply store not sold by the case.

"Oh. Yeah. That's right."

"What'd you get that could've cost this much?"

Say it, she encouraged him in her mind. Say it's none of my business. Say it.

"Because you know those wineglasses you like have no place in a bar like the Half Moon."

She knew she sounded like the exact kind of wife she swore she'd never be, speaking to him like she was his boss, or his mother. Did she want to speak to her husband like he was a child? Of course not. But when a person dreams of partnering with someone for life, no one ever considers the fact that there's no dependable way to communicate a thought except to say it.

"Five ounces will look like one sip in those things. Every bartender will overpour. Customers will complain because even a heavy pour will look short."

She couldn't stop herself. "People will wrap them in napkins and tuck them into purses. Fine to steal pint glasses if Smithwick's is supplying them, but these? Mal."

"Jesus Christ," he muttered, as if she'd arrived at a party just to knock over the cake.

"What?"

Say it, she thought.

He glared at her.

"Tell me what I'm supposed to do. Keep quiet? Even though we already talked about this? And agreed to the exact opposite of spending a few hundred bucks on glasses? The Half Moon isn't the Plaza. I'm exhausted, Mal. I've been working sixty-hour weeks for fifteen years. And at this moment we have—" She glanced down. "Nine hundred and twenty three dollars in checking."

"Yeah I know it's not the Plaza, Jess. I'm working hard, too. Always have. You think you're the only one who works hard around here?"

"Oh my God that's not what I'm saying and you know it."

He was making the face that made him look like his mother. Whenever he made that face, she saw so clearly how he'd look when he was old. Sometimes Gail claimed that Malcolm got his broadness from her, and then she'd roll her shoulders like she was proud to have the build of a man. "A lot of models have broad shoulders if you notice, makes clothes look nicer," Gail said to Jess once, and Jess almost choked on her sandwich.

"Can you return them?"

"You know, Jess? It's really none of your business. You mind your career and I'll mind mine."

Boom, Jess thought. There we have it. She felt a rich, thick heat rush from her center to every part of her body. "It's not my business?"

"You don't believe in me, in the bar, any of it. You've made that clear."

"If that's how you're taking this, then we have a serious problem," she said at the same moment the car pulled up. Instead of kissing her good-bye, he walked through the house and slammed the back door.

Jess's only real job at the conference was to show her face at cocktail parties, sit along the back wall during panels. Arguing with Malcolm and then getting immediately into a car and brought to the airport left her feeling off-balance. She wasn't angry, exactly. Or even hurt. It was more like she felt dazed, like everything she was doing, every part of her life, existed at a greater distance from her real self than she'd previously thought. Standing on the security line, lifting her bag onto the belt, her mind was a complete blank. At least I don't have to worry about fifteen hundred dollars' worth of fertility medications getting confiscated, she thought. At least there's that. She touched her back pocket to check for a hair elastic just as she stepped into the body scanner, so they flagged her, but she didn't quite tune in to the fact that she was being patted down until it was over, and she was swept up once again into the current of people rushing toward the gates. If she read a magazine or sipped a coffee while she waited to board, she couldn't remember. On the flight, she pulled up a playlist, put on her headphones, but didn't notice for a full hour that no music was coming through. When she stepped onto the sidewalk at SFO, she felt a relief that was different from her usual relief at having landed safely, more like a surprise pleasure in glimpsing the true size of the world. Thinking about the distance between where she was standing and home—the fact that Malcolm, the Half Moon, the empty rooms in their house, her mother's comments, their friends, were all three thousand miles away—felt like something heavy being lifted from her shoulders. She took a deep breath and hailed a cab.

In her hotel lobby she noticed a group of men around her age, not affiliated with the conference. A bachelor party maybe, Jess figured, though they seemed a little too old. They drew her attention at check-in because there were seven of them, and though they weren't rowdy exactly, she noticed there were no women among them. They were attractive guys, early to mid-forties, all in relatively good shape, all well-dressed, clearly happy to be with each other. They weren't intimidating, like a group of men can be. She noticed them again when she went down to the hotel bar for a quick drink before the keynote dinner, a moment to gather her thoughts. They were at a table behind her, talking over each other. She eavesdropped and learned they were supposed to have spent the day golfing somewhere in the Presidio but changed plans because of the rain.

Just as she was finishing her drink, one of them came up to the bar and stood next to her, waiting for the bartender. He was close enough for her to notice he smelled good. She was glad she put on a dress for the dinner instead of just changing her blouse.

He nodded at her and put his credit card on the bar. He leaned forward on his elbows. He had nice hands. Where his cuff rode up she could see a scar, right above his wrist. She snuck a glance at his face. A nice face, too. There was no one aside from Jess at the bar, but he stood only two feet away.

"Hey," he said. "Could I ask you to—?" He nodded at his credit card and then pointed quickly at the bartender, who was all the way on the other side.

"You want me to give it to her?" she asked. She hadn't expected him to speak to her.

"Yeah, I—"

"Oh, got it. You're picking up the tab."

"If one of my friends hasn't beaten me to it. In a second they'll notice I've been gone too long."

"No problem," she said, and slid the credit card toward her napkin.

"Tell the bartender to keep it and I'll settle up later. They'll catch on if I get up again to sign."

"I'll sign for you so she can close it out."

He looked amused. "You will?"

"Sure. There's probably a new bartender coming on soon."

"She won't care?"

"Nah, she'd probably prefer to close," Jess said.

He was studying her face as if he'd noticed she was a woman and not just a person sitting in a convenient spot for his task.

"Okay, thanks. I'm Fred."

"Frederick, actually," she said, tapping his credit card.

He smiled, and she liked that his face was so open, that he wasn't trying to hide the fact that he was enjoying talking to her. Something about his appearance, his bearing, struck Jess as careful. He was not Southern, she decided. Definitely not from the Northeast. Beyond New York and New Jersey she wasn't good at identifying accents.

"Well, thanks," he said, and as he turned back to his table, Jess noticed the wide column behind them and realized that was the reason he was standing so close, so he could be a little hidden from his friends.

Later, after the meet and greet, after the most boring dinner during which speaker after speaker made dark jokes about the end of print media, a bunch of people from the magazine went off to a dance place they heard about and invited her along. Jess had an immediate vision of

Christopher from sales throwing his blazer over a chair, losing his mind when Flo Rida came on. She didn't know them well enough yet, and she was technically senior to all of them so she'd have to buy rounds wherever they ended up. Buying rounds was not something she could do at the moment because even if Bloom reimbursed her, that reimbursement would take six weeks.

When she got back to the hotel, it wasn't even ten o'clock, so she figured one drink, she'd charge it to her room. She checked her phone to see if Malcolm had texted, but all that popped up were photos of her friend Maria's daughters in the outfits Jess had given them for their birthdays.

She chose a seat just a few down from where she'd been sitting earlier. The bartender, a different one, had just placed a vodka soda in front of her when a man's voice said, "You tipped thirty percent."

She startled, her hand shook, the liquid sloshed inside her glass and splashed her cuff. She lowered the drink to the coaster without sipping.

"I'm so sorry," he said, laying a hand on her shoulder. With his other hand he grabbed napkins, wiped the drops that landed on the bar. "I didn't mean to scare you."

"I thought thirty was only fair," she said, pressing a napkin to her wrist, "considering the drama you made out of paying." She switched the way her legs were crossed. He leaned on the edge of a barstool, facing her.

"You're with the magazine group? The conference?"

"Yes, but I'm in legal. I'm an attorney."

"Named Jess," he said, and she remembered she was still wearing her badge. "Short for Jessica?"

"Ugh. Yes. Awful."

He made a wounded expression. "My mother's name is Jessica. And my grandmother's."

Flirting was as she remembered, like smacking a beach ball back and forth, trying to keep it aloft. It came back like muscle memory, effortless, more fun the faster they played.

"Then they know," she said.

He dropped his chin to his chest when he smiled, and as he did she had the strangest feeling, like the whole conversation was inevitable, like something had remained unspoken when they chatted earlier and the second part of that conversation was unfolding exactly as it was always going to unfold. He held out his hand for her to shake, and when she did, he shook it slowly, held on for longer than necessary. His group was there and seemed rowdier than they'd been earlier in the evening.

"Your friends are having fun. Bachelor party?"

"Ahhh, sort of the opposite." He turned his back to them as if he were about to divulge a closely guarded secret.

"Divorce party. See the guy in the blue button-down?"

Jess craned her neck to see over his shoulder, as if it were important to her to know which one was divorcing, as if she hadn't just been making conversation.

"Three out of six are in blue button-downs."

"Okay, a beard."

"Two of those have beards."

"They do?" he looked over. "Okay, the one closest to us. The shorter one. His divorce just went through."

"Sort of a sad thing to celebrate."

"That depends." He shrugged. "It's been bad for a long time."

Jess considered that.

"One kid. But he's almost eighteen."

"Ah."

"Want to join us?" he asked. He was wearing a wedding ring, she saw. Just being friendly. She was wearing a wedding ring, too.

"No." She shook her head. "I'm just finishing this and heading up. But thanks."

He didn't say anything.

"And I'm leaving tomorrow. Early flight."

"Okay." He paused. "Well, thanks again, Jess." When he was a few feet away, he turned back. "My mother's name is Elise, by the way."

"Lucky her," she said.

She watched him in the mirror as he fell into whatever conversation his friends had been having without him. Light-headed, she pressed all of her fingertips to the bar as hard as she could. He was watching her, she was certain of it, and out of nowhere she had a thought of Malcolm and how they used to sleep facing each other in a tangle of arms and legs. Part of her was relieved she no longer woke up three times a night because a limb had fallen asleep under Malcolm's weight, but another part brimmed with sorrow that the period of their lives that burned brightest might be over. Last time they had sex she couldn't focus, so she asked him to stand up, to stand behind her, to hold her tighter.

"Tighter," she kept saying that afternoon. "I said tighter." But Malcolm only drew away, put his hands to his head, annoyed.

"Pretend I'm someone else," she said, hoping that would ignite something in him, throw him out of his routine. "Pretend I'm Emma."

"What?" he said, looking at her with shock, reaching for his boxers. "What did you say?" But he didn't actually want her to repeat it. "You're really losing it, Jess."

And then he got dressed, walked out of the room, and she was too embarrassed to go downstairs until she was sure he'd left the house.

Early on, when she was still in law school and he was the star of the Half Moon, the one everyone went there to see, she forced Cobie to come to Gillam for a weekend to meet him. They'd gotten together a few times by then, nothing serious, or so she told herself. The first time, straight from the bar, he worried he stunk of cigarettes, and offered to take a shower first. To think that someone as beautiful as he was could be self-conscious about any aspect of himself was a revelation. He said that her skin smelled like citrus and then he seemed so pleased with himself when she told him that he was the one who did that, his hands handling limes and orange slices all night, and then touching her.

Cobie, who hated the suburbs, who as a rule did not transfer from one form of transportation to another, made an exception for Jess and joked that this guy would have no power over her, that she was already annoyed at his existence, this person who was pulling Jess away from the city all of a sudden. Jess had to explain to her friend how it was that she didn't know Malcolm growing up, because he was just those critical few years older than she was, and though Gillam was small in some ways, it wasn't *that* small.

"Okay, well, let's get a look at him before you work on your origin story," Cobie said, and rolled her eyes.

But even Cobie found herself watching him, she told Jess after, and not only because meeting him was her sole purpose for visiting Gillam. She took in the bar, the crowd, the music, Jess's other friends from home, but somehow, for some reason, when she wasn't paying attention, she was always searching for Malcolm.

"Exactly," Jess said. "What's that about?"

"He has a lot of presence. And the two of you together?" Cobie asked. "You're like the prom king and queen."

"Him, maybe," Jess said. "Not me."

"Not you alone, no. But with him?" Cobie paused. "You're different here."

Jess met Cobie on the first day of college orientation. They'd both complained about their hometowns—Cobie's all the way in Texas—how the rules of life were prescribed from birth, though the families they'd been born into couldn't have been more different. Jess asked, tentatively, if it had been hard coming out to her parents, and Cobie laughed and told her she was never "in"—her parents knew she was gay before she did. No, it was something else about home that was strangling her, the notion that what's important to one person must be important to every-one. All of Jess's classmates saw themselves as the ones who'd broken free, but oddly, the more the others griped about their hometowns, the more Jess saw that hers wasn't so bad. The Ryans hadn't had money, but that wasn't Gillam's fault, and in general, she remembered kindnesses. Teachers telling her she was bright, encouraging her along.

She'd gotten a decent merit scholarship but had still needed a sizable loan. She ended up deferring repayment to go to law school full-time. She paid for law school with a new loan, and the loan officer seemed pleased to tell her that when the time came she could bundle her loans together, as if it made any difference to her whether she repaid with one check or split the amount into two. At twenty-two, money was still only theoretical to her, and the higher that loan amount climbed, the more abstract it seemed.

"God," Jess said the first time she saw Malcolm, standing behind the bar, "who's that?" It was her friend Jenny's birthday. They'd been co-captains of the track team their senior year of high school, and they still ran together sometimes when Jess was home. Jenny had just broken off an engagement, and Jess had just broken up with a classmate she'd been see-ing half-heartedly. He always finished her sentences and he was always wrong. So they were due for a night out. They'd rounded up a few other friends from high school Jess hadn't seen in a while.

"Oh," Jenny said, with sympathy in her tone. "You've never met Mal-colm?"

"Hello, Jenny's lawyer friend," Malcolm said to her later, when it was her turn to buy a round. "Your friends were bragging about you before you got here."

"I'm not a lawyer *yet*," she said. "Working on it."

"Well look at you," he said.

"I'm Jess," she said.

"I know," he said. "I'm Malcolm."

"I know," she said, and laughed. "You're a big hit around here."

When Jess returned to the table hugging eight bottles of beer and wearing a dopey smile, Jenny said, "Don't even think about it. He's been with everyone."

"Think about what?" Jess asked. But every time she got a chance, she looked over at him.

She found an excuse to go home again two weeks later. And then again two weeks after that. Later, when they were together but no one knew, Jess would shout her order over the din and he'd lean very close, as if to hear her better. It wasn't true that he'd been with everyone. He had rules about never getting together with girls who hung around the bar too much, girls he'd have to see too often when it ended. He wasn't interested in girls who wore their designs on him too bluntly, the girls who got too drunk and sagged against him at the end of the night. He liked the girls who kept it together, he said, who could hold a normal conversation at midnight. Like Jess.

Once everyone knew, the same friends who'd stood alongside her in sympathy the first night started side-eyeing her, sizing her up. Was she in fact too tall? Could her breasts stand to be a bit bigger? Was she actually all that pretty or was she just skinny with good hair? Sometimes it was hard to tell the difference.

Occasionally, to give her a break from all the back-and-forth, he came to her apartment in the city, but Jess knew he hated giving up a weekend night at the bar, hated circling in search of a parking spot. If she and Cobie had friends over, he asked Jess's classmates for stories of what she was like in law school, if she was very serious or if she ever fell asleep in the back row. He said it was unfair that she could picture his day but he couldn't quite picture hers. When they went out he always had plenty of cash and kept it neatly folded in a clip. He made the guys searching the opens maws of their wallets look like little boys.

In her third year, Jess was selected to represent her school on a tour of Southeast Asia as part of an international law initiative. She was twenty-five years old. She wore one of Cobie's silk blouses to a meeting in Myanmar and ate the best meal of her life in Singapore. She went swimming off the coast of Cambodia and saw the towering Golden Buddha in Thailand. By then she knew she was in love with Malcolm, and sent him a postcard almost every day, mostly about food. She woke up ravenous every morning and asked her classmates if it was the same for them, if they thought it was the time difference, perhaps their bodies didn't know when their meals were supposed to be and so wanted to eat all the time.

She was sick on the plane home, which was embarrassing. She hoped her classmates didn't hear her retching into the tiny toilet. When she stepped out of the bathroom, a very kind flight attendant handed her a gel ice pack, told her to hold it to her face and neck, it would make her feel better. When she finally got to New York, dragged her suitcase up four flights of stairs to her apartment, she sat up late with Cobie just to talk about all the things they wanted from their lives, all the places they wanted to go. And then she slept for twenty hours, waking only to pee. When she woke up for real she was so hungry that she felt nauseated. Malcolm was on his way to see her.

Cobie said she'd clear out as soon as he arrived, but before she left she wanted to add one extra point to that conversation they'd had last night. She said, and asked Jess to please not be mad at her for saying so, that with Malcolm, Jess's boundaries would always be Gillam's. She thought Jess would have ended things with him by then, but instead it seemed to be getting more serious. Cobie said it was something she'd been thinking about and she'd be a bad friend if she didn't make sure Jess knew that.

"You've just been to all these places," Cobie said. "Is Malcolm interested in going anywhere besides Gillam and the Jersey Shore?"

"That's not fair," Jess said. "You need money to travel. Each year of that high school you went to cost more than most people pay for college. So there are things you just do not understand, Cobie. You think regular people can up and fly to Vietnam? I wouldn't have gone to Asia if someone hadn't picked my name out of a hat or whatever. If all my expenses hadn't been paid."

"There you go," Cobie said. "They didn't pick your name out of a hat and you know it."

"He's not dumb," Jess said. "Far from it."

"I didn't say he is."

"Okay."

"Okay."

"And there's nothing wrong with the Jersey Shore. It's beautiful. A lot of people don't realize."

"I said okay."

"Or Gillam, for that matter."

"I know that."

"Anyway," Jess said. "He's ambitious. His plan is to own his own bar one day." She laid a hand on her stomach and tucked a pillow behind her head.

"Great," Cobie said. "Awesome."

What happened in the five minutes between Fred wishing her a good night and getting up from her seat, Jess wondered later, on the flight back to New York and then a thousand times in subsequent weeks. What exactly had she been thinking on the long walk from the bar, across the lobby, past reception, to the elevator bank? Her hands had been shaking, she remembered that. She had to clasp them together and remind herself to breathe.

When Jess left the bar area and turned for the elevators, she counted to five—one, two, three, four—and then turned. And there he was, standing in the lobby, looking at her. Just where she knew he'd be.

"Hey again," he said. He didn't seem the least bit nervous. He stopped about three feet away from her, shoved his hands deep into his pockets, and raised his shoulders to a shrug. "Want to get a drink?" he asked. "Not here," he added.

Jess glanced over at his buddies, and if they'd all been turned toward them, watching, she would have walked away. But they didn't even seem to have noticed that he left.

"Where?" Jess asked.

"Upstairs?" he said, pressing the elevator button. He didn't touch her, he just stood very close. "If you want to."

"Just a drink?" she asked.

"Probably not just a drink, no." He smiled, and it was a kind smile.

She wanted to seem like a woman who found the invitation to be no big deal, like it happened all the time.

"Tell you what. I'm going to room 704. If you want to join me, great. If not, then it was very nice to have met you." He paused. "In case you don't come up, I want to tell you that you are very, very lovely, Jessica-who-hates-her-name. I hope you have someone who tells you that."

When the elevator door closed, she stood there for what felt like a very long time. She listened to the machinery turning, carrying him to his room, steel cables straining and pulling. Then silence. The whole building was waiting for her to decide. She put her palm to the door. She pressed the button and the system sprang to life. When the elevator arrived, she pushed number seven.

She thought she'd have a minute to collect herself, but when the doors opened, he was sitting in the armchair across from the elevator.

"Okay, I'm nervous," she said.

He closed the space between them, took her elbows, and walked her backward slowly until they arrived at the wall. And then he kissed her. He seemed cautious at first, testing, but then she kissed him back. He pressed his whole body against her, and she could feel his knee between her legs. He had her dress partly unzipped, and she didn't even notice until she felt his hand on the bare skin of her back.

"We should probably get out of the hall," he said.

But it struck Jess as they moved toward his room that he might be different in there. He might hurt her. Or she might see his toothbrush on the bathroom counter in a pool of murky water and know that the way he appeared to strangers was false, that the wife he left behind in Seattle, or Toronto, or Minneapolis was sick of cleaning up after him, was working up the courage to leave him.

"Hey," Jess said, pulling away from him. "I'm sorry. I'm going to head to my room. I'm really sorry."

"Don't be sorry," he said, immediately taking his hands off her. He sighed, but he was nice about it and that made her feel worse.

"You're sure?" he asked.

"Yes," she said.

"Okay. Let me just—" Frowning, he reached around and zipped up her dress. He patted her back as if to say she was all set.

"Do you do this a lot?" she blurted. "I noticed your ring."

She didn't mean anything by it, but she could see he didn't like the question and wouldn't be answering. He called the elevator for her, waited politely until the door opened.

The next day, checking out, Jess waited in her room until the very last moment. Then she arranged her hair in front of her face, put on sunglasses, and got out of the hotel as quickly as possible.

During the flight home, she thought of the flight attendant on the long journey from Bangkok all those years ago. Jess tried to remember what she'd been like at twenty-five, what she thought about, what she worried about, how quick she was to speak her mind. How sweet that woman was, handing her that ice pack, later bringing her a cold can of ginger ale. How she'd asked, the second time Jess had to rush to the toilet to vomit, if she always felt ill when flying or if perhaps she was expecting. She said Jess's face was very pale, but she said it with a small smile, as if encouraging Jess to share a secret. Jess remembered how the woman's colleague had said something to her sharply in Thai, and the attendant who'd been so kind suddenly looked flummoxed.

"Expecting what?" Jess had asked, and only much later, in the frigid darkness of coach, thirty thousand feet above Africa, in a tube traveling five hundred miles an hour, did Jess register what she meant.

When she arrived at their little house in Gillam after a delayed departure from San Francisco and her driver from LaGuardia taking a wrong turn, she walked in to find Malcolm there, even though it was a Saturday. His face, his stance, the slight cowlick over his left eye that he tended to so carefully in the mirror each morning, the way he tilted his head and rubbed the stubble on his cheek when he was nervous, when he was trying to think of what to say, it was all as familiar to her as her own reflection.

"I returned the glasses," he said, taking her suitcase, moving it to the landing so he'd remember to carry it upstairs. "They said the credit will show up in about a week."

"You didn't call," she said. "You didn't text me even one time."

"Neither did you," he said. And that had hurt, she could see. It wasn't a sentence he was capable of saying.

Jess felt a sob gathering in her chest, so she put her hands over her face and doubled over like she'd been punched. She made a keening sound that she'd never made before, not even when she lost the baby she'd come to think of as Nora. Malcolm's Nora.

"Jessie," Malcolm whispered, sliding his hand through her hair, pulling her as tight as he could. The solid hulk of him compared to that stranger in a hallway. How could she have gone that far.

"Jessie. Honey. Don't cry. Please."

"The glasses are not the problem."

He was quiet for a long time and then he said that he knew that, of course he knew that, but he didn't know what to do.

five

They met at a barbeque at Siobhán and Patrick's house, Memorial Day weekend. Siobhán called Jess at work that Friday to say that Patrick's best friend from college had moved to Gillam, she was sure she'd mentioned that to Jess. He didn't know anyone. He'd moved there because Patrick had talked it up so much over the years and he had to find a place fast, get the kids settled, get them enrolled in school. They'd only ever known the city but Neil liked the idea of a big yard, somewhere commutable to Midtown. Siobhán assumed he had plans for the long weekend, but it turned out he didn't. So now they all had to come over.

"How do you know I don't have plans?" Jess asked.

"Do you?"

"No."

Siobhán was positive Jess had met him at some party or other, their wedding at the very least. As if Jess would be able to recollect all three hundred people who'd attended Siobhán and Patrick's wedding seventeen years ago, after an entire bottle of prosecco and a mishap with the shuttle bus. As if she ever talked to anyone at those parties other than the people she already knew. That was Malcolm's thing. He was the host of their table. He was the host of the elevator that brought everyone to the top floor. He was the host of the line that snaked its way to the buffet, cracking jokes and pumping the hands of everyone he knew and hadn't seen in ages. Neil and Malcolm had both been groomsmen, Siobhán reminded her. But Patrick had had ten groomsmen, and Jess had been seeing Malcolm for only a few months. She and Siobhán were friendly at the time but not close yet. She spent most of the night waiting for Malcolm to wrap up his duties so they could hang out.

Siobhán said he was worried about his kids, the poor guy. "His ex should be in jail," she added. "Can you imagine Patrick picking back-to-school clothes for Cara?"

"I'm sure he'd figure it out," Jess said.

"Anyway, he's a lawyer," Siobhán said, in the soft voice she used when she was trying to sound innocent. "I think he does something very similar to what you used to do at the firm."

"Oh no. No-no-no. What did you say about me? There are a zillion different types of lawyers, Siobhán! As soon as he hears how long I was at the firm and then this sudden pivot, he'll know I left because I didn't make partner."

"Well," Siobhán said. "I wanted him to know he has things in common with people here. He claims he'd never even been on this side of the Hudson before he came to look at the house he bought. He relied completely on Patrick's stories about Gillam, so now the people in those stories have to show up! He doesn't care why you left the firm!"

"Also," Siobhán added. "We're having those ribs you like. I'm making the marinade right now."

"Oh really?" Jess said. She'd just eaten a dry turkey sandwich at her desk. "I could drink that marinade."

"I know you could."

"Okay, we'll be there. But stop discussing my résumé, please."

"I love you."

It wasn't that he'd care. It was just embarrassing. Jess had been at Bloom for a few months by then. They owned the Half Moon but it was still so new. They weren't behind yet, though a simple comparison of the profit and loss sheets month over month, charted on a graph, predicted very clearly where the line was headed if something didn't change. She'd followed that line to its obvious conclusion, had stayed late at work one evening creating a spreadsheet so she could show Malcolm. And she'd been generous! There were expenses she didn't know about, surely. The unpaid tabs. The unspoken etiquette of cash put down on a table and then pushed away. The macroeconomics of an entire industry, how to tip and why and when and to whom and how much. Cash passed in envelopes or folded into thick wedges and tucked into shirt pockets. Stacked in a safe deposit box, sure, but also removed in denominations of one inch, two inches. But when she brought home this presentation of facts, he glanced at it exactly once and then told her to just tell him what it said. When she explained, said they'd be in the red within six months, said they'd be up an actual creek if they didn't make a change—get an investor or sell or come up with a brand-new idea for how to get bodies in a dingy room, buying drinks—he said her work was too binary, what with its columns for profit and loss, success and failure. His world was full of nuance, determined by moods, weather, current events. If the Mets made it to the World Series, the bar would kill it in October. Things like that couldn't be captured on a spreadsheet, he said, and she said yes it certainly could, she'd done it, all he had to do was look.

On the day that Siobhán called to invite them to the barbeque to meet Neil, Jess and Malcolm hadn't had sex in almost three months. Afternoon talk shows and morning radio would have her understand that was normal for some couples, but it wasn't normal for them. She could count exactly how long because the last time was the day she returned from San Francisco, and every day that passed felt like an alarm ringing deep inside her center, keeping her up at night. There was no way he could know what had happened in San Francisco, but part of her wondered. He was eerie like that, the way he could feel in a room if someone was sad, if someone was in a mood to pick a fight. Maybe it was the same way he could detect something not right in her, a wobbling of loyalty, the fraying of a bond. To look at him, no one would think he was thinking about anything at all.

By the time Jess started at Bloom, she and Malcolm both knew that their therapist Dr. Hanley was turning out to be a disaster. She'd sought him out to help them sort through their conflicting feelings about fertility—or rather, to convince Malcolm that he wanted what she wanted—but then there was so much more that she didn't know bothered her until she spoke in that office. They didn't tell Dr. Hanley that they'd stopped having sex. Every other week, he asked about intimacy, and every other week they just slid right by it, said that everything was fine. Jess wondered how many of his clients were like her and Malcolm, raised to keep all troubling thoughts to themselves, and then, as soon as they possibly could, to bury them. When Jess said that intimacy was fine, and Malcolm looked anywhere but at either of them, Dr. Hanley said that was good, a sign of health, a sign of a solid foundation.

After hanging up with Siobhán, she saw the time and had to move fast or she'd miss her train. They were supposed to be at Dr. Hanley's at five o'clock, the latest he was willing to meet at the start of the long weekend. That day felt no different from any other appointment. Jess got to the train in the nick of time, Malcolm was waiting for her at the station, only to sit in the vestibule for five minutes while the previous couple wrapped up and exited through the other door so they wouldn't encounter each other. Sometimes Dr. Hanley's white noise machine played ocean sounds and sometimes rain.

"You know he says the same stuff to everyone," Malcolm said while they waited. He seemed particularly put out to be there that day. Memorial Day weekend could go either way at the bar, could be slow with people away until Monday night, or busier because those who had not gone on vacation would want to go out.

He never wanted to be there, clearly—who did?—but on that evening, something about his whole attitude made her angry. The weather was gorgeous—a perfect, cleansing May day. Would she prefer to blow off their appointment and go get a cocktail, sit outside somewhere? Of course. But this was supposed to be good for them. She noticed he'd gotten a haircut at some point that day. There was a pale line at the back of his neck.

She was about to ask him if he came to these appointments for himself or for her, if he agreed that there was something between them that needed fixing, when Dr. Hanley ushered them in and they sat down next to each other on the love seat. Malcolm glanced at his phone, and Jess felt her temper flare. So she crossed her legs, leaned forward, and before Dr. Hanley could ask how the last two weeks had been, Jess blurted out that she thought Malcolm had a problem with porn. Malcolm was so surprised he made a sound like a squeak, a sound he'd never made before or since, and then he looked up at the ceiling and sighed. She just wanted to say something new, and they both knew it. A few times over the years he'd suggested they watch together, and though she didn't object—sometimes she criticized his choice, sometimes she covered her eyes and said "la la la la" until the wet sounds were over, sometimes she tilted her head and looked closely and said she could be in medical school for gynecology, this was probably exactly what it was like—they both knew that she'd never once implied that she was upset or offended. And she wasn't, really. When she said the word "porn" in Dr. Hanley's drab office, six miles from their home, in a room that smelled like Pine-Sol and was full of particleboard furniture made to look like mahogany, just days before Dr. Hanley would close his office for three weeks of fishing in Maine and she knew Malcolm was thinking, finally, he'd get a break from the guy, the doctor intertwined his fingers across his belly and tuned way in.

Jess could see that Malcolm was trying to seek out the doctor's eyes to see if there was something to be understood between them. He did *not* have a problem with porn, he said. *Some* of what she said in that room might be true, but that? No. Okay, so he watched porn once in a blue moon, he said, turning red, and then he challenged both Jess and Dr. Hanley to find a man in the universe, okay any man with access to the internet, who did not, on occasion, watch porn.

"My father," Jess said. Malcolm looked at the ceiling again, as if for help. He was, as she knew he would be, hamstrung by the fact that her father was dead.

"Sure" was all he said.

"You're saying he did? Where would he even get porn?" Jess asked. He'd died after a long battle with cancer, and had never once, as far as she could recall, used a piece of technology other than the television.

"Where did anyone get porn before the internet?"

"I think we're getting off base here," Dr. Hanley said.

"You're saying my mother rented X-rated videos for him? Are you remembering that he couldn't drive for the last four years of his life?"

"I'm not saying anything, actually. You're doing all the saying here."

"Listen," Dr. Hanley interjected. He leaned over his knees to tell them there was nothing wrong with anything, as long as both parties were in agreement. But it sounded to him like Jess was not in agreement.

Jess could almost see the adrenaline coursing under Malcolm's skin and thought he'd either walk out or say something dirty just to get Dr. Hanley to change his expression. Instead he said, "Jess, I think it's pretty standard."

"Standard what?"

"Standard fare? For two people who've been having sex for as long as we have?"

"Are we having sex?"

He ignored that.

"It's lazy. You're hoping you don't have to put in any work, so you pull up a porn and hope it does the job."

"And it does. Sometimes. Doesn't it?"

Jess felt mortified for three seconds, and then absolutely furious.

"If we're going there, we should go there. Right? Isn't that what you said? Jess? Have you not been pretty turned on by a porn a few times?"

She turned a fraction so that he was talking to the back of her head.

"I'm confused," he said. "Isn't this where we come to say honest things to each other?" He looked at Dr. Hanley, and then because he was already in trouble, he looked at his phone to read a text.

"I have to get to the bar."

When he came home that night, he woke her by lifting her shirt over her head. He tugged down her underwear and she told herself to refuse, he'd been such a jerk in Dr. Hanley's office, and that would teach him. He hadn't even texted to apologize. But this was the apology, she supposed, or if not an apology it was some kind of message, and it was up to her to decipher it. She couldn't help looking at him when he sat back on his heels for a moment to take off his shirt. She couldn't help noticing that he was beautiful, still. He was the kind of man who'd get better with each passing year, because along with age would come a little wisdom, discipline, a flame trimmed back so neatly he could control its height, its heat. It was all there in how he carried himself, how he stood, how he listened. He was immovable, a rock. It was the worst thing about him and the best. But he was angry now—unusual for him to show it—and it was even more unlike him to stay angry for so many hours. He barely looked at her. His skin smelled like gin. It was like he was in a daze, not really seeing her at all, and though her mind and heart felt a little hurt, felt more than a little worried, her body didn't seem to care. He gripped her hips. He splayed his hand against her chest and pressed her down. It was so fast, and once it was over, instead of collapsing next to her as he normally did, instead of drawing her close and breathing into her neck, he stood and walked into the bathroom, turned on the shower. She closed her eyes and could see his bare shoulders, how he'd hunch them toward the heat of the water, how he'd dip his head, how that long muscle across his abdomen would tense when he reached to clean himself, when he lifted one arm and then the other. She, on the other hand, was fading fast, or so it felt. Her youth was streaming out of her as if from a puncture she couldn't find, couldn't patch. After showering, he went downstairs to watch television without even glancing in her direction.

Siobhán had started out as Malcolm's friend—she, Patrick, and Malcolm had been hanging out since high school—but over the years had become just as close to Jess. As Malcolm told it, it was Siobhán all those years ago who pointed out that Jess was different from the other girls, that she brought out the best in him. Once or twice Jess tried to talk about what was happening between her and Malcolm to Siobhán and their friend Alice—Jess's best friend from high school. That her body had become a cage. That something sick was taking root, she could feel it.

Her friends would have good advice, no doubt about it. But every time she felt herself winding up to begin talking, she suddenly became protective of their secret, as she'd come to think of it. Where would she even slip it in? After which sentence? They'd tune in closely. They wouldn't interrupt. They'd tell her it would all be okay. She imagined herself saying it: He sleeps on the couch at least two nights a week. He went months without touching me. Siobhán would insist it was all normal, my goodness, only to be expected, but an alarm would ring in her expression. So Jess always pulled back, hard, like a sluice of water rushing up against a dam.

Also, they'd discuss it after, with each other. They'd do it out of concern, but she didn't want concern; she wanted a concrete solution. She wanted a cure for grief and she wanted someone to tell her where to find it. Siobhán and Alice and every other woman in her life were sensitive to what she'd been through and never brought it up explicitly unless Jess did first, but even small talk, even the most careful arrangement of information, was a reminder of their bustling families. It was there in the cars they drove, always full of crumbs and shin guards and orphan socks. It was in the food they stocked in their refrigerators, particularly the drinks: juice boxes and lime green sport-aids and rows of water bottles with floral prints. It was in the way they had to keep a cell phone on the table when they went out to dinner, and had to keep looking at it in case a babysitter texted, in case a kid called from a sleepover to be picked up early.

Cobie wouldn't understand, either, because she grew up in a family where they all said what they felt, and then had follow-up discussions to make sure problems were being addressed. Whenever anyone in her family visited New York, Cobie hugged them tight and said, "I've missed you so much." Jess had witnessed these greetings and had barely known where to look. Cobie's wife had conceived their twins through intra-uterine insemination—"via turkey baster," as she always put it—and it had all been very straightforward, as far as Jess could tell. Sometimes Cobie seemed to lose track of the reason it had not gone the same way for Jess.

Siobhán and Alice grew up more like Malcolm and Jess, but whenever Siobhán had a few drinks she let her guard down. Very recently, over glasses of wine on Jess's patio—the first time Jess had invited friends over in a while, Malcolm at work—Siobhán made a crack that her kids were conceived nearly the exact moment it crossed their minds to try.

"Oh God," she said immediately after, placing her wineglass down on the table. It was as if a cold wind had swept through. Every woman looked chastened, and that's when Jess glimpsed the extent to which they must discuss her when she wasn't around. "I'm so sorry. That was an incredibly dumb thing to say. What the heck is wrong with me?"

"What?" Jess asked, as she always did, the many, many times it happened in ways big and small. "Don't worry about it." Siobhán was better at protecting Jess from other people's stories than she was from her own.

Alice, too, had stories about the lengths she and her husband, Jack, went to have sex, always hiding from the kids, being quiet because of the kids, making sure no sounds were uttered, no bedsprings creaked, the time recently that Jack, usually so thrifty, drove her to a hotel fifteen minutes from their house and paid for the night even though they stayed for only three hours. "I would have spent the time watching TV in peace," Alice joked, but her expression—if not smug, exactly—bordered on self-congratulatory.

One morning, Jess decided to surprise Malcolm in the shower, but when she opened the door and slid aside the curtain, he was just standing there with both hands flat against the tiled wall, his face taking the full brunt of the water, his eyes closed, not washing himself, not doing anything. He looked sad, and Malcolm rarely looked sad. Jess stepped backward out of the room, shut the door, tried to wipe the image from her mind. There was a time when he would have felt the slightest tickle of the draft on his skin and known she was standing there, would have pulled her in.

He was worried about the bar, she knew he was, even though he acted as if all her worries were built on a foundation of sand. But then he didn't act like a person who was worried. She heard him humming under his breath when he dragged the garden hose around the yard, and his pleasantness, his general good mood, grated on her as if he'd been clanging symbols and yodeling. "Hey!" he said to anyone who shouted hello to him from a passing car, and pumped his fist. Sometimes he called out a specific name. "Johnny B! What you got?" and when she looked out, he'd still be talking through someone's car window fifteen, twenty minutes later.

After everything happened, Jess tried to remember what things had been like at home on the morning of the barbeque where she first met Neil, as she and Malcolm were getting ready to head over to the Hills' house. She tried to remember what they talked about. They arrived separately because Patrick texted Malcolm to pick up a few bags of ice, and Jess made a Buffalo chicken dip she wanted to bring over early in case Siobhán wanted to pretend she made it. They passed each other in the hallway in their haste, each hustling to their separate assignments, Malcolm in a new T-shirt that still had the size sticker on the sleeve. She put her hand on his chest and he looked at her with alarm, as if he had to brace himself every time she took a breath to speak. She saw everything he feared she would say pass through him, and he knew she saw it and neither of them said a word. She peeled the sticker off and held the little XL circle on her fingertip to show him. He stood there, his expression different now, full of relief, though he would have denied it. He looked at the top of her head for a moment before they both motored on. The day was already warm and the Hills' yard wouldn't be fully shaded until late afternoon.

An hour later, Malcolm was ripping open bags of ice and pouring them into coolers while Jess was helping set chairs on the lawn. The walk over had left her sweaty, and she was fanning herself with a package of napkins when Neil walked into the yard, his son in an infant carrier, only six months old, the two older girls in matching sundresses, sticking so close to their dad that Jess thought they might get tangled up in his legs. She saw him hesitate by the hedge, reach for his younger daughter's hand. She thought she saw him take a breath, as if girding himself, even though it was just a backyard barbeque, just friends of his friend, and he was an accomplished guy, everyone was on his side, there was nothing to be nervous about. Jess noticed he changed his expression for his daughters, whose faces were tipped up to study his. Out of habit she watched the hedges a moment longer, as if a woman, a wife, the mother of these children, might stride in behind him, but then she remembered.

Siobhán had told her how young his kids were, but Jess didn't really take it in until she saw them. "Hello." She waved, about to introduce herself, but next thing Patrick was there, clapping Neil's back, crouching to look at the baby, and she didn't want to interrupt.

"He's here," Jess leaned into the kitchen to tell Siobhán, but instead of going out to greet him, Siobhán waved her over to the corner of the kitchen, where she was huddled with Toby's wife, Amanda, and another woman named Laura, the mother of a friend of one of Siobhán's kids, and who was always at the Hills' parties now.

"She didn't even try that hard to keep them," Siobhán was saying. "Final straw was—and don't ever repeat this—she had the kids in the car after having a few drinks. I forget some of the details, but the story I heard was that one of the girls was supposed to sleep over at a friend's but started crying to come home, so next thing Christine—that's his ex—heads out to pick her up, and rather than leave the other two alone she put them in the car with her."

Siobhán paused so they could take that in. Jess didn't like this side of her friend. Her true motive, Jess knew, was getting everyone on Neil's side, getting them to welcome him and accept him as if he'd been there hanging out with them all along, but she just ended up seeming like a gossip.

"Those poor kids," Amanda said.

"Ugh," Laura said.

"Didn't you say they lived in the city?" Jess asked. "Why would she be driving?"

"They have a house on Cape Cod," Siobhán answered, giving her a look that told her she was missing the point. Jess made her eyes wide to tell her friend, Stop talking, but Siobhán ignored her.

"Had a place, I should say. Chatham. Just sold it. The kids have friends there."

"Selfish," Amanda said, nodding, as if she knew the type very well.

"Where was he?" Jess nodded toward the slider to indicate Neil. "Why didn't he go pick them up?" The yard was getting crowded. Siobhán must have invited everyone they knew. The women would share with each other what Siobhán told them, and they'd tell other people, and before you knew it Neil would walk into Food King and the seas of people would part, would begin a slow clap in their minds. What a man, to take full responsibility for his kids.

"At work I assume," Siobhán said in a tone that asked what that had to do with anything.

"At night?" Jess asked. "While on vacation?"

Siobhán gave her another look, and Jess shrugged.

"It's not the drinking per se that I don't understand," Amanda said and then paused. Jess alone recognized she was making a little joke, but when no laughs came she turned serious again. "It's the neglect."

"Absolutely," Siobhán agreed.

Malcolm would ask why Jess's first instinct was always to argue with people, but Jess was tempted to recall that it wasn't all that long ago that she had to wake Patrick at two in the morning to come downstairs and help get his wife up to bed. Patrick came down in his boxers, wrapped his arm around Siobhán, and said, "That's it, babe, you got it," every time Siobhán climbed another step. Jess grabbed the decorative bowl off the entry table and followed them up, holding the bowl under Siobhán's chin.

Neil was a nice-looking guy. He carried himself like an athlete. He was settling the kids, trying to do four things at once. After moving the baby to the shade of the hedge, he led the girls over to the corner of the yard where other kids were congregated. He went down on one knee to speak to them when they seemed hesitant, and Jess liked that he made his face level with theirs. More people arrived, and when he returned to the adults, he moved a chair to make room. He checked on the baby, who'd fallen asleep. He loosened the straps of the boy's seat and moved him further into the shade. Jess saw in his movements a certain shyness maybe, like he was out of practice mixing with a large group and didn't quite know how to be. There was a woman out there in the world who'd either lost him or given him up. Jess wondered what the ex was doing at that exact moment. If she felt her family had been ripped from her or if she felt free.

A few moments later, when he came in to ask if he could heat up a bottle and Siobhán introduced them, Jess spoke to him just like she'd speak to any of the men at the party, spouses within earshot. If anything, she decided later, she was more formal with him because she didn't know him. More formal because she'd already decided he was attractive. Later she wondered if she already sensed her curiosity taking root, if she already felt a premonition about the degree to which she'd wonder about him—his habits and preferences and the music he liked and whether he drove fast or slow and what he thought about when he had a moment to himself. Siobhán introduced her simply as Jess, without mentioning whom she was connected to, so Jess was the one who added "Malcolm's wife" when she shook his hand. At that moment, Malcolm was over at the makeshift bar. He shouted for Siobhán to bring him honey if she had any, bring him the bottle of hot sauce he saw on the counter, too, and she shouted back to get it himself.

"Jess," Neil said as if the name rang a bell. "You're the one who was at Kinney-Bartle?" Jess felt him appraising her. She felt him deciding that she was not quite what he expected. "I think I work with one of your old classmates."

He named a guy Jess had been in school with, someone Jess hadn't thought of in years. They'd gone on one very awkward date and had never spoken again.

"When I said I was moving here, he mentioned you. That you'd grown up here."

"How in the world did he remember that?" Jess asked, not really expecting an answer.

"Well," Neil said, making sort of a small bow, as if in deference to something. He smiled and Jess blushed. He didn't seem half as serious as he'd looked out in the yard.

"Siobhán said you switched to a media company. How's it going?"

"Ask me in a year," she said. "It's too early to say. The hours are better, I can tell you that."

Later, when she was trying to figure out how much to lay at her own feet, she considered whether that was presumptuous of her, that they'd know each other in a year. As they were talking, the other women kept interrupting to ask if he needed anything for the kids. They used words Jess didn't know. Do you need a Boppy? A binky? Do you have a Tommee Tippee? A Boon Orb? They were all impressed with him—a man who could bathe and dress three kids, get them to a party in a presentable state. A man who could tell when his baby was about to start fussing. "Sorry, Jess," they said when they moved on. Amanda handed out plates with hot dogs that had been cut lengthwise first and then into smaller pieces.

"I have a friend who wants a change, and his background sounds like yours. Did you work with a recruiter? I'd put him in touch if you don't mind giving me your number."

"Totally fine," Jess said, and watched as he tapped the numbers she recited and then typed J-E-S-S, as if she were the only Jess in the world.

Later, when they were walking home, Malcolm asked her what she thought of him. It was their standard review after meeting a new person, and she wondered if he'd forgotten how tense things were between them. Malcolm noticed that Neil hadn't had a drink. "You think he's on the wagon?" he asked. Later, Jess found out that he didn't drink that day because his kids were with him, and he said it shocked him, upon moving to the suburbs, how often people strapped children into the backseats of their cars and crossed their fingers. "It's only three turns!" they joked. "All back roads!" When he said that, Jess wondered what she and Malcolm would have been like if they'd gotten so lucky. Would they have been careful like Neil or would they have been like most and have no idea how lucky they were? The smaller girl was crying at one point and ran up to the deck where it was mostly women sitting around. "Hey," Jess said. "Can I help?" She smoothed the girl's sweaty hair away from her face and without the least bit of ceremony the girl placed her hot hand in Jess's and told her she needed her daddy.

"I bet he grew up with money," Jess said.

"Definitely," Malcolm said. "Weird how it's always obvious. I think the ex got a huge settlement. Maybe to stop her fighting him about the kids."

"Who'd agree to that?" Jess wondered. "What woman?"

There was a section of street between the Hills' house and theirs, where there were so many branches overhead, all thick with May blooms, that it felt like walking along an enclosed corridor. For a second Jess was sure Malcolm would take her hand, but instead he hooked his arm around her shoulder, pulled her in roughly for a kiss, and then he let her go. This was him calling a truce. This was him telling her that he hated arguing with her, that he loved her. She circled her arm around his waist and lay her head on his chest. That was her way of saying she agreed.

"He seemed a little blah," Jess added, and didn't know why she said that because she didn't believe it.

"Well, he didn't know anyone besides Patrick," Malcolm said.

At the party, when she and Neil were talking, they were both looking toward the Hills' old trampoline, so full of kids Jess was worried the bottom would give.

"Are any of those yours?" he asked.

Jess squinted at the trampoline as if searching for a particular child. "No," she said eventually, as if hers might be in the bathroom, at soccer practice, inside taking a nap.

She heard nothing from him for several weeks, had forgotten she'd given him her number. And then.

A few group texts first, about getting together. A beer garden in River-side. Dinner in a nearby town or in the city. A band they all liked at the

Forest Hills Stadium. Did anyone want to go? His was the only number without a contact assigned. She didn't know who it could be at first.

And then a direct text. Did I see you running by the train this morning?

For a moment she thought it was meant for someone else. Except she had gone for a run that morning, and her route took her by the train station. Then she remembered.

You should have honked! I could have used encouragement.

"All good?" Malcolm asked. She'd been at the counter dicing celery when Neil's message came in. They were making dinner together for the first time in a very long time.

"Oh, fine," she said. "That was just—" And then she turned her phone over so it was facedown on the counter. She thought of the show she'd fallen asleep to earlier that week, on National Geographic, about spiders, how they're born knowing how to weave a web, without ever having seen one, without imagining what a web could be for.

Later, as they were washing up, she checked to see if he'd written again.

They exchanged maybe two dozen meaningless texts, spread out over many weeks. Mostly about town, Jess's recommendations. She assumed he was asking Patrick these questions, too. Or Siobhán. Or his new neighbors. She assumed he had so many questions that he had to assemble a dozen people to answer because it would be too much for one person. Best sushi, best dry cleaner, whether the Y was clean. He probably had a thousand questions related to the kids, and school, and their activities, and it occurred to her that he was probably asking someone—a parent—for advice on those things. There were probably so many of "those things" that he was texting that person more than he was texting her. Once, she was driving when she saw his name pop up, and she pulled over to reply. Later, she wondered why she hadn't simply waited until she got home. It was a little heartbreaking, when she considered it; having to make new friends in his forties, hoping to be included in things, hoping for his kids' sakes to make inroads in a place that was not his home.

His messages ended with three exclamation points, sometimes. Sometimes no punctuation at all. Sometimes he mixed up "you're" and "your." And yet he seemed fastidious in other ways—she'd glimpsed the interior of his car, she'd seen the diaper bag. Some texts were strictly professional. He sent an article he read about Bloom. He sent an article from a law review he subscribed to. She once mentioned a band she liked, and several days later he sent her a Spotify link to a song by a band she'd never heard of because he thought they were similar and wanted to know if she thought so, too. He was over at the Hills' house when Siobhán called to wish Jess a happy birthday. Jess heard two male voices in the background, and then Siobhán switched to speaker so everyone could shout their good wishes. "Who's there?" Jess asked casually, as if she didn't feel an electric current down her spine as soon as she heard his voice, and just as she knew she would, Siobhán listed Neil and his kids alongside the rest of her family. Alice and some other friends had suggested getting together for drinks, but Jess didn't feel like it. It was a beautiful August night, the cicadas making a racket. Her father used to say that meant the next day would be very hot. "You still won't come over?" Siobhán asked, taking her off speaker, and Jess felt a little taken aback, like Siobhán knew that Neil would be a particular draw for her and was surprised she held out. But Malcolm had already promised they'd do something to celebrate on his night off. She curled up in her bed with a book and woke up sometime in the middle of the night to the jarring brightness of her bedside lamp.

She saw him around town a few times, and noted the car he drove—a white SUV, the same as so many others—but his had a royal blue decal on the bumper in the shape of Cape Cod. She found herself looking for that sticker when she was running errands.

Thirty-nine is too young to give up on trying for a baby, the Facebook groups told her, even when she typed her whole history, six and a half years of heartbreak summarized into two paragraphs. She read compulsively and then closed her tabs and cleared her history. Women having miracle babies in their forties. One woman at forty-seven with numbers worse than Jess's.

He was back at the Hills' house for a Labor Day barbeque—they rented an enormous Slip 'n Slide for the kids—and Jess saw him glancing over at her a few times before he walked up to say hello. They were shyer with each other in person than they were on text.

"Where's Malcolm?" he asked after they chatted for a bit. "Working?"

"Yes, working today, probably home tomorrow."

"So many of Patrick's stories are about that place. Fun times."

"I'm sure."

"Is it hard though?"

"Sorry?"

"All the nights and weekends?"

Jess laughed. "He loves it. He's a night owl. Never complains."

"No, I mean for you."

"Me?" Her stomach tightened. He was looking at her so intently. Her heart knocked as if trying to tell her something important. "No, not really. We're used to it. We have our rhythm."

When he walked away—called over by Patrick, who wanted him to show the guys something on his phone—Jess felt shaky, like something had happened that she couldn't describe.

He found her on Facebook a week or so after Labor Day, went on a tear of liking her photos one night. She screenshotted the notifications, wrote "psycho," and almost sent it to him, but something told her to pause, to think for a second. She slowly deleted the letters of his name. She deleted the screenshot.

She put her phone down on her bedside table. She looked at Malcolm sleeping in a heap beside her, his cheeks heavily shadowed though he gave himself a close shave every afternoon. Malcolm lived and died by his routine. He woke up, went to the gym for an hour, stopped by his favorite deli for an egg sandwich on his way home, salt-pepper-ketchup, no cheese, had a quick chat with Jay, with his wife, Carmen, who worked the register, he asked about their kids, about Jay's brother who had Parkinson's and had moved in with them, he chatted with whoever else happened to be on line waiting for their own sandwiches, and then he headed off to buy three scratch-offs from the mini-mart. At the mini-mart he usually stayed for a minute to chat with Lorenzo, but if it was Rick at the counter, he just took his tickets and headed home because as Jess knew, as Jess alone knew, Rick gave Malcolm the creeps. He kept a specific scratch-off penny in the cup holder of his car and always scratched the tickets in their driveway, against the steering wheel, his sandwich and coffee getting cold beside him. When he lost, he stuffed the tickets in the pocket of his car door, only emptying them when they began to overflow. Once inside the house, he stood at the counter and read the newspaper for twenty minutes, the crumbs of his sandwich falling all over the pages. Then he showered, shaved, headed off to the Half Moon once again.

"Are you happy?" she asked him once. Long before San Francisco. Before they stopped trying for a baby but after it was clear that it was not likely to end happily for them. Before he gave her a firm no to donor eggs, to adoption, but after she sensed he was backing away, recalibrating what he imagined their life would look like.

When she asked whether he was happy, he acted as if he didn't understand the question, like he didn't even know how being happy or unhappy was relevant to a life like theirs. "What do you mean?" he asked.

"I mean, you always seem upbeat but are you really? Do you ever want something else?"

"Something else?" he asked. "What are my choices?" She saw that he'd never asked himself that question, or if he had, he'd refused to answer. She saw him wondering if what she was really asking was whether she was happy.

"You mean go somewhere else? To live? Do something else for a living? Or do you mean someone else?"

"Somewhere else. For a start."

"Where?" And then he looked around their little house as if to ask where could be better. "And what do you mean 'for a start'?"

She told herself to respond to Neil's texts more slowly going forward. She began setting a timer each time one came in. She told herself she was not allowed to respond within two hours. Anything after two hours was okay. But then sometimes he'd send a second, and she didn't know if she should start the timer over again with each new one.

One morning on the old rail trail, she recognized him running toward her, finishing his loop. Couldn't women and men be friends? Wasn't she still close with her guy friends from high school, and God knew there was nothing going on between them? It was nearly Christmas, and they were texting enough by then that she stopped herself from polling her girlfriends to find out whether Patrick's friend from college was texting them all the time, in case the answer was no (in case the answer was yes). Her breathing quickened when she saw him. She decided the best thing was to say something friendly, something forgettable, but to not break her stride. All runners understand not stopping. And it was so cold. They were both wearing knit hats, gloves. But once he reached her, he turned around and ran alongside her without saying a word. He was not as tall as Malcolm. His build was leaner. He had large eyes the color of a faded penny, thick lashes, high cheekbones, full lips. She kept glancing at him and then away, and he kept doing the same. His running watch beeped. Even in the dead of winter his skin had a gold tone and didn't turn ruddy and pink like hers did, like Malcolm's did, too. His hair was buzzed to the scalp, and she imagined if he took his hat off right then, the cold would feel like a slap.

That morning on the trail, after they'd panted side by side for maybe a quarter mile, he said he was glad he ran into her. His younger daughter needed a haircut but he wasn't sure which of the local salons would be okay with him bringing in a little girl. He couldn't exactly take her to the barbershop. Jess imagined him walking into a salon and every woman looking up. She imagined them catching each other's eyes in the mirrors without betraying a single thought. The older daughter had curly hair and didn't need it cut so often, he said. But the little one's hair was long and fine and was always slipping out of the barrette.

Jess pictured him fixing his daughters' hair in the mornings, helping them pick out their outfits. The fathers Jess knew, the fathers Jess and Malcolm had, they weren't even the same species as this sort of man. Jess tried to imagine her father saying the word "barrette." She tried to imagine him watching a video that would teach him how to braid her hair.

"Her mom doesn't—?" Jess began, not knowing quite how to put it.

"She said she'd take care of it. But she hasn't yet." He paused.

They were nearly at the first mile marker, their rhythms matched exactly.

"We only communicate through lawyers." He turned to smirk at her. "They love us." A lawyer joke. The fighting was so bad that they were keeping two firms afloat.

"God," Jess said. She couldn't help it. It was shocking to think two people could love each other enough to get married, and then be rendered incapable of having a conversation about trimming a girl's hair.

And then he said, "Fuck her," like it was nothing, like he was making an observation about the weather. Jess's pace slowed. She moved a little farther away from him on the path. For the rest of the day she kept hearing him say it: his tone, the anger that bubbled there. Fuck her. She decided to keep her distance. He was Patrick's friend. No need to be hers.

And then, more than a year after they met in the Hills' backyard, he texted late. Malcolm was at the bar.

I'm watching that new movie about the plane crash and the actress reminds me of you

It wasn't dirty. It wasn't suggestive. She knew the movie. There was some resemblance on her absolute best day. But reading it made her feel like she'd accidently tugged a trip wire.

What was the problem, she asked herself in her silent bedroom. That he'd noticed what she looked like? That he was thinking about her? Hadn't she noticed him? Weren't they all checking each other out almost all the time? Just a few weeks ago didn't Jess say to Phil Colombo, whom she'd known since middle school, that she noticed he'd lost weight and that he looked really great—younger and even more handsome than he'd been at twenty? Didn't she say something to Phil like "go get 'em, tiger," and didn't he growl at her before lifting her off the ground in a bear hug? And didn't all of this happen in front of everyone going about their business in the bread aisle of Food King and not one person felt an antenna rise?

So why was there nothing wrong with that, but something a little wrong with Neil's text?

She deleted their whole history.

The problem was her response, an immediate drumbeat of desire that started in her belly. Even as she told herself not to text back, she knew she'd text back. She knew whatever this thing was, she wanted to keep it going.

But she decided to go to sleep instead. She'd let it fade away and when they saw each other next, she'd make sure to keep the conversation cordial. A few days later, she drove up to Patrick and Siobhán's and he was there, helping Patrick dig out a tree stump. It was the end of summer. His kids were heading into their second school year in Gillam. Jess was dropping off a selection of shoes for Siobhán to choose from for a wedding they had coming up. Neil was in an undershirt, his dress shirt draped over a bush, and so Jess imagined he stopped by straight from work for some other reason—maybe Siobhán was minding his kids—

and then Patrick had roped him into helping. Siobhán was making fun of them a little, the veins in their foreheads protruding, struggling to pry the root up with their spades, but Jess found it hard to laugh or speak. She found it hard to follow what her friend was saying, as surprised as she was to see Neil. He seemed startled, too. Patrick called out hello but Neil didn't. He looked over at her but stayed across the yard. Jess told herself it would be insane to feel hurt by that. They were sweating, streaked with dirt. She barely knew him.

But there was something in that moment, a mutual recognition, maybe. If a judge were to catalog the grand total of the exchanges between them, it would read as completely bland, except for the fact of their existence in the first place, why there'd been exchanges at all. Later, Jess knew that was the moment something shifted. She recognized him and he recognized her across the space of maybe forty feet. There were no drinks to sip. No phones to hide behind.

"You okay?" Siobhán asked that evening in the yard. It was almost twilight, the days getting shorter. And then in a lower voice, she asked, "Do the supplements still make you feel sick?"

"No, we stopped all that," she said lightly, as if she hadn't owed her friend that news for a whole year by then. She spun her car key on her finger and pretended not to notice how closely Siobhán was looking at her. She let herself into the house, lined the shoes along the floor. When Siobhán joined her she described which ones were most comfortable, which were best for dancing, all the while keeping track of where exactly Neil was standing in Siobhán's yard.

"Jessie," Siobhán said, her eyes soft with concern. "Want a quick glass of wine? The kids won't bother us for at least twenty minutes." She held up a bottle of Sancerre she knew Jess liked.

Jess was tempted. Staying meant the men would come in, maybe. Maybe join them. She'd get to see him, sit near him.

"Or a cup of tea? It's been a long time since we've hung out just the two of us," Siobhán added. "Come on."

"I wish I could, Bon-Bon," Jess said. "But I have to go."

"Malcolm's at work!"

"My mother. I'm taking her to dinner."

"You're acting kind of odd."

"I know."

"What's up?"

"Nothing. I don't know."

"Okay. But soon, please? I feel like we haven't had a good chat in a long time."

She called out a goodbye to Patrick and Neil as she all but jogged to her car. As soon as she drove around the corner, out of their line of sight, she pulled over and parked, tried to make her body stop trembling. Nothing happened. You stopped by your friend's house. You dropped off shoes. Nothing happened. But she couldn't make her bones hear a different tune.

She was sure she'd get a text, but nothing came. When she was invited to a party where she assumed he'd be, she declined.

She saw him here and there over the next few months, but always kept the conversations light and quick. It was good to see him but she was on her way somewhere. Dr. Hanley was starting to help a little. The Half Moon's balance sheet made gentle swings back and forth between red and black each month, but never too widely, never too far. Jess started to wonder if maybe it was possible to dance at the edge of a precipice and keep dancing for the rest of your life. By the time they got their invitation to Amanda and Toby's annual New Year's party, she told herself that she was cured of whatever feeling had come over her the previous summer. Hormones. Grief. Boredom. The growing sense that life was passing her by and if she didn't do something she'd leave nothing behind to prove she was even there.

Malcolm always said that New Year's was the one night a year when normal people turn completely feral, so he wanted to be at the bar. He'd hired a DJ, had cleared out the low-tops. He sold tickets in advance and would sell more at the door. The cops would be all over town, giving Breathalyzers. He suggested their friends have New Year's at the Half Moon but they didn't want to, the crowd would be too young there, they said, the music too loud. Jess knew he'd never push the idea on anyone, so he didn't ask twice. Between just the two of them, they compromised. They'd both go over to Toby's for a while, and then when the time came for Malcolm to head to the bar, Jess could either go with him or stay at the party.

"I really will be working though," he warned her. "You might want to rope a few people into coming to hang out." But Jess knew no one would want to change locations, not if they were having fun.

Neil was the first person Jess saw when she walked into Amanda and Toby's kitchen. He was leaning against the counter with his arms folded across his chest, and she saw his eyes jump from her to Malcolm and then back to his conversation in one split second. Malcolm walked right up to him and shook his hand. Jess followed and he said hello to her, kissed her cheek just like he would any other woman on New Year's Eve. Every conversation Jess had, every circle she stood in, she knew where Neil was and she knew where Malcolm was, without even looking. Malcolm kept stepping outside to call the bar, and every time he returned Jess expected him to say he was leaving, but he stayed. Toby's daughter came stomping up from the basement in a swivet about how the kids were supposed to know when it was midnight since there was no TV downstairs.

And then the power went out. Someone shouted at Toby in the dark, asked if he'd paid his electric. Everyone laughed. It was only around ten o'clock. Malcolm made for the porch to call the bar, to find out if the power outage was all over town. The rest of them held perfectly still, afraid to bang a leg against a chair, afraid to bump against someone's glass, and then she felt it: a hand pushing aside her hair, the warm press of a kiss on her neck. She was so surprised that she barely registered it in the moment, but after, a minute after and a week, she conjured up that press and release over and over and over, his breath on her skin.

"You look pale," Malcolm said when the lights came back on.

"Just tired," she said. Used to be that every time she said she was tired, they both wondered if she was pregnant.

Malcolm blew a party horn, and the thin plastic unfurled by her ear. "Party pooper," he said. "I guess that means you won't come to the bar."

"No," she said. "But will you drop me at home on your way?"

"You're sure? I could give you Hugh's old throne. Free cocktails all night?"

"But then I'll be stuck there until closing."

"I'll call you a cab!"

"Nah," she said. "It'll be impossible to get one tonight. Home, please."

"Heading out?" Neil asked a moment later, appearing in the doorway of the spare bedroom where everyone tossed their coats. "It's so early." Malcolm was still making his way around the living room, saying his goodbyes.

"Yes," Jess said, without looking at him. She pretended to search for something in her purse. The sound of glass shattering came from the other room, a scurry for a broom and dustpan, peals of laughter.

"Hey I'm sorry about that," he said. "Before, I mean. I just . . ."

He took a step and staggered. He held the back of a chair to steady himself.

Oh, Jess thought. There you go.

"I'd like to talk to you," he said.

"Neil," she said, and they locked eyes.

"All set?" Malcolm came up behind Neil and clapped him on the back one final time. Neil wished them goodnight, returned to the party, to the endless circling about of stories and old jokes and drinks poured with a heavy hand as the night wore on. Amanda was handing out beaded necklaces and plastic glasses with frames that made the numbers 2018. Out on Toby's porch, Jess pulled the collar of her coat tight and looked up at Malcolm, caught a frown pass across his face. He patted his jacket pockets as if searching for something.

"What?" Jess asked.

"I don't know," Malcolm said. "I just got the weirdest feeling."

She kept going over it. She kept putting her hand to the place on her neck. What a prude she was turning out to be. Everyone knew boundaries shifted on New Year's. He'd had too much to drink.

Next time she saw him was at Penn Station, mid-January. It wouldn't have taken much to cut through the crowd to say hello, but she didn't. He looked different in the city, in his work clothes. He was reading something on his phone, a messenger bag crossed over his chest. She saw him again when she transferred at Secaucus but he was ahead of her and didn't look back. The whole ride to Gillam she imagined him somewhere on the same train, staring out at the same view, and it was only when they disembarked at Gillam's station that he saw her.

"Oh, hey," he said, surprised. The circle of light cast by the streetlamp enclosed them together. How lonely he must be. How much courage it must have taken to break his life open and change it. The other commuters had already scattered. They each made a bunch of standard complaints about the train. "Was your day okay?" he asked. He seemed to have genuine interest in her answer, so she told him a little about it, then asked about his.

He had to go, he said eventually. The sitter was due to leave. His younger daughter needed a rock to paint for school and couldn't find a good one in the yard. The older girl needed a particular color T-shirt for spirit week and he promised to take her to the mall.

"It's a lot," Jess said.

"It is a lot," he agreed. "And by the way. I've been meaning to apologize about, you know—"

"It's fine."

"You know what I was going to say?"

"I think so."

That was a Thursday. On Friday, the very next night, he texted for the first time in a long time, to ask if she was home, if he could stop by. He must have known Malcolm would be at work. Everyone knew where to find Malcolm Gephardt on a Friday night.

When he arrived, he closed the door behind himself but just stood on the mat. He wouldn't take off his coat. Jess thought, maybe he's dropping something off. But he had nothing in his hands. She was nervous, her voice loud when she offered him something to drink. How cool she was trying to be, how badly she wanted to seem at ease. But instead of answering he put his hands on his head and clutched it like he was trying to hold it together.

"Jess," he said, dropping his arms to his sides.

She waited, the electric hum inside her body getting stronger. It was now, she knew. It was now. She had a decision to make. She was in cotton joggers. Her old R.E.M. T-shirt. A ponytail. No makeup.

He took a step closer and then reached past Jess to the panel of light switches behind her. The cold air from outside rolled off his clothes. He turned off the light in the hall, and Jess knew that he'd decided, that whatever he was about to do he couldn't have people see if they glanced at her house.

"What are you doing?" she asked. She felt like she was breathing through a straw. His coat was unzipped, and she put her hand flat to his chest, over his heart. He went perfectly still, maybe to figure out if she was pushing him away. But she slid that same hand to his shoulder and he groaned like an animal, like she'd injured him somehow.

six

On the second morning after the storm—Sunday—Malcolm woke in the clothes he'd been wearing the day before, his knit hat twisted up with the bedsheets, his coat on the floor. His phone was dead. He remembered getting up in the middle of the night to search the medicine cabinet, and then Jess's bedside table for an old Xanax that might have escaped the bottle. She never took one until she'd truly tried to sleep on her own, and she made a rule that she could never take more than one a week. But all he found was a tube of self-tanner, a pile of bobby pins, an empty baggie labeled "folic acid." He could see his breath in the slant of moonlight.

He wondered if Neil Bratton knew by then what trouble she had sleeping, how she fell asleep easily but couldn't stay asleep, how her thoughts found a loop and stayed there, night after night, all the things she would have done differently, like a marble rolling down a run, the same twists and turns over and over and over.

Surely the power would come back that day. Surely something would happen, because he wouldn't be able to stand another like the previous one, no markers to go by, no beginning, middle, or end. He stood up, from his bed, his shoulders aching, and went to the window, first the back and then down the hall to the front, his new snowstorm ritual. The plow had come through—there were grooves on the road—but it must have snowed more because the tracks were blurred. He tried to tell from the sun what time it was, but every corner of the sky was gray.

Downstairs, the wall clock showed it was just after ten. He lifted the smaller of the two pots of water on the stove and chugged as much as he could. He placed the pot back down on the range and took a deep breath, pressing his fist to his chest. He opened and closed cabinet doors, looking for something to eat. He ate a bit of the cold meat loaf his mother had wrapped for him on Friday, and hoped she had a good fire going, that she knew to close the doors to trap the heat. He could feel his temper stirring, like chop on the surface of a shallow pond. Amazing to consider the situation he was in, stuck in his house while his bar sat empty and his wife played pretend across town. He closed his eyes and conjured the scene that always calmed him: a vision of the Half Moon packed from end to end, a cover band playing songs everyone loved. He thought of his friend Adrian who worked at the Half Moon for a few years but then moved down south, Nashville first, and then Miami. He'd called Malcolm twice recently. Left voicemails for Malcolm to call him back without saying what he wanted. Malcolm hadn't gotten around to it, and then just a day or two before the storm, he opened *Neat* magazine and whose face did he see but Adrian's, looking at him from his bar "on the edge of the world." It wasn't really on the edge of the world. It was on St. John, basically a pergola set over a stone patio from the looks of it, up-lighting, the Caribbean shimmering in the background. The article was mostly about the hurricanes that had hit the previous year, and what the rebuilding effort looked like. Malcolm imagined having no heating bill. No cable. No windows to break. Just a steel drum and a nightly sunset. He wondered how Adrian protected the back bar and the stemware when it rained.

Maybe Adrian had heard the Half Moon was struggling. He wasn't a bragger, so Malcolm was sure whatever he wanted had nothing to do with the feature in *Neat*, but Malcolm couldn't quite bring himself to call back and hear how well Adrian's place was doing. Maybe he should visit St. John. He could get out of town for a few days and get some perspective from a friend who knew Gillam, knew Hugh and the Half Moon, knew what it took to run a place.

"Jesus," he said aloud, and wished for something, anything, to distract him. There was nothing to clean, nothing to organize except the attic, but he wasn't going back up there, no way. Malcolm closed his fist against a vision of Bratton's face collapsing when Malcolm made contact. Patrick's, too, for inviting him in. Everyone knew, he supposed. Like he didn't have chances? Like he didn't have very appealing options every weekend night of his life?

He wondered if his mother had gotten anyone to plow her driveway. Last snowfall Mr. Sheridan rode his quad with the plow attachment around the block to clear her driveway after doing his own. Malcolm had just gotten over there, hadn't started shoveling yet when they heard the quad coming. Seventysomething years old and Mr. Sheridan's taking corners on two wheels, the plow's blade scraping the road. His mother suggested it was a little wrong to bypass houses where the people inside also needed help, but Mr. Sheridan said screw that, he wasn't in charge of the whole neighborhood, and from the way his mother blushed Malcolm knew that she loved the idea of him speeding by Margie Strand's four-car driveway to get to her. Malcolm was sure she had plenty to eat, at least, but maybe she was scared over there by herself. His sister had called twice in the last few weeks, saying she wanted to talk to him "about Mom," but he hadn't gotten a chance to get back to her, and now his phone was dead. Anyway, he knew what she wanted to say: little mistakes—names, places. He'd noticed, but he wasn't quite sure how much to worry. She seemed confused, sometimes, about basic things— had she eaten at the diner that morning or was that several days ago? But then a moment later she was razor-sharp again. His mother-in-law had called, too, the only time he heard from her since Jess took off, and left a long message about a raccoon in his mother's basement but then said there was no raccoon, the basement was fine. He deleted it and figured he'd check it out himself next time he went by, but then he'd gotten tied up at the bar every night, and last time he saw his mother had been in his own kitchen on Friday, late afternoon, when she showed up with dinner. She sat and talked with him while he ate. She seemed totally fine to him except for one tiny thing, a funny thing, really, when he thought about it. When Malcolm teased her for making a meat loaf so big, how would he ever get through it, she said it wouldn't go to waste, it was her son's favorite.

"Your son?" Malcolm laughed. "Hello? Do you have another?"

Jess used to say that he wasn't himself until he had people around, until he had other moods and personalities to react to, and he resented when she said that, as if he were incapable of self-reflection, but now he sort of knew what she meant. It wasn't that he disliked being alone, it was more like he felt muted, not completely awake. He held a bag of ground coffee, considered whether he could rig up a percolator on the stove if he found matches to light the pilot. And then, after standing there another minute, he heard the crunch of snow under tires, as if from his dreams.

A police SUV was rolling slowly up the street, the snow so high it looked like it was floating. Malcolm imagined all his neighbors rushing to their windows, praying that a cop car meant something that would distract them for ten minutes, break up the morning. It kept coming, rolling past the other houses, and stopped at Malcolm's driveway.

Malcolm tried to see who was driving, but the young officer who eventually got out of the car was one Malcolm didn't recognize. He began making his way across the snow to Malcolm's door.

"Malcolm Gephardt?" the officer said when Malcolm answered his knock.

"That's me."

Jess was dead. No one could call. His mobile wasn't listed. They didn't know how else to reach him.

"You own the Half Moon on Seneca?"

"Yeah?" Malcolm said.

"You were there on Friday night?"

"Yes. What's going on?" So it was the bar, then, not Jess. The bar had flooded. The bar had filled with carbon monoxide and exploded, taking out half the town.

He gestured for the officer to come inside.

The cop stomped the mat several times. "Cold out, huh?"

Malcolm led him down the hall to the kitchen. He stayed on one side of the island, the officer on the other. He wiped down the counter like he was at the bar, about to serve a drink.

"So? What's up?"

"Do you know a Charles Waggoner? I understand he was at your bar on Friday night."

Charles Waggoner. Malcolm felt his body relax. Jess was fine. The bar was fine. It was just some guy named Charles Waggoner who was not fine.

"I know a Tripp Waggoner. Any relation? We had a pretty good crowd Friday night. Why? What happened?"

"Tripp. That's his nickname. He hasn't been home since Friday. His wife talked to him around six o'clock, and he was headed to the Half Moon. He told her a friend was dropping him off."

"Sorry, today is Sunday, right?"

"Sunday, yeah," the officer said as he reached into his pocket and drew out his phone. "It's the power being out, the days are blending together. Anyway, this is him. A photo from last summer."

Malcolm nodded. "He almost got himself into a brawl. He never made it home?"

"No."

"Sorry to hear that." He should be careful now, he knew. A pair of cops in uniform had come into the bar one afternoon years ago, asking questions about a guy who'd driven his car into a house. He blew right through a stop sign and into the den of a family of five, all of whom were sleeping. There was an eleven-year-old boy whose headboard was not eighteen inches from the front of the car. The guy had been drinking at the Half Moon for hours that day.

Did Hugh panic? No. He asked after the officers' families. He changed the subject every which way. He told André to throw two steaks on the grill. When they left, Hugh shrugged and said, "No one died and insurance will pay for the house to get fixed."

"Can you shed any light?" the officer asked now. "What time he left? Did he mention where he might be going?"

He'd gotten dropped off, Malcolm heard as if on a delay. So there was no fear of Tripp having plowed his car into someone. He tried to remember—there was a bar in the Bronx recently that made the news because a patron had left on foot—on *foot*—and assaulted someone, maybe an hour later. The bar had still gotten sued. Maybe whenever he left, whichever way he'd gone, some of the young guys in the group from earlier in the night spotted him. Maybe they caught up with him, continued the argument they'd been having at the bar. He tried to remember the guy who punched Tripp, how young he was. Tripp had taken the punch like all drunk people, like he barely noticed, as numb as he was. But he would have felt it Saturday morning.

"Sorry, I don't know. He never made trouble before, but on Friday he got into it with a group of young guys, so we had him cool out for a bit. I guess that was about nine thirty or so. But then he ended up leaving before we called a cab for him."

"'Cool out' meaning what?"

"Meaning we took him aside, set him up in the kitchen. I figured he

142

should sober up a little. He was at the bar alone, otherwise I would have told whoever he was with to get him out of there. And we kinda know him, he comes in a lot. But anyway, he just left."

There were times, after cutting someone off, when somehow that person seemed even more wasted after an hour of doing nothing than they had while drinking. As if whatever last gulps of alcohol took precisely that long to enter the bloodstream and reach his brain. Maybe that's what had happened to Tripp.

"When you say 'got into it,' what do you mean?"

"Ah, you know. Taking digs at each other about dumb things. People around him were getting sick of it."

"He didn't mention any plans?"

"Most people were planning on being snowed in, I think," Malcolm said. "It was a weird night."

"I mean in general. Life plans. Or any trouble he might have been in."

"No. Not that I remember."

"Okay," the officer said.

"That's it?"

"That's it."

The day before him was too long, too shapeless. He hadn't talked to another person since Friday night. He didn't want the officer to leave.

"You know, he usually does go on about how he wants to move somewhere far away. Get off the grid. How we're all suckers for living the way we do, the constant hustle. Stuff like that. He likes to say there are places where it's spring all year-round."

"Yeah? Where would he go?" The officer was interested.

"He seemed really into South America."

"To Peru? Did he say Peru?"

"Yeah, Peru. You knew that?"

"What else did he say?"

"Just how beautiful it is there. He'd looked into how much land costs per acre in one particular area, how he'd make his money stretch. Stuff like that. He seems to really hate his job."

The officer waited, as if hoping for more.

"I just let people talk. He does something in finance, don't ask me what."

He thought of Jess, the time she asked him if he was happy, how he'd reacted as if he didn't know what she was talking about, as if he'd never asked himself that question, the closed expression on her face when she thought she was the only one. Later he thought it was probably mean of him to make her think that, how she might feel lonelier, but if he forged on as if there were no other choices, then so would she. Only it hadn't worked out that way. Over the past week, Malcolm had gotten bills for a new year of disability insurance, workers' comp, his permit from the Department of Health, the company that serviced his fire extinguishers and the exhaust hood. He'd owe first-quarter sales tax pretty soon.

"Did he ever mention specifics? How he'd go about it if he were to do it?"

"Not that I remember. I didn't take it too seriously, to tell you the truth. You should hear the things people talk about when they've tied one on. People don't realize they'll bring their exact same problems to a new place, new relationship, new career—whatever it is they think will solve their problems.

"He seems like a pretty nice guy," Malcolm added, "but put a few drinks in him and he's an expert in everything. You know the type? He'll tell me how to run my bar. He'll tell you how to be a cop. He'll tell a fish how to swim." Malcolm shrugged. "He was definitely unhappy. A little angry underneath, but that's everyone. I hope nothing happened to him.

"You want coffee?" Malcolm asked, and then remembered he had no power. "Oh wait. Sorry."

The officer closed his notepad and put it in his pocket. Malcolm followed him to the door. He noticed the new four-foot-tall ridge of snow at the end of his driveway. The plow must have pushed it across while they were in the kitchen, and now that ridge was no doubt transforming into a solid block of ice.

"Is the power out all over town?"

"All over the county."

"The roads are okay though?"

"No, the roads are terrible. An alert went out to stay home. We've been doing rescues all night."

"But the forecast said the freeze will last days."

"People are getting stuck. For real. Don't go out if you can help it. Anyway, thanks for your time."

He began to high-step his way down the path, in the same footsteps he'd made on his way in.

"Hey. Do you think I could get a lift? To my bar? Since you're driving over that way and your car is on the other side of that mountain?" He glanced again at the enormous ridge of snow where his driveway met the road. "It's an old building. I have a generator there but I need to set it up. The lever on the water main broke off a few years ago and I never got it fixed so I'm worried about a pipe bursting."

The officer hesitated.

"I'd really appreciate it."

"Yeah okay," he said.

"I just need one minute," Malcolm said and then moved as fast as he could through his house. He layered on clean clothes, grabbed his wallet, his keys, his phone. He stepped into his boots and went out the back door to the shed, picked up the canister of gasoline, looked around for what else he might need. He half expected the car to be gone when he got back around to the driveway, but it was still there, waiting. The officer had just summited the ridge of snow and was stumbling down the far side. When it was Malcolm's turn, he rested the gas can on the crest and climbed over on hands and feet.

The car was warm. The street was freshly plowed but Malcolm could see from the way the sun glinted off the surface of the road that the thin layer left behind was all ice.

"Your bosses are so worried about Tripp that they sent you out in this?"

The young officer didn't respond at first. He rolled slowly through the stop sign at the end of the street and took the turn without tapping the brake.

"You call him Tripp. Did he tell you to call him that?"

"I guess so. I didn't come up with it myself."

"It's a childhood nickname. He usually introduces himself as Charles. He probably likes you."

"Yeah?" Malcolm said.

The car rolled right through the red light on Raritan.

"He's my father."

"Ah," Malcolm said, trying to remember what exactly he'd said about Tripp. Nothing too bad, he hoped.

"I'm supposed to be barricading the hill on Overlook Drive. I'm Rob Waggoner."

Malcolm had never pictured Tripp's kids.

"For a couple years now he's just been talking crazy about going away. He pulled me aside maybe six months ago, but he's so full of it in general that I didn't really tune in to what he was saying. But now he's gone. Just like he said. I mean, I can't imagine anyone getting very far after Friday's storm, but on the other hand we think he's been planning. He might have looked into getting papers. You know, false documents."

"False documents," Malcolm repeated. "You're serious?"

"I know it sounds crazy. My mom thought he was having an affair. He was being secretive, always closing his laptop when she walked into the room. She sometimes saw him looking through a file folder but when she searched for it when he was at work she could never find it. The little things she did manage to find never had to do with women."

"What were they?"

"Places he wanted to go and how to live there. Patagonia. Mongolia. Northern Canada. Really rugged places. But his favorite was Peru."

"If you're worried can't you check? Put out a description?"

"Like in the movies?" Rob glanced at him. "Send out an APB? Our captain made an announcement to be on the lookout for him and we can alert other police departments, but that's pretty much it. And it's busy right now. People getting stuck in this cold, in houses without power."

"Listen, people talk all sorts of nonsense they don't mean," Malcolm said as they glided down Seneca, the storefronts so peaceful with snow piled on the sills, sticking to the plate glass. "I hear it all the time. I'm going to leave my wife. I'm going to quit my job. I'm going to write my memoir and sell it to Hollywood. But very few people actually do the things they say they're going to do. And it feels a little dramatic for a guy like Tripp. Plus remember the weather on Friday night? I'm sure he's holed up somewhere and he'll be back soon. I bet his phone died."

They pulled up to the Half Moon.

"I'm going to take a look around if that's okay," Rob said. "I want to picture his night."

There were no other cars around, so Rob left the cruiser running in the middle of the road.

"Yeah sure," Malcolm said. He couldn't remember exactly how he'd left the place, but knew it was in a state, the floors unwashed, glasses grouped here and there.

"Might be a bit of a mess," Malcolm said as he unlocked the door. Just as he feared, he pushed open the door and the first thing he saw was a napkin on the floor, stained with hot sauce. In bright daylight, brighter than usual because of the reflection off the snow, he could see rings on the high-tops. He set his stuff down and listened for the sound of water. He went into the kitchen, opened the mop closet, got down on his knees, and gripped the old pipe. Cold but intact. He walked over to the sink and flipped it on, got the water moving just in case it was icing up in there, ready to bust. It was a good building. Ugly but strong. Sound construction. Hugh wasn't wrong about that. But it felt colder in there than it had been in his house.

"So anyway," Malcolm said when he returned to the dining room. "Tripp or Charles or whatever we're calling him—your dad—was sitting over there." He pointed.

"And then like I said we took him into the kitchen to put a little distance between him and the group of younger guys he got into it with." He led Rob through the kitchen door, showed him the chair where Tripp had rested. "The guys moved on. I don't know where they went."

"Okay." Rob looked around. "And then?"

"Then he was just gone. I was in and out, my staff was busy. He must have gone out this door because he didn't come through the main room. I would have seen him."

Rob pushed open the door that led from the kitchen to the alley. Malcolm saw his snow shovel leaning up against the dumpster, exactly where he knew it was. Both men leaned as far as they could out the door and looked left and right. If they were in a movie, this would be when they spotted him, sitting against the far side of the dumpster, frozen solid, icicles hanging from his nose.

"The commuter lot is right there," Malcolm said, pointing over the flimsy chain-link fence that separated the back of the Half Moon from Metro-North property. He scanned for a body over there, too, and the blinking seriousness of Rob Waggoner's face told Malcolm he was doing the same. But the snow was thinner there because of the trees, and Malcolm could already tell there was nothing there but the same empty soda bottles and torn cardboard boxes that had littered that spot for years. Rob knew where the commuter lot was, of course. The point was that Tripp could have gone either way. He could have cut left from the kitchen door and walked to the sidewalk around front, or he could have turned right and walked through the parking lot, away from town.

Malcolm noticed Rob looking up at the motion-activated light in the alley. There was a small canister underneath that looked like a camera, but the only real camera was on the front door, trained over the bouncer's shoulder. To install a working camera at both doors was double the price, and Malcolm figured a fake would be good enough. He told Rob that, and apologized, a real security camera would have helped. Together they took a few tentative steps outside, testing the frozen surface of the snow to discover whether it would hold them. Malcolm broke through first, and then Rob. One after another they stamped a path down the alley to the sidewalk. Nothing. They retraced their footsteps, and circled around the back of the building. Malcolm had left his gloves on the bar and his hands felt so cold he was starting to feel pins and needles in his fingertips.

"You should probably check his route home. Just in case."

"I already have." Rob squinted up at the trees, the lacework of frozen branches. After a moment he said he was heading out but he'd come by later to see if Malcolm needed a lift back home.

"Nah, don't worry about me. I'll crash here."

"Yeah? Okay."

"Don't forget to barricade the hill on Overlook."

"Oh yeah."

Once Rob left, Malcolm sat at the bar and ate an entire bag of party mix, pouring it into his mouth directly from the plastic pouch. He found two oranges, which he peeled and ate. He checked his phone but all he'd gotten were dumb memes of people wiping out on ice and two from Toby complaining that he was in his third hour of family Monopoly. Nothing from Jess.

He used the landline to call his mother—thank goodness he kept the old, corded phone—but it rang and rang. He walked through the bar and flipped chairs over on tables. He swept. Nearly forty-eight hours after losing power the water in the slop sink still ran warm, so he filled a bucket, cleaned every corner of the floor. It was good to be moving, doing something productive. He scrubbed the bar, the back bar. He wiped down the bottles. He got down on the hex mat and cleaned under the rack. He got so warm while he worked that he took off his coat. He imagined Emma walking in, surprised to find him there. He imagined what he'd say, and then what she'd say, and what might happen. He imagined Jess walking in and his body locked up. He wouldn't make it any easier for her. He'd just stare at her until she spoke, and then he'd tell her it didn't matter to him in the least what she did with her life. He cleaned the bathroom, emptied all the garbage cans, brought the bags outside, and since he was out there anyway he shimmied his shovel loose from the spot where it had frozen, and then walked around front to clear the sidewalk. He purposely left his phone inside, but after a few minutes he let himself check. Nothing.

The water in the tank wouldn't stay warm forever, so he went to the men's bathroom and splashed his face, not caring about the puddle growing on the floor. He used the hidden key to open the supply cabinet where the spare hand towels were kept, and he found three fresh undershirts, plain white, still with cardboard inserts. He slowly unfolded the top shirt, held it against himself. "Well okay," he said, taking off the T-shirt he was wearing and pulling the new one over his head. He used his stale undershirt to wipe down the sinks, wipe up the water on the floor. He wiped down the urinals. Then he dropped his old undershirt into the garbage can and scoured his hands.

Fully dressed once again, he went down to the storage room to get the generator he bought in a panic after a freak hurricane, not long after the bar became his. The generator was on the cheap end, not meant to keep the place running, and Jess had argued at the time that they'd be better off spending more on a good one than any money at all on one that would prove near useless in a crisis. The guy who was helping them piped up that he agreed with Jess, that the one Malcolm picked was barely better than a camp generator. Malcolm wanted to ask the guy what business it was of his, but instead of engaging, instead of making his case, he heaved the thing up to the register without using the hand truck, and slapped their credit card down. Jess went silent, staring dead-eyed out the window the whole ride home. Now, two years later, looking at it as if for the first time, he knew Jess was right: the old 1980s space heater he'd inherited from Hugh's day would pull all of the power. He shook the canister of gasoline he'd grabbed from his shed and wondered how long the gas would last.

He found a bottle of engine oil that had never been opened, carried the oil and generator outside, and knelt down in the snow. The air was pale, cold-blasted, and hung more thinly than it did out front. "Come on," he said as he pulled the start cord once, twice, and then finally the engine kicked on, as loud as a small airplane.

Back inside, after setting up the heater, he found matches and lit the pilot on the gas stove. He turned on two burners and held his hands above them for a minute before setting a pot of water and a skillet on top. He opened the walk-in, assessed what would be easiest to cook, and emerged with a pack of burgers. He cracked two off the stack and placed them in the skillet. The buns were frozen, too, so he placed them alongside. He found a dozen votive candles on a shelf and lined them up on the counter to be ready when night fell.

Almost five o'clock. His phone's charge wouldn't last very long. He looked up the weather forecast and then the local patch to see if they'd estimated when power would return. Why hadn't he ever gotten that lever fixed on the water main? Because he was too ashamed to ask whether the guy would work on credit. The whole system was so old that the basement needed to be dug up, the entire line replaced. Insurance wouldn't cover it.

Could he forgive her? The question dropped into his mind as if whispered into the quiet. No, he thought immediately, the obvious answer, the answer that had been there on Patrick's face, on Siobhán's, when they told him on Friday night. Of course not. Not after being made a complete fool of. And yet there was something that trilled between the thoughts that rung out in his head in complete sentences and the shapeless feelings that bubbled underneath, not even close to coherent yet.

There was that one night, so many years ago.

Jess had switched to the firm, deciding several years later than her classmates that she wanted to be on a partner track. She loved working for the union—she *knew* those men, she understood better than anyone what protections they needed, and don't get her started on the few women who were in the Laborers' International, the work and politicking it must have taken to get accepted—they needed her even more. But that job didn't pay nearly enough for her to get ahead of her student loans. All of a sudden she made a switch in paths, and was working even longer hours, trying to make up for lost time. She was traveling, having dinner with colleagues in San Diego and Seattle. Every time he called her, he could hear voices in the background but couldn't match them with faces. At home she was always surrounded by files and folders. They wanted to buy a house but it felt out of reach, still. One of them was always at work.

While Jess tried to make herself essential to the firm, he was where he'd always been, at the Half Moon, trying to make sure everyone was having a good time, but also feeling a little stuck for the first time, like he'd eliminated options at some point without even realizing it. John was still there, but other bartenders had moved away, gone back to school, become electricians or stockbrokers or pharmaceutical sales reps. Were other careers better? No, but they had things that Malcolm never cared about before, things that used to make him want to fall asleep from boredom whenever they came up: health care FSAs, 401(k)s.

"If we have a baby," Jess said when she was making insurance selections from the packet HR had mailed, just before she started at the firm, "we want it entirely covered. Right? We don't want to deal with a deductible. It'll be more out of each paycheck but I think it's worth it. Right?"

"Right," Malcolm said, without really thinking.

That night. Not even a night. An hour. Jess was nearing the finish line on a case she'd been working on for years. She'd seen a doctor, had gotten a few tests. They had no idea what was ahead of them, but he already felt the weight of it rolling toward them. Work, all they did was work. They went days without seeing each other awake, and that morning he noticed she'd circled two upcoming days on the desk calendar, like he was a prize horse and those were the dates he had to perform. He cracked a joke when he saw it. What happened to spontaneity? Meanwhile, Erica Delfino had been after him for probably fifteen years and made no secret of it. At John's coaxing, he had a bunch of drinks behind the bar, something he very rarely did. Hugh had been in earlier in the evening, so they could be sure he wouldn't be back, and it had been so long since Malcolm had gotten truly drunk. That night, when he came out from behind the bar to clear the high-tops and Erica leaned into him, he placed his open hand on the small of her back like it was the most natural thing in the world.

"Kitchen," he said, and had not the first inkling he was about to make the suggestion until it was out of his mouth. She went in first, and a moment later, he followed. It was late, the bar was busy, but the kitchen was closed, the food wrapped tight and put away. Everyone on staff had left except for Malcolm and John and the bouncer, who would stay on the sidewalk by the front door. She hopped up on the counter, and he remembered driving his hand through her hair, which felt different than Jess's. Her face was a perfect heart. They weren't friends, her and Jess. He'd never seen them talk. He cupped her neck and felt her pulse fluttering under his thumb. Just as he was telling himself it was not a big deal, it had nothing to do with Jess or the life they were building together, just after he reminded himself that he was better behaved than most, look at John for example, my God, Jess walked in.

Erica was gone instantly.

"What's up, Mal?" Jess said, cool as could be, taking a slow look around the room. He knew that expression on her face. And surely, she knew his. He assumed she was at home by then, but it turned out she'd gone out with a few friends, ended up going dancing somewhere in New Jersey. When they got into taxis at the end of the night, Jess told her driver to bring her to the Half Moon, to surprise him. She must have stood there and told him that because he knew it afterwards, the next morning and every time the memory popped up unbidden, leaving him with a feeling in his belly like the floor had fallen out from under him. In the moment, inside his brain was nothing but static, white noise. She studied him with a calm so measured that he knew she already knew the answer.

If he responded in that moment he couldn't remember what he said. He remembered only pushing through the swinging door back to the bar, letting himself be absorbed by the noise, the heat, their demands.

How many years ago was that? He counted back.

For weeks after he could barely stand himself. It crossed his mind at odd times, and every time it did Erica's face became more common, her willingness more off-putting. He was dumbfounded at how stupid he'd been, how much he'd risked. And for what? To step outside of his life for an hour? To be shored up by someone who meant so little to him? How could he have imagined that would even work?

"What was all that last night?" Jess asked the next day as she spread peanut butter on a slice of apple and he tipped back two Advil. She'd hung out for an hour after finding him in the kitchen. She'd chatted with everyone and had a few laughs, and he made sure he was way in the weeds behind the bar, too busy to talk. Even as she was chatting, keeping everything light, he could see her mind working it over.

"All what?" he asked, the coffee percolating, their mail piled on the counter.

"You know," she said, looking at him steadily. "Just tell me. It's okay if you just tell me."

"I have no clue what you mean."

Why hadn't he just said he was sorry? That he was obviously out of his mind and it would never ever happen again? Why couldn't he say that he missed her and he was worried about some change he felt coming over them?

He checked what time sunset would be and figured it would take a while for the light to fade completely. The heater was doing its job, but his hands were still so cold. When it became too dark for him to read the credit card receipts, he found a flashlight. He knew he'd never fall asleep on the floor, not considering all the mouse traps he pulled from under the sink and behind the garbage, the squeals of the live ones giving him chills. So he pushed three chairs together so that he could sit up and have his legs supported when he stretched them across.

Up until Patrick and Siobhán's visit to the bar on Friday, up until the moment they told him what they knew, it felt to him that as long as no one addressed whatever was happening, as long as they didn't say the actual words, then it could go on the way it was forever, sort of stalled between spaces, like a hallway between rooms. Were they separated now? The word carried weight, had legal implications, so he'd never used it. But other people had. "You've been separated for months now," his mother said not long ago, and he got unreasonably mad at her, as if she were forcing whatever was happening between him and Jess into a category where they didn't fit.

He picked up his phone and searched the name Neil Bratton and got seven thousand results. The one that was relevant to him was at the bottom of the first page. There wasn't much. Two professional photos. Senior partner. The website said his practice focused on civil litigation, government investigations, employer responsibility, and white-collar criminal matters. Impressive, Malcolm thought, though the words sort of washed over him, and then he thought about how smart Neil must be. Jess probably talked with him about things she could never talk to Malcolm about, things he couldn't even guess because he didn't know about them. He didn't like the empty feeling that left him with. So he closed his eyes, pictured a rooftop full of customers, a three-piece band, a starry sky, people laughing, sitting close. He imagined himself at the center, surveying his small kingdom. How great it would be if he could make it happen, somehow.

He did quick calculations in his head, and when he didn't like the answers, he searched Peru. Temperature highs and lows. The government. The price of real estate. His phone was at five percent. Four percent. He searched for a place like he remembered Tripp talking about. He searched for places where the water running off the Andes was so cold it would numb a person's hand if he reached down to feel it flow.

seven

Azalea Estates, where Neil lived, was considered the posh section of Gillam, but to Jess it had no personality. The houses were different from one another but perfectly so, as if there'd been three models to choose from when the development was being planned and the builder made sure to never put two of the same next to each other. Stone, brick, shingle, repeat. Tan, gray, blue, repeat. Over in her neighborhood, the one she grew up in and the one where she and Malcolm bought a house and imagined they'd raise a family, every house was different because each generation that lived there tacked on an extension, or added a sunporch, or converted a garage to a bedroom. The Dunleavys recently painted their house a bold lilac color, the shutters eggplant, the front door and mailbox a pale pink. For weeks, cars slowed as they passed. Neighbors restrained dogs on leashes as they considered whether a purple house was cheerful or bizarre. Down the shore maybe, but here in Gillam? There was a broken-down RV in the Dunleavys' potholed driveway and two rusted quads sitting on the lawn for so many years that most of the neighbors had stopped seeing them, until against a different backdrop they were suddenly obvious again. "A train wreck," Malcolm called it when the paint job was complete. But Jess said at least the whole scene told you something about who they were.

There were no strip malls in Neil's neighborhood. There were no pizza places or ice cream shops kids could walk to unless they crossed the four-lane parkway that at one time marked the boundary of Gillam, and then walked another mile into Gillam proper. The town border moved when Jess was in law school, something to do with the local utility, so a corner of Riverside became Gillam overnight. "Technically, Gillam," people said. "But." Even in March, when the rest of town was scalded with salt and coated in grit, the spruce trees and boxwoods over in Azalea Estates looked as welcoming as a Christmas movie.

She hadn't set foot in Gillam in over four months on the day she left Cobie's to stay at Neil's for the first time. He drove his car to the city that morning instead of taking the train, just so he could pick her up after work. She brought her bag to the office, and all day she considered canceling. It was happening too fast, and she wasn't ready. She'd lost control of the situation and needed to get it back. She could say something came up. She could say that Cobie and Astrid needed her to babysit. They'd been tense lately—disagreeing on everything from how to break down a box for recycling to where they should go on vacation—and Jess felt sure her presence was causing the strain, though Cobie insisted having her there had made things better, gave her and Astrid something to focus on aside from their kids and each other. Jess had offered to watch the boys for a few days if they wanted to get away somewhere together. "Go for a week!" she said. "Why not take advantage of me being there?" Astrid had looked at Cobie like she wanted Cobie to say yes, and Jess's heart broke for her.

"It's a bad time at work," Cobie said, and all the hope on Astrid's face disappeared in one instant. She didn't say a word. She just loaded lunch boxes into backpacks and said she was taking the dog for a walk.

"You're not always that nice to her," Jess said one night when she and

Cobie were alone, sipping wine on the terrace. The boys were inside playing *Minecraft*.

"Oh!" Cobie laughed. "You're doling out relationship advice?"

"I'm just saying," Jess said. "She's a good one. Don't forget."

"Yours is a good one, too," Cobie said. "Malcolm I mean," she added, with a droll expression on her face.

"You've never said that before. Not once in all these years."

"I'm saying it now." Cobie shrugged. "I don't like this new guy."

"You've never even met Neil."

"I don't need to meet him to know. And another thing—"

"Oh boy."

"It's not one or the other. You know? There's a third choice. You can just be alone for a while."

She could say to Neil that she simply could not go to Gillam. That something in her had folded since he told Patrick what was going on. But he arrived at her building ten minutes earlier than planned and told her to hurry because he was in a bus lane. She jumped into his car so fast that she blinked and next thing they were ticking off miles along the West Side Highway. She thought of the mums she'd planted back in October. She wondered if Malcolm had gotten rid of them when they shriveled and went brown, or if they were still sitting on the front step, their pots full of damp leaves.

Once in Gillam, the lights of a car approaching from a side street lit up the interior of Neil's, and she dipped her head, hoped she hadn't been recognized. A moment later, they waited at the ludicrously long light on Dearborn while a car of the exact make and model as her mother's waited on the other side. She arranged her hair in front of her face and asked Neil to please tell her if the plate of that red Camry started with HGX. It did not.

"Jess," Neil said.

"I know," she said.

"What am I supposed to do? You've barely said a word since Manhattan."

"Honestly, maybe drop me at the train."

He went to pull over, not at the train but so he could look at her. The streetlamps grew brighter as dusk settled in. She might as well have been onstage. She slid down in her seat.

"This is so dumb."

"I know."

"I gave the kids a talk. Even Ethan." Ethan was only two. Jess was especially looking forward to spending time with him. Neil said Ethan seemed to miss his mother most at night, which was a little baffling. They'd split when he was an infant, and the kids were only with her two weekends a month.

"I'm sorry."

"Didn't we talk about making this really happen?"

Jess was silent. He had raised the idea of her moving in with them, but in the same conversation he'd also asked if she had a divorce lawyer in mind, because if she didn't he had a few names. They were standing in the vestibule of a crowded restaurant downtown the first time he said the word—"divorce"—so she turned away, pretended to read the menu, asked the host how long it would be until their table was ready. Later, after their meal, he called her on it, said she was avoiding the issue. But it was her issue to avoid.

"I said I'd stay for the weekend. I never said I'd stay longer than that. I have to go to my mom's. I have to figure it all out from there. I have to see Malcolm and face the music. It's different for you. I have to do this right."

"*Now* you have to do this right?" he said.

She was tempted to get out of the car right then.

"Sorry," he said, reaching for her. "Sorry. I'm just tired. And impatient, I guess. The minute you make this decision, our lives will be better. We can stop hiding. My girls have questions, I know they do. I'd love for you to meet my parents. But I can't introduce you if you're still married. Once you have everything squared away, we can make this really happen. We can be a family."

A messy family, not exactly the one she always wanted but pretty close. She thought of Malcolm, his leisurely Sunday mornings, how they used to pack sandwiches and go on long hikes together before he headed over to check on the bar.

Not for the first time, Jess wondered why Neil and his wife had really broken up. It was as he described, no doubt, but his side of the story was surely just one layer in a multilayered plot. Once in a while, when she was sprawled out on Cobie's enormous beanbag chair with her boys, watching the baking show they loved, she forgot her resolution to only take life day by day and accidentally thought about waking up next to Neil in the middle of the night, his bedside water bottle, his contact lens solution on the bathroom vanity, his reading glasses folded on the table when she went downstairs in the morning. How long until the little items that made up his life seemed familiar to her, part of the backdrop of her day? Where do you put your recycling? she'd ask upon moving in, and then, after being told just once, that's where she'd put her recycling for the rest of her days.

"It's being here," she said. "You know that. If you lived anywhere else, it would be different. You have to understand the position I'm in. I'm *from* here. Even if we face this, it's not as if we'll be going out to dinner in Gillam. It's not as if we'll do our grocery shopping at Food King. I can't stand the idea of people talking about us."

"Well," he said, and she decided if he said she should have thought of that sooner, she'd open the door and walk away from him forever.

"If I lived anywhere else, we never would have met."

He looked at her, and whatever she was about to say next fell away. The road ahead of them curved gently to the left, and after that, she knew, a stop sign would appear. After the stop sign would come a bump that made her stomach drop when the car rose and fell. She knew every inch of the town, knew it in her blood and her bones. She wondered for the hundredth time what she was doing.

Her mother had made a little comment last time they spoke, that Gail Gephardt seemed confused lately. Gail had called Maureen Ryan when she couldn't get hold of anyone else because she kept hearing a sound in her basement and was convinced it was a raccoon. "What a panic," Jess's mother reported. "What about her friend Artie Sheridan? What about one of Malcolm's buddies if she couldn't get hold of her boy? What about *animal control*? But no, she called me and expected me to hop to it. What am I going to do if I come face-to-face with a raccoon? Anyway. When I went down there I didn't see anything."

"Does Malcolm know that?" Jess asked.

"And there she is at the top of the stairs waiting for me to report back."

"Mom."

"Did she even go down there herself? No clue. But she sure thought I should go down there. Like I don't have my own problems."

"Mom. Hello?"

"Does Malcolm know?" her mother echoed. "I'm not Malcolm's wife. You are. You'd better call him and tell him his mother needs him."

Shortly before Jess left, Gail Gephardt had been on her way to the same hairdresser she'd been seeing for twenty years when she got confused by a detour and called Malcolm from the side of the road. Nothing looked familiar, she insisted. She kept turning like the signs said but then there were no more signs and she didn't know where she was. Malcolm tried to talk her through how to drop a pin on her phone's map but she just shouted, "Malcolm!" So he told her to drive until she found a place to buy a cup of coffee, ask the exact address, and then call him back. He told her to sit in her car and enjoy her coffee while she waited, he'd be there before she knew it. It turned out she was less than a mile from her hairdresser, so he led her there at twenty-five miles an hour. When she got out of her car, he could see the fear was gone. She said now that she knew where she was she'd be fine, but he knew she'd encounter the same closed road on her way home, so he bought a paper and waited.

"Look at you," the stylist said when he came in to check how much longer she'd be. "Haven't seen you since you were in college."

And from under her crown of foils Gail said, "That didn't last long."

"I'm sorry, too," she said to Neil as the memory faded. "I'm just nervous."

"It's going to get better."

I doubt it, she wanted to say, but instead she said, "I hope so."

She was still living with Malcolm the first time she saw Neil's house. His kids were at their grandparents' for the night, and Jess felt like she was back in high school, sneaking into a place she shouldn't be. She couldn't stay there, no way. She imagined people looking in the windows. She imagined a parent he might know through his girls dropping something off unannounced and spotting her there. It was insane that she had even come as far as his driveway. She ducked down in the passenger seat like a criminal. Jess planned on telling Malcolm that she was going to dinner in White Plains with a college friend and didn't want to drive home late so she'd crash on her friend's couch, but he never asked. He had live music at the bar all weekend, was hoping for a solid crowd. She and Neil were headed to dinner an hour north, near Cold Spring. She only agreed to come inside his house because it was dark out, and being inside seemed less risky than waiting in his car. As she waited for him to get whatever he'd forgotten—his wallet or his phone or what?—she took in the tray ceilings, the large, curtainless windows. She'd imagined a masculine space, something modern and sophisticated, something that looked like an extension of the way he dressed, but instead the house seemed like the waiting room of a dentist's office. In the front room were two ugly, overstuffed couches in mismatched florals pushed up against the walls. A few dark wood tables placed here and there.

"Walk me through your thinking here."

"My mother's," Neil said. "Stop making that face. I wasn't going to fight with Christine over couches."

"I wasn't making a face."

"The funny thing is I only noticed how bad it was once I started picturing you here, making that face."

"I'm not," she said.

"You are."

Now, only her second time inside his house, his kids chattering in a nearby room, she felt butterflies. They were standing close together in the doorway that led from the mudroom, and Jess knew that he would never take one more step without removing his shoes, not even by accident. How appalled he'd probably be if he could peek inside her memories and see her house in high school, her brother's cleats leaving little perforated chunks of grass and dried mud all over the house, the sink always full of food scraps that her mother cleared out with her fingers bent like a claw.

Meeting out as they'd been doing, hours stolen here and there, meant they always arrived at each other already armored. Neil clean-shaven and impeccable in a white dress shirt, his watch peeking out from beneath his cuff whenever he reached for anything. Jess in mascara, a pencil skirt, a swipe of lip gloss, three dots of concealer under each eye, expertly blended so that there was never any line. But at home, the gold seams of his dress socks against ceramic tile, the vulnerable looseness of his neck that she never noticed before that moment, she wasn't so sure she wanted that layer exposed. As she got to know him better, she got a strong impression of habits that would reveal themselves more fully with time. "His ways," her mother would say. Neil's ways were to press the door closed behind him until it clicked and then press a moment longer to be sure; to immediately look around with an eye out for what needed to be tidied; to lick his thumb and rub a spot on the mudroom wainscoting that only he could see; to carefully place his briefcase on the end of the bench and then look to see where Jess placed hers.

These small things, she knew, were the end of a vein that ran strong and deep through the bedrock of his personality. She brought a cup of coffee into his car once, when he was a few minutes early picking her up, and after looking at it he said, "Yeah, that's fine," as if Jess had asked. I don't know him, she reminded herself then and now. Not really.

Since stepping inside his home, all she could think about was Malcolm, whether he'd heard yet, if it were still possible that he had not, how she would tell him. Now that she was back in Gillam, Malcolm close by somewhere, she felt all the guilt she'd been holding at bay come sweeping over her. That the bar was struggling, that he'd gotten them into something she hadn't agreed to—that was old information. There was no need to get mad all over again. She pictured him taking the news of her and Neil by crossing his arms and refusing to look at her. Every other man in the world would have guessed, but Malcolm? It probably hadn't entered his mind.

"Come on," Neil said, when she said that to him. But it was true. Malcolm never imagined people doing things to him that he wouldn't do to them. Look at Hugh.

"You've said he's cocky. There you go, I guess," Neil said. And it was the strangest thing, every time Neil even hinted that he agreed with her assessment of Malcolm, she wanted to shift it so he'd understand that he'd never have it exactly right. Malcolm had good reason to be cocky. He was handsome and charming, and when he loved a person he loved that person with his whole heart. He wasn't demonstrative, but he never complained about anything, ever, and he was always there where you expected him to be. It was why his friends loved him, it was why they'd stuck by him for forty years. In this dramatic divorce, where Neil's ex was in the complete wrong according to him, who'd gotten all the mutual friends? It was a detail that only occurred to Jess recently.

It was weird to think that their friends and neighbors still saw Malcolm all the time, that in the last four months he must have brought in the mail and put gas in his car and bought his usual weekly roundup of scratch-offs. He must have put up Christmas lights and taken them down and carried the ladder on his shoulder. She hadn't seen any of it, but other people had. Thinking about it gave her the same feeling she got when she jolted awake at night to save herself from falling.

She followed Neil down the hall to the kitchen, where the babysitter was lining dirty dishes in the dishwasher. When Neil referenced the sitter, Jess had pictured a teenager. But of course a teenager had to be in school, couldn't mind children all day. This was a grown woman. Her face rang a bell; Jess either had overlapped with her in high school or had seen her at the Half Moon. Jess hung back, inspected the recessed lighting as if she were there to redecorate the place, to take a few measurements and head out. Neil told the sitter not to worry about the dishes, that she could go, but right in front of her he quickly turned the plates to face the direction opposite to the way she'd loaded them.

Maybe he was fastidious to a fault and he'd get that way with her, too—her body and her habits. By the time she stepped inside Neil's house, they'd been together in hotel rooms, in his office after hours, in his friend's empty beach house. Almost but not quite in a loaner Jeep when they drove upstate, his car at the dealer for new brakes. Twice at Cobie's when Jess had the place to herself for a weekend, Cobie and family in Texas for a wedding. He hadn't liked that, being in someone else's home, said it made him feel jumpy. But five minutes inside his home, the place where he clipped his nails and nodded off in front of the television, already felt far more private than any of those encounters. She looked away from the kitchen cabinets, where he kept his alternate flours and his vitamins. She looked away from the books piled on the fireplace mantel in case she caught a glimpse of Ayn Rand or Milton Friedman.

"I got snipped," he said at one point, fairly early on. "You haven't asked but you should know. In case you were worried. Or in case you were hoping—"

It was right around the time they began discussing the idea that whatever was between them wasn't just a passing thing, that they should probably own it, give it a chance to live. "You should know I'm not up for that."

"No, of course not," she said, but saying it aloud left her with that same bereft feeling she thought she'd left behind, like wandering into a pocket of cold air.

"Anyway the problem was me. With all that. Not—"

But she didn't want to say Malcolm's name. Didn't want to bring a thought of him into the room, not in this context, not with this person who'd given himself the freedom to have a few thoughts about what had happened between her and Malcolm, what had gone wrong.

"I have no hope of getting pregnant. Don't worry."

But she did have hope—vague, unreasonable. It wasn't the main draw, but it was there for sure. Nothing concrete, just a passing thought: maybe. A new person, a new combination. What did the private discussion rooms agree on if not this: conception was a mysterious process. She only called herself on it when he told her about the vasectomy and she examined her disappointment. Still, there were the kids already born. The kids who needed a mother more than two weekends a month.

When they walked into the family room, the kids didn't move. The TV was tuned to a woman dressed like a child, dancing.

"You guys," Neil said. "This is Jess."

"We've met Jess," said the older one.

"At Cara's house, right?" Jess said. Cara was Patrick and Siobhán's youngest child, the one who lined up with this girl. Suddenly, Jess saw the other way the whole town would find out. This girl would tell everyone in school, and the teachers would hear, most of whom had grown up in Gillam.

"Yup," the girl said. "I remember you from there."

"But you haven't formally met," Neil said.

"We have, actually," the girl said.

Well, well, Jess thought.

"Hi!" the younger girl said. Ethan raised his arms for his daddy.

The babysitter, Jess noticed, did not meet her eyes when she passed by on her way out, and Jess saw the first five minutes of the woman's drive home unfold in her imagination like a scene in a movie. By the time she got to the red light on Main, she'd have texted her eight best friends to let them know that Malcolm Gephardt's wife just walked into Neil Bratton's house with the obvious intention of staying. Five of them would text back to say they'd heard something about that, hadn't Malcolm and his wife broken up back in the fall? One would ask whether Malcolm was the hot bartender at the Half Moon, or was she thinking of someone else? That's him, six out of eight would reply, and then each would follow up with a flames emoji. One would say that he and his wife always seemed like a mismatch, hotness-wise. One would ask the babysitter-friend to please snap a good pic of Neil next time she was there. He didn't have much of a social media presence, and they'd like to discuss how he stacked up against Malcolm.

"From there the whole town will know," Jess said, once the sitter was gone and she shared her worry.

"And?" Neil had asked. "Who cares?"

Jess tried it on for size. Who cared?

Well, she did.

For four months she'd been trying to make herself scarce in Cobie's guest bedroom, hovering like a satellite at the edge of their endless family discussions of who'd take whom to soccer, who'd take whom to chorus, believing when the time came to make a decision it would be obvious what she should do. And then, out of nowhere, Neil spilled everything to Patrick. He and Patrick went to some ski shop up in Warwick that was liquidating. Patrick was the one who heard about it—crazy deals—and roped Neil into going along. They each bought new skis, boots, bags, and then they went out all afternoon. After Neil confessed, his misgivings were enough to sober him up, to prompt him to call Jess from outside the bar. For some reason she pictured him wearing ski boots. "Three Manhattans and it just came out" was how he put it, and didn't seem all that remorseful.

Malcolm could drink twenty Manhattans and still remain a vault. That's why people told him things.

"Wait, what?" Jess asked, pressing the phone to her ear, as if that would help. It was windy wherever he was standing. It sounded as if he were yelling at her from across a field.

"Patrick was pretty shocked," Neil said, shouting over the wind.

"What did he say?"

"He said you guys have had a really tough few years. He said maybe he should have seen it coming."

"He did?" Jess said, and felt defensive, wondered what Patrick would have seen if he'd looked.

"Where's he right now? Can he hear you?"

"No he's inside. He's hitting the head and then getting us another round."

"Another round? He's not mad at you?"

"Mad at me?"

"Well. Yes."

"He's surprised. He doesn't approve, obviously. But no, he didn't storm out or anything."

Jess felt a dull ache spread from her center. She felt like she might get sick.

"I told him that I know he's a good friend of Malcolm's. I told him I knew it put him in a bad spot."

Good friends? They'd been best friends since they were six years old. Patrick used to be afraid of the wind, and Malcolm would hold his hand as they ran across the school parking lot to their bus. When Malcolm's father died out of the clear blue, Patrick slept on Malcolm's bedroom floor for a week. But Neil didn't know any of that. As Neil was talking, Jess's phone started lighting up. A text from Patrick, asking her to call him, followed by a call, which she declined. Then a call from Siobhán. Then twenty texts in approximately fifteen seconds, all from Siobhán.

Holy shit

Jess what's going on

Call me

Or Call P

Are you okay?

What's going on w you Jessie?

You said you needed space

That's what you said so I figured everything you've been thru

Here's me and P feeling so bad for you!

And thinking M might be to blame

With everything, you know

He can be so M and not exactly a talker etc

Neil told P

What in the world?

now I hear it's been going on for ages? W the actual F

Jess!

I'm not judging would just love to talk

Could be a little thing that got carried away, right?

Considering everything

Just call me asap

Neil called again from the Uber he and Patrick shared to get back to Gillam, once Patrick got dropped off. Patrick left his car and their skis behind for pickup the next day.

"I think we'll both feel better when everyone knows, don't you?"

"No," Jess said. "I don't feel that way at all."

"Jess," he said simply. "You were going to tell Malcolm soon, right? I mean, it's long past time."

He repeated the thought the next day, when he surprised her at her office and asked her to lunch. He apologized, said if it made her feel any better, he had the most ferocious hangover of his life. He seemed less put together than usual, and halfway down Fifty-Ninth Street he stopped walking, said he actually wasn't sorry. That she was stalling was something they were both smart enough to understand, and it was time to acknowledge it because otherwise it would just go on and on and on. Did she want to make a go of it or not? Because he did. He wanted a family. A complete family. Not the lopsided thing he'd been living inside since his divorce. And he wanted her, specifically. How many people did he meet that day at Patrick's Memorial Day barbeque? How many women crossed his path every single day? But it was Jess his mind snagged on. Jess that he couldn't stop thinking about in the days after.

"So you took matters into your own hands," Jess said.

"Yes," Neil said, and shrugged. "It's my life, too."

That Patrick hadn't seemed angry with Neil kept Jess up all night. She didn't want anyone to be angry at anyone. She wanted everyone to take it in and try to understand. And yet. She had two missed calls from Patrick before eight o'clock that morning. Plus Toby, who was not a texter, wrote to say he thought she was disgusting and to never show her face in his house again. Who told him? Jess wondered. Patrick or Siobhán? Had they called him late the night before or first thing in the morning and either way: Why? Had they called Malcolm, too? It wasn't Toby's business. *Disgusting.* She never even liked Toby and long wondered why in the world Malcolm and Patrick let him tag along with them their entire lives. All he did was steal their jokes and brag about his job, as far as she could tell. She kept looking at his text to confirm that's what he'd written. She'd been heading into a meeting when it popped up. Working to keep her face a blank, she left her files on the conference room table, closed her laptop, silenced her phone, and went into the ladies' room to stand in a stall for two minutes with her forehead pressed against the faux wood wall.

"I don't know what I'm doing," she said on the day she left, as she began transferring the piles of clothes to her suitcase. She had an ache at the back of her neck, and her head was splitting.

"You're leaving," Malcolm said, and just stood there, watching, his thick shoulders hunched, and for one split second it crossed her mind that he might punch a wall or something. It was in there somewhere, that possibility, but he kept all extreme emotions neatly in line, and he'd sooner pretend it didn't matter to him at all than to make a scene, even when there was no one around to see it but her. She thought about pointing out that it was the first time in a long time that he'd paid attention to a single thing she did, but she knew she'd sound like a petulant, attention-seeking child, so she swallowed it back. She wasn't looking for a fight.

"I'm not *leaving* leaving." She paused what she was doing but didn't look at him. "We just need a break."

Why had she said that? That she wasn't *leaving* leaving. She didn't know that. She didn't know anything.

She kept having the same memory of the day she and Malcolm bought the house, how desperate they were to get a down payment together. And then they had it and they felt invincible, twenty-eight and thirty-two, writing a check bigger than either of them ever thought they would be able to. With the deed and keys in hand, they drove to the house immediately after signing, let themselves in, made their way to the living room before Malcolm remembered what he meant to do. He marched Jess back outside so that he could carry her over the threshold. She said she was pretty sure that was a wedding night thing and they'd been married for three years already, but then she was off her feet, laughing, and he was trying not to knock her head against the doorjamb.

Inside the empty house, they opened cabinets and turned on faucets. They went down to the basement and scrutinized the furnace. They walked upstairs and listened to the floorboards creak. They climbed into the attic, where Malcolm poked at the insulation. The inspector had said the house would need a new roof soon, but not yet, it would hold out for a little while.

"What now?" Malcolm asked when they were done with the tour, and were standing in the bare upstairs hallway, smiling at each other.

"We have so much to do," she said, but half-heartedly.

He smelled like shaving cream. Everything about him—from his brow line, to his hands, to the way his pants rested on his hips, was completely masculine.

"Here?" she said as he took hold of her hip. "The floor is too hard."

"You can be on top."

"My knees!"

"We can stand," he said.

"I need something to hold on to," she protested, but she was laughing, had given in. "Besides you."

"Jesus Christ," he said, pulling her into the bathroom, where there was a long counter for her to grip if she needed something, mirrors on every wall.

When she thought of her child, the child that would have been born, absolutely, had she lived her life differently, that child was all ages at once. He was four, running to keep up with the other trick-or-treaters, his plastic pumpkin bucket knocking against his knees. She was a ten-month-old, the surprising weight of her sitting on Jess's arm. He was an adolescent and Jess was the age she was now, walking into his bedroom and telling him to crack a window, my God.

She dreaded telling her mother she was leaving, the questions that would come, and even in her mind, explaining it was like pinning down a cloud. Car packed, she drove away from her house without looking back at Malcolm, at the bewildered expression on his handsome face. She drove straight to her mother's, said she couldn't stay, said she had something to tell her that she didn't want her to hear around town or from Malcolm if she happened to go by the house, but then her mother clapped her hand over her mouth and Jess saw that she thought the news had to do with a baby. So she had to let her bring out the Vienna Fingers, make a pot of tea.

She heard herself say it again, that she wasn't *leaving* leaving, they just needed a little time apart, and her mother pointed out that Jess had probably never expected Malcolm to stay a bartender, not deep down anyway, no matter what she might have told herself. Jess could see by the way she sat, the way she raised her eyebrows and fixed her mouth, that she'd been wanting to say that for a long time. Maureen claimed that she saw it all coming ages ago, the very first time Malcolm strolled into their kitchen at eight thirty in the morning, not one shred of shame on his face. "You'd stand up to look at him, my goodness, it was like he filled a room just by walking into it, but—" she said. "Anyway, I tried to tell you."

All those bright men Jess had been in school with! From all over! What was the point of that student loan debt if not to tie her life to one of them? They were from states you never even hear about! That redheaded guy—what was his name?—smart as a whip, who knew what he was even talking about half the time, and didn't his mother's side of the family have a vineyard in Washington State or someplace? Oregon?

"He loved you," her mother said. "I saw the way he looked at you." But what did Jess do? Maureen Ryan mused. She dumped him and fell for the local bartender.

"Cobie," her mother said, when Jess told her where she'd be staying while she thought things out. "She's still with that woman? She's still—"

"'That woman'? You mean her wife? Are you asking if she's still gay?"

"Don't go getting mad at me, but maybe you should have hung around with girls more like you. Maybe that was your mistake. You could have been on the lookout together."

"Oh my God," Jess said, looking out the kitchen window. She could see streaks where the sun hit. She had no energy left to argue.

"Anyway," her mother went on. Wasn't it at least possible that women shouldn't be working like men? It was wonderful to earn a living, sure, she guessed so, Maureen had worked her whole life, too, but was it right? Did it not, in fact, do something *maybe* to a woman's body? All those hours and that stress? Running for trains? Have women possibly ruined things for themselves?

Jess went to the cabinet where her mother kept her vitamins and prescriptions. She reached past four bottles of super omega-3 capsules, cod-liver oil, women's dailies, the various antibiotics Maureen never finished because why ever listen to the doctors she demanded to see. She plucked out a bottle of ibuprofen, fished out two, swallowed them dry. She glanced at the expiration date—four years earlier—and took one more.

"You know more than a fleet of medical experts, I guess."

"Well, tell me what doesn't add up," Maureen said. "Two young, healthy people."

Jess sighed. "It's more than that. There's more than that now."

"Oh," Maureen said, and for the first time since Jess came in, there was silence. Jess counted the ticks of the old clock. "I don't know, Jessie. But look. At least there aren't any kids."

Jess was angry driving away from Gillam, like she could toss a match behind her and watch the whole place go up and not feel one bit bad about it, but once she got on the Palisades, got as far as the gas station right before the bridge, and then the toll plaza, she could feel something else move in, like weather she was helpless to watch come and go. Malcolm had the Halloween party at the bar that night, and he'd been so worried it would be a flop. He'd put out money for decorations, for prizes. He had a cover band going on at 9:00 p.m. He'd had Roddy put it on Facebook and then take it down because everyone said Facebook was lame, and then put it back up again because someone else said it was still good for community news. Roddy told him the bar should have its own account, but maybe not Facebook, which was for old people, and Malcolm had said he didn't know places had accounts, he thought it was just people, and Roddy had said, "Oh yeah, brands, buildings, pets, anything." Roddy was good at the internet, getting info on his phone. Malcolm hoped the kid eventually went back to college.

Malcolm had Roddy post on social media, but he still went over to the office supply store and printed a hundred flyers like it was 1998. He divided the pile among everyone on staff and told them to post them at bagel shops, Laundromats, Dunkin', bus stops, everywhere they went. Roddy said there'd be a good crowd. He could tell by the metrics. And he turned out to be right.

Malcolm never knew what to do with himself when he was alone in the house. And Jess was pretty sure she'd used the last of the half-and-half. He probably wouldn't notice until he made his next pot of coffee, and then what?

Jess pulled over to the shoulder just after the toll plaza and rolled down all the windows of her car. Just ahead was the helix that would carry her to the bridge, and then to Manhattan, then down the West Side to Cobie's. He'd feel less nervous about the Halloween party if she went. He'd feel even less nervous about it if she put on her old Mia Wallace costume—her bangs at that moment were the exact right length, she

176

might not even need the wig—and made it her mission to have a great time. She could always leave him again tomorrow.

A Port Authority Police cruiser pulled up to her bumper, blipped the siren, and flashed the lights.

"Okay, okay," Jess whispered to her empty car and then drove on.

She spent seventeen weeks in Cobie's guest bedroom and tried to think of it as time outside of time, like a burl on a tree is part of the trunk but also its own thing, complex and apart, created in response to injury or illness, the tree's way of healing itself. She didn't answer any calls, except from Neil and sometimes not even his. She almost never responded to texts. She took long walks after work to give Cobie privacy with her family. Sometimes she took the twins to the movies and for milkshakes, watched them flip their skateboards, listened to them play their instruments. When Cobie and Astrid argued, they usually did so via text, often while sitting in the same room. Cobie said it was so the kids wouldn't hear them, but once, when both Cobie and Astrid were hunched over their phones with miserable expressions on their faces, furiously pecking away, the boys looked over at Jess as if to ask whether she understood what was happening. They rolled their eyes. But then, almost as often, she caught either Cobie or Astrid looking down at her phone and then looking across the room at the other with a grin.

And then Neil had gotten hammered with Patrick, spilled everything, and the burl was cut away, leaving only the damaged trunk.

The first night she spent at Neil's, the Thursday before the storm, she stayed downstairs when he went up to manage baths, toothbrushing, pajamas, books. The kids were off from school the following day—a conference for the teachers—so Jess and Neil took off, too. The plan was to play games with the kids all day, bake, watch movies, let them get to know Jess better ahead of the snowstorm that was due to arrive on Friday evening. The latest forecasts showed the storm would be bigger than the news had first estimated, but there was time still, projections changed, it wouldn't be the first storm the weather people made a big drama about that didn't end up materializing.

Listening to the bedtime routine, she had the same thought she'd had her first night at Cobie's, that a house where kids lived felt full even when the kids were out of sight, even when their toys were tidied away for the night. There were always whispered footsteps, bedsprings squeaking, doors opening and closing, faucets turned on and off. When these kids got older and had more freedom, they'd show up from school with their friends in tow, their bodies suddenly too big, their bikes abandoned to the front lawn, and like a descending army they'd look through the cabinets, clear out the snacks. Then they'd sit around saying all the obnoxious, self-important things teenagers have been saying since the beginning of time. Later still, they'd pull up in cars, run inside with breezy shouts of where they were going, where they'd been. How lucky for the person listening, to have that energy sweep through. What company to walk in to find all those scuffed bags and worn-out sneakers piled up in the front hall. Even the performance of being annoyed—"Clean up your shit!" Siobhán often yelled at her kids—had joy at the heart of it, exhausted and fed-up though that joy may be.

"Mom, you said 'shit,'" one always replied, and Siobhán would pull that one to her thickening midsection and hold him tight. On college breaks, all these kids would bring friends home. Someday they'd bring their husbands or wives. Their children. Neil, Siobhán, Cobie—they'd have full tables at Thanksgiving for the rest of their lives. Jess could see it, see all of it, including herself, in sort of a split screen, living in an ordered quiet, always turning on the radio for company.

I shouldn't be here, she thought. These people were blanks to her. They moved to different music, were formed by different clay. They were appealing for those differences, she reminded herself—but now that it was time to color them in, color herself in beside them, she couldn't see how the picture would ever look right. And she wouldn't be able to do this again. It's a thought that hit her at some point while she was staying with Cobie, and which she immediately tried to silence. Because if this was real between her and Neil, why would she care about that? Most people got one chance in life, and she was stealing a second. But to use that second chance and end up in a house only three miles from where she started? Why hadn't she thought bigger, gotten farther? She didn't have the excuse of being young anymore.

Because it was him I met, she remembered. Him I liked. She recalled the strange feeling she got, locking eyes with him from across a room when they barely knew each other's names, recognizing him, feeling recognized, long before anything happened. A line pulled taut. A tug. A whole life that was hers to step into, if she wanted to.

She could hear Neil's low murmur coming from upstairs, though not what he was saying. She could sneak out now, head back home, beg Malcolm for forgiveness. But whether that made her brave or cowardly depended on what was actually the right thing to do, and that's the part she couldn't decide. She could take the flashlight she'd spotted in Neil's mudroom and make her way back along the ruts and inclines of the roads she knew so well until she arrived at her own door and apologized for trying something new. A new backdrop, new rooms to move through. A new way of being touched, looked at—that was part of it, too.

As she listened to him soothing one of the kids, she pictured the long walk home, how she'd rehearse her apology. But then even in her mind she stopped walking. The bouncing light stilled. She was at the exact point in the road where kids used to crawl through a broken section of the chain-link fence to find a sheltered spot to drink beers, to make out in the mossy patches between the trees. She was also not sorry for trying. For feeling a way and doing something about it. She had a problem and she was trying to solve it.

And anyway, she couldn't leave. Neil had already carried her bag upstairs, and she'd already taken out her hairbrush, left her toiletries case on the sink. She'd already emptied her pockets of change, put it in the kids' change jar. Next thing Neil was back downstairs, searching a drawer for menus, and from across the room he looked like a stranger to her, as if she'd met him not ten minutes before. "Let's order dinner," he was saying. "Your first night. Let's open a bottle of wine. Hey," he said, coming over to her. "I'm really happy you're here."

But she couldn't keep her thoughts on track.

"Hey," he repeated, so that she'd look at him. "Everything is going to be okay."

"They say once a cheater always a cheater," she said. "Did you know that?"

"Do you count this as cheating?" he asked. "Jess, this is not wrong, and I'll never be convinced otherwise."

She liked him best when he said things like that, when he was insistent about it and seemed absolutely sure.

The next morning the kids said hello when they padded into the kitchen, but wore puzzled expressions, like they were just remembering, Oh yes, that's the stranger who arrived yesterday and is still here, pouring our milk into her coffee.

eight

His whole life, he'd had good luck. Hadn't he?

"Well aren't you the luckiest boy!" his mother said to him in August 1987, shaking him for joy when he found a twenty-dollar bill not once but twice in a single month. He remembered the moment because what she said felt so true. Of all boys, he'd been chosen. Ordained. Picked by fortune. Two twenties, just three weeks apart. What were the chances? There were dozens of kids his age who biked around town all day, but he was the only one who'd spotted that folded bill on the grass beside the bandstand, and then, on a different Friday, another, folded almost exactly the same way, on the sidewalk outside Buster Brown. His father asked him if he mugged two different people or the same guy twice.

His mother told him to put the money in his sock drawer for a rainy day, but he was afraid if he kept it she'd get ideas about spending it on something practical. So instead of waiting around for her to tell him he was in charge of buying his own notebooks and pencils that school year, he marched every kid in the neighborhood up to Two Scoops and bought a round of ice creams. Siblings tagged along, which he hadn't expected or calculated. He didn't want to leave anyone out, so he ended up pedaling full speed back to his house to beg his mother for $1.75 or else he didn't know what would happen. She said no at first, let it be a lesson to him, what a fool, treating the entire neighborhood when his father was busting his hump and the propane tank needed filling. But the kids had already started licking their cones! He couldn't exactly return them! "You're joking," his mother said, furious, peeling two dollars from the fold that lived in the blue cookie tin over the fridge.

"You mean to tell me you got one, too?" she said to him not fifteen minutes later, when he came cruising down the dead center of the block on his BMX, the soggy end of a cone in his hand.

"Well, I wasn't going to leave myself out!" he said. "It was my money."

"And sprinkles?" she said, eyeing his T-shirt.

He shrugged.

Another time, when he was even younger, the Gephardts went to the Jersey Shore for a few days. They usually rented a house in the Catskills for a long weekend every summer—Malcolm and Mary played with the kids of their parents' friends from the Bronx, while the adults played cards and told loud stories that ended up with drinks rocking off tables and glasses shattering on the floor. But his dad had struck up a friendship with a guy who owned a motel in Margate, on the Jersey Shore, and Malcolm overheard him tell his mother that he liked that it was close to Atlantic City in case he got bored sitting on the beach. On their third day there, Malcolm woke up very early, odd to have his entire family sleeping in the same room, so he decided to go for a swim despite the warning sign outside the manager's office, despite his mother's cautioning that the ocean was not the town pool. The motel's floating dock looked so close, hardly a risk, and he'd watched people swim back and forth the previous afternoon. If it really was rough he could always turn around. He wasn't scared at the time, but since then the feeling he had that day sometimes returned to him without warning: having to fight for a full breath, feeling his body pulled by some mysterious force, glancing at where he'd come from and then ahead at where he was going, unable to decide whether to push forward or go back, and all the while knowing that the longer he took to choose the more precious energy he wasted.

The landline in the bar rang, cutting through the silence and jolting him back to the present. Malcolm staggered up from his arrangement of chairs and pressed his palm to his chest to stop his heart from pounding.

"And what did you decide?" Jess asked, when he first told her the ocean story. That vacation was the only time he could remember his father wearing a bathing suit. His sister was embarrassed because the bathing suit was almost the exact same color as their father's skin, and from far away he looked naked. Jess laughed, said her father must have had the same one, said she remembered wanting to die the one and only time he came to the town pool. They were in bed, somewhat new to each other still, the windows wide open, a humid summer afternoon. They'd been lying there for hours, telling stories about growing up. Jess's family had had less than the Gephardts. There were ways to tell. Which sports a kid played. Whether a kid had birthday parties at McDonald's or whether all the photos were of their siblings crammed around their own kitchen table, a defrosted Sara Lee in the tinfoil pan. Her family wasn't poor, Jess was always quick to say. There were a lot of kids who had less.

Something about the smell of a storm in the air made him remember that swim he took at ten or eleven years old.

"What happened? Did you end up swimming to the dock or did you turn back?"

"Neither," Malcolm said. An old man zoomed up to him in a motorboat, reached out a hand, and heaved Malcolm on board. He scolded him over the buzz of the motor until they reached shore.

Back at the beach, the man bought him a fountain soda from the crab shack, told him to use his head.

"So I lived, plus I got a soda," he bragged to Jess.

"But you didn't have to make a choice," Jess said, and seemed troubled.

He never understood why that was such a thing for her. He was rescued because he was always going to be rescued, was his point, and by that logic had never really been in danger. She seemed to consider it a sign of something else, and only now, in the silence of the bar, the ringing phone calling attention to the silence, did her point move into slightly clearer focus. He was surprised he slept that deeply. He was surprised he slept at all.

The sound of the boat was almost identical to the noise of the generator running in the alley beside the bar all night, and Malcolm's brain made the link out of the most delicate filament, where it became briefly incandescent and then broke. It must have run out of gas at some point just before dawn. The heater was cold to the touch.

By the phone's third ring he'd shaken off every dark thought and was in work mode, all business. He slipped through the swinging door quickly, to keep the warm air trapped in the kitchen, and the cold of the main room felt like stepping outside. He'd taken off his boots to sleep, and the feel of the hex mat under his socks was like a massage. Who could be calling the landline? Jess. Patrick. His mother. He should have checked on his mother on Saturday. Now it was Monday. He hoped she had enough wood stacked beside the slider on her deck. He hoped she hadn't had to wade through the snow to the pile in the backyard. What if she slipped and fell out there? He had to get over there as soon as he could.

"Half Moon," he said when he picked up, in the same harried tone as always, as if there were a dozen hands reaching for him.

"Malcolm Gephardt?" a woman's voice asked.

"Yeah?"

It was an officer from the local police department, but he didn't catch her name. She and her partner had been by his house already, trying to track him down. They wanted to ask him a few questions about a patron. Would he still be there in ten minutes if they came by?

When the police cruiser pulled up, he expected Rob Waggoner to be one of the two officers, but instead it was Jackie Becker with an officer he didn't recognize. Jackie was the youngest sister of a friend of his from high school. She used to come to their baseball games and run after the foul balls. Whenever he spoke to her back then, she would blush a deep violet. He hadn't seen her in years. She and her partner were both in uniform and both looked exhausted.

"Hey, Jackie," Malcolm said. "Was that you on the phone? You should have said."

"Hi, Malcolm." She smiled. "I wasn't sure you'd remember me."

"I thought you worked in the city. How's Tom? Still down in DC?"

"I transferred up here last year. Yeah, he's good. Three kids. I'll tell him you were asking."

Malcolm stuck his hand out to the other officer. "Officer Navarro," the man said.

"So," Jackie said as she reached up and straightened the Hennessy sign by the door. "What can you tell us about Charles Waggoner? We heard Rob filled you in a little."

"He hasn't turned up yet?" Malcolm was surprised. He figured Tripp would have shown up one way or another by then, that he'd either found his way home or been discovered somewhere between there and the Half Moon. If he'd attempted the walk home on Friday night, he might have stopped for a rest, fallen asleep like drunk people tended to do. And then the snow, the extreme cold that followed. It wasn't a bad way to go, really. There was also the creek that ran along Jefferson, the water moving fast under the surface ice. A body had been fished out when

Malcolm was in ninth grade, and he was certain that every person his age who grew up in Gillam could name the place they were when that news went out. They'd played in that creek all summer.

"No, and we really need to track him down before this next storm gets here," she said.

"One more biggie and then spring," Officer Navarro said. "Next thing the tulips will be pushing through."

"That's March for you," Jackie said.

"I hadn't heard that," Malcolm said. "About another storm. My phone's dead."

"Tomorrow, supposedly," Jackie said. "They might be wrong. It doesn't have that smell, if you ask me. You know how you can smell snow coming?"

A Tuesday storm would be better than another Friday storm. He needed to be up and running by Thursday, latest. He had a birthday party coming in. Plus the rolling St. Patrick's Day parades that took up most of March—Hoboken, Jersey City, Woodlawn—would mean people returning to Gillam and going for a drink in town. The rowdy groups opened tabs, stayed for hours. He had a band scheduled for Saturday night. They were probably awful but they'd agreed to play for drinks and tips. March was usually his best month.

Malcolm told the officers more or less the same things he told Rob the day before, that Tripp had gotten drunk, cooled out in the kitchen, walked off. They took Emma's and Roddy's names. He went to the kitchen to get his phone so he could give them their numbers, forgetting it was dead. They asked if he knew the names of any of the people Tripp had been arguing with, but Malcolm didn't.

"What's upstairs?" Jackie asked. She looked at the ceiling.

"You ever hang out here, Jackie? I've never seen you."

"I don't think I've been here in years. I like going to Riverside or into the city. That new place on Oak is nice. Have you been?"

"Nope," Malcolm said, and pulled on his tight shoulder. "Well anyway, there's nothing up there. Odds and ends. I thought I'd use it as an office, but I really don't need one. There's a door from the sidewalk, or a staircase in the back, if you walk past the men's." Malcolm pointed.

"You never had a renter or anything?"

"No. Thought about it, but I'd need to renovate, put in a full bath and a kitchenette." And who in the world would want to live above a bar? They'd have to soundproof it, bring it to residential code. "I've been thinking of opening a wall, having outdoor space, a rooftop bar. You can see the lake from up there."

He watched for their reaction.

Jackie turned her face north and tilted her head. "Wouldn't it over-look the commuter lot?"

"There are things you can do about that. Decorative things."

But she'd already lost interest. "You mind if we look around up there?"

"Sure," Malcolm said, and then apologized for having to lead them back outside to the door that led upstairs. A policy leftover from Hugh's time; they kept the interior door to the second floor locked so that peo-ple didn't sneak up when the bar was full.

Upstairs, the light was brighter. The walls were scuffed and the floor was pitched badly, needed to be leveled. But there was something cheer-ful about it, something promising.

"What's all this?" Officer Navarro asked. Malcolm was across the room, imagining the wall gone, some sort of wood trellis to prevent a person from looking left. "Is someone staying here?"

Malcolm turned to see what he was talking about. There in the corner of the room closest to the door they'd entered through was a duffel bag, and next to it, a short stack of clothes, neatly folded. A phone charger. Two battered paperbacks. A clip-on book light. A camp mattress, rolled up into a cylinder. A sleeping bag. As a group they moved toward the tiny bathroom and looked in. There was a cup on the windowsill that held a single toothbrush and a travel-sized tube of toothpaste. Deodor-ant. A striped towel hung from the doorknob.

"Whose stuff is this?" Navarro asked, looking at him carefully.

Malcolm shrugged, astonished. For some reason his first thought was of Jess. But if it was her stuff, there'd be the face wash she liked. There'd be her floral makeup case. She didn't wear men's deodorant, mountain fresh scent.

"Someone's definitely staying here," Jackie said, looking at Malcolm. "You didn't know?"

"No idea," Malcolm said, glad he didn't have to lie but also feeling a strong sense of trouble looming. They stood over the duffel bag. There were two boxes of peanut butter protein bars. Jackie picked up a sweatshirt, held it so they could all read what was written across the front: "Fall Classic," a drawing of a fish underneath. One of the books was a spy novel and the other a guidebook of sorts: *Alone: How to Break Free of the Grid.*

Navarro picked up *Alone,* flipped it open. "'Dig a well before you're thirsty,'" he read aloud.

"You don't need a warrant?" Malcolm asked, and immediately wanted to kick himself. He sounded defensive, but really he just wanted to make sure they did everything right because if they didn't, it would end up becoming his problem.

Both officers looked up.

"Nah," Navarro said. "If Charles Waggoner wants to jet off to the South Pole or wherever, that's his business. We just want to feel pretty sure that's what happened."

"For his wife's sake," Jackie added. "The family is wondering."

"Trespassing is a crime, isn't it?" Malcolm asked.

"Yeah," Jackie said in a tone that said, Not really.

"You're certain he was on his own on Friday night?" Navarro asked.

Malcolm shrugged. He wasn't certain about anything anymore.

"Who else might be staying here?" Jackie asked. "Someone on your staff maybe?"

Malcolm ticked through his staff face by face. He paused on Roddy for a moment, always broke, always disheveled, but he moved on.

"I'm just confused. Why would he need to stay here? He has a house."

Jackie looked at Navarro and he shrugged as if to say, Go ahead.

"Rob found an itinerary for Toronto in his father's email, early Saturday morning departure. Or rather, Rob's mother found it, showed Rob. That's when he looped us in."

"Saturday morning as in two days ago? I would think flights were canceled. How'd he even get to the airport?"

"You'd be surprised," Navarro said. "Planes get above the weather pretty quickly. Getting to the airport would have been hard but not impossible. We confirmed the flight took off from Newark at 7:35 Saturday morning and he purchased a seat several weeks ago. We also confirmed that he checked in, but anyone can check in remotely, so it doesn't tell us all that much. Maybe he went straight from here Friday night and slept at the airport. We're waiting for the passenger list. That'll tell us if he was actually on board. There was also a bunch of stuff in his search history about a village in Peru." He pronounced the name of the village slowly, syllable by syllable. "Ollantaytambo. Rob said Tripp and his mother went there once, years ago. His father's been obsessed with it ever since."

"He told me about that place," Malcolm said.

"So Rob's thinking Canada might just be a rest stop," Jackie said.

"That's assuming he made it as far as the nearest traffic light," Malcolm said. "You checked the snowbanks between here and his house?"

"Looking into all possibilities," Navarro said.

"And there's been another development that's sort of interesting," Jackie said. "He changed his life insurance beneficiary, about eighteen months ago. The beneficiary is now a person named Mark Duro. You ever hear that name? All the people who come through the bar? We figure if anyone would know him you would."

The name didn't ring a bell.

"Could be a fake name, right?"

"Could be."

"I still don't get why he'd have his stuff up here." He pictured Tripp brushing his teeth, settling in for the night.

"Yeah, you're right," Navarro said. "Why stay here? He lives on Acorn. Big house. It's not that far." He walked to the window, peered down at the street. "He takes the train to work every day. His wife said he'd been coming home every night until Friday, unless he's out of town for business. He'd been having trouble at work, was really stressed out. She didn't think much of it until he never got home Friday night."

Malcolm thought of a regular from Hugh's era, an old-timer everyone called Mr. Met who used to spend his days bouncing from the deli to the library to the OTB to the Half Moon, because if his wife saw him sitting down in the middle of the day, she'd come up with something for him to do.

"Maybe this was his daytime spot. A place to be instead of the office. Are you sure he's been going to work?"

The officers looked at each other.

"I can call," Navarro said.

With music on, the bar was loud even when it was empty. A person staying up there could move about freely without a worry of being heard. They would have to be careful at opening, Malcolm moving through the quiet, getting ready for another day. Any unusual creak of a floorboard and he would have noticed. Was Tripp listening when he negotiated with his suppliers last week? Had he been eavesdropping when Malcolm called the bank for a third time to ask about a line of credit, and then how did he interpret the silence on Malcolm's end when the loan officer explained equity to Malcolm like he was a five-year-old?

"Will you be here later? Or tomorrow?" Jackie asked. "We'll need to get back in at some point."

"Depends on this next storm. I have to run a couple errands and I have to check on my mother." As he was talking, he was making his way to the staircase at the far end of the room, the one that led down to the bar. He jogged down and went to unbolt the door, but it was already unlocked.

"That's weird," Malcolm said. He opened the door, stepped through. "This door has been locked for years."

He turned to face the officers standing at the top of the stairs.

"Maybe he came and went through the interior door when the bar was full," Navarro suggested.

The bar was rarely that crowded, Malcolm thought, especially not during the day. Someone would surely have noticed if a guy went down the hall to the men's and never returned. He pictured the money lying around in the mornings sometimes, if he was counting out payments. He pictured all the bottles left out when deliveries were made. He was short a bottle of Jameson around Christmas and he thought it odd, figured one of the delivery guys had nabbed it. He lined up all the bottles along the bar, thinking he'd missed it, checked the lineup against the packing list, but then he'd just let it go, figured the delivery guys were in as bad a shape as he was and it was Christmas.

Then he remembered the clean pile of undershirts just sitting there in the men's room cabinet the night before, how he hadn't even questioned it. The men's room downstairs was a lot bigger than the tiny bathroom upstairs, and a man of Tripp's size would need space to clean himself.

"You might as well come down this way," Malcolm called up to them but Navarro said no way, said it was bad luck to leave a place by a different door. So Malcolm left the door unlocked, went back up, and exited with the cops by way of the street stairs.

"If I'm not here, you can always let yourselves in," he said when they reached the sidewalk. He hoped they were noticing how cooperative he was being. "This door seems locked but it's actually just jammed. If you shove hard, it'll open." He lowered his shoulder and rammed it against the door to demonstrate. As he did, it occurred to him that Tripp might have figured that out.

"Better if you're here, though," Jackie said.

"Sure, okay," Malcolm agreed. "Hey, can you guys give me a lift home?"

Malcolm grabbed the empty gas canister, his phone, the cash pouch, and hurried to the backseat of the cruiser. Sitting inside the warm car, he noticed how cold he was, pinpricks of pain at his fingertips, his toes. He hoped his mother had a fire going. He hoped she had the sense to close the living room door and trap the heat, to sleep on the couch down there. He needed to get his car out of his driveway, no matter what it took. He had too many stops to make. He needed to charge his phone. He needed to refill the generator, get that space heater going again.

The roads were better than they'd been twenty-four hours earlier, and there was movement about, the occasional car, kids playing despite the bitter cold. He noticed lights on here and there. "Is the power back?" he asked.

"Some blocks but not many. And it'll be tricky with more snow coming. They're saying another foot, minimum."

"It's not too cold to snow?"

The officers looked at each other. "We were just talking about that. Is that a real thing?"

All three shrugged.

At home, he went directly upstairs, stripped, dipped a washcloth in the cold water he'd collected in the tub, and rubbed his face roughly, brushed his teeth. As he did he thought of Tripp off the grid somewhere, squatting next to a campfire, perhaps, until he figured out how to live. Next Malcolm pictured Tripp stiff as a board, dead since Friday night. Either way he had no worries about roofs leaking or pipes bursting. No worries about a mortgage or filing quarterly tax estimates or where he and his wife were in their health insurance deductible or getting his car inspected or cutting the stupid lawn and getting the edges just so. No worries about Hugh Lydon and getting a payment to him month after month after month.

Once he was dressed in fresh clothes, Malcolm went to the window and looked at the sky, wondered what muted parts of a person's DNA were possible to reawaken given the right circumstances. Life was ticking by, day by day, and it was dawning on him lately that the distance between his present life and his future was getting shorter every minute. Malcolm's grandfather in Galway had been able to smell rain a day away, could probably tell by the particular shade of the sun what weather was coming across the meadows and fields, but Malcolm had lost all that, had never been taught how to look for these things, had never known how to live any life but the one he was born to. Had Tripp really been drunk on Friday? Malcolm was almost certain it was no performance, but maybe this guy was that good. He must have been sober to have disappeared so completely, to have gracefully slipped away into a window so narrow that he'd have to have very steady hands to pull it off. Brilliant, really, when Malcolm thought about it. He wished he knew the whole plan. Maybe even the fight he'd gotten into was designed so that everyone would remember he'd been there, would swear to it should it ever come up when the police came knocking.

It felt urgent to dig out his car. He rebundled, walked over to the Colemans' garage to take back the same shovel he'd returned on Saturday. It felt a little warmer than it had earlier, not quite as bitter, or else he was getting used to it. He started his car to let it warm up as he worked, set his phone on the charger. He hacked and hacked and pried plates of ice from the surface, tossed them to the street piece by piece.

When he finally cleared enough to get his car out, he sat in the driver's seat and saw that his phone had come to life. Four times, Jess's name appeared on his screen. More texts: his mother, Emma, Patrick, his mother again, André, a local number he didn't recognize. He read all of them and purposely skipped Jess's, saving hers for last. Emma and André wanted to know if power was back on in Gillam, when they should report to work. His mother wanted to tell him she had plenty of food in her fridge if he wanted some of it and that Mr. Sheridan had cleared her driveway. Patrick wanted him to come for dinner, said he had a bottle of scotch they could open. The unfamiliar number was Rob Waggoner, to tell him some police officers might be coming around. Finally, he tapped Jess's name.

You home?

I'm stopping by

Are you in there? Your car is here.

Ok I'm going

He looked up. She'd been there while he was gone. He got out of the car and stood there, imagining where exactly she'd walked, what path she'd taken. He imagined her opening the door of their house, stepping inside. She'd been in there and he hadn't even sensed it.

"Jess," he said aloud.

"Malcolm," a voice responded, and Malcolm wheeled around to find Hugh's guy Billy standing behind him in a jacket too light for the weather, a flat cap pulled low over a gaunt face.

"Jesus," Malcolm said, and out of habit almost went to shake his hand.

"What's the story?" Billy asked Malcolm, as if he'd just come by to shoot the breeze.

Malcolm steeled himself. He was tempted to make fun of the guy. His whole look seemed copied from a bad movie.

"What do you want, Billy?"

Billy laughed. "What do you think?"

"Yeah, tell Hugh it'll be all good in a few weeks."

"By this weekend."

"This weekend?" Malcolm said. "That's a joke. Look around. Nothing's moving. And there's another storm coming."

Billy reached for his pocket and Malcolm swallowed, felt his whole body tense up. But Billy only drew out a pack of cigarettes, followed by a long search in the other pocket for a lighter.

"Where is he anyway? I tried calling him. I'd like to talk to him."

"You left messages?"

"Yes, but if you'd let him know, I'd appreciate it."

Billy smirked. "Sure."

"Because what I want to know is why'd he go to so much trouble talking me into buying the place if he knew how it would go. He knew about the new place opening on Oak. There's no way he didn't. He knew the vendors wouldn't grandfather me into those old contracts. He said we'd work it out, not to worry about it, but then he comes up with an interest rate that's impossible to get ahead of? What's the point?"

Billy shrugged. "The only reason he's been as patient as he's been is because of how far back you go. But his patience has a limit."

"You know, we didn't sign anything," Malcolm said. "I have a letter that says the money was a gift. Free and clear. I could stop paying him right now and there's not a thing he could do about it."

Malcolm followed Billy's gaze to the little house, top to bottom, how cozy it looked capped in snow. Of course there were things Hugh could do about it.

"We started around the same time," Billy said.

"Started what?"

"Working for Hugh. I started and then a few weeks later there you were."

Malcolm hadn't realized that. Billy seemed like a guy who was born the age he was now, in the clothes he was wearing. When Malcolm started at the Half Moon, he remembered seeing Billy along with Hugh's other guys and thinking they'd all worked for him forever.

"He put me on his other jobs but he put you in the bar."

His point was there somewhere, but Malcolm couldn't pin it down.

"Did you hear what happened to Pete Spear?" Billy asked.

Pete Spear, town manager, had come by the bar maybe four times in a short period, looking for Hugh. He wanted to catch him for a sec, he said to Malcolm the last time he was in. He just wanted to talk. Malcolm wondered if the guy was losing it a little, how many times had he explained that Hugh didn't own the place anymore.

"Got mugged I heard," Billy said. "Beat up pretty bad. In Midtown. Lost sight in one eye."

They both squinted into the glare that rose off the surface of the snow.

Back in his car after Billy drove away, Malcolm took deep breaths. He cupped his hands over the heating vents. He tried counting to a hundred but he kept losing his place. He used to ask himself what he was going to do, but the question was too large, and had no answer, so at some point he decided to just get through each day. The days would add up to weeks, weeks to months, and maybe everything would be fine. But it looked as if that plan would not work after all. He scrolled through his contacts and tried calling Hugh again. No answer.

The main road was crunchy with sand and salt, but the side streets were slippery, and Malcolm could feel the wheels of his car losing traction. He drove to his mother's first, felt relief at the sight of the perfect boxed cuts Mr. Sheridan's snowblower had made along her driveway. She tried to get him to stay, and when she saw he wouldn't settle, she suggested she tag along with him, help at the bar and keep him company.

"Ma, no," Malcolm said. "Just keep the house warm."

"Well, you should sleep here tonight at least. I have the fireplace."

"I can't. But I'll come back."

"Is everything okay? Besides the weather, I mean. Besides Jess."

"Yeah, everything's fine," he said as he imagined Jess showing up at the house again. Four texts in a row was something. Four texts in a row was more than he'd gotten in months. So she knew she had some explaining to do. If she did show up at the house again, he wanted to be there.

"Fine," she said. "Go. Darren will be—" She stopped speaking so abruptly that he looked up.

"What were you going to say?" Malcolm asked. He left Billy and Hugh and the Half Moon and Tripp Waggoner and even Jess outside in the cold for a moment. "Something about Dad?"

She looked at him as if he were the one who'd confused things. "I'm calling Mary. They didn't get one flake of snow in Boston. Can you believe it?"

Malcolm waited until he heard his sister's voice on the line, and then he shouted hello from the background. He told his mother that he was taking the empty gas can out of her garage because he needed a second. A few minutes later, taking turns slowly, he made his way to the gas station and filled both canisters. Then he rolled along Seneca to the Half Moon. The façade looked damp and forlorn, badly in need of new shingles. There were thick icicles hanging from the roofline. He pictured one breaking off and impaling a passerby. The place needed so many things— new gutters, a whole new roof, the list was too long, and if he stopped paying attention for even one day, it grew longer. He looked up at the second floor windows and imagined someone looking down at him.

None of the other businesses had bothered clearing their sidewalks, not with the power still out and another storm coming on the heels of the last. Power was on at the bank. He asked the teller to write his balance on the receipt. Outside, he looked once and then tore it into a dozen pieces. He'd have to ask his mother for a loan. He had no choice. He'd get it back to her on a payment plan somehow. No one could ever know. Not Mary, not his friends, not Jess, not anyone. She had to have more than social security and her little salary from the school district. She should see a doctor, he knew. A specialist. He'd called her regular doctor a few weeks ago to ask what he recommended, but that doctor hadn't thought much of what Malcolm described. She was forgetful at times, sure, but she was seventy-two. Malcolm searched on the internet, but it led him nowhere except to wonder what exactly a doctor could do for her anyway. There was no medicine that would help long-term. Everything he read online about signs of memory loss—or not loss, exactly, more like confusion—all had to do with prevention. A diet and exercise program she should have been on since she was thirty.

Aside from the bank, nowhere seemed to be open except Food King, a smattering of cars in the lot. Casually, without realizing he was doing it, he looked for shoes sticking out of the snow, looked for any lumps that might be shaped like a human man. He slowed as he passed the bus shelter, the long bench that might appeal to a person staggering home late at night in bad weather. He looked carefully at the clutter of cans and bins and stored landscaping equipment behind the mechanic's shop. The door of the Salvation Army bin was warped. Had anyone checked in there? He left the car running in the middle of the street and walked over, peered inside. He pictured Tripp sleeping peacefully, tucked into a pile of old winter coats and sweaters, but the bin was empty. The traffic lights had all been switched to flashing yellows. The trains weren't running, the signals still out.

He drove slowly past the library, and then, seeing a half-buried realtor sign advertising an open house, he remembered something from a few years before. He kept driving toward the edge of town, where the houses were set farther apart, and then turned toward the busy road that separated one small part of Gillam from the rest. It was a vague memory, but it was growing sharper in his mind. A few years before, Patrick had looked at a house over in the new development, and made Malcolm come with him. "Fifteen minutes," Patrick said. "Tops. Just a little detour." They were on their way to a golf course in Westchester to celebrate their buddy's fortieth, but first Patrick wanted to walk through an open house, get a quick look at the place for his college friend, to see if it was worth his friend driving from the city to check out.

"Nasty divorce," Patrick explained that day. He told Malcolm to stay in the car if he wanted, no need to come in, but Malcolm followed anyway and stood patiently aside as Patrick peppered the realtor with questions. He followed Patrick up the stairs and down the hall as he glanced into bedrooms, opened closet doors.

"Your friend has this kind of money?" Malcolm asked as they were walking back to Patrick's car. The house was huge and expensive, the area it was in far nicer than any other section of town. Divorces were expensive, too, but apparently this friend could afford both.

"Yeah," Patrick said. "But he's a good guy. I guess I've always talked this place up. Gillam, I mean. He's curious. And he has to decide pretty quick because of school and everything. They're in the city now. The kids are in private school. So it'll be a big change."

It was a habit they'd inherited from their parents, the second half of the sentence laid out in opposition to the first. He had money *but* he was a good guy. To both admire money, want it, and be suspicious of it, too. To consider anyone with money a species slightly different from their own. Anyone in their crew could make a billion, but they'd still understand what it meant to worry. It was present in them no matter where they ended up, just the same as their eye color, their height; the patina of a childhood made up of hand-me-down sneakers and overhearing their parents discuss layoffs, strikes; buying the expiration day meat and their mothers saying it was fine as long as it was cooked to well-done. When people were raised without that worry, you could feel it just by standing near them; something about the way they spoke and moved. It couldn't be learned.

"He won't want to be in the suburbs, though, will he?" Malcolm had asked at the time. "Newly single?"

"He got the kids," Patrick said.

"Ah," Malcolm said, and immediately imagined Jess calling him out for something, his old-fashioned assumption that the wife always got the kids.

"But why Gillam? If I had this kind of money, I'd get one of those sick houses on the water in Mamaroneck."

They were still within the bounds of Azalea Estates, Patrick driving slowly so they could look at every house, every yard. There were no weeds, not a single sprig of boxwood that rose up above the rest. "You? No you wouldn't. You'd stay right here. And anyway, what do you mean? Gillam's a great town. You don't like it here?"

"I really don't know whether I like it or not. It's just home."

"You'd get it if you had kids," Patrick said. Sometimes Malcolm knew what Jess meant about people being smug when it came to their families.

Malcolm shrugged. "I get it. Even without kids."

"I know you do." Patrick glanced at him as he put his blinker on and turned. "Sorry. I don't know why I said that. Is that stuff, you know, the doctors, you and Jess—"

"Nah, we're done."

"Yeah?" Patrick nodded. "And you're good with that?"

"I'm fine." Malcolm shifted in his seat. "I mean. The last time—"

"I know. That was really tough. You guys were stoked. Everyone was."

"Yeah. Jess is struggling."

Patrick frowned, kept his eyes on the road. "Siobhán said something about adoption maybe? Are you guys thinking about that?"

"Jess has brought it up a few times, but I don't think she's all that serious. She sort of raised the idea and then dropped it. It would take years and we've already put in so many years. At one point maybe I'd have considered it, but now? I'm just tired. I need a break. We need to move on."

"I get it. You feel how you feel. When Siobhán was pregnant with Jack, it was as if she completely loved him as soon as she got pregnant and kinda got mad at me that I didn't. I said I did but she knew. It took until meeting each one of them if I'm being honest, and sometimes a little longer. So assuming Jess is more like Siobhán, I guess what I'm saying is that she's going through something slightly different, losing this baby."

They turned onto the main road.

"But what do I know?" Patrick asked after a mile or so. "I was never in your position. I can't imagine going through what you guys have been through."

Malcolm nodded. He'd been through it, too, not just Jess. He felt a heaviness pressing in on them and didn't want to ruin the day they'd been looking forward to.

"I'd probably get a weird one anyway," he said, trying to lighten things a bit.

Patrick smiled. "You'd get one who can't keep his finger out of his nose. Or who can't stop fiddling with himself in school."

"Remember David Hoyle?" Malcolm said, and they both cracked up. David Hoyle had been in school with them until fourth grade, and then switched schools halfway through the year under mysterious circumstances. He used to press down on his crotch with both hands when Miss McConaughey walked up the aisle. None of their mothers would ever explain why he left so abruptly.

"Jack told me this morning that he can't be in the kitchen when I'm eating because my chewing is gross," Patrick said. "He told me it sounds like a swamp in my mouth. Can you imagine saying that to your father? Can you imagine what would happen? But that's the way it is now."

"And you have good ones! I mean, they're normal. More or less."

"Depends on the hour."

"Toby's kid is pretty odd, right? That middle one?" Malcolm pulled a face that mimicked Toby's second son's expression whenever he interrupted the adults.

"Oh my God," Patrick said, taking quick glances at Malcolm's impression as he merged onto the highway. "How have I never seen this before? Mal! You know what? That kid's eleven years old and has yet to flush a toilet in my house. Unreal."

Malcolm did his impression of the kid's face once more, and Patrick laughed so hard the car swerved.

"He deuced on our trampoline when he was maybe seven. Did I ever tell you that? I didn't, right? Siobhán said not to. Why do I listen to her?

She made me clean it up and told me to pretend to myself it was the dog and never tell anyone."

Malcolm laughed so hard he felt beads of sweat spring up under his collar. It was a beautiful spring day, perfect for golfing, perfect for a beer outside, what did it matter that they all stunk at golf, it was just an excuse to be together. Jess was so miserable, absolutely gutted, and he was heartbroken for her, but he just wasn't as sad. He wasn't, and he couldn't pretend he was. He didn't see the sense. He was relieved that they were finally moving on. They were still young. There was time to make a good life with each other. All around him, in every part of his life, he saw pretty good fortune. And the day before him was one reason why. Hour by hour, day by day, it was possible to will oneself into feeling better.

"Skip it," Patrick said. "The bar is your baby anyway."

"Oof. Can't say that to Jess."

"No. Jesus. Definitely not."

Malcolm didn't know if he'd be able to find the house again. The whole neighborhood looked different in the winter, the velvet green lawns covered in snow. The lots in that section of town were divided precisely, far bigger than in his neighborhood. He made turns as his instincts dictated, and next thing he saw it: Bratton's car.

He pulled all the way into the driveway, which was cleared to a perfect asphalt rectangle and showed exactly zero signs of the weather. A curtain moved in an upstairs window. Let him come outside, Malcolm thought. Let him fucking come outside. In another moment, it was Jess who stepped out, wearing a pair of snow boots he'd never seen before. Her hair up, without makeup, she could have been twenty-five years old. When he just kept staring straight ahead, refusing to look at her or roll down his window, she walked around to the passenger side and opened the door.

"Hey," she said, sitting. For some reason she put on her seat belt. "I stopped by. You got my texts?"

But he said nothing. He would not make it easier for her. He felt something rise up in him, a choked-off feeling, like all the things he wanted to say were bottlenecked in his sternum. He pushed back from the steering wheel, took a deep breath. He glanced at her quickly—she was pale, far too skinny, purple pockets under her eyes. He imagined how he probably looked to her, after the weekend he'd had.

"How are you?"

"Fuck you, Jess."

She flinched, looked at her lap.

They sat side by side in silence, the car's engine humming. She should talk first, he decided. Let her come up with something. Let her work for it.

But then. "He knows you're out here with me?"

"Yeah."

"He's okay with that?"

"I don't know. It wasn't up to a vote, you know?"

"No, I bet it wasn't. I bet you just went ahead and did whatever you wanted."

"Well," she said, in a tone that said she had a few things to say about *that* but she'd give him a minute.

He imagined barging in, finding Bratton, throwing him through his giant picture window. He didn't give one shit if the guy's kids watched him do it. He had twenty people who'd vouch for him, say he'd been on their couch playing Go Fish with their families all day. And Jess. What a liar, what a— But none of the usual words felt right. And it hadn't felt good, even in his imagination. As soon as she opened Bratton's front door and stepped outside, he felt most of the rage evaporate, and instead he felt hollow, tired, adrift. There was his girl. She was just standing in a different house.

"Where's your car?"

"In the city."

"So? You're sleeping with him. And what else? Do you love him?"

"Malcolm," she said like a plea, quickly turning her face away from him. "I don't know." He accepted her answer like a blow. He folded it up and absorbed it and waited a moment to see how it would take.

She reached for his hand, squeezed it tight, but he pulled it away.

"What are we going to do?" he asked.

"I don't know," she said again.

Two older men walking dogs passed on the street behind them, taking slow, deliberate steps on the ice. Malcolm watched them in the rearview. Hot air blasted from the dashboard vents but his hands refused to warm up.

"You should have seen the bar. You should have seen it on Friday when I pulled up. I knew right away. I just felt it. If I could figure out how to make it like that every night. Or not even! Four nights a week. And it was only half a night, really. We closed before midnight."

"Really?" she asked. She was humoring him maybe, but he didn't care. Her favorite nights in Hugh's time were the nights when tables and chairs were spontaneously pushed aside to make room for dancing. The bottoms of her feet would get filthy because she always took off her heels, and then after, when they got home, she'd have to lather and rinse them in the tub before she got into bed, before she let him pull her there. "Just put on socks!" he used to plead. Remembering this, he described everything that was still vivid about Friday, and he knew by the way she looked at him that she could see it, that he'd done a good job, that she believed every word.

"You look good, Mal," she said. "You look okay."

"You look awful," he said. "Sorry."

The sky was changing. Still bright blue for the most part, but a line of gray was advancing from the north. The air, which all day had smelled so clean, so dry, like pine and bare branches, now had a faint earthy scent, humidity settling over the land. They shivered at the same time.

"I can't believe you." He intended to sound disgusted, to let her know where things stood, but the words came out in a near whisper.

"I know."

"How could you? And not a fucking word. I'm waiting here like an idiot for you to come home. Four months. And then to hear about this from someone else. You know how stupid I feel? After all these years. And with Patrick's friend. Aside from losing you, what's this going to do to Patrick and me? You just wanted to take everything down with you?"

"No of course I didn't want that. I wasn't thinking about Patrick."

"No you sure weren't."

"I'm so sorry." Her face had that stricken look that came just before crying. He was so affable, so easy in so many ways, but if there was one thing he wouldn't forgive, it was being made to feel stupid.

"And you know—" It was getting difficult to shape the words; his breath kept getting squeezed into the pocket at the base of his throat. She turned away to give him privacy. He banged the steering wheel with the heel of his hand. "When I said I was worried that working so hard for a kid would mess things up between us, and I felt a little protective of the great thing we had going, *you said* that we were already a family. I asked you and that's what you said."

"I know."

"But if you really believed that, about us being a family, you and me, then you wouldn't have done this. So that means, deep down, you felt we were only a family *if* we had a kid. A kid would *turn us into* a family. But without one we're not. Is that right?"

"No."

"Well, explain it to me then. Looks to me like you went out and got yourself a family. So where does that leave me?" But before she could make any sort of attempt to explain, he held up his hand. "You know how many people I could have cheated with? You want to know how many? I don't even know. Remember Meg? She was gorgeous, but I didn't."

He could see the pale oval of her face in his peripheral vision as she turned to study him. It wasn't quite his point. It hadn't come out right. She should know what he meant without him spelling it out.

"Good for you, Mal," she said after a minute. "What a guy."

"Sorry. That was a dumb thing to say."

"I seem to recall interrupting something a few years ago. Remember Erica Delfino? Because I certainly do. But we never talked about that, did we? And Emma? You can barely make eye contact with me when her name comes up. Come on."

Malcolm's stomach dropped. "Nothing has ever happened with Emma. She's a pretty girl and my best employee. That's all."

"If you saw your chance you wouldn't take it?" And then she sighed. "Don't answer that. I'm sorry. I mean, Jesus. Look where we are."

"Wait, I want to say this. I'm sorry about what happened with Erica. I'm really sorry. I don't know what I was thinking. You and I—there was only one subject, you know? Nothing happened, but it could have. I'm not making an excuse. I just—I've been sorry since that night and I feel sick every time I think about it. It was completely meaningless."

"I know that. I know you, Mal. But that doesn't mean it didn't hurt."

He cracked the window, took deep gulps of cold air.

"How'd we get here, Jess?"

She'd been thinking about that exact question for seventeen weeks. She pressed her fingertips to her temples and felt far too tired to cry. Neil's kids were warming to her. The plan was for her to stay just two nights and then head over to her mother's, but then the snow arrived, far more than expected, and the thought of being trapped with her mother and all her comments, without even being able to go for a drive or take a long walk—no, that was not something she could face. Being in Neil's house was like time suspended. No need to decide anything because it was not real life, not until the snow melted and the power was restored. The train signals were still out, and Bloom announced everyone in the NYC office could work from home until further notice. Neil's office said the same. The kids openly stared at her face, her clothes, her hair. Just that morning the girls came downstairs with cheeks covered in blush, eye shadow up to their brows. Jess imagined the contents of her makeup case scattered all over the bathroom floor.

"You two look a little different today," Jess said, as if she couldn't quite put her finger on what had changed. They froze, medium and small versions of each other, waiting to see what Jess would do next. "May I just—" Jess said, reaching out with a tissue to wipe the lipstick from where it had passed the boundaries of their lips, and they glanced at each other in relief. The oldest one was still a little reserved, but the younger girl and the baby climbed up to sit on her lap even when there was an entire empty couch available. "Sorry," Neil said, and told them to give her some space. But it was a heady thing, having these small people place a portion of their love and trust at her feet. They didn't hold anything back to protect themselves.

Their mother was supposed to take them on Sunday after the storm and keep them overnight, so Jess and Neil made dinner plans. Christine liked her weekends, Neil said, so she preferred having them on Sundays even though it meant a long drive to get them to school on Monday. There was a shortage of road salt in the entire lower Hudson Valley, but Azalea Estates was only half a mile to the entrance to the highway, which was always better than the local roads. Neil packed up their little things and drove them to their mother's at twenty-five miles an hour, only to discover she wasn't home. Turned out she flew to Nashville last minute, ahead of the storm, forgot to tell him. She got confused, she told him when he called, irate, and Jess could believe that, she supposed, but then she said the airfare was just too good to pass up, which sort of contradicted her claim of having forgotten. In the meantime, there were three little kids with their teddies clutched to their chests, wondering what was going to happen. When Neil recounted it for Jess, an hour after he packed them up and two minutes after he returned with them, he was afraid she'd be annoyed. They had an evening planned. A movie picked. But all Jess could think about was that the kids were down the hall only pretending to watch TV. She could feel them watching her, ready to take in her reaction.

"So what are you supposed to say?" she asked Siobhán later, once she got up the courage to call her friend, begin to explain. She was in Neil's bedroom, the door closed. She told Neil whom she was calling and he wished her luck, told her it would be fine, but added that if Siobhán couldn't accept it, forget her. He pointed out that she had her law school friends, her college friends, her high school friends who'd always been more hers than Malcolm's. And she had him now. She didn't need Siobhán.

"Well, no," Jess said, looking off into a blank distance as she tried to get her mind to catch up with the bad feeling that had sprung up in her belly. "I won't be dismissing Siobhán with a 'forget her.'"

"You know what I mean."

"I don't, actually," she said as a cold, bewildered feeling enveloped her whole body like a caul. Siobhán had welcomed him, arranged what were essentially playdates for him, a grown man. She wondered whom he loved, if he could name them, how many there were. And if he could say why. She wondered again what his ex-wife's version of their breakup story would look like, what picture she'd paint.

Siobhán was trying her absolute best to listen to Jess's explanation without interrupting. Jess could tell she wanted to understand, but she loved Malcolm. There was that old story about how she'd gotten her period in his car when they were driving down the shore together at nineteen, years before Jess knew either of them. There were three other people in the car, all boys, but somehow Malcolm figured it out—he had a sister, he was no dummy—so he covered for her, dropped off the others at the house they'd rented and then made up some reason why he needed Siobhán to stay in the car, help him with a beer run. He drove to a gas station restroom, and as she rinsed her shorts, dug out a fresh pair from her duffel bag, he bought a gallon of water and scrubbed the cloth-upholstered seat. He never said a single word about it until more than twenty years later, when Siobhán recounted it for Jess and he was at the table, listening.

When Siobhán realized Jess never heard the story she shouted, "You never told her?" punching him in the arm.

"You told me not to tell anyone." He shrugged.

Siobhán insisted Jess could have talked to her all along, and Jess knew it was probably true. She wouldn't have stood in a circle at a party and told anyone what Jess was feeling. Siobhán loved Malcolm but she loved Jess, too. She might have helped steer her away from the mess she was currently in. Even talking for ten minutes or so, she could feel her friend soften, feel her listening closely. "What do you say when he returns home with the kids," she asked Siobhán, "knowing they're listening? Knowing what they've been through and that it's quite possible their mother would prefer being anywhere else than with them. Knowing none of this is their fault?

"So what I said was 'That's great, I'm so happy they're here, I'd rather hang out with them anyway.' And I could sense their minds grow easy." Morning until night, the house was full of their voices.

To which Siobhán said, after a long pause, "Oh, honey. What an absolute mess."

"I still can't believe it," Jess said to Malcolm in the quiet of his car. "I could feel a baby in my arms. I'm not trying to be dramatic. I'm just telling you the truth. All that time, I thought I was seeing a future. So what was I seeing? It was so vivid. I would have been a good mother. I would have been really, really great."

Malcolm wished he were better at putting words on his thoughts, but they came to him as feelings outside of language—static electricity that ran down his arms, tightening in his chest. She had to make her mind change the subject, like he had. She had to take what was dark and fill it with different light, Or maybe that was what she tried to do, maybe that's what she was still trying for with Neil Bratton and his kids. It was the most astonishing thing, when he looked back. To think that when they first said they loved each other, when they got married, when they bought the house and filled it with furniture and plates and bowls and lamps and all the clutter of domestic life, that all of that was aimed at a future they had no guarantee of reaching. It had occurred to him since she left that each day, each hour, was a place he'd never been, that he'd have to find his way through. It was too obvious an observation to say aloud, and yet it had left him shaken.

"What are we going to do?" she asked after a moment.

"You're asking me?"

"Well, yeah. We have a serious problem."

"More than one," he said.

"More than one," she agreed. "Speaking of which—" She took his phone off the dash and punched in his password as if they'd never spent a day apart.

"The snow is supposed to start tomorrow midday."

"I know."

"The power is still out on Seneca, right? That whole section of town?"

"Yeah." And then he noticed the lights inside Bratton's house. He looked down the block and there were lighted windows dotting the fronts of every house.

"I have an idea. It came to me yesterday. That's why I stopped by the house."

"What?"

"First I want you to listen. We can talk about all this"—she indicated the house before them, the people inside—"and we have to, obviously. But we have a more pressing issue."

He looked at her. "More pressing than this?"

"He was here. That skeevy guy. What's-his-name."

Malcolm was a total blank, and then he gaped at her.

"Hugh's guy? Billy?"

"Yeah. Scared the hell out of me. I think he was outside our house when I went by, and then he followed me. Anyway, he just parked, and looked. And made sure I saw him looking. Don't get mad, just listen."

"Okay."

"Okay, so I have an idea."

"You said that."

"And it's so obvious I don't know how I didn't think of it before."

"Okay," Malcolm said, waiting.

"But before I tell you, I think you should go home and think about the bar. Think about yourself, about Hugh, about Gillam, the whole situation."

"Huh? You're sending me home to think? What's this about, Jess?"

"Along with the bar," Jess continued, "think about me and you, all that's happened. You know what I read on one of the fertility sites recently? This woman commented that someone else was the luckiest person in the world to have had a healthy child, and a hundred people piped up and agreed. But then this one woman way down in the comments said the luckiest thing, actually, was that each of us got born in the first place, that we should all remember that. Because what were the chances? I've been thinking about that. I'm mourning the babies I didn't have, but to get you, to get me, for our mothers to have conceived us—us *specifically*, you and I, and not the gazillion other possible combinations that could have gotten mixed up in there. It means something. And then to have been delivered safely, to have been raised safely, too. Whether we stay together or stay apart, it means something. I'm just trying to figure out what. We're messing up. We're wasting time. We have one life, and it's a miracle when you think about it. I want to stop messing it up."

"But how? We can't exactly start over."

"Look, Malcolm." She turned fully in her seat and stared at him straight on. She wanted to put her hands on his beautiful face. She wanted to climb onto his lap. As if reading her thoughts, he took hold of her wrist and held her hand against his cheek.

"That's what I'm asking," she said. "That's what I'm working up to. Are you sure about that?"

nine

Was he sure about that? He asked himself that question as he drove, once again, by the Half Moon. He didn't bother going inside. He told Jess he'd meet her over there in the morning, before the snow, so she could explain her idea. He stayed in Bratton's driveway long enough to watch her pull her navy coat tight around her body and walk back inside. Once she closed the door, he took his coffee from the cup holder—long gone cold—lowered his window, and flung it at the back of Bratton's car. It exploded against the rear windshield, the cup skittering in one direction, the lid in another. He waited a few seconds to see if anyone—if Bratton—would come running out the door, but the world was as still as it had been before. As he drove away, the announcer from the local radio station was asking people to look in on each other, especially the elderly. There were warming centers set up in various parts of the county, but the problem was getting people there. He suggested those with fireplaces and generators take neighbors in. It was not advisable to drive, but a car with gas could be turned on for heat. The announcer warned that running cars should be in well-ventilated areas, that tailpipes should be checked for ice or packed snow.

Malcolm drove by his mother's house again because he forgot to check how much wood she had stacked on the porch, but she didn't answer, so he stomped around the house to the slider, which was always unlocked.

"Ma?" he called. The wood-burning stove felt warm to the touch, and the place smelled strongly of smoke. He walked quickly through the house, not caring about the snow he was tracking, expecting to find her slumped somewhere. Would it be better to drive to the hospital himself or call an ambulance? But the house was empty. Her car was parked in the driveway.

He drove over to Mr. Sheridan's house and knocked.

"Oh, hi, Malcolm," Mr. Sheridan said when he opened the door. "Your mom is here. Were you worried? I'm sorry. She just—" He stepped out and pulled the door shut behind him. He spoke in a low voice. "She just seemed a little confused. I figured, why not set her up here? If she's here with me, then I won't have to worry about her."

"Oh," Malcolm said. Mr. Sheridan worried about her? Malcolm said he appreciated it. Then Mr. Sheridan opened the door wide and used a loud voice. "Hey, Gail, Malcolm found you. You were afraid he wouldn't."

"Is that you, Malcolm?" his mother called.

"Hi, Mom," he said, following Mr. Sheridan into the living room. He tried to remember when Mr. Sheridan's wife died, if it was before or after his dad. He felt a little confused, too, like he was slow on the uptake, but they were just friends, surely, they'd been friends for years. His mother was seventy-two and Mr. Sheridan was probably older. He wanted to call Jess immediately, tell her to forget their troubles for two seconds so he could get her take on this. There was his mother, sitting on the couch with her knees tucked up on the cushion like a kid. She was clutching a mug of tea, and Mr. Sheridan's German shepherd dog was at her feet. The fire was roaring.

"I went by the house."

"Look how handsome," his mother said, her face lit with pride.

"You okay, Mom? You good?" He made a point of glancing at Mr. Sheridan so she'd understand.

"The smoke started coming inside. Just pouring in! I opened the flue."

"Well, that shouldn't happen," Malcolm said. "Maybe the ice—"

Behind her back, Mr. Sheridan shook his head almost imperceptibly, gave Malcolm a look that asked whether he was really buying it, and the rest of Malcolm's thought fell away.

"I'll check it when I can, Gail," Mr. Sheridan said.

"Or I will," Malcolm said.

"Everything's gonna stink of smoke," she said.

"It'll air out, Mom. It's good you're here."

"You heard there's another one coming?" Mr. Sheridan asked him. He seemed younger than his years. Boyish, with that head of hair. What did he want with his mother?

"Yeah. I'm worried about the bar. I've got a generator running, but—" He shrugged. "No word on the power coming back?"

"I keep calling. The recording has been predicting eight to ten hours for the last three days."

"Great."

"Well, listen, you go on, do what you have to do. It's getting dark. We're like pioneers now, have to do everything before nightfall. She's okay here. Honestly. Aren't you, Gail?"

"Are you sure?" he asked, directing the question to his mother, trying to get her to meet his eyes so he could really see. Where would she sleep? If Jess were there, she'd find a way to ask.

"I'm fine! Look!" She showed him the paper tag of her tea bag hanging over the edge of her mug. "He has Lady Grey."

Malcolm woke early the next morning, and went straight to the Half Moon. When he pulled up, Rob Waggoner was standing outside, holding a paper bag. This again, Malcolm thought.

"Figured you'd be camping here," Rob said. "Brought you an egg sandwich. I was just about to take off."

"Thank you, no, my bed is more comfortable than a barstool. I appreciate this," he said, taking the bag. "What's going on?"

"I heard you had a guest and didn't even know. I just want to get in there and take a few photos. Becker and Navarro will be here in a minute."

"Yeah, sure. Any news?" Malcolm asked, popping the street door open like he'd demonstrated to the other cops the day before.

"Ah." Rob Waggoner pulled off his knit hat and rubbed his hair. He was dressed in plainclothes and looked far younger than he had the first time they met. Malcolm had no idea if he had kids of his own, if he hated his father or what. "Yes, actually."

"Oh, yeah?" Malcolm said. He began leading Rob up the stairs. "Are you allowed to say?" If he wasn't, Malcolm knew he could probably get it out of Jackie.

"They told you he was booked on a flight to Toronto? Well, it looks as if he also booked a flight to Panama City, departing from Toronto a few hours later."

"I don't get it," Malcolm said.

"He wanted us to think he was in Canada, but was really aiming for Panama City."

"And was he on both flights?"

"We have confirmation he was on the first flight, but we're still waiting on the passenger list for Panama City. We're looping in the police up in Toronto."

"Hey, no offense, but shouldn't there be real detectives involved maybe? The FBI?"

Another police car pulled up.

"Oh they're definitely involved. It looks like he was in pretty big trouble. There was an SEC investigation into his company, and apparently they presented their findings to the commission this past week.

His partner will be arrested any minute, and I'm sure they'll issue a warrant for my dad."

"Wow," Malcolm said. "Jeez. Tripp."

"But until there's a warrant, he's just a missing person, and it's still with our local department. He's just a guy who flew to Canada in bad weather without telling his wife. Changing his beneficiary is not illegal. Booking flights isn't illegal."

Malcolm thought people told him things when he was behind the bar because they considered the relationship sacred, separate from their real lives, protected. And because they were drinking. But maybe it was just something about him that made people want to talk.

Jackie and Officer Navarro jogged up the stairs to join them.

"Hello again," Jackie said.

Malcolm stood aside in the doorway as the other officers joined them, so Rob could see his father's pile of things. But Rob just looked at him blankly. And then Malcolm noticed the stuff was gone.

He looked in the bathroom. No toothbrush. No deodorant. He walked the room from end to end as if there were any places a duffel bag might have gone to hide.

"Where'd the stuff go?" Navarro asked.

"I don't know," Malcolm said, feeling accused. "I didn't touch it."

He went to the other stairs and jogged down, opened the door first to the hall, and then to the men's room. He removed the hidden key from its spot and looked in the storage cabinet. The undershirts were gone, too.

"I don't understand," Malcolm said, returning upstairs just as Navarro's phone rang. He turned his back to take the call.

"You were right," Navarro said when he hung up. "He hasn't been to his office since December."

They all looked around the room.

"Who cleared out his stuff?" Jackie asked.

"Mark Duro?" Navarro suggested, and Malcolm noticed all three officers were looking at him funny. The air pressure in the room shifted just a fraction but Malcolm felt it.

"Who else knows about this space up here?" Navarro asked.

"Ahhhh, the former owner, every person who ever worked for him, everyone who works for me, anyone who passes by and notices, oh, that building is two stories."

Navarro nodded. Rob was looking back and forth between them.

"How's the bar doing?" Navarro asked. "I heard you're having a hard time." He withdrew a pad and pen from his jacket to make a note.

"Bullshit. Where'd you hear that?" Malcolm said. Ridiculous. "You think I helped this guy? Like I don't have enough problems?" The place certainly didn't look as if he poured much money into it, but it looked exactly the same in Hugh's day, and no one doubted Hugh was minting money. Navarro couldn't pull his financials without a warrant, and why would he have done that before that very moment. He wondered if they could have checked with the liquor authority.

"I don't think so," Jackie said slowly, looking carefully at Malcolm but directing the comment to Navarro. "I really don't."

"Me neither," Rob said.

"You guys," Malcolm said. "I'm not sure you're understanding how hammered he was on Friday night. There's no way he pulled this off, whatever it is."

"He might have been pretending."

"I seriously doubt it."

"Well, he was on that flight."

"I don't know what to say," Malcolm said, suddenly annoyed to be even talking about this. Tripp was almost a stranger to him, and he had plenty of his own worries. What if he didn't have things shipshape for the party coming in Thursday night? What if power stayed out for another week? What if Billy was serious about getting Hugh his money by the weekend? Impossible.

"If anything occurs to you, call us."

"Of course," Malcolm said. When they got back to the sidewalk, he spotted Jess's mother's car pulling up across the street. Jess must have borrowed it, but how did she get over to her mother's in the first place? Suddenly he could picture the scene, Bratton driving her there and meeting Maureen Ryan, who sprayed her hair into a perfect shell for the occasion. Bratton was exactly the type of guy she wanted for her daughter all along.

"What was that about?" Jess asked as the officers got into their cars. They all got on their phones immediately, which Malcolm didn't like one bit.

"Nothing," Malcolm said.

"Nothing?"

"Give me a break, Jess. It's a long story."

"Sure, okay."

"Why don't you just tell me what your idea is."

She glanced at the cars, still idling. "I should probably wait until they leave."

Inside, she looked around the place as if she'd never seen it before. She walked through the kitchen, looked in the mop closet. She went downstairs to the storage room, and he followed her.

She got down on her hands and knees to look more closely at the ancient furnace. She crawled over to the shelf where he kept leftover construction supplies—half-empty cans of paint in case the walls upstairs needed touch-ups. Thinners. Polyurethane from when they refinished the wood floors. Random pieces of lumber. Old rags. Light bulbs. A drill. His toolbox. On the next higher shelves were boxes of alcohol, mostly fruit-flavored vodkas he'd over-ordered in the summer and that would now sit there until warm weather. He'd tried to sell them over the winter, save him from buying more of the unflavored, but people weren't interested. She began piling empty boxes. She kept stacking until the pile touched the crossbeams over their heads. When she finished, she started another tower, this time against a wood support beam.

"What are you doing?"

Without answering, she carried an old barstool over to the wall with the window, climbed up, peered out.

"We have an extension cord, right?"

"Yeah it's upstairs."

"How long is it?"

"Why?"

"Why didn't you put the space heater against the main? Down here? Warming the pipe that far up the line doesn't protect the sections down here from getting frozen."

"It's too dangerous down here. All this stuff. Plus buildings freeze from the top down. Down here will be okay because it's underground."

"Hm," she said, thinking about that. "Is that common knowledge? And why didn't you get the valve on the main fixed? It's been broken for what? Two years? How much would it cost? A few hundred bucks?"

He crossed his arms. "It's been broken since Hugh's day."

"But why didn't you fix it. I mean if someone asks you. What would you say?"

"Why would anyone ask?"

"Humor me."

"I would tell them the truth. That I was waiting until I had more room in the budget. You know as well as I do that one thing leads to another. I had a plumber take a look at some point, but he wanted to dig up the whole floor. I've been working here for a lot of years and I never remember the pipes freezing, so I figured it would be fine for a while longer."

"But we've never lost power for this long. Not as far as I can remember. And another storm is coming."

"And? What's your point?"

"You said it would be too dangerous to set up the heater down here,"

Jess reminded him. "But it makes sense, right? If you wanted to protect the whole system?"

"No, I don't think it does make sense."

"What I mean is, if you explained your train of thought to someone, it would ring true."

He waited.

"It's part of my idea."

She walked over to the metal file cabinet, pulled open the bottom drawer. That cabinet was where they kept the deed, the receipts from vendors, contracts, permits, licenses, employee 1099s, insurance policies. She ran her fingers along the tabs, removed a file, flipped it open, read silently for a moment, and then nodded as if to confirm something to herself. She handed the file to Malcolm, but he didn't know what he was supposed to be doing with it.

"What?" And then he knew. "No," he said, handing the file back to her. "No, Jess. No way."

"Listen."

"You're nuts."

"I'm not."

"You've completely lost it. Jesus Christ."

"Statistically, this would be the time when it would happen. I've been reading since yesterday. A basement like this is ideal for producing a large fire. There are so many ways it could ignite accidentally. It would rise straight up and destroy the whole room above us. Everyone knows you love this place, that you're worried about it, that you'd want to protect the plumbing and might not have thought out the consequences."

"But I did think about it. Which is why I put the heater upstairs."

"But what if you were in a panic and made a bad decision?" She looked up at him. "It's believable, isn't it? That you would have set it up down here?"

"Believable that *I* would do that? Malcolm Gephardt? Or that a person would do that?"

She hesitated. "A person. Anyone. Think about it. A power outage. A thirty-year-old space heater. What were the safety standards on those things back then? You know how many fires they cause every year? I looked up the stats. Who's to say you don't store gasoline for the generator down here? So what if you moved the generator outside that window, snaked the power cord through, pushed the space heater up against the main here in your hopes of keeping the whole system warm. And let's say, oops, it was set up too close to that tower of boxes, all those chemicals. Let's say the heater throws a spark."

He stared at her. Together, they looked at the crossbeams over their head, the low ceiling. Together, they thought about the floor above.

"Several people can attest to the fact that the lever broke years ago, and that it was never fixed."

"Please stop."

"An accident caused by your best efforts to protect the place."

When he didn't say anything, she pointed to the document she wanted him to see. "Read it. Look at the numbers. Our fire coverage is better than our flood coverage. There's loss of business income coverage, too. Add it up. We can get square with Hugh, with the bank. Then tell me that this is crazy."

She could see she was breaking his heart for the second time.

"You want to go to prison, Jess? Because I definitely don't. Stop. I don't want to talk about this anymore."

"It'll be deemed an accident. I know it will. We won't have to worry about that."

She had that preternatural calm she always had when she was right.

"And we'd be free. You could do whatever you want. Take everything you learned here and start from scratch. Me too. We could sell our house."

"Sell our house?" He couldn't read the expression on her face. "And go where? You'll stay with Neil? At his house?"

"No," she said, looking away. "I don't think so." She hadn't even said it to herself so plainly yet, but she knew almost the moment she stepped inside his house that it was the end of something, not the beginning.

"You don't think so?" He was embarrassed at how he clung to this small hope, not that he knew what to do with it.

"Thing is, Mal, this idea—it's time sensitive. This storm will be here in a matter of hours. The utility company is working around the clock, but even they will have to call it when the storm hits. The moment the power comes back on, this no longer makes sense. And by the way, the snow, the freeze, those conditions would also prevent the fire trucks from getting here quickly. Everywhere is closed. No one will even notice the place is burning until it's fully involved. The local patch said every town in the county is out of salt. The sand they trucked in has almost run out, too. No one can get anywhere quickly."

"Fully involved," he repeated. "You really have been reading."

She walked over to him. She was so close they might as well have been touching.

"Plus," she said. "Did you notice? Where are the hydrants?"

He pictured the street outside. "They're all covered in snow."

She told him to just read the files. One problem at a time and this would be first. When he walked her out, she turned and faced him once more. Her expression was all business, like it always was when she was worried about something.

"If you search anything online, make sure you're on private mode but try not to because I don't know to what extent those searches are protected."

"Jesus," he said.

She looked up Seneca, and not a single thing was stirring. "The fire department will know there's no one inside. They won't go into a dangerous situation for no reason. I'll meet you at our house in"—she looked at her phone—"at three o'clock. We'll take one car. It's probably best yours stays in your driveway. The snow will be coming down hard by then, and people will be home, hunkered down."

"And then what?"

"Then we wait."

It was just after eleven a.m. Several flakes drifted down, early harbingers of what was coming.

"What if you're wrong and someone gets killed? They're volunteers. What if they don't have the training paid firefighters have? There are very young guys who do it. Like barely out of high school, I think."

What he didn't say: There was a person staying upstairs who I didn't even know about. That whatever Tripp had done, he'd used the Half Moon as part of his plan. He was distracted by the thought of her coming over. At three o'clock she'd stand in their kitchen, walk through their rooms.

"If this goes the way I know it will, they'll just let it burn and protect the other buildings. No one's going to get hurt."

She looked to the left and right of the Half Moon. No shared walls. The alleys on either side were at least ten feet wide. There was the tiny deli to the right with the offices upstairs. On the other side was Primavera. All closed since Friday.

"I don't know what else to say. This is our only option."

"That can't be true," he said. He'd already been thinking about how he might get Hugh's address in South Carolina. He hadn't seen John since the day he fired him for stealing, but he bet John was still in touch with Hugh, maybe even working for him again. If he could only get a few minutes with him in person, they could surely sort it out.

"Well." She looked at her phone. "You have a few hours to decide."

He stood there for a while after she left, watching the traffic light turn yellow, then red, then green, then yellow again. He wondered what she was doing in the meantime. Going to see her mother, she said, but how could he ever know what she said was true? She told Malcolm she wanted to see Siobhán in person, but Siobhán had said that with Patrick home her house was most definitely not the place to chat, and with the new storm coming and everywhere closed, they couldn't exactly go out. They'd have to do it another time. Malcolm felt a flare of satisfaction at that, and when Jess saw it pass through him, she closed her eyes and shrugged as if to say that was his right, he'd earned it, there'd be a lot more where that came from. Patrick was his. Toby, too. ("Toby's all yours," Jess would say.) Everyone in Gillam, probably, except for Neil.

But she was the voice in his head, even when she wasn't there in front of him. The men are yours, Jess might say. But the women? She'd make that face meant to warn him not to be so sure. They might understand: her girlfriends, her mother, any woman who listened to her whole story and really took it in. They'd never admit it to their partners—no, they'd never do a thing like that, risk their families, risk their predictable lives, my God, what had she been thinking—but to each other? To themselves, in the privacy of their own thoughts? There were those who'd sympathize with following a temptation to its conclusion. There were those who would admire a woman who had a problem and did what she thought might fix it.

When Malcolm went back inside, he went straight to the file she left flapped open on the basement floor. He took a good look at the numbers and then closed it, returned it to the cabinet. That was all her doing, the insurance policies. After she found out about his side deal with Hugh, she went out and purchased coverage for every possibility.

He shivered though he didn't feel cold, exactly. He could sense her there, in the light she'd just been standing in, the red glints in her dark hair. Even as he insisted to himself that the whole thing was completely insane, he felt himself brush up against the lure. He closed his eyes and made himself picture it, the entire place aflame. He waited for the memories to come at him like echoes down a long corridor, but instead he felt peace. A new chapter. A chance to start over. Waking up in the morning without feeling like he was scrambling uphill before he even opened his eyes. Moving through his day without a physical weight pressing on his chest. He thought again of Tripp. Look at what he might have pulled off, assuming he wasn't dead in a ditch somewhere. Instead of whining to his bartender for the next twenty years like most people would do, he'd taken action. Instead of waiting for the Feds to come arrest him, he'd taken off. And now where was he? A place so far from a city that he could finally see the stars. In Malcolm's mind he tried to place this village he'd never seen—sun-drenched, quiet—and next to it he placed Gillam, the endless jockeying for parking spaces, the relentless moaning about traffic and taxes.

When people asked whatever happened to the Half Moon, he wouldn't even have to say it failed. It had been doing just fine up until the moment tragedy hit.

At home, he tried to think it out, every possibility, every reason it was a bad idea. He pulled the shades and stretched out on the floor. He stared at the ceiling. He was starving, but he was too tired to get up and hunt for a snack.

At three o'clock Jess knocked twice on the side door and then let herself in. The flurries had multiplied. He watched her notice the wire fruit bowl was now on the opposite end of the counter. She glanced out the window over the sink. "Those branches fell very close to the house."

"I know," he said, without moving.

"Are you ready?" she asked.

He drew himself up to full height. "How is it you're so calm?"

"Because we don't have a choice."

"We could file for bankruptcy."

"I thought about that. That could solve the debt with the bank. It might even solve our debt with the clinic. Our credit would be destroyed, but it can't get much worse anyway. Problem is I don't think Hugh accepts Chapter 11 filings."

"I was also thinking my mom probably has something tucked away."

"Stop," she said, looking at him finally like the old Jess. "You're not serious."

He shrugged, held up his hands.

"Your mother's going to need every cent she has. She's only seventy-two. She makes eleven dollars an hour, Malcolm. No, we won't be asking either of our mothers. We got ourselves into this, and we're going to get ourselves out."

He sighed. She was right.

"Look," she said. "It's not as if we're going to have to sprint up the stairs with a fireball at our heels. We're just placing things next to each other. Think of it that way. If a fire inspector finds evidence of gasoline, of chemicals, yes, that makes sense, that's what was stored down there. We're not trying to hide that. The whole staff knows what's down there. In fact those things were part of the backdrop for so long that we stopped seeing them. You were so worried about pipes bursting that you just went ahead and put that ancient heater in the spot where it made the most sense to you."

"But—" he said.

He tried to pinpoint exactly what he wanted to say, tried to find the precise thing that was nagging him. People didn't get away with this, or else they'd do it all the time. Everywhere, times get tough, buildings would be burning. But they weren't. Or were they? He thought of what happened at the café on Vanderbilt. Three in the morning, an electrical fire. They had to close the place for a few months, but when they finally reopened, they had a new kitchen, state of the art. They had beautiful custom shelves installed in the dining room.

He imagined being interrogated. All of his answers would be right there, adjacent to the truth. Such a strange set of days, all the rules were different until the power came back on.

They took Maureen Ryan's car. Jess drove with her mouth pinched into a straight line. As they passed each house, he understood what she meant about people hunkering down, looking only to themselves and the people they were stranded with. No one was thinking past getting salt on their own driveways, a way to get a hot meal into their kids. There was chimney smoke coming from a few houses, not many. The roar of generators churned up the silence. Driving through town, Jess cruised by the bar as if it didn't mean anything to her and parked a block away. They entered through the alley door, out of range of the camera trained on the front door. Once inside, he was relieved that she didn't go directly to the stairs.

"You want a drink?" she asked.

"Now?" he asked.

"Sure. Fifteen minutes won't make much difference."

"Okay," he said. One drink and then they'd begin the plan. One drink and then he'd put one foot in front of another, and then again, again, come what may. But for now the bar was still standing, he'd done nothing wrong, he was just there with Jess, company in hard weather. She moved seamlessly as she made them each a Manhattan, her slender hands. She placed the napkin down in front of him first, then the glass on top. She would have made a great bartender.

He drank slowly, small sips, long pauses, but he reached the bottom anyway. He said he'd go move the generator while she moved the space heater downstairs, but told her to take her time, finish her drink. He took a detour on his way outside to jog up the back stairs and check the second story, to make sure whoever had been crashing there hadn't come back. But it was still empty, and he stood by the window for a moment to watch the street fill with snow. When he returned downstairs and carried the generator around to the back, he knocked on the basement window from outside. She had to hammer it with the butt end of a screwdriver to get it to pop open. For a second he thought it was all over, the plan wouldn't work if they couldn't get the window open, and he couldn't decide whether he was disappointed or relieved. But then she shimmied it open a crack, just enough to snake the cord through.

"What are you going to do after this?" he asked when he joined her in the basement. He didn't know how to frame the question except to simply ask.

"Go to my mom's I guess."

"No, I mean what are you going to do, Jess? What am I going to do?"

It was darker outside now, the snow coming down harder.

"I don't know."

They both walked to the window, stood on tiptoe and looked out. The second canister of gas was at Malcolm's feet.

"You want to do it?" she asked, holding out a book of matches.

"No way," he said. "This was your idea."

She seemed to have expected that. He watched her light a match. He watched her crouch down and hold it to a corner of the bottom box. Malcolm's heart was beating very fast. He wanted to warn someone that this was happening, someone who could manage the next steps without putting anyone in danger but who wouldn't rat them out. But who? The flame grew brighter for a few moments but then burned out, leaving only a wan curl of smoke. Jess rearranged the boxes and reached for a second match. But she hesitated for just a second, and Malcolm felt something tighten in his chest. He thought of Emma's cardigan on a hanger in the broom closet. He thought of the picture of Scotty's kids that was taped to the side of the microwave. He thought of the framed photo of Gephardt's that he hung over the bar when he took over: 1982. His father standing under the sign with a cigarette hanging out of his mouth, the blur of a yellow cab as it sped out of the frame.

"Hang on," he said, staying her hand. "Hang on a sec."

He knelt down beside her on the packed dirt floor. "We need to think for just a minute."

She dropped the book of matches into her pocket and let out a long breath.

Was she relieved? He couldn't tell. It was harder to read her than it used to be. She'd always been a doer, that was one of the things he loved about her. She was a worker, a problem solver. If someone got dumped, then she set them up with someone new. If someone needed a job, then she asked around until that person got one. She paid attention to how things were done so that she'd know how to do them herself. When they bought their house and had zero money to spare after the down payment, she took classes at Home Depot to learn how to tile, how to grout. When they were short on food at Siobhán's baby shower, it was Jess who took everything to the kitchen, cut what they had in half, and rearranged it on more platters so it seemed as if it had doubled. "It was just like the loaves and the fishes," Siobhán said when she recounted it for Malcolm later. "A miracle." She felt stuck in her job, so she left. She felt stuck in her marriage, apparently, so she left that, too.

They sat in silence for a while.

"I'm out of ideas," she said eventually.

"I know," he said. "I just have to talk to Hugh. I have to make him talk to me. I've called and called but—" He shrugged. "Listen. Let's just go, okay? The snow must be coming down hard by now."

"This is our chance. We won't get another. You need to be sure."

"I'm sure." Malcolm unplugged the power cord, pushed it back through the window. He told her he'd move the generator back to the original spot, and asked her if she wouldn't mind carrying the heater upstairs.

"I can't move," she said. "What's wrong with me. I can't move. It's like I'm stuck." She was sitting there hugging her knees in the dark. So he carried the heater upstairs, set everything up as it had been. He filled the motor with gas and started it up.

"Jess," he said when he returned to the basement. "Time to go. Come on." She held out her hand and he took it, gently pulled her forward.

Outside, the snow was pounding hard. Malcolm used his sleeve to clear the windows.

Jess stood there without helping. She kept rubbing her face with her cold-reddened hand. "Jess?" he asked, and then he reached into her coat pocket and fished out her mother's key. He opened the passenger door for her and guided her in. He went around to the driver's side and started the car.

"You're fine." He looked over at her. "Nothing happened. We're fine."

"We're fine," she repeated. She had her forehead pressed against the cold glass. The rear wheels fishtailed a little and then found traction.

"Malcolm," she said. "Do you ever think about what would have happened if I hadn't gotten pregnant?"

Somehow, he knew that she meant the first time. At twenty-five. If they hadn't rushed into marriage. If they hadn't been so giddy as they applied for the license without telling a soul, Malcolm stuck in traffic coming from Gillam and Jess glazed with sweat after a short walk from the subway, unseasonably warm for May. He caught sight of her crossing the street that day and tried to decide whether she looked pregnant yet. There was a blank on the application where she had to write her new name, if she chose to change it. "Oh," she said. "I have to decide right now?"

"You can always change it later on," the woman behind the desk said.

"I haven't thought about this," she said, the pen still poised above the blank.

"I like your name," Malcolm said. His way of telling her that it didn't matter to him either way.

"And I like yours. And we're getting married," Jess said, and quickly wrote Jessica Lee Gephardt in the blank space.

"Holy shit," she said when the woman collected the forms, told them where to wait. She threw her arms around him and squealed.

They drove to Gillam together after, riding a wave of momentum, of raucous joy.

When they finally got back to the house, the wipers barely able to keep up with the snow, Jess said, "I'm coming in."

It felt as right and natural as anything that had happened in four months.

"Okay," he said. "Listen. We're going to figure everything out."

She looked at him. "How?"

"I don't know, but we will."

Once they were inside, he reminded her that she had plenty of clothes upstairs if she wanted to change.

She went up and he soaked in the sound of her moving around above him. She eventually came down in her old leggings, a long flannel shirt he hadn't seen her wear in years peeking out from beneath a wool sweater. She put her coat back on.

Inside they sat close together on the couch for warmth. He pulled across their laps the heavy down comforter he'd carried downstairs several days earlier.

"Didn't we talk about getting a fireplace?" she asked.

"Yes, but—" he said, and figured they could both fill in the blank. They'd talked about lots of things, all of which were put off until until until.

The snow tinkled against the windows.

"Hey, Malcolm?" she said. Her head was somewhat below his. He breathed her in and realized he probably didn't smell too fresh. He didn't want to talk about anything big. He didn't want to get into it. He was so tired, and so cold, and so hungry, and he just wanted to rest there for a bit, her body fitted to his despite all their bulky layers. Whatever might happen, he wanted to be quiet there with her for a few hours.

"Yeah?"

"I know I made a mess of things."

He didn't say anything, so she continued. "I know what I did is not the same as what you did with buying the building."

He thought about all the things he saw at the bar and looked away from. The little nods of agreement and the silences because that was his job, to be dependable and neutral. To have no opinion. Would he have told her about his side deal with Hugh? If she hadn't figured it out so fast? Probably not.

"I made a mess of things, too," he said eventually.

She didn't say anything, but he felt her shift, felt her relax against him.

"Freezing in here," she said.

ten

In Malcolm's dreams they heard sirens. They ran to the window to listen and then they tried to remember their prayers, as if God would help a pair like them, two sinners who'd not stepped inside a church since they were kids except for their friends' weddings. Mr. Sheridan was in his dreams, too, pushing a snowblower with huge, muscular arms that unsettled Malcolm. Dr. Hanley appeared with his notebook. Hugh showed up, squeezed behind the steering wheel of his Cadillac. Emma was there, pulling at the end of her ponytail. But in reality, during the many times he woke during the night, he heard nothing except wind, the trees outside groaning as they swayed. It felt right sleeping side by side on the couch instead of upstairs. They'd reached not a truce, exactly, but more of a pause, a taking of breath.

Over and over, as she slept and he stared at the blank ceiling, he tried to pinpoint the moment when the line that had been rising so steadily year over year reached a summit and began to fall. All that promise. They just frittered it away, and they didn't even notice until it was too late.

Until it was *almost* too late, Jess would say. "Almost too late" was actually the same as "in the nick of time."

When Malcolm opened his eyes next, the world outside was brighter and Jess was still sleeping, heavy against his shoulder.

"Hey," she said, hoarse, when he stood into the cold. It was very early, he could feel it. They both looked at their phones.

"Mine's dead," Malcolm said.

"Mine too."

He walked to the front door and looked out, but there was nothing but a bracing white, so bright Malcolm had to shade his eyes. The snow had stopped. His skin was so cold under his clothes. He wondered how his mother had fared at Mr. Sheridan's.

"Your mom is okay in this?" Jess asked, as if reading his thoughts.

"She went to stay with her friend."

"Oh, good."

What she didn't tell Malcolm: that she'd invited her own mother to come to Neil's, since he had heat and lights, but her mother had declined out of loyalty to Malcolm. Malcolm would be surprised by that, moved maybe, but to tell the story she'd have to say Neil's name.

"The power's been out for too long," he said. "Some people aren't going to make it."

"It's crazy. I don't remember anything like this."

"I'm starving."

"Me too. Is there any food here?"

"Some old meat loaf I meant to throw away," he said. "I can't find matches to light the pilot." He'd had a splitting headache the day before but now he felt light-headed. Neil Bratton probably kept a half dozen travel chargers on hand at all times. He probably had a ten-thousand-dollar generator.

Besides the meat loaf, the fridge was empty except for a jar of pickles and a tub of butter. That was where Malcolm's search usually ended, but Jess went over to the pantry, reached into the way back, and withdrew a can of black beans. She rustled around some more and came up with a large can of diced tomatoes. She went to the drawer where they threw random things to search for matches hidden beneath old bills, menus, and dried out pens.

"Oh wait," she said, remembering. She reached into her coat pocket and withdrew the book of matches from the previous day.

She went to the spice rack and removed this and that. She measured rice into a small pot, covered the rice with water. Never in a million years could Malcolm have looked at the random things she assembled and make his mind see a meal.

"Plenty here," she said. Malcolm lit the pilot on the stove and in twenty minutes they had hot food. Just like the story of the baby shower, she'd made something out of nothing. When they finished their first bowls, eating in silence, they each had another. It was so elemental. Cooking. Eating. Washing up after with the water Malcolm had collected. Two white bowls left to dry on a worn kitchen towel. A cobalt blue sky beyond the window. It was an extravagance, thinking only about the present moment. There was Jess, next to him. He already felt warmer, his headache fading.

"We're in trouble," Jess said. "What are we going to do?"

"Let's not talk about it. Let's not talk about anything until later. Okay? For this morning let's just pretend nothing's wrong and then maybe something will come to us. I know that's nuts but—"

Whatever Jess might have said to object, she swallowed back. "Okay," she said. What harm? He was different than he was before she left. She'd first noticed when they were in the basement of the bar. Something in the way he held himself apart from her. Something about the solemn way he listened as she spoke. And now she was seeing it again. Where was the guy who clapped a dozen backs when he walked into a room? The guy who parted the air just by walking through it? Where was the kid who sprang for ice cream cones for the whole neighborhood, without having the first idea what the tab would come to? Gone, as far as she could tell. Humbled. Crushed. By her and what she'd done, yes. She made herself acknowledge that fact. But also, the slow-motion failure of a dream. She'd seen that failure coming, but he hadn't. She saw that it hadn't just been denial; he truly had not seen. And then it hit her that it was the same for him when it came to her dream. He knew long before she did that she would never deliver a baby. But he'd stood aside and hoped she'd arrive at that conclusion on her own.

Outside, they worked in synchrony. Jess put Malcolm's phone on his car's charger first, said she didn't want to hear from anyone anyway. Not even Neil, Malcolm added in his mind. He shoveled while Jess used a broom to clear the car windows. What are we going to do? he thought over and over. What are we going to do what are we going to do what are we going to do? He knew she was asking the same. They discussed the weight and texture of the new snow, how it felt different from the heavy, sticky snow that had fallen on Friday. It was like they were in a play, acting like normal people, making their faces calm for the world. Jess asked Malcolm if he knew the Inuit people have fifty words for snow, and Malcolm reminded her that they watched that documentary together.

"Oh, yeah," she said. Once the cars were clear, she went at the steps, at the windowsills. She reached up and waved the broom overhead to knock down icicles, one hand clutching the broom's handle, the other crooked over her head to shield herself.

"Why don't you check my phone," he said, wincing as an icicle almost caught her in the eye. If he simply told her to stop, she wouldn't. He wondered where Neil thought she was.

"Anything?" he asked, when she sat in his car to check.

"Emma," she said. "She said, 'How's it there?'" Jess squinted over at him. "Do you want me to reply?"

"Nah," Malcolm said. "Anything else?"

"Roddy. Wants to know if he left his headphones at the bar. He said they'd be next to the register."

"Oh my God that kid. What else?"

"Mary. Wants to know where your Mom is. She's not answering the landline at home."

"Can you write back? Tell her she's fine. Tell her she's staying with a neighbor. Ask her if she remembers Artie Sheridan. Ask her if she remembers when his wife died."

"Gail's staying with Artie Sheridan?" Jess asked. "That's interesting."

"Is it?"

"You don't think so? Come to think of it I stopped by there once and he was in the kitchen heating soup. She was upstairs and he called up to tell her I was there and that the soup was ready." Jess looked at the sky. "I never thought about that until right now."

"When was that?"

"Two or three years ago I guess."

"They're friends. Good friends."

"He's attractive for a man his age."

"Aren't they kind of old for that?"

"Gail in her old bras that make her boobs pointy. Her big underwear."

"Please."

"I can see it. I'm being serious right now, I really can. I'm happy for her."

"But she's been so forgetful. Have you noticed? The other day she said something as if she expected my dad home soon."

"I've noticed. Here and there. But, I don't know. Last week I spent five minutes looking for my phone and it was in my hand the whole time."

"I think this is different and Artie Sheridan isn't going to sign on for that," Malcolm said. "Why would he?"

"Maybe he loves her. Maybe he's loved her for a long time and we never knew."

Was it possible? Malcolm wondered. The way he looked over at her and her crazy hair that she could never make lie flat the way the other mothers managed to do. Her button-down shirts that she bought in the men's section at Costco. The way he shook his head to signal Malcolm that he knew better, her chimney had not malfunctioned, but it was okay because he was there to set things right.

After an hour or so the driveway was mostly clear. In the distance came the sound of steady beeping, growing louder as it moved toward them.

"It's just the plow," Malcolm said, as he looked down the street.

But behind the big town plow with its flashing orange lights was a police car. And following the police car was an unmarked SUV.

"Oh," Jess said, suddenly pale. They left an ember behind without realizing. The place had lit up despite their change of heart. It was astonishingly dumb. One look at their financials and anyone with a brain would be suspicious. Malcolm immediately saw how guilty he would look, a fire just after they discovered Tripp was staying upstairs.

The cars stopped at the end of their driveway. The plow stopped, too, and Jess was soothed by the sheer racket of it combined with the roar of the Colemans' generator. It felt like a physical barrier, like the drivers of these vehicles would actually have to press their hands to their ears to see her and Malcolm clearly.

"How you doin?" Malcolm called over, when it was clear theirs was the house they were aiming for.

Jess recognized the female officer from around. The other two were trailing behind her, one of whom looked young enough to be in college. Malcolm shouted something to the driver of the plow, and next thing the beeping stopped. Immediately, Jess felt exposed. As the men in the SUV approached, she heard the female officer tell Malcolm that they were federal agents.

"This is my wife," Malcolm told the group as Jess came up beside him. He glanced at her quickly as if to say if there was a different word for what she was to him, then he didn't know it.

They had questions about Charles Waggoner, who still had not turned up, and Jess felt relief wash over her. "Who's that?" she asked, but Malcolm said he'd fill her in later.

"Did you ever confirm he was on that second flight?" Malcolm asked. "To Panama?" The agents ignored the question, and the local cops looked a bit sheepish, like maybe they shouldn't have told him so much. The two Feds asked how often Tripp came to the bar, whom he spoke with, his drinking habits, topics he went to, if he met friends there, if he ever talked about his job, if he ever talked about financial trouble, if he ever talked about a particular stress he was under or a decision he had to make.

"Sorry, but no," Malcolm said. "I already told them"—Malcolm nodded at the three local cops collectively—"that he talked about how much he hated living around here, the routine of work eat sleep repeat, you know, who doesn't feel like that? And that he seemed to have a dream of living in Peru. But specifics about work? No, nothing."

They looked at him as if he might say more. Eventually, the shorter of the two offered a detail. "His partner was arrested this morning."

"Okay."

"If you were in touch with Charles—"

"I'm not in touch with him. He drinks at my bar sometimes. He was there on Friday. That's it."

"Wasn't he staying at your bar? Upstairs?"

"Well, we found some stuff." Malcolm looked at Jackie to help him out, but she gave him a look that said she couldn't. "But I don't know if it was his. I never go up there, which I guess someone knew.

"And also, I'm sorry," Malcolm said. "But he just didn't seem savvy enough to disappear. I always had the impression that he was pretty good at his job, which might seem crazy given that you're probably here to arrest him. And he was a know-it-all about some things, yes. But this stuff about checking in remotely and taking a flight north to go south, I just don't buy it. There was this one time, he was complaining about his phone's battery life and I told him to try closing all his windows and apps. He asked me how to do that. When I took his phone, there were like two zillion windows open. He said he'd never closed one, not once, ever."

Malcolm paused. "Some guys would be sort of defensive because no one likes feeling dumb or out of date or whatever. Especially a guy like him who was heading up a big company. Most guys like that would be like, 'Oh, I kept those windows open on purpose, I love having a bazillion pages open on my phone.'"

Jackie laughed.

"But Tripp just said technology wasn't his thing and thanked me for figuring it out. And trust me, if I know more about phones than he did, that's saying a lot."

"He had help," the agent said. "For sure he had help. Which is why we're here."

The agent walked to his car to get something and while they were distracted, Jackie whispered to Malcolm, "He looked into renting an apartment in Panama City. A company ran a credit check on him. He also looked into opening a Panamanian bank account."

When the agent returned, he held out a driver's license. "Do you recognize this man? We think he and Charles probably connected at the bar."

Malcolm took the license from him, brought it close. An instinct kicked in and he made his face a blank, the face that drove Jess crazy.

"The photo is pretty small." He could feel Jess at his side, also looking. The name on the license said Mark Duro. Tripp's insurance beneficiary. An address about an hour upstate from Gillam.

"Duro has a bunch of social media accounts. When you search his name you see references to past employment, a charity 5k he ran. But no photos. His profile pic on most accounts is some famous temple in Japan. The interesting thing is that one of the accounts—the Facebook page—liked a post about the Half Moon a few months ago. A Halloween party."

"Really," Malcolm said. He brought the license closer still, as if he could communicate to the face in the photograph, as if he could speak to him in his mind. Roddy. His hair slicked back. A dress shirt. Glasses. But it was Roddy. His heart was hammering. Jess was leaning on him hard. He handed her the license.

"If it's fake it's a very good one," one of the agents said. "It was in a drop box he rented at UPS."

"Do you recognize the man on the driver's license?" Jackie asked, looking back and forth between him and Jess. "Would you remember seeing him on Halloween?"

"I don't think so," Malcolm said. He thought quickly. If they found out it was Roddy and that he worked at the Half Moon, then Malcolm would ask how they could expect him to identify a face when he was worried about the bar, and when his estranged wife was standing beside him, a fact that anyone would confirm. He had bigger things on his mind. And the Roddy he knew didn't look anything like the one in that photo. He made a mistake.

"You sure?"

Malcolm shrugged. "Sorry."

"How about you?" she asked Jess.

She shook her head. "No, me neither. But I'm not at the bar much."

Malcolm didn't dare look at her.

He thought of Roddy clutching his phone, posting the Halloween party on five different social media platforms in under ten seconds. He was always looking at the thing, ordering this or that, figuring out new apps. He wasn't dumb, his uncle had emphasized. He just didn't seem to know how to apply himself. He remembered Roddy on Friday night, walking off into the storm in his ratty running sneakers, declining a lift because he preferred to walk.

Mrs. Tyrell from a few houses down came outside in her bathrobe and snow boots to yell at the driver of the plow, to ask if he was aware that he had taken out her mailbox on the last go-around, said the town should reimburse people for that, what a pain in the ass, her husband had sunk the post in concrete and now it was splinters, he'd have to dig the whole thing up.

None of them could hear the driver's response, but his arm hung limply from the window of the cab, and whatever he said made Mrs. Tyrell even more angry.

"We need you to call us if you remember anything else," the taller of the two agents said as he handed Malcolm his card. As the group broke up, the local officers made a plan to go eat. They mentioned two diners that were open as of that morning, and Malcolm made note of which one they decided on. Rob begged off, said he had to touch base with his mother and sisters about everything that was going on.

As they made their way to their cars, Mrs. Tyrell called over to Malcolm and Jess. "Am I right? Ridiculous the way they operate these plows. You guys don't have any damage?" When the Tyrell boys still lived at home, the whole neighborhood used to hear her yelling at them.

Then she shaded her eyes and called over, "Is that you, Jess?" and began making her way up the driveway.

"Dear God," Jess muttered as Malcolm said, "Christ."

"How are you, honey? I haven't seen you in so long!" Her long, bottle-red hair looked like it hadn't seen a brush since the first snowstorm. "Want to come down to my house and sit by the heater? Have a visit? Jimmy has the kitchen snug as a bug. I can make you a cup of coffee? It's just Nescafé in the saucepan but it's hot."

Malcolm waited for Jess to say no, to find an excuse. She looked exhausted, battle worn, pale. He thought of her at the hospital that time, the worst time, her legs in stirrups, the green of the paper gown harsh against her skin. How she looked beyond sad, like she had no life left, no fight. She didn't speak. She didn't cry. He saw her notice the tray of tools the physician's assistant rolled in, saw her glance at them once more when the doctor came in a moment later.

But instead she said, "I'd love that. Give me a minute."

"Really?" Malcolm said when Mrs. Tyrell was out of earshot.

Jess shrugged. "Sure. Why not?"

"If I go see about Roddy." Malcolm tried to think of how best to put it. "Will you be here when I get back?"

"You think that's smart? Going straight to Roddy? Can you explain all of this to me please? Don't say it's nothing."

"I will. I swear. But not now."

Backing out of his driveway, he realized she never answered his question.

He tried to remember where exactly Roddy lived. He knew it was in one of the apartments where the railroad tracks crossed the creek, but which? It was not nice over there. People piled junk on their balconies, and the natural shingle that had probably looked fresh thirty years earlier was now black with weather. A big OxyContin dealer had recently been arrested from there; his name and mug shot went out over the local patch.

Once he got to the parking lot, Malcolm texted Roddy, asked him to come outside if he was home. Three dots came up as if Roddy was typing a reply, but in the meantime Malcolm looked up, saw someone come to the window on the second floor.

You there? Malcolm texted, and the figure stepped back. I'm coming up, he wrote.

Upstairs, the hallway smelled like cats and mildew. He knocked on the door he estimated to be the right one but heard movement in the apartment next door, so he moved down one door and knocked again. He leaned forward and could hear breathing on the other side.

"You might as well open up," he said.

The locks slid, a chain was drawn aside, the door opened.

"Oh, hey, Malcolm," Roddy said, his hair the usual mess. He was wearing a long wool coat with a blanket draped around him like a shawl. "You didn't have to drop them off."

"Drop what off?"

"My headphones?"

"That's not why I'm here."

Roddy stared at him.

"Have you eaten?" Malcolm asked, glimpsing the chaos of Roddy's apartment. "I heard Slice of Life is open. Let's go see if they'll seat us."

If it occurred to Roddy that he could decline, that Malcolm was not the school principal, not his dad, he showed no sign. He followed Malcolm to his car. They drove to the diner in silence, parked between two utility trucks. There was a coffee station outside for utility workers to refill their travel mugs, and the line extended to the edge of the parking lot. Inside, it was warm. Malcolm greeted Sebastian, the owner, made small talk for a minute, and then asked if he could get a table. Once seated, Sebastian waved over a waitress who was circling with a pot of coffee. They put in their orders so she wouldn't have to come back. Malcolm waited until the waitress walked away before he spoke.

"Roddy," he said, sitting square to the kid. "Do you remember the guy giving us trouble on Friday night?"

"Yeah," Roddy said, and Malcolm could see caution pass over his face. Like an animal he felt another animal circling. "Tripp."

"It's the craziest thing. No one has seen him since then. I've now talked to the police four different times in—" He looked at his wrist. "Five days. Turns out he was in big trouble with the SEC, probably about to be arrested. Do you know why I'm mentioning all of this to you?"

Roddy placed his spoon carefully next to his coffee and pushed the saucer away.

"The cops know someone helped him, and now they have a driver's license with a photo of that guy," Malcolm continued.

"They do?"

"Oh yes. They showed it to me not even an hour ago."

"I should have known you wouldn't come all the way over just to return my headphones."

"Where is he? Panama or something? And how much of whatever this is got dreamed up at the Half Moon? Do I need to worry? Because I'm a little worried."

Roddy looked surprised. "Is that where they think he is? Panama?"

"Yeah. It sounds like he rented an apartment there. He tried to open a bank account, and he used his passport as identification. For a guy who wants to disappear, he's not that good at it. He used his real name."

"Wow," Roddy said. "They know about the bank account already? That's really good."

Malcolm had already lied to the cops once. That one could be explained away, but another lie and he could be charged with a crime. He knew it, but it was hard to think that way with Roddy sitting across from him looking as he always did, so helpless, so guileless. When he hired him, Malcolm had promised Roddy's uncle that he'd look out for him, but he hadn't, clearly, and now he was in this mess. Tripp had dragged him into something he probably didn't understand.

"How in the world is that good?"

Roddy hesitated. "First tell me how they found the license. Tripp was supposed to leave that in our spot."

"Where's your spot?"

Roddy rubbed his chin.

The waitress appeared at their table with more coffee, told them their food would be out shortly. Once she moved on, Roddy said, "I guess I can tell you since you already saw the license."

"Yeah I would think so."

"Don't be mad. It's at the Half Moon. Was. Upstairs. Nothing's there now, don't worry. No one ever goes up there. Tripp couldn't have it at home in case his wife found it."

"Where upstairs?"

"In the bathroom vent. The cover pops right off."

"You're joking."

Roddy shrugged. "Sorry."

"The cops saw Tripp's stuff."

"When? Did they see papers? Or a laptop?"

"No, just a bag. Clothes. Some books." Malcolm had so many questions it was hard to know which one to begin with. "They found the license in a box he rented at UPS."

"Ah," Roddy said.

"What's the plan here? You really thought you were going to pull this off with a fake license?"

Roddy stared at him for a moment. The waitress came over with their food. Bacon and eggs for Malcolm, chocolate chip pancakes for Roddy. When she walked away, Roddy asked, "You think I'm dumb, don't you?"

"What? No. Why would you ask that?"

Roddy shrugged. "Did you tell them?"

"Tell them what?"

"That it's me. The license."

What was with this kid that made Malcolm so annoyed. Yes I think you're dumb, he thought, but then he remembered the feeling in his belly when he watched the thin strand of smoke curl up toward the basement ceiling, Jess reaching for a second match.

"No."

"Are you going to tell them?"

Malcolm hesitated. "No."

"Why?"

"Trust me, I do not know."

Roddy dropped his chin and let out a long sigh. "Thank you," he said. "So tell me."

Something sparked in Roddy, a confidence Malcolm had never seen. "Mark Duro has pay stubs, tax returns going back ten years, a lease, his own company, a retirement account, a social security number, a passport. It took forever. Tripp picked up the license from my guy last week. I guess he put it in his box for safekeeping."

Malcolm gaped at him. "Look, Tripp's partner has already been arrested. You have to figure out how to bail out of this. How did it even start?"

"He approached me just a few weeks after I started working at the Half Moon. A year and a half ago I guess. I had a really bad night. You know that regular Emma calls Limp Bizkit? He called me a faggot when I asked him to settle up. He threw a fifty in my face."

"I didn't know that," Malcolm said. "I would have banned him."

"You would have banned him?" Roddy smirked. "I don't think so. You would have told me to deal." And Malcolm realized he was right. He thought about how Bridget regularly cried in the walk-in and he never made her feel bad about it. Was Roddy allowed to cry in the walk-in, too?

"He threw the money in my face but it fell on the ground and I had to come around the bar to pick it up. It was embarrassing."

Malcolm felt chastened but wasn't sure what to say.

"Me and Tripp got to talking. He seemed disappointed that his son ended up a local cop. It was important to him that I knew he earned a lot of money and that he'd started with nothing. I didn't mind listening. He asked me what I'm going to do with my life, if I'm going to stick around Gillam. He warned me about getting tied down, how one little decision might mean I'm trapped. I told him about my idea for an app. But what do I do with an idea? I can't call up Apple. I have to build it, but my mom won't help after everything that went down at school. And my uncle has helped enough."

All around them, thanks to the warmth of the diner, people had removed their jackets and coats for the first time in days, and there was a vague scent of bodies needing to be washed.

"Anyway. I'm good at research. Tripp wanted to disappear because of something to do with work, and he didn't love his wife anymore, and he said his kids are all on her side about everything. But to disappear you need a plan. You need a whole system that closes up on itself after every move. And you need money unless you're okay with living rough for a while. Tripp isn't the kind of guy who'd take a job that doesn't require papers. He isn't going to sweep streets."

Roddy's uncle was right. The boy was smart. "I hope he paid you cash up front, because I think the Feds are about to arrest him."

"I plan to take my fee before I pass his money on to him. He can't rob me because it comes to me first."

Malcolm felt dread spring up in his gut, and a slow dawning that the way things looked was not the way things were.

"Is he in Toronto, Roddy?"

"No."

Roddy looked at Malcolm with such clear-eyed seriousness. "I like Tripp, but I don't trust him. I mean, look at what he's doing to his family. I met his wife once. She seems like a nice lady. She raised their kids, stayed home with them, and he seems to think nothing of that, like it wasn't work. I don't know what he's so mad at everyone about. He wanted to just pay me a fee at first, half up front and half when it was all done. But I didn't believe I'd ever get it. And I need this money to live on while I build this app."

Roddy swirled his last sip of coffee around the bottom of his cup. Malcolm was shocked at the recklessness of it but also, at the bottom of that, impressed. There was far more to Roddy than he thought.

"What's the app?"

"You really want to know?"

"Yes."

"Well." He tried to boil it down. "It knows your mood and predicts your patterns before you realize you're in a mood or have a pattern. It takes in your searches, your social media—everything from the amount of time you scroll, to the pages you pause at, to the speed at which you click. It listens to your conversations, reads your messages. It can tell how much you've sat still or stood or walked in a given day. Based on all that data—and it gets smarter over time—it will start sending you messages after about a month of use. If I build it right, it will be like advice from a trusted friend. Don't have that drink. It's okay to skip your spin class. Don't cancel lunch with Becky because you need the social interaction. People will be shocked that the app knows what they're thinking of doing before they've even really admitted it to themselves."

"You can build something like that?"

"Yeah. I think so. But now the problem is there's already an app that's similar. Not quite the same but enough to make me nervous. I'm sure there are more in development. I have to get going on this. Like I said, I need time and I need money. I've been thinking about it for about three years now."

"And that's where Tripp came in. So he's in Panama?" Malcolm wished none of it implicated the Half Moon, but his curiosity was too strong. If he was going to lie, he wanted to know what he was lying about.

Roddy hesitated. "Not exactly. But—"

"But?"

"If things go as planned, in about three days there's going to be a car accident in Panama City. There will be a fire. Charles Waggoner's body will be so burned up that they'll have to identify him by the papers left behind at his hotel room."

Malcolm remembered a late-night documentary he saw once. Part of it was about the black market for dead bodies, how people trying to really disappear could arrange the purchase of a corpse approximately the same size, age, and gender, set things up to look like an accident, and next thing you have a death certificate for a trusted loved one to present to your life insurance carrier.

"Then where is he really?"

"I don't think I should tell you."

"You've already told me this much."

Watching Roddy decide, Malcolm saw that he wanted to tell him— that he'd probably been wanting to talk to someone about all of it for a long time.

"You think I'll get in trouble? Is that it? Don't worry about me," Malcolm said.

"He's in Peru."

Malcolm slapped the table. "I knew it. He loves that place. He talked about it all the time."

"He did?" That was the first thing that seemed to alarm Roddy.

"Yes. And I told the cops so. Every time he got lit he'd talk about whatsitcalled. Ollan—"

"—taytambo. Shit. I didn't know that."

"So he's going from Panama to Peru?"

"No. He was never in Panama. Or Toronto for that matter. He flew directly to Lima yesterday morning, just a few hours before the second storm. He used his new passport." Before Malcolm could ask, Roddy answered the question on his mind. "He stayed upstairs at the bar on Friday night. That's why no one saw him leave. He just went up through that door by the men's room. Late Saturday I drove him to a hotel in Secaucus. He stayed there until he left for the airport on Tuesday."

"So who packed up his stuff from the Half Moon?"

"I did."

"But the passenger list for that Toronto flight had him on it."

"Come on, Malcolm. You know that there's always someone who'll do what you need them to if you have the money to pay them."

Malcolm looked at his plate, the food grown cold. He picked up his fork and slowly ate every morsel before he spoke again. He signaled the waitress to refill his coffee.

"Roddy. You know you can't ever claim that life insurance money. Right now you're just an accessory to Tripp's mess, but if you claim that money, you're as guilty as he is. You get that, right? Stay up in Binghamton with your mom for a while. Get a job there. You were never Mark Duro. You want a bartending job? I have a buddy in Ithaca who's always looking for help. You want to go down to Miami and bartend there? I have a friend with a place in Coral Gables. I'll put a word in. But honestly? You're not a bartender. Get a job at a cool store or something. You're only twenty-two years old."

"What would be a cool store?" Roddy looked at him with the same expression he wore the night the urinal got pulled out. Overwhelmed, as if he might cry.

"I don't know. But you're a smart kid. Why don't you go back to school? You can still build the app."

"What does it matter? Being smart?" Roddy asked. "You need way more than that. My uncle paid the first semester of college and my mother was supposed to take it from there, but she kept trying to get me to ask him for the money and he'd already done so much for me. The bursar was calling me every day. Like, oh sure, I have seventeen thousand dollars rolled up in a coffee can or something. I got a job with a skip tracer to make some cash. When I learned how it worked, I took a few clients of my own. I liked it. I could do the whole job from my dorm room. I once found a guy who was delinquent for child support by tracking down his loyalty card at a tackle shop. All his ex said was that he loved fishing. But then—"

"What?"

"There's the flip side. You get some really bad guys looking for their wives or girlfriends. And I could find them. You know? I could see how hard a woman tried to cover her tracks, but it was so easy. I didn't like that. One guy, he just seemed evil. I wanted to reach out to the woman to warn her that she was way too easy to find, and to help her. I never told that guy that I found her."

They both looked out the window at the dark space under the highway overpass. Kids drank there in the warm months, and there was a collection of broken bottles and crushed cans pushed against one of the pilings. A bright red cardinal alighted on a plow's blade, and Malcolm watched it look around for a moment before it flew away.

"Are you okay?" Roddy asked.

Malcolm felt so incredibly tired.

"I really don't know. Are you?"

Roddy shrugged. "Same I guess. The bar's not doing great, is it?"

"No it isn't. But promise you'll drop this thing. Will you? It's insane."

"He really talked about Ollantaytambo? How dumb. He never told me that. I told him to go to Cambodia or Vietnam, but he wouldn't hear it. He said his heart was in Peru."

"Yes. Even if it takes a little while, I know they're going to figure that out."

When Malcolm got home the house was empty. Jess left a note to say she was at her mother's but to call her because she wanted to hear what was going on with Roddy. The utility trucks had finally made it to their street; the linemen were up in buckets, working on the wires. Malcolm didn't want to ask them what everyone else had been asking, but one of them called out his name, took off his hard hat. Malcolm recognized him from the bar.

"Lights on within the hour," he said.

"Thank God," Malcolm said. "You guys must be beat."

"Loving the overtime," he said. "My wife is already pricing a trip to Turks."

"Why not," Malcolm said. "You've earned it."

"Yeah," the man said as he looked up the street. "Listen, there was a guy parked in your driveway for a bit. Asked if I'd seen you."

"Okay."

"He didn't say who he was or what he wanted."

Billy, Malcolm knew.

When the power returned, it was a click and then a surge, and everything came alive at once. The microwave clock flashed. The oven showed an error message and the refrigerator started purring. He stood in the kitchen for a minute, and then he turned right around and left.

—————

"Hey, Ma," he said, standing at Mr. Sheridan's door.

His mother invited him in like it was her house.

"I can't, the car's running. I just wanted to see if you're okay."

"Artie went over to check on the house," she said. "He went to see about the smoke."

"Oh good," Malcolm said. She was wearing the same clothes she'd worn the day before, but what had she worn to bed? Her hair was twisted up, pinned in some complicated way, but a fringe still stood straight above her forehead like a tiara.

"You look exhausted, Malcolm."

"Listen, Mom," he said. "The bar isn't doing so well. You might as well know that. I feel like a huge loser and I don't know why I didn't tell you sooner. I just don't know what's going to happen."

"What? Would you please come in? Come in here this minute and don't say that."

"I have to go see Jess. I'm sorry. We'll talk later. I'll come by. I promise."

"Jess is back? Okay, but, Mal? Honey? You could never be a loser. I just said to Artie that something's wrong with Malcolm. I know everything with Jess and all that, but I said to Artie it's more than that, he's not himself at all."

"Hi, Maureen," he said when he got to Jess's mother's house.

"Malcolm," Maureen said, solemn as a funeral director. She kissed him on the cheek and then she hugged him tight, something she'd never done before. "Come in. You want something to eat? You have power? Ours just came back."

When he walked into the kitchen, he found Jess sitting at the table spreading jam on a piece of toast. Her hair was wet, and she was wearing the same Gillam High School sweats she'd worn to breakfast the first time he stayed over.

"Malcolm," she said, astonished, as if he'd traveled a thousand miles and not four blocks. She jumped up to take a stack of magazines off a chair, but he refused to sit.

"Are you staying here tonight, Jess? Or coming home? I thought I'd check since you don't have your car." He sounded gruff. Formal. He could hear it in his voice, but he couldn't take it back.

Jess looked at her mother, but Maureen Ryan was slowly backing up toward the stairs. A moment later they heard a door click closed up there.

"What do you want me to do?" Jess asked.

"What do you want to do?"

Had she called Neil? Had she filled him in?

"I want to come home."

He nodded. Good. That was good. He sat heavily. He leaned over his knees. He felt her hand on his back.

"Malcolm," she whispered. "I'm so sorry."

"Then come home," he said.

eleven

Malcolm got through the Thursday birthday party he'd booked—the power came back on at the bar in the nick of time—but André couldn't make the appetizers the group had picked because their supplier was delayed by the double storms. "I can run up to Food King," he offered. And when the whole staff looked at Malcolm, waiting to hear what he'd say, he realized they'd known for a very long time how precarious things were. It was one thing for him to live like that, but they had families and lives, too. "Good idea," he said, plucking two twenties from his wallet. How much did a few boxes of frozen pigs in a blanket cost? Malcolm worried Billy would show up, but he didn't, and it ended up being a decent night. There was a lot of laughing, in any case, and the group stayed late. Roddy didn't show.

"Has anyone heard from him?" Malcolm asked, but no one had, not since the previous Friday, the night of the first storm. Malcolm hoped that meant he'd heeded his advice and taken off.

When they were closing, Malcolm told Emma he'd be out of town for a day or two, so she'd be in charge. He was sorry to leave her stranded on a weekend. "Not that you'll be running," he said. A joke, but it had no mirth behind it.

"You never know," she said. A kindness.

It was a plan that had formed that very hour, as he was cleaning up after the party and trying to figure out what to do. He couldn't wait around for Billy to show up at his house, not with Jess back home, not with things feeling like they might get better now. Surely, he had a card to play, if only he could come up with it. He had to see Hugh face-to-face.

"If something else comes along for you," he added. "Any of you. I—"

"Hey," Emma said. "You think I'd stay if I didn't want to be here? That any of us would? No."

The next morning, Friday, a full week after the first storm, Malcolm drove Jess to the city to pick up her stuff from Cobie's. While Malcolm waited in his car, Cobie tapped on his window and said she just wanted to say hello. She'd been walking the dog when she spotted him.

"Hey," he said, slightly embarrassed when he remembered the last time they'd spoken. "Glad to have your guest bedroom back?" he asked.

She smiled. "I'd forgotten how much space she takes up for someone so skinny. How many sweatshirts does one straight woman need?"

Malcolm relaxed. It was fine. Cobie didn't think he was a jerk. She said she'd like to visit sometime soon. Malcolm said they'd like that, anytime, he knew how much Jess loved Cobie's boys, and he hadn't seen Astrid in ages.

"It'll take a while, probably," Cobie said. "Day by day right?"

"Right," Malcolm said. It was something he'd noticed himself. He was so happy to have her home, so completely relieved, that he was confused about why it also made him feel like something he'd been wanting to say had been muffled. Like they'd gone through so much, the worst period of his life, and within twenty-four hours old patterns were already emerging. Malcolm put an empty box of cereal back in the cabinet. Jess left her sneakers on the stairs where one of them would trip on them and break their neck. They were both swallowing all those petty domestic grievances, but neither one had any doubt that they'd return. And then what?

What did all the heartbreak get them if not a little wisdom? She wanted to ask him if he forgave her, he knew she did. But it wasn't a question he could answer, most likely for a very long time. Had she forgiven him?

Patrick was almost as shocked at Jess's return home as he'd been by her departure. "She's back in the house? You're back together?" he was incredulous. Before Malcolm could answer, he added: "*Why?*"

And then he said sorry, but it just didn't make sense. They didn't have kids. There was no reason to stay together. And then he apologized again.

Why? Malcolm thought. It was a good question. Another one he couldn't answer.

"By the way," Patrick added. "Me and Siobhán, all of us, no one is talking to Neil. I had no idea—"

"I know, I know," Malcolm said. Day by day, like Cobie said. Eventually, the burden they were carrying would become lighter.

"I did things, too," Malcolm said. "Things that hurt Jess."

"But not that," Patrick said. "No way would you have ever done that."

Jess drove straight to Neil's after they dug out her car. Malcolm didn't offer to go with her, though she saw the thought cross his mind when she said she'd see him at home later. She squeezed his arm to remind him that there was no reason to worry.

Neil answered the door with a cold expression, and for a moment she thought he might not let her inside. He followed her around as she gathered her things, and told her it was stupid to go back to Malcolm, that she'd already done the hard part by leaving, it didn't make any sense, that maybe she didn't want to be happy, did she ever think of that, that she was making a huge mistake. He told her he guessed he was wrong about her. He thought she was a smart, levelheaded woman who'd married a man below her and out of loyalty and kindness had stayed with him far too long but in fact she was a drama-seeking woman just like his ex, just like all women, maybe, and he guessed she didn't care whom she hurt in her pursuit of attention. She was just another woman panicking about middle age and trying to grasp one last high, and that high had come at his expense. At the expense of his children, who'd gotten to know her.

And then he said he didn't mean it, he just didn't understand. But she didn't quite understand either. It was just something she knew. It was time to go home. She was truly, deeply sorry.

He told her that no one would ever love her like he did. She wanted to say that she agreed, but that it wasn't relevant. No two people ever loved each other the same way. It was the kids she'd miss the most, though she didn't say that, either, because it would hurt him for no reason. And it wasn't even that she'd miss the real, actual kids but rather the idea of them. If she stayed, she'd become a fixture in their lives.

He told her to go, he didn't care, get the hell out. And then he tried to put his body close to hers and persuade her to stay. But that had lost all power over her, too, and she wanted to cry when she realized how lost she must have felt only a few short weeks ago. Everything about him that was different from Malcolm repulsed her now, and it had happened overnight. His build, the way he smelled, the texture of his skin. It wasn't his fault, but it wasn't her fault either. She missed Malcolm so much that she felt it in her muscles, in her blood.

"Now things are going to be so weird with Patrick," Neil said.

"*Now* they'll be weird with Patrick?" She couldn't help herself: she laughed. The kids were back at school, finally, after so many days at home, and Jess considered leaving something behind for the girls—a lipstick or a necklace. But in the end she decided it would be best to clear out completely, to leave no trace.

While Jess was at Neil's, Malcolm drove over to Hugh's house in Gillam, but no one was there. He flagged down a neighbor and asked if he'd seen

Hugh lately, if he knew his address down south, but the man said the only people he ever saw at the Lydons' anymore were the landscapers and they hadn't been by since November. He went by Little Hughie's house next—a huge, plastic-looking monstrosity—but no one answered the door. He drove home and called a few of the regulars who'd been coming to the Half Moon since Malcolm started there, but all of them assumed if anyone knew Hugh's new address it would be Malcolm. He realized how little he knew about Hugh, how little he'd ever known. The few times he met Mrs. Lydon were when she came to the bar to decorate for Christmas. He'd never been to their home or to their family parties, and they'd never been to his. He was staring into space at his own counter when he heard something outside. His mother. She was leaving a box of donuts on the step.

"Oh, hi, sweetie," she said when he opened the door. "I didn't want to bother you guys."

"That's okay, Jess isn't here."

His mother handed him the box, and he asked her if by any chance she knew of anyone who was friendly with the Lydons. Someone who might have kept in touch after they moved. The Lydons were around the same age as his mother, after all. They must have had friends who had nothing to do with Hugh's businesses.

"A woman in my gardening club is good friends with Josephine," she said.

"Really? Can you get their South Carolina address for me?"

"I can try," she said. "Is everything okay?"

"Yeah everything's fine. Just bar stuff."

"Everything's fine? The other day, you told me the bar's not doing well, and you said you'd come back and we'd chat. But you never came back."

"I know. Sorry. There's so much going on right now and—"

"I want to ask you something and I want you to tell me the truth. I'm your mother, Malcolm, and I'll know immediately if you tell me a lie."

261

"Okay."

"Is Hugh Lydon holding the note on the Half Moon?"

Malcolm didn't answer.

"Why didn't you ever tell me?"

"I don't know."

"Malcolm, your dad and Hugh had a history. Did Hugh ever tell you that? I don't know all the details but I know it was a big thing. You and Little Hughie were only babies. I used to think that was why he took you under his wing when your father died, maybe to make up for something, but now—" She shrugged.

"What was it? Do you want to come in?"

"I can't. I'm meeting Artie at Pappy's. They'll give us a free glass of wine with our pasta if we're seated by five."

Standing on his cold step with her knit hat pulled down to her eyebrows, the bright white snow made her eyes a vivid blue. Her hands were red.

"You need gloves, Mom."

"I'm fine," she said, and shoved her hands deep into her coat pockets. "I only know parts of it because you know how your dad was, and it was a long time ago. I never told you because it was ancient history and you were doing well at the Half Moon, earning a living at least. And when you bought it, I assumed you were done with Hugh. From what I gathered back then, Hugh made a big bet. A really dumb bet, and everyone knew about it. He used to show up at Gephardt's every once in a while and get really lit, who knows why, little kids at home made him nuts maybe. He'd opened the Half Moon but you can't really get drunk in your own bar, as you know. Anyway, he lost the bet, but they worked it out. That's what your dad always said about everything. 'We worked it out.'"

"Dad let him welch."

"Not a chance. No. He couldn't! That's just not how it worked. If he let him welch next thing everyone who owed him would think they could just walk away. I don't know what agreement they came to, but all I know is after it settled, he told Hugh to never show his face at Gephardt's again. And as far as I know, he never did."

Malcolm took it in, tried to make this young, stupid version of Hugh fit with the Hugh he knew.

"The Lydons lived a few blocks from us back then. Their house was so pretty and Josephine was proud. She invited a bunch of women over for sandwiches when they wallpapered their kitchen. Darren didn't like mixing worlds and he hated that Hugh used to drink down at Gephardt's sometimes. He didn't like that Josephine was sort of my friend. He kept certain parts of his business away from me and I didn't like to think about it too much if I'm being honest. But I know he wouldn't have wanted to ruin someone so close to home, kids in the same school. Our marriage was different from yours. I wasn't as clueless as Josephine, but Darren and I didn't talk much about work."

"So how'd they settle it? Hugh must have paid up somehow."

"I don't know. Honestly. I'd tell you."

Two hours later, the box of donuts still taped closed on the counter, she called. "I got the address. Do you have a pen?"

Malcolm wrote it down.

"And will you have Jess call me as soon as she gets home? I thought of something and I want to talk to her."

"About what?"

"About none of your business. I've missed her. I want to say hello."

Jess said she was coming with him. He didn't want her to at first, but when he thought of her home alone and Billy coming around, he agreed.

Two round-trip plane tickets would cost a fortune on such short notice, so they took fifteen minutes to gather a few things and then they drove through the night. She had to do a little work, she said, and connected something to her laptop to get an internet connection. After a rest stop where she made a few calls while pacing the refrigerated section of a Quik Mart, she moved to the backseat, and every time he looked in the rearview mirror, she was staring at her laptop or out the window.

"Okay to play music?" Malcolm asked.

"Yes, of course, sorry," she said. She climbed over the armrest into the front passenger seat. "I'm waiting for someone to call me back."

"At this hour?" Malcolm asked.

"A friend in records. She's doing me a favor."

Malcolm was about to ask more but just then Jess's phone rang and she put on headphones to take the call. She said something about joint tenancy, the right of survivorship. If she were still at the firm, he would assume it was a case, but it didn't quite line up with the work he imagined she did at Bloom.

The town where the Lydons lived was less than an hour from Charleston, a place Malcolm had always wanted to see but hadn't gotten to yet. Fort Sumter, the antebellum mansions, a sense of somewhere totally different. After fourteen hours in the car, they stopped at a gas station and washed up as best they could, put on fresh clothes.

"What are you going to say?" Jess asked.

"I don't know," Malcolm said.

The house was more modest than either of them expected it to be. It was nine o'clock on Saturday morning, and Hugh's Cadillac was in the driveway, a cat sitting in the shade of the bumper. By the time Malcolm turned off the engine, Hugh was standing at the door. From a distance of forty feet, he looked like any overweight old man. Why had it come to this? Malcolm wondered as he felt the long fuse of his temper ignite. Hugh could have just answered his phone, returned his call. They could have come to an agreement. But Hugh wanted him to beg, Malcolm understood. He wanted Malcolm to feel a little ridiculous. Maybe that's all he ever wanted, making Malcolm wait so long for the chance to own the bar. How long between Hugh first mentioning it and actually walking away? Twelve years of hoping and expecting it to happen any day. A place that meant so much to him that he didn't realize it was on its last legs.

"Wait here," Malcolm said.

"No way!" Jess said.

"Malcolm," Hugh said, holding the door open for them. He turned to call into the room behind him, "Josephine, look who came to see us." Neither of them seemed the least bit surprised.

"Is your phone broken, Hugh?" Malcolm said, and felt Jess press his arm.

Josephine Lydon showed them to a screened porch out back, where there were several ashtrays filled with butts. The temperature was already near seventy and muggy. Hugh settled into an armchair, and Josephine asked if anyone wanted tea. Hugh seemed heavier than he'd been in New York and had a rosy sheen on his skin. Malcolm had never before seen him in shorts, short sleeves, his dimpled joints, the coarse rust-colored hair that covered him.

"Now," Josephine said when she'd arranged muffins and teacups. She looked at Jess. "Will we leave them to it?"

"Thank you, but I'm fine here," Jess said.

"Oh," Josephine said, and looked at Hugh.

"Jess," Malcolm said.

"Malcolm," Jess said.

"It's all right," Hugh said, and Josephine disappeared somewhere inside the house. "I hear you're having some weather up there."

"The whole town lost power for almost a week and it's crazy cold, single digits. Everything is shut down. Part of the high school roof collapsed."

Jess looked back and forth between them as if to ask if they were really talking about the weather.

"But the Half Moon is okay? Didn't I tell you that place had good bones?"

Malcolm nodded, took a breath.

"I assume you're here because you can't keep up with your end of our deal. I've been in touch with Billy. I don't understand. When I stepped away, the place was doing great."

"I'm not trying to get out of anything. You know me. You know I wouldn't do that," Malcolm said. "I just thought, given how long we've known each other, if you could make the monthly payments lower, or if we renegotiated the interest. You told me that I'd get grandfathered into your vendor contracts and I took your word for it. But you must have known that would be impossible."

"You don't do your research before making an investment so big?" Hugh said. "And it's my fault that you didn't? I heard you got rid of the pool table. People loved that thing."

"It was filthy," Malcolm said. "And it took up too much room."

And then Hugh turned his attention to Jess for the first time. "I'm surprised to see you here, Jess. Aren't you living over in Azalea Estates now?"

Jess looked stunned, and her face flushed a deep red. Malcolm spoke quickly. "I was thinking we could work out a percentage of what I bring in each month. Slow months you'd get less, okay, busy months more, but you'd always get your cut and then I'd chip away at the note and you'd have income. The way it's structured now—I just can't do it. I need time to come up with a strategy to bring people in and build a little buzz. None of the usual things are working."

"Slow months I'd get nothing, is what you mean."

"I'm trying, Hugh. You'll get everything you're owed, it'll just take longer than I thought."

"Or," Hugh said. "You could sell your house. You've owned it for what? Thirteen years? Values have gone way up. There must be quite a bit of equity. That would take care of it."

"My house?" Malcolm repeated. His house wasn't part of Hugh's world. His house was Jess's domain, all her patterned throw blankets and bowls, all the vases and candles she placed around to make it look sweet. Her stacks of books. Her running pants on the drying rack. He stood up as he took in what was happening, as it sank in that he was powerless in this situation, and anything he suggested would be received with total disregard, as if no one had made the suggestion at all. Nothing mattered to Hugh. Not their long history, not the fact that he'd been his best, most loyal employee for so many years.

"You're an asshole, Hugh, you know that? I don't get what the point was. Of any of it."

"I'm sorry, but the house is your only asset. I'd never have lent you that money if you didn't have it."

"Hugh?" Jess said, but the men ignored her.

"And I'm the asshole?" Hugh went on. "You think you deserve something better than what you got? You're every bit as arrogant as your father was. You're what? Forty-five years old? You're blaming me because you don't have your life together? Hughie says you were always decent to him when you were in school together, and I appreciate that. But if one of my boys failed as miserably as you did with the Half Moon, I'd be embarrassed to know him. At least your father knew what he had to do to make a place really work."

"Hugh," Jess said again with some force. She stood, stepped in front of Malcolm. Hugh looked at her like he might look at a child who'd walked in and interrupted the adults. "Are you completely sure you were within your rights to sell the Half Moon in the first place?"

"What?" Hugh said.

Malcolm could feel the momentum that had been building skip a beat. He felt a chill, as if a ghost had come striding through.

"If I were to pull the property records right now, are you sure I wouldn't see any names except yours and Malcolm's?"

It seemed for a moment like Hugh was going to heave his giant body to standing, but instead he stayed seated, looked at Jess. "What are you talking about?"

"The land the building is sitting on."

The land, Malcolm repeated in his mind, the words becoming tactile, like something he could touch.

"What about it?" Hugh asked, but Malcolm knew that sneer. Something about what Jess was saying had him rattled.

"You signed the land over to Darren Gephardt in 1975 to make good on a debt."

"What?" Hugh asked just as Malcolm had the very same thought. *What?*

Malcolm wanted badly for her to look at him, but her eyes were locked on Hugh.

"I have no idea what you're talking about," Hugh said, glancing at the screened door to find out if Josephine was listening.

"It didn't come up in the sale probably because Malcolm didn't hire a lawyer. Things get missed, especially if an ownership structure is rare, like this one. Just yesterday I found out about a case in Manhattan where this exact thing happened. The current owner of a bar called Bluebird did a bunch of really nice renovations when he bought the place, and everything was great. But then one night he kicked out some jerk who was acting up, and that guy was embarrassed and furious. Turns out the jerk was a property lawyer—that was the owner's bad luck—so he decided to dig into the old city records to mess with the owner. And jackpot! The owner didn't own the land under his building and he had no idea. It never came up when he bought the place. The land had been sold off back in the 1980s and had its own deed. So the new owner panicked, hired a lawyer. He was furious and felt he'd been swindled, which he sort of had been. He had his lawyer track down the owner of the land to make it square. Problem was the man he bought the building from was dead and the owner of the land was dead by the time it all got figured out."

"Bluebird," Malcolm said. "I've been there."

"You want to know who owned the land?" Jess asked. Hugh stared at her. "Darren Gephardt."

"Wait," Malcolm said. "I remember going there with him."

"Right," Jess said, turning to Hugh again. "Darren gave the owner of Bluebird the same deal he gave you in the seventies. He couldn't let you welch because everyone knew about it, so he took something that wouldn't ruin or humiliate you. Gail only found out about Bluebird recently. The new owner's lawyer got in touch with her when they were tracing Darren's next of kin. I think Gail felt sorry for the guy, so she settled easily. I wish she'd told us it was happening, but she said she didn't like discussing certain aspects of your dad's businesses. Talking with Malcolm yesterday got her thinking, so she suggested I look into it."

Jess turned to Malcolm. "She didn't want to get your hopes up."

To Hugh she said, "You legally separated the land from the building in 1975."

"So what?" Hugh said. He tried on his normal bravado, but Malcolm could see he didn't quite fit.

"So here's what we're going to do," Jess said, looking back and forth between the two men. "Malcolm is going to sign that land over to you, and you're going to take the whole thing back. Land, building, business. It's all yours. But we're clear. That land is worth at least as much as what Malcolm owes you."

"Hang on, Jess," Malcolm said, pulling on his shoulder. Didn't this mean he could keep the Half Moon somehow? But the look she gave him told him to think, to unspool it all the way out.

"You're joking," Hugh said.

"You'll get your bar back without that caveat you've been hiding all these years. If you'd sold to anyone else, they probably would have discovered it. It's a good deal. You can keep it or resell it, whatever you want."

Malcolm felt he was taking everything in on a delay, two beats behind the action. Just hand over the Half Moon? Hugh appeared to be thinking about it.

"You're saying I clear your debt and take title of the land."

"Correct."

"My lawyer draws everything up."

"Sure," Jess said. She'd be ready for any funny business. "Malcolm?"

He'd walk away with nothing. Not the Half Moon, not the time and energy he'd already invested in it. Just before the first storm he'd taken a photo of his TV screen at home as he was watching a movie. The premise of the movie was dumb but the scene showed the characters seated at a rooftop just like the one he imagined. He needed a few days to think. He wanted to talk to his mother about what else she remembered about his dad and the deal he'd made with Hugh. But Jess's expression when she turned to look at him read like a plea.

"Malcolm," she said, not a question this time.

"Let me think for a second."

"Mal, please."

"Yeah okay," Malcolm agreed.

Hugh said the paperwork would be waiting for them by the time they got back to New York. The taxes would get complicated, but Jess could figure that out. They approached the exit for downtown Charleston, and Malcolm reminded her it was Saturday, they couldn't make it all the way home anyway without getting some sleep, why not make this the place they stayed? As they were driving, Malcolm asked how in the world she'd figured it out, but she gave all the credit to Gail. She'd researched, yes, she'd used her contacts, but it was Gail who had a hunch.

And the crazy part, she said, was that she hadn't been sure. Her contact in the county records office hadn't found the document she needed by the time they walked into Hugh's house. Records from the 1970s were in off-site storage and predated the electronic files. All her friend could see was a note that read "1975" and a code that indicated what box the records could be found in. So Jess just assumed that meant there was a transaction of some kind in 1975.

"You were bluffing," he said, amazed.

"But I was right." She grinned.

"Jessica Ryan!" he said, grabbing her hand as he merged onto the highway. He kissed her knuckles. He'd lost the Half Moon, but he'd regained Jess, and all of that had happened in a matter of days. It was almost too much, how quickly things could change. He wanted one day out of his own life to process everything, one day of wandering around a place where he didn't know the streets or anyone's name. Jess didn't have to be at work until Monday, and Malcolm didn't have to be anywhere, apparently. He tried to let that fact sink in, but it was impossible. They went to breakfast while they waited for their room to become available—it was only eleven in the morning after all—and could barely keep their eyes open. When they were finally allowed to check in, they immediately went to sleep.

Jess woke first, confused about where she was since it was still daylight out, and then she turned to find Malcolm sleeping on his side, facing her, his jaw slack, his hands tucked under his cheek like a little kid. She studied the graying hair at his temples, the breadth of his rib cage as it expanded and contracted with his snores. She tried to decide whether she'd ever really stopped loving him or if she'd just convinced herself that she had. She believed her love had run out because that was how it felt—a petering out over a long, long time, an exhaustion settling in the space that used to be taken up with joy, and then one day finding a thought of him stirred nothing in her, not even fury, and who was it who said the opposite of love was not hate but apathy?

But yet here she was, beside him again. She thought of what Cobie said about there being a third choice, which was being alone for a little while. That there were more choices than the ones she'd set before herself. A mere week ago she had no expectation of when she'd next see him, and here she was watching him sleep, in a hotel room eight hundred miles from home.

She stepped into the shower and when she came out, Malcolm was awake. "Hey," he said, and tugged at the edge of her towel until finally she let it fall. As they moved around each other, she tried to decide what was different, what he was holding back from her now that he'd never held back before, but there didn't seem to be anything except maybe a new seriousness, a sense that they'd come very, very close to losing each other, and also, underneath all of that, a sense that they still might, nothing was guaranteed.

Once they were dressed, they wandered until they found a restaurant that had a good vibe, as Malcolm put it, and as usual he chatted up the bartender. A band started playing almost as soon as they sat, so they didn't have to talk. After dinner they walked back to the hotel, watched a movie, slept. The next day, she spent the long drive home trying to convince him that it was a win. He'd had a job for twenty-six years, and now he was stepping away from that job, and that was it. A lot of people stepped away from their jobs after twenty-six years with nothing of the place where they'd worked all that time. He'd get something else. Without that massive pressure on them, they could pay down their debt with the clinic, their credit cards, Jess's student loans.

"We could sell our house," Malcolm said. "If you really want to talk about starting over. Hugh isn't wrong. It's worth something."

The same thought had occurred to Jess.

The paperwork was waiting for them, as promised. When Malcolm told his staff at the Half Moon that Hugh was taking over again, that the place would likely close for a while, he thought they'd be angry with him, but instead they wanted to comfort him. They all told him to let them know if he ended up opening a new place. Malcolm took a few of the framed photos that meant something to him. He told the rest of them to take what they wanted.

"What are you going to do?" Emma asked.

"I don't know," Malcolm said.

The snow melted, though enormous dirt-encased hills lasted in parking lots until late April, taking up crucial spaces at Food King, at the mall. His mother told him more of the story when he got back from South Carolina. "You were still in a playpen," she said. Gail remembered him pressing his fat cheek against the netting while Darren told her what a dumb loudmouth Hugh was and how he'd gotten himself into a situation. According to Gail, Hugh had never liked Darren and for some reason always acted like he had something to prove when he was around him.

"And did Dad like Hugh? I mean before this dumb bet?"

"Honestly, I don't think he thought anything about him at all."

Malcolm avoided driving down Seneca, but one morning he turned out of habit. Already the building was under construction—a major renovation from the looks of it—a chain-link fence circling the lot. He thought signing the place over would feel like amputating a limb, but all it had taken were five minutes and a few signatures. The land was a bit more complicated. Darren's next of kin was Gail, so it was Gail who had to sign it over. When Malcolm apologized, said he'd make it up to her, she shushed him, said if he'd only told her how he'd been struggling, she might have thought of it much sooner.

Now, several weeks after the paperwork was finalized, he pulled over to look more closely, and without realizing he was doing so, he clutched the steering wheel. He was still there, and he was still Malcolm, no matter what was becoming of the Half Moon. How had Hugh gotten plans drawn up so quickly? He made himself think of the dozen mouse-traps in the basement—the ones that smelled of rotted flesh if he didn't find them right away, and the mice that shrieked for hours until they died—and he then made himself find some gratitude that he'd never have to deal with them again.

Siobhán said to each of them separately that she was glad they'd worked it out. She said it to them together, too, one night when they were hanging out in Jess and Malcolm's backyard. A test run, as Jess described it, to see how their friends would be. She ran into a few of her other girlfriends, and most seemed a mix of nervous and sympathetic. She went for a run one morning, and a couple she knew crossed the street when they saw her, pretended to be examining a tree so they wouldn't have to look her way. On the night that Siobhán and Patrick came over, they left their kids at home with instructions that if there was an emergency to just run over to Malcolm and Jess's. Siobhán joked that there was probably already blood on the walls. Jess made stuffed jalapeños and bacon-wrapped dates, and kept jumping up to refresh drinks. They talked. They laughed. But Patrick never addressed Jess directly.

"He won't even look at me," she said to Malcolm when they passed in the kitchen.

"Well," Malcolm said, and raised his shoulders as if to ask if she could blame him.

"You said you wouldn't do that."

"Sorry. It's hard."

Later, they cleaned the dishes side by side at the sink. They'd had a nice enough time with their old friends, had a few laughs, but Jess felt grief hanging in the air among the four of them. Malcolm insisted their larger circle would come around eventually, but Jess wasn't so sure. Some friends—two to be exact—reached out to say they hoped she was okay and if she ever wanted to talk. Jenny, whose birthday Jess had been celebrating the night she and Malcolm met all those years ago, was one of them. She was divorced now, living in Toms River, and emailed to say that people having opinions about what happened even though they didn't have the first clue would be the hardest part, but that Jess should just remember that they don't know anything, it was no one's business but hers.

"Jenny," Jess whispered aloud when she read that, and it stopped her breath to think what she must have gone through to have gained that wisdom. And where had Jess been for her? Nowhere. Jenny had gotten pregnant so young. They'd drifted apart.

When they finished drying the dishes after Siobhán and Patrick left, Malcolm leaned back against the counter and looked at her. They were paying more attention to each other lately, as if all past assumptions were open to question.

"What?" she asked. It had been six weeks since she moved back in, six weeks since their trip down to South Carolina.

Malcolm's phone rang, and he glanced at the number quickly before declining.

"Who's that? Kinda late."

"Do you remember Adrian? He's called a few times."

"What does he want?"

"To catch up, I'm sure. He has a place down in St. John. Apparently it's doing pretty well."

Jess tilted her head, looked off like she did when she was thinking.

"You know?" she said. "You should call him back."

Malcolm shaped for per diem work with the sandhogs. He was a little on the old side, but he had a hook, and he appreciated the money. He liked the chumminess between the guys, but it was so vastly different from the work he was used to. There was no performance to it. No electric energy. It was just getting to the end of eight hours and then doing it again the next day. Owners of other bars who knew he was free called and offered him shifts, but he couldn't face it yet, slinging drinks in a place that wasn't his, taking his cut of the tips again like he hadn't ever held his dream in his hand. On days he didn't get work he went to the gym, got his paper and coffee, and then drove over to the Half Moon, to see how the renovation was progressing. Emma worked at a place in upper Manhattan and was dating a sommelier. André had been hired as sous chef at a place much nicer than the Half Moon. No one had heard from Roddy, and Malcolm decided no news was good news.

Sometimes, out of nowhere, he thought of Patrick's question and the astonishment in his voice when Malcolm told him that Jess had moved back in, that they were staying together: *Why?*

They heard that Neil put his house on the market. His kids would complete the school year in Gillam, but then he was moving to Westchester, to be near his mother, who would watch them after school. Jess heard it from Siobhán, who heard it from some other parents. Siobhán added that she never said hello to him if he was at pickup. She'd noticed other parents had followed suit, maybe sensing her dislike of him.

"Don't do that," Jess said as a wave of shame came over her. "Don't mobilize people against him." These waves came at moments she expected but also out of nowhere, and sometimes left her momentarily paralyzed. She was reaching for a bag of coffee beans at the grocery store one recent morning when a woman passed by pushing a cart with a boy around Ethan's age sitting up top. It hit her, what she'd done, and she withdrew her hand from the coffee like she'd been bitten. The reverberations went on and on.

Patrick said to Malcolm, "Thank God he's leaving. You won't have to worry about running into him."

"He's the one who should be worried," Malcolm said, but almost every time he went to Dunkin' or the deli or any of his usual spots, he searched for a white SUV in the lot. And if he spotted one, he kept driving.

One morning, late May, Malcolm ran into Jackie Becker at the bagel shop. She was in plainclothes, her day off, and he didn't recognize her until he lined up behind her and she turned.

"Malcolm," she said. "I was thinking of you the other day."

"Oh yeah? What's going on with the investigation? I've been curious."

She turned to face him. "You didn't hear? Charles Waggoner was killed a few weeks ago. An accident in Panama City. He was in a taxi."

Malcolm's stomach seized. "That's insane. After putting together that plan he had?"

"Exactly. The Feds have their doubts. I think Rob has his doubts, too, but the family is fighting for the insurance money, so having an actual death certificate makes it a lot easier."

"Ah," Malcolm said. "Makes sense. Seems like it would be an easy fight, no? Given all the evidence of a fraud in the making?"

"You would think so, but"—she shrugged, was looking up at the sandwich menu—"it's entirely with the Feds now, so I don't have the full story but I think it got pretty complicated once Mark Duro filed. There was a tiny window—if he'd waited another few days the case would have been flagged up the line—but he filed and got a partial payment. Apparently when a policy is beyond a certain dollar amount, they release some of it immediately and the balance a month later. So the rest is being held but, boy, he got a chunk."

"Sorry. What?"

"What what?"

"Mark Duro did what?"

"Filed his claim. Got a partial payment."

"I'm confused."

Jackie looked at him closely. "I assume he's out of the country at this point."

She leaned over the counter to order her sandwich. Malcolm tried to remember if someone told him that Roddy was staying at his mother's or if that was something he'd decided in his own mind.

"But the reason I thought of you was because I was at a rooftop bar the other weekend. There was this wall of ivy, and when I peeked around to see what it was hiding, there was this really ugly parking lot below. I thought of what you said about a rooftop bar at the Half Moon. I saw it's under construction. You going for it?"

"Oh," he said. This had been happening lately. "I sold, actually."

"Are you opening a new place?"

"I'm still figuring it out," Malcolm said, stepping forward for his food when they called his name.

But as she turned to leave, he stopped her. "Will they catch him?"

"Catch Duro?"

"Yeah."

"Honestly? I doubt it. They're interested in Duro only insofar as he might lead them to Waggoner, but from what I understand, it's cheaper for the insurance company to just eat a fraudulent claim than hire an investigator to chase a ghost all over the world. Waggoner's old partner is in prison. He insists that Waggoner is alive and probably living in Peru. They seem way more interested in that."

Walking to his car a moment later, his coffee warming his hand, he scrolled through his phone to call Roddy's uncle.

"He's traveling," the uncle said, and Malcolm heard frustration in his voice. "Backpacking through Asia. There's some famous route. I honestly don't know what to do about this kid, Mal. What's he doing with his life? He's lost. I tried to help him but he won't listen. He warned us we wouldn't hear from him for a while, but I can pass on a message when we get word?"

"No," Malcolm said. "Don't worry about it."

Management offers came in but he declined. He bartended the wedding of a friend of a friend, and they handed him a nice stack of cash at the end of the night, so he worked two more weddings. He looked at a place in Yonkers that was for sale. Another in Riverside. Both were total wrecks. He didn't even know why he'd gone to look. They were a long way from making that leap again. On the way home from the place in Riverside, he stopped to watch a Little League game on the field where he'd grown up playing. The boys were young, maybe nine or ten. In another life he'd be standing among the dads, coaching first base, maybe keeping the book. In another life he'd watch his boy walk up to the plate and hope he remembered the speech he'd given him about courage, the fortitude and mental strength it takes to keep trying your absolute best. He remembered stepping up to the plate as a kid, already having struck out twice, wondering what the hell he was doing, how embarrassing, standing up there by himself just so twenty kids could watch him whiff again. And then, a moment later, connecting, the perfect thwack of bat to ball, the feeling of rightness in the palms of his hands as the ball flew down the third base line.

"Are you happy?" he asked Jess one night after she came home from work and changed into leggings and a hoodie. He made salads and had roasted a chicken. It was Memorial Day weekend, warm; they decided to eat outside. It was the exact question she had asked him years ago and he hadn't known what she meant. He told himself on the day she came home that whenever he was in doubt, he'd ask.

"I think so," she said. "I'm working on it. I don't regret being here if that's what you mean."

But it wasn't what he meant, exactly.

"Do you ever think about what Tripp pulled off?"

Malcolm had been checking the papers to find out if there was news of his arrest. He googled Charles Waggoner and Mark Duro and Roddy Horan almost daily. He searched Tripp Waggoner and Roderick Horan and also Rodney because he'd never asked what Roddy was short for. He searched Tripp's company. He tried to understand Tripp's crimes.

Jess looked surprised. "No. Do you?"

"All the time. Almost from the moment I wake up until the moment I fall asleep. He has a totally different life now, wherever he is. We would have heard if he'd been caught." He kept expecting to see Roddy's face on the news. His dumb T-shirts. He kept thinking of how disappointed his uncle would be, how he'd decide that the kid's father was right about him after all.

"You really do?"

"Yup."

"You have to pay attention to that."

"I know. I think that's what I'm getting at."

And then, the first week of June, he was at his mother's trying to remove some stubborn vines from her side yard when out of nowhere he thought of Adrian Walsh. He went inside to get a glass of water, and as he drank it, he looked through recents on his phone until he found Adrian's number.

"Malcolm?" Adrian said when he picked up. "About time. I've been trying to get hold of you."

Malcolm liked Adrian and had no idea why it took him so long to return his call. "I know. I'm sorry. It's been a crazy few months. But I saw your place in *Neat* and I wanted to say congratulations. How cool is that?"

"That's what I was calling about. But now it might be too late."

"Too late for what?" Malcolm asked. Through the window, Malcolm watched his mother open a little spot in the dirt with her hand trowel. He watched her lower a zinnia into the hole, the perfect cube of roots and soil. He watched her pat the topsoil around it like she was tucking it in. Mr. Sheridan had dropped off the flats of flowers for her, left them on the back porch.

"How'd he know what to get?" Malcolm asked when he saw them. Mostly zinnias and impatiens. Some marigolds. "How'd he know what colors?"

"I get the same every year!" she said. "Of course he knows!"

"I have a possible opportunity for you," Adrian said. "I know you're tied up with the Half Moon, but I think it might be worth your time to meet. At the very least we can hang out for a bit. I'm actually in New York for my cousin's wedding."

"I'm not tied up with the Half Moon. I sold it. You didn't hear?"

"No. I heard it wasn't—I heard it was struggling, to tell you the truth. That's why I thought of you for this job. That you sold is even better. Do you have an hour or two today? But it has to be today."

"Sure," Malcolm said to Adrian. "Why not." Jess wouldn't be home until dinnertime.

"Great. I'll meet you—where? The Alibi Lounge?"

"I'm dressed to do yard work. Somewhere casual. How about Stella's?" Malcolm liked their grilled cheese with tomato.

As soon as he saw Adrian, he wondered again why he hadn't called sooner. Adrian was a nice guy, got along with everyone. He was smart, went to Fordham for college and started bartending for extra cash. Like Hugh always warned, cash was a siren song too seductive for mortal men, and Adrian fell prey. He graduated from Fordham and got a day job at a big ad agency, but quickly figured out he'd give up a third of his salary in taxes. He'd be better off bartending more instead of less. Malcolm couldn't remember why he ended up in Gillam, but he put in maybe four years at the Half Moon.

Adrian showed Malcolm a photo of his baby daughter on his phone.

"She's beautiful," Malcolm said.

"You and Jess?" Adrian asked. "No kids, right?"

"Right," Malcolm said. "Jess is good though. Things are good." If Adrian had heard the Half Moon was struggling, he'd probably also heard about Jess. Like all good bartenders, he had an excellent poker face.

"That kind of makes it easier," Adrian said.

"Makes what easier?"

"I'll just get right to it," Adrian said. "Have you ever been to St. John?"

The island was still recovering from being hit by two back-to-back category five hurricanes in September 2017, Irma followed by Maria. Adrian showed him photos of the devastation in general, and of what the property looked like when he started. Of course, Malcolm had already seen the end result in *Neat*.

The place is doing really well, Malcolm recounted to Jess later. Jess gave him a look that said she'd heard that one before. Adrian didn't own it, he managed it, and now the owner wanted his help opening a new spot in Maui. He already had bars in Anguilla and Turks and had plans to open one in the Maldives. He was looking into property by some famous lake in Guatemala. Ecotourism was booming. The owner was CEO of a technology company in the Bay Area. He had no interest in the day-to-day of his bars, but he loved the idea of having them, an antidote to the rest of his life. He knew an absent owner in a mostly cash business was asking for trouble, so he was careful. He ran his bars the way he ran his company, offered contracts and benefits, a housing allowance to salaried hires who had to relocate. He held annual meetings where the managers of all locations got together for a few days, shared ideas. He relied on the people he trusted.

"So I'd take Adrian's place in St. John now that it's up and running. A contract would protect us since we'd be uprooting our lives. If it doesn't work out and he wants to fire me in six months, I'm guaranteed a year's salary. We get free housing for one year. If it does work out, I'd potentially be asked to stay or oversee opening one of the new places. That's what's happening to Adrian.

"Or," Malcolm added when Jess didn't say anything. "I could be done once the contract is up."

"So if you did this—"

"You'd come, too." He faltered as he searched for the right words. "I mean, I hope you would. You kind of hate your job, Jess. I know you do."

"I hate the commute more than I hate my job. Besides, I can't just quit. We can't afford it."

"We can't afford it here, you mean. But there? We'd sell this house. We'd live for free for a whole year. After that, yeah, okay, St. John is expensive so maybe we stay, maybe we go somewhere else. Don't they need lawyers everywhere?"

"It seems crazy."

"Maybe. But it's certainly not the craziest idea either of us has had lately."

Jess grimaced, pretended to look behind her like he might be talking to someone else.

"I mean, everyone else here feels stuck. I hear it all day long. But us? We're not stuck like they are. So why are we here?"

Jess frowned. "What about your mom?"

"I know. I've been thinking about her. All I'm saying is that I don't want to look down the barrel of the same routine for the next forty years, if we make it that long. And I know you don't either."

"You love your routine. I've never known a single person who enjoys going to Food King on a Sunday afternoon except for you."

Malcolm stood, started pacing. "I do love it, you're right. But, I wouldn't be sorry to take a break from it. Can't a person want two things at once? I need to see something else. I need to go to a place where no one knows us. And with everything that's happened? I have to get out of here. I have to do one interesting thing. I have to hit the reset button."

"I get that," Jess said, leaning back to take it all in. She could tell he was already picturing himself in flip-flops, sand between his toes. If they left New York for a year, she'd never get her position back. But she could already feel it: walking along a sunny street in a place she'd glimpsed only once, a stop on a three-day cruise she'd taken for someone's bachelorette. Somewhere no one knew them.

"And what? You just have to decide? This amazing job is yours for the taking?"

"Well, I have to meet the guy. I have to interview. But I'm sure I'll get it."

Jess stared at him for a moment, and then laughed. "It's unreal how cocky you are. You know that, right?"

Once they had all the information, Jess did a search of the owner's name and whistled after the first result. "He's a total nerd," she said, but then her eye caught on something. "Oh, he's from the Bronx. His dad was a bus driver. His mom died when he was a kid."

"He's like us," Malcolm said.

"Give or take a hundred million," she said, though she knew what he meant.

The owner's name was Noah Grayson, and he and his assistant had interviewed four candidates in total, flying each down to Key West for a day. Malcolm would be the fifth. The interview went pretty well, Malcolm thought. He answered their questions about budgeting, negotiating with vendors, keeping staff in line. He regaled them with stories about the Half Moon's wildest nights. He did less well when it came to questions about marketing and promotion. He had no familiarity with social media but he made them laugh at least. They had him make three drinks. Two to their specifications, one that Malcolm could improvise. They took a walk by the marina, and Noah asked him if he knew much about boating. Malcolm watched the boats bobbing in the water as he admitted he didn't. Then Noah asked where his favorite beach was. Malcolm said Beach Haven, New Jersey.

"I know Beach Haven. We used to go to Long Beach Island," Noah said.

But Malcolm had said Beach Haven because almost everyone who named the nicest beach on the Jersey Shore said Beach Haven. It was a safe answer. And he didn't want to risk lying, pretending he'd been somewhere he hadn't.

"Sorry. That's not true. My real favorite beach is called Sunset Cove. My friend Patrick calls it Cigarette Cove. It's on a lake, about three hours north of the city. The beach itself is not nice, honestly, but I love it there. Maybe it's cleaner now. I haven't been there in a long time."

Noah leaned back in his chair. "Never heard of that one."

"No, you wouldn't have."

"Why do you love it so much?"

But how could Malcolm explain love?

"For you it's more about who you're with," Noah said.

"Of course," he said. "What answer did the other people give?"

He got the call from Noah's assistant first thing the next morning. They wanted him to start in three weeks. As soon as Malcolm hung up with Noah's assistant, his mind immediately became a flip board of all the things he had to do. It stopped flipping when it landed on his mother, how he'd leave her, if he really could. He'd have to loop in Mary. He'd have to have a frank conversation with Mr. Sheridan. He asked Noah's assistant if there was any flexibility on the timing, but they'd delayed the decision already because it took Adrian so long to connect with him.

"I totally understand," Malcolm said. "Three weeks is plenty of time. I just need a day to think about it, okay?"

"Take the weekend," the guy said.

He was going to call Jess at work to tell her but decided to drive to Midtown and surprise her instead. He'd never even seen her office and she'd been there three years.

"You're where?" Jess asked when he called from the lobby. Then she told him to hang up and have the guard at the security desk call her. When he got his security badge and reached Jess's floor, she was there by the elevator waiting to lead him across the expanse of gleaming hardwood between the huge glass doors and her office. As she did, she noticed everyone they passed sit up straighter. He was tan from all the yard work, from his single day in Florida. He was trimmer than he'd been in years.

He smiled when she glanced over at him, and just like that every other man in the building looked pale and sickly from sitting too long under fluorescent lights.

"Guess what?" he asked as soon as they got to her office door. He grabbed her at the waist, and her admin giggled.

"It's like the boat story, Jessie. Remember I told you? When I tried to swim to the dock and the boat picked me up?"

"How is this like that? You mean the job? You got it?"

"It was always going to work out."

Maureen Ryan thought the plan was a fine one, as good as any other, said she'd be happy to look in on their house until it sold. She said she'd probably end up leaving Gillam herself pretty soon. Her friends were all moving to the Villages in Florida, a fifty-five-plus community so big it had its own zip code. They were drinking Bloody Marys by eleven and whizzing around on golf carts all day. Dinner was a rotating potluck. No one ever wanted to stay home.

"I didn't think I'd end up moving there. If you guys had—" She stopped herself from explaining the rest. If they'd had children. If she had a granddaughter a few blocks away who needed to be walked to school. But now.

Gail Gephardt was surprised, seemed far less sure that it was the right thing.

"Yeah?" she said when Malcolm told her everything. "Well, that came out of the clear blue."

They were alone in her kitchen, the radio tuned to the Fordham station. She liked the Irish music program on Sundays. "But it sounds exciting," she said, though her voice was hesitant. "And Jess will go?"

He saw worry in her face. He saw how many of her thoughts went to him, her boy. This was what having kids was like, he wanted to tell Jess. You worry sick over your child even when he's forty-five years old.

"Yes," he said, and she looked relieved.

"Oh good," she said, reaching over to place her hands on his ears and press. That had been their thing since he was little. "You were always such good company for each other, you and Jess. You used to chat out on the deck half the night. Remember? I used to love listening to you two. I'm so glad you figured it all out."

Patrick's question swept through his mind, as it often did now: *Why?*

"But what about you? You'll be okay here?"

"Me?" she laughed.

"You get confused sometimes. You know you do. What will you do when I'm not nearby?"

"I don't think I get any more confused than anyone else. And if I feel a little mixed up, I'll call Artie. He's usually who I call anyway. I only call you if he doesn't answer. You're so busy, but Artie's always around. A year is nothing. At my age a year goes in a blink. Nothing will change in a year. And if you decide to stay longer . . ."

She let the thought go unsaid.

"I don't want you sticking around here for me, kiddo. I'd really hate that."

"You call Artie first?" Malcolm felt like he'd stepped into a fog. "Ma, do you have something going on with Mr. Sheridan? I mean, like, *something*?"

"Like *something* something?" she said and shimmied her shoulders. She didn't have her bottom bridge in, so she covered her mouth as she laughed.

He called Noah's assistant to tell them he accepted, and they immediately scheduled a call between him and their relocation coordinator. Later that afternoon, he was making a sandwich at the counter, the TV blaring, when he heard the name Charles Waggoner. Holding a folded slice of ham, he walked slowly into the living room and there was Tripp, being led down a dark sidewalk and into a waiting car, hands cuffed, a gray beard down to his sternum. The reporter said he'd been charged with eight counts of fraud, money laundering, perjury, and theft. Authorities found him at an organic quinoa farm in the Sacred Valley, where he'd been living under a false name and consulting as a wholesaler. They'd searched for him in the area previously, but were led back when they got an alert that several Google searches at an internet café near Pisac were for Charles Waggoner and each of Charles Waggoner's children.

He'd been extradited from Peru overnight and would face trial in New York City within six months. There was no mention of Roddy.

Within minutes came a flurry of texts from Emma and the rest of the gang from the Half Moon. They sent news clips back and forth, giddy about being so close to a major crime, a news story. They included Roddy's old number on the chain, but Malcolm noticed he didn't reply.

Holy shit, Jess texted soon after. Did you see?

He waited four full days, the longest he could stand, and then he texted Roddy's uncle to say he had some stuff that belonged to Roddy but that he wasn't returning his calls. Did he get a new number? Was he back from his trip?

Immediately, the uncle called. He sighed into the phone, said Roddy had met someone apparently, wasn't coming back for a while. He sent his mother a postcard to say as much. He didn't even have the decency to call, which was a garbage move if you asked him.

"So just toss the stuff," his uncle said. "Whatever it is."

"Yeah okay sure."

Malcolm stood perfectly still for several minutes after he hung up. My God. He was going to get away with it.

They packed up everything they could to make the house as neat as possible for showings. On weekend mornings they drove upstate for a hike and breakfast while strangers walked through and noticed how small their closets were, how badly the kitchen needed updating. Everyone so far was a newly married couple, or a couple with one small child and plans for another. Malcolm asked Jess if she wanted him to pack up the contents of the attic by himself, the things she'd collected all those painful years, but she said no, they'd do it together. She told him not to worry about her. She was fine. Was he?

Up in the musty attic, they combined the contents of all the small bags of hand-me-downs into two giant boxes. And then they looked to the toys, seats, play mats, things that defied categorization. They agreed they'd donate all of it, rather than leave it on the curb to watch it get picked over. Jess found a women's shelter that would be happy to take it.

"I had something like this," Jess said, spinning the wildly patterned ball bolted to a rimmed seat with wheels. It was for learning how to walk. One of her first memories was of her father grabbing the edge before she went tumbling down the stairs and then smacking her thigh, hard, and telling her to never go near the stairs again.

"I had one, too," Malcolm said. The seat had a complicated system of belts and clasps. He couldn't imagine a life where he'd find it second nature to understand how these things worked.

"It's funny," he said.

"What is?"

But what was it he was going to say? It was so hard to capture a feeling and then make it understood, even to Jess, even to himself sometimes. He remembered being a kid, all the things he felt capable of, all the streets and avenues that branched away from his body, all the possibilities. But in the end you can only have one life. One at a time, at least. You could turn, you could pause for a while, but you couldn't go down two streets at once. The things they didn't end up doing, the places and people they decided against, all defined them as much as anything else, in the way negative space defines a photo or a song. The lives they didn't lead were there, too, always with them. Only recently did he begin to see the shape those choices had made.

While Malcolm was getting settled in St. John, Jess would square away what was left to organize in Gillam and at her job, and then follow a few weeks later. Mr. Sheridan came by one evening and talked to Malcolm out on the patio. He stuck to practical things—that Gail needed a sump pump at the house, that it was dangerous for her to trim her hedges on her own, up on a ladder, but they both knew there was no stopping her. He said he wished she'd let him take out the bathtub in her main bathroom and replace it with a walk-in shower in case she fell. He made his whole house senior friendly years ago, no sense pretending life wasn't headed full speed toward the inevitable. He repeated what Gail had already said to Malcolm, that a year was nothing, it wasn't like he and Jess wouldn't be back and forth—holidays, other visits—and if Malcolm didn't mind, he and Gail would like to come down to St. John to see them. Neither of them had ever been.

"Anyway, the whole point of me stopping by is to say you don't need to worry. I'll look out for your mom," Mr. Sheridan said. "Always have. Lately when I make my doctor appointments I make one for her, too, so we can go together."

"You've looked out for her ever since my dad died," Malcolm said. "I'm sorry I didn't realize."

"Longer than that even," Mr. Sheridan said, and Malcolm decided to say absolutely nothing but to hold it in his hands and carry it to Jess for discussion later.

"I'm glad about you and Jess," he said. "Your mom is, too."

"Yeah, me too," Malcolm said, not wanting to get into it. "Life is complicated, right?"

"Funny," Mr. Sheridan said. "I was about to say exactly the opposite. I was just about to say how simple it is. Life is actually really simple when you boil it down."

Why?

Because he loved her.

Malcolm's flight was early, ten past seven in the morning. He offered to take the bus to the airport but Jess was an early riser, she wanted to drive him, plus they wouldn't see each other for a few weeks. They decided five fifteen was early enough to leave—a summer Friday, little traffic. But they were still home at five thirty, groggy, the airport forty minutes away, so it was a mad rush and then they got lost in Queens—road construction, a detour—and Jess kept saying it was insane to be lost so close to home, going to a place they'd been so many times. He could hear the panic escalating in her voice. She'd been up late reading about how the island was evacuated in an emergency. She'd looked at a hundred images of the destruction after the last hurricane. Now, she kept leaning over the steering wheel to check the sky for planes, as if one of them might guide her.

She didn't used to worry so much.

"We're not lost," Malcolm said. He read aloud the directions along side streets, narrow one-ways, wide boulevards. Next thing they were back on track.

When they got to the airport, everything was quiet, like it was not yet open for business, the coffeepots cold in the terminals, the planes still resting out back. Jess pulled up to the curb and no cops shouted at her.

"You have everything?" she asked.

"I think so," he said. He was looking ahead at the pedestrian bridge that connected the terminal to the parking deck, and then at the bright cobalt sky above everything. An older man pulled his roller suitcase behind him as he crossed at the light, a pleasant expression on his face. "Good morning!" Malcolm said to him as he got out of the car.

Jess shook her head. Leave it to him. He'd have to sprint to his gate, but he'd probably say hello to everyone he passed on his way.

She got out of the car and walked around for a hug.

"You okay, Jess?"

"I'm just thinking, what if it doesn't work out? This 'reset button' as you call it."

Suddenly, or so it seemed, the lane filled with cars, the cops found their whistles, reps from the airlines were tagging suitcases and directing people to the correct doors. It was like witnessing the day swing open, usher everyone inside. Malcolm patted his pocket to confirm his wallet was there. He checked his phone. The driver of an enormous black truck blasted his horn as a low-flying plane passed over their heads, white bellied, and Malcolm imagined himself and all the people around him becoming smaller as it climbed higher, hauling whatever it carried deeper into the blue.

"We're not even there yet. Why do you worry so much?"

"We haven't really talked about it though. What will happen if we don't like it or I can't find work or they don't renew your contract or—"

As she spoke, she ran her hands along his arms to his shoulders. She laced her fingers at the back of his neck and held fast. He felt overcome for a moment—all they'd been through, all that lay ahead. He kissed the part in her hair.

"What will happen? We come back home. That's all. We just pick right up and head home."

acknowledgments

Thank you with all my heart to my longtime first and best readers: Eleanor Henderson, Brendan Mathews, and Callie Wright. I truly can't write anything without you three telling me all the ways it's bad before it's good.

My deepest thanks to Jeanine Cummins, Catherine Keane, Annette Keane, and Anna Solomon, for feedback on later drafts. Your enthusiasm helped me believe this story had promise.

Thanks to Seamus Keane, Danny Keane, and Jimmy McMorrow, for answering a thousand questions about bartending.

To Taylor Duck and Callie Wright in particular, and to the many anonymous women in various online fertility support groups, for speaking to me about your most private struggles.

Thanks to my brilliant editor, Kara Watson, whose careful questions made this novel so much stronger. To my agent, Chris Calhoun, and everyone at Scribner and Simon & Schuster who helped bring *The Half Moon* to the world: Jon Karp, Nan Graham, Brian Belfiglio, Wendy Sheanin, Stu Smith, Jaya Miceli, Emily Polson, Ashley Gilliam Rose,

Katie Monaghan, Jason Chappell, Hope Herr-Cardillo, and so many others. I truly appreciate all the hard work you put into this.

Thank you to Jess Leeke at Penguin Michael Joseph (UK) and Jenny Meyer at Jenny Meyer Literary Agency. This makes four books together and counting!

Thank you to my parents, for always rooting for me. And most of all, thank you to Marty and our boys, for putting up with my preoccupation with this book when we were in a very real lockdown. The strange and shapeless loneliness of early Covid is in this story. I wouldn't want to be trapped at home with anyone but you three. And I'll never see a Monopoly board again without thinking of you dirty cheaters.